LORD EDGINGTON IN

BOOK 9

WHAT THE VICAR SAW

A 1920s MYSTERY

BENEDICT BROWN

COPYRIGHT

For my father, Kevin,
I hope you would have liked this book an awful lot.
And to my new son, Osian,
I hope you want to read this one day.

Fig. 2.1: Detail of the window to Saint Bartholomew in the south transept of St Bartholomew's church in Condicote, in the region of Tatchester, England.

READER'S NOTE

I write these books to be self-contained mysteries so that new readers can dive into the series at any point. They are spoiler free but, inevitably, the characters grow and change over time, and there are minor references to previous cases.

All you really need to know to enjoy this book is that a distinguished detective (who shut himself away from the world for a decade before the beginning of the series) and his well-meaning grandson work together to solve dastardly crimes.

At the back of the book you can find a character list, a glossary of unusual and antiquated words, and notes on my research and inspiration. I hope you absolutely love it.

CHAPTER ONE

Part One – End of December 1926

Baron Stamford Fane had never been a popular man but, on the day of his funeral, the church in the village of Condicote was full to bursting. People were packed in, ten to a pew, and villagers lined up in the aisles to witness his last rites.

Mr Oldman, the school master, whispered to his ever-silent wife that, "It isn't hard to imagine why there are more people here today than there were at Reverend Oldfield's Christmas service."

His neighbour, Mrs Grout the grocer, leant forward from the pew behind and, in her typically gruff voice declared, "That's right. Condicote never knew a more malignant fellow than Stamford Fane. I'm only here to make sure he's really gone!"

This caused Mayor Hobson to tut rather loudly and pat the dead man's widow on the shoulder.

Perhaps the most damning testament to just how great a scoundrel the baron had been was the fact that his own wife couldn't muster a single tear for him. She stared straight ahead as her companions on either side made a fuss of her, but her eyes were dry. Sitting not so far away at the front of the church, I had to wonder if she was just as shocked as everyone else. The stories of her husband were so wicked, and so numerous, that it was hard to accept that he had finally met his Maker.

At eleven o'clock on the dot, Mrs Stanley, the organist, cracked her knuckles, straightened her back and began to play. The congregation rose accordingly. There weren't enough hymn books for everyone and, in some cases, whole families were huddled around a single copy, but the people of Condicote were in fine voice that morning as we thundered through one of my favourite hymns.

Guide me, O thou great Redeemer,
Hold me with thy powerful hand.

Admittedly, there were those towards the back of the fine old church who couldn't hold a tune. I was fairly certain it was the first time that some of them had set foot inside St Bartholomew's, but the overall effect was appropriately stirring.

Perhaps feeling it was his duty as the highest-ranking aristocrat present that day, my grandfather, the Marquess of Edgington, sang loudest of all.

> **Bread of heaven, bread of heaven**
> **Feed me till I want no more.**
> **Feed me till I want no more.**

The only problem was that, as we approached the end of the hymn, there was still no sign of Reverend Oldfield. We'd made it through all three verses and, as the vicar hadn't appeared, the verger, Bob Thompkins, gave a quick bang on the vestry door and signalled to Mrs Stanley to repeat the final refrain.

> **Songs of praises, songs of praises**
> **I will ever give to thee.**
> **I will ever give to thee.**

A whisper spread about the church as there was still nothing happening, and so Mrs Stanley's fingers went tripping across the keys one final time.

> **Songs of praises, songs of praises**
> **I will ever give to thee.**
> **I will ever give to thee.**

It was no good. We could have kept singing until Michaelmas and it wouldn't have done the trick. The reverend was known to be fond of a glass of wine from time to time – those times being morning till night – and everyone in the church must have come to the same conclusion. With a shake of the head and a few well-disguised words, the verger threw the door open and disappeared inside.

"Well, that was a short service," some likely fellow grunted, which earned him a few laughs and just as many disapproving looks. Silence fell and, when the verger still hadn't appeared, my grandfather's tundra-white moustache drooped. He pushed his way along the row and didn't need to snap his fingers to tell me to join him, but he did it anyway, and I went scampering to his side.

He pulled open the entrance to the vestry without looking back and, when the door closed behind us, it was clear that Reverend Oldfield had more to worry about than just his love of communion wine.

Standing as still as one of the stone angels in the graveyard outside, Bob Thompkins was pointing at his boss. "He…" the man attempted. "The reverend, he's…"

The great bell rope around the priest's neck and the bloodshot eyes in his battered head told us all we needed to know, but the great detective beside me couldn't resist finishing that sentence.

"He's dead."

CHAPTER TWO

We might never have become embroiled in the whole affair if my silly brother and his lovely fiancée hadn't decided that Condicote had the prettiest church in England. They were determined to get married there and, if it weren't for them, the first few months of 1927 would have been very different indeed. Of course, the only reason I'd even heard of such an unassuming town as Condicote was because my father's mother lived there.

A few days after a perfectly traumatic Christmas, my family piled into Grandfather's convoy of exquisite cars, and I charted a course towards Tatchester in the Yock Valley. Tatchester is one of those lesser-known cities in Britain, the kind that few people talk about. It's somewhere not too far from Newminster. And it's really very close to Yockwardine, if you know where that is, but it certainly isn't the easiest place to locate on a map.

"I'll get you driving again one of these days," my maternal grandfather assured me as he stood outside his palatial property, admiring the seven cars that were packed for the journey. We could have got away with two at a push, but he simply couldn't travel without a footman, a cook, his beloved golden retriever, a maid, a page boy... Well, he liked to make a big expedition out of just about every journey.

"You can think that if you like, Grandfather," I replied quite cordially, "but I'm really so much happier being a passenger. For the sake of pedestrians everywhere, I believe it's better that I remain one for as long as possible. And besides, why would I deprive you of the opportunity to enjoy the country lanes and by-ways of this fine nation? It's bad enough that you allow Todd to take the wheel from time to time. If I drove too, you'd never get the chance."

He was about to produce a clever response when our chauffeur opened the door to the Aston Martin. Once our dog Delilah had leapt inside, the old lord climbed aboard. "Very well. I'll see you in Condicote. Bon voyage, Chrissy. Bon voyage."

He said this in a very grand manner, but the rest of the cars needed their engines cranking and so he had to sit on the drive for a few minutes longer, pretending he couldn't see me.

My father would be accompanying us on the journey for once, and so I went to join my family at the front of the pack. On the one hand, I would miss the fascinating conversation that my grandfather, Lord Edgington – famed detective and owner of one of the most elegant estates in England – was sure to provide, but on the other I would be less likely to die in a horrific motoring accident.

"What's taken you so long, boy?" My papa was still cranking the navy-blue Bentley, which he treated like a fragile infant. I would have said that he treated it like his own son, but he hadn't ever shown me such care. He'd certainly never spent hours washing and polishing me.

"Don't fuss, Walter," my dear mother intervened on my behalf. "We're all here now and we're going to have a magnificent trip together. It's been too long since we did anything as a family."

My brother Albert might have contributed to this conversation, but he was already seated in the back of our car, gazing romantically at his future wife. This was fairly standard behaviour on his part, and I could only hope that he would get over the novelty of Cassandra Fairfax's unparalleled beauty once they were married.

"Jump in next to me, Chrissy," my sister-in-law-to-be declared as she shuffled her dumbstruck fiancé further along the wide seat. "I'm simply over the moon to be visiting another branch of the illustrious Prentiss family. I've only one grandparent left, and he's as friendly as a walrus with a swollen flipper."

"Oh, really?" I must admit that she was rather enchanting. I found myself drawn to her eyes as though they were fine works of art hanging in the National Gallery. "Then he'd get on perfectly with my grandmother."

"Chrissy, that isn't polite." Mother had climbed into the front seat and was watching me over her shoulder.

"You're absolutely right. It's terribly rude of me to say such a thing." I paused just long enough for her to think I was serious. "Quite accurate, of course, but rude nonetheless."

Cassandra giggled at this and, as his beloved had showed her amusement, so did my brother. With the Bentley now purring, Father leaped into the front of the vehicle, put on his leather gloves – like a surgeon preparing for a delicate operation – and released the squeaky brake.

"As much as I would like to defend my mother, Chrissy's words do bear a grain of truth." This was a rare compliment by my always serious father's standards, and I listened intently to what he would say next. "I'm afraid that my mother is as welcoming as a pond full of leeches. My advice, if you wish to win her over, Cassandra, is to say very little and stand up straight."

This was the first time I'd seen the newest addition to the family betray a hint of apprehension. Since I'd met her approximately eight days earlier, Cassandra had become a beloved companion to each and every one of us. I'm sure that most people fear the sort of lunatics that marry into one's family, but she was an absolute gem. In fact, the only flaw in her that I had detected was her really very poor taste in men.

Albert was more of a nervous procrastinator than an out-and-out thinker. He was a good fourth to make up a game of bridge, rather than the spark of a party. And he was less an Adonis than a... Well, I'm sure you get the idea. He was definitely not the kind of man whom beautiful, ambitious young women – kin to the Duke of Hinwick, no less – usually marry. I doubt I was the only one to question how the pair had fallen in love.

"My mother-in-law is a very strong person." Dearest Mummy is the most diplomatic human I've ever met and couldn't bring herself to say a bad word against anybody. "A strong, capable person with many opinions and..." She faltered once more. "...and high expectations."

By the end of her little speech, I was fighting off a bout of laughter. It fell to Father to put her out of her misery. "Yes, yes, darling. Mother is a real one-of-a-kind. I'm sure it will be just wonderful to spend a few days with her."

Perhaps it was this false positivity that brought an air of gloom to the car. My laughter faded, and I contemplated what the week might have in store. On our visit to see her the previous summer, Granny had decided that, instead of a birthday present, she would give me the details of an exercise regime used by soldiers in the desert.

"You must also watch what you eat, Christopher," she had explained as she handed over the weighty tome. "If you don't change your habits, you'll be mistaken for a prize pig and win first place in the village fete."

"Thank you, Grandmother," I responded with all the enthusiasm I could muster. "It goes so well with the skipping rope you bought me for Christmas."

Perhaps it's the fact that I was her youngest grandson or, like a ravenous hyena, she enjoyed preying on the weakest member of the herd, but she always picked me out for special treatment. I rather hoped that Cassandra's presence would deflect her attention from me, but I wouldn't have placed any money on it.

In the car, a ruminative silence had fallen before Mother spoke in little more than a whisper. "We can think ourselves lucky, Chrissy. At least we didn't have to spend Christmas with her."

Father stared at his wife in disbelief, and Mother looked just as shocked.

"My goodness. Did I say that out loud?"

No one uttered another word until we'd left the rolling (but soggy) hills of Surrey behind. The snowstorms that had attacked the country just a week earlier were long forgotten, and, in their wake, they had left dark clouds, muddy fields and unceasing rivulets running down every gutter.

I traced our route on the map past Hope-under-Chesters, Gabbett's Cross and Radsoe. Signs for tiny hamlets flashed past us, and I spotted Mudstone Hillock, Duckswhich Peverel and Bishop's Knockerdown, proving once more that towns across my motherland were named by madmen. The journey took anything between two and seven hours (I couldn't tell exactly how long we were in the car as my father drove so slowly and smoothly that it was impossible to stay awake). All I can say is that it was Thursday when we left, and that was still more or less the case when we arrived.

"Mummy!" my father beamed when we pulled up in front of The Manor at Condicote. It was a poorly named property as, although my grandmother liked to pretend she was the only landed citizen for miles around, there was another, equally grand house on the other side of the village. "It's so nice to see you!"

"You're late." Granny was a spindle of a woman with a slender neck that was as long as any swan's. There was a harpyish aspect to her pinched features and, standing in front of her looming gothic home, she looked as though she was as much its guard as its owner.

"Yes, Mother. You have my apologies." Her son searched for an explanation. "But it is quite some way to drive."

Her lip curled. "There is no need to be pert, my boy. And as for the distance, your father-in-law and a large cohort of his staff arrived in good time. What's your excuse?"

As the heir to the family estate, Father was in thrall to this Valkyrie's every whim and clearly didn't know the best way to avoid upsetting her. Luckily, my quick-witted mother was there to save him.

"We were stuck behind a herd of cattle at Thames Bottom. I think a cart must have overturned as they didn't clear for some time."

My grandmother narrowed her eyes and looked at her daughter-in-law as though deliberating upon her suitability. My parents had been married for a quarter of a century, but it was never too late for Granny to show her disapproval.

"I suppose you must come in," she finally conceded, without leading us inside. Instead, she came closer to the car and waited for her grandsons to line up for inspection. Uncertain of the protocol, Cassandra did the same. Granny was most regimental in her interactions and demanded a similar attitude from her subordinates.

"Albert," she began, turning his chin from side to side with one claw, "you should take more sun. No one likes an anaemic young man, and you have the complexion of a deceased white rhino."

Next in line, I was dreading what new insecurity she might foist upon me.

"Christopher, you…" She looked for the right words to cut through any layer of confidence I might recently have constructed. "You… you look rather well for a change. Have you been following the exercise regime I gave you?"

The only exercise I'd done since I'd left school the previous summer was lifting heavy pies towards my mouth and chasing after my grandfather on his myriad investigations. Of course, I had no desire to tell her that.

"Religiously, Grandmother. I've turned my room at Cranley Hall into something of a training camp."

She looked rather impressed. "I should think so. Though don't go too far and end up starving yourself. I do not approve of gaunt, gangly young men. You are not a Parisian waif and should not be mistaken for one."

As she moved on to Cassandra, I wondered whether this would be the only time in my life that I was neither too skinny nor too fat for her liking. I can't say her fleeting approval made me feel a lot better about myself.

"And who do we have here?" She tilted her head back to look at the interloper.

"I'm so very pleased to meet you–" Cassandra would not get another word out.

"That is not what I asked, Mrs. Nimble-Chops. I have no interest in chatterboxes and you would do best to leave the twittering to the birds." Without pausing for breath, she moved from censure to advice. "Assuming that you are Albert's fiancée, I can only recommend that you spend your time here paying close attention to the way in which we in the Prentiss family conduct ourselves. You clearly have much to learn."

She gave the poor girl one last withering look and spun to ascend the front staircase of the uninviting house. The Manor was rather distinctive in that it was all very neat and tidy but looked like the gloomy edifice in practically every ghost story. Black ivy, of a kind that I was sure existed nowhere else on Earth, grew on the façade. There was always a cackling posse of crows on the roof of the great tower, and the light of the sun reflected off the dingy glass in each window to give the impression that there was someone gazing out from beyond the net curtains. I'd never been anywhere quite like it and hoped I would never find its equal.

"Walter, bring your bags," she shouted after her son, who mumbled helplessly in reply.

"Isn't that why we brought staff?"

Leaving him with a pile of luggage to transport, the rest of us chased after my grandmother up the steps. Of course, the exterior of the building was as inviting as a picnic on a sunny day compared to its suffocating interior. The decor was all in the limited spectrum between red and black and the dim lighting turned anyone who entered a similar colour.

"Grandfather!" I beamed, running ahead of the others into the largest of many salons on the ground floor.

My mother's father was sitting at a small, round table with a chessboard resting upon it and didn't look up as he was too busy examining the distribution of the pieces. "Grand to see you, my boy. Just grand." He betrayed none of his usual enthusiasm, and I wondered what dark magic our hostess had practiced upon him.

My mother was an experienced Granny-tamer and would not allow such witchcraft to take place in her presence. She ran to her father and, placing herself between the old lord and the game, managed to break the spell.

"How was your journey?" she asked. "Has Delilah recovered from your driving?"

I hadn't noticed her until now, but the cherished golden retriever was sitting beneath an armchair, looking rather down in the mouth.

"She'll be fine," he said, finally rising to greet us. "She does insist on fussing about these things. I've told her it will do her no good, but whenever it's just the two of us in the car, she moans and whimpers if I go past sixty miles an hour."

My grandmother sat down in the free chair beside the chessboard and seized her rook to topple the old man's king. "Checkmate, I'm afraid, Edgington. I thought you said you were an old hand at this game?"

I very much doubted that it was down to her skills at the chessboard that she had defeated the genius detective so much as the psychological manipulation he had undergone. It was a good thing that my grandmother had never taken to a life of crime, or I feared that Lord Edgington would have finally met his match.

"Now that you're all here, perhaps we should have a look at this church we've come such a long way to visit." He was trying to change the subject, and I didn't blame him in the slightest.

"What a disappointment! I thought you'd come here to see me." Granny allowed herself a short cackle. "Either way, you won't be able to visit the church until the morning. The vicar will be on his rounds in the neighbouring villages at the moment. I think he rather fancies himself on a par with the doctor. He hopes to heal the souls of his parishioners as he cycles about the place."

"Tomorrow it is then." Grandfather rubbed his hands together, and I imagine he was about to find an excuse to leave when his would-be nemesis kept talking.

"There's a funeral tomorrow that I do not want to miss." She spoke as though such an occasion was a real treat. "You will never guess who died? It's simply too marvellous."

"Really Mother," my father admonished her as he passed the room with a stack of cases under his chin. "Must you always take such pleasure in the deaths of your fellow villagers?"

She ignored his critical tone. "I don't always take pleasure, Walter, but this is a special occasion."

My mother is as good a detective as her more celebrated father and realised what the crotchety old lady was implying. "Not Stamford Fane?" Her jaw hung open for a half-moment. "Surely he can't be dead."

"He is!" Granny made no attempt to hide her glee. "That scoundrel is on the last leg of his iniquitous journey, and one thing is for certain, he'll be travelling down, not up." She pointed to the infernal realm beneath our feet and a brief shudder passed over me.

"Who's Stamford Fane?" Cassandra asked in an innocent voice.

"Observe, child!" Granny snapped in reply. "I said you should observe, not speak."

The poor girl appeared to shrink a few inches, and my brother sat her down on the nearest black brocatelle chaise longue. Albert had long since learnt it was better to keep one's counsel within twenty feet of the widow of The Manor.

Despite her initial reaction, Granny could not resist answering Casandra's question. "Baron Stamford Fane was my sworn enemy. He possessed a somewhat meagre property a little way from here and acted as though Condicote had been built for his pleasure."

"The devilish Stamford Fane!" I said to myself more than anyone as I pictured Granny's longstanding foe. "Surely your description is missing a few rather significant details, Grandmother."

Unable to accept that I might have something valid to say, she shook her head. "I suppose most people would focus on his gambling, womanising and the rumours of his criminal behaviour, but those had little impact on me now, did they? What always got my back up was how arrogant he could be. I've met peacocking thespians with smaller egos than Stamford Fane."

If there was one thing my grandmother loathed, it was actors… and butchers. Oh, and she really didn't like her postman, although it was hard to say whether that was a personal issue or it was the profession in general to which she objected – "Coming onto my property at some ungodly hour each morning, traipsing through my garden with his big, muddy boots: it's simply not acceptable!" – It's safe to say that there were a lot of people that Granny didn't like, but Stamford Fane was at the top of the list.

"He was the very definition of a solipsist," she murmured.

"Sorry, what's the definition of a solipsist?" I don't know bothered asking such questions.

"*He* was."

"No, you misunderstood me. I'm asking— Actually, never mind."

"How did he die?" Grandfather turned the discussion to a more significant point.

Granny looked a little crafty for a moment, and I concluded that we had stumbled upon yet another suspicious death for the inimitable Lord Edgington to probe.

"He died…" She paused to pique our interest. In fact, she held that pause for fifteen long seconds. Mummy moved a few steps closer, perhaps to check that her mother-in-law wasn't speaking in a whisper. Albert and Cassandra leaned forward on the sofa, and Father had returned from depositing our cases upstairs by the time she finally continued. "…in a car accident."

The whole room emitted a sigh. Even Delilah looked unimpressed by the revelation and closed her eyes to go to sleep.

"No, wait, wait." Granny evidently wished for a bigger reaction and added some more details. "The drunken swine was on his way home from the Drop of Dew Inn when he crashed his car into a lamppost between here and Yockwardine. They say it went up in flames, and the mayor heard his cries and went running. I hope that odious fellow was cooked like a Christmas goose."

"Mother!" Even my normally kowtowing father couldn't tolerate the old lady's sadism.

"Yes, Walter?" Her gaze was like a needle that poked him back the way he'd come. "I doubt you have collected all the bags. Chop chop!"

Grandfather seemed to be off somewhere far away but returned to the present to ask another question. "Are the police certain there was no sign of foul play? The brakes on the car were intact, I suppose?"

Granny was clearly enjoying the attention. "Oh, yes. P.C. Brigham checked all that sort of thing. In fact, he even sent for an inspector from

Scotland Yard, what with Fane thinking himself such an important person, but they're confident it was an accident. It happened on Boxing Day, and he'd been drinking non-stop before he got into his Lanchester 40. Half the village saw the state he was in."

"What a waste," Grandfather declared. "The Lanchester 40 is a truly beautiful car."

"Daddy!" his daughter complained. "A man is dead."

"Yes, my dear. I gathered that much." My maternal grandfather could be just as heartless as my paternal grandmother, and his esteem for an automobile over a debauched and dissolute man did not surprise me.

"So you'll come then?" Grandmother peered at each of us in turn. "There's nothing quite like a good funeral!"

CHAPTER THREE

I may have given something of the story away by beginning with the most exciting part. As you already know, we did accompany my grandmother for her morbid entertainment the following morning and, to everyone's surprise, there wasn't just one dead man in the village of Condicote, but two.

Poor Reverend Oldfield. He'd been my grandmother's vicar ever since I was old enough to remember her complaining about him. I would imagine that he was approximately sixty years old, though it's a lot harder to estimate such things post-strangulation. He had a rather monk-like appearance, with his (admittedly now caved-in) bald head and fuzzy eyebrows, and I recalled that he travelled everywhere by bicycle, but I knew little else about him.

"Mr…?" Grandfather asked when the shock of that violent scene had worn off a little and, out in the church, the organist had started a new hymn. "I'm sorry, I don't know your name."

"Bob Thompkins," Bob Thompkins replied. "I'm the verger here."

"Mr Thompkins, can you tell me how the vicar's death went undetected until now?" Grandfather moved closer to feel the temperature and examine the state of the corpse. "The man has been dead for some time."

Thompkins began to shake in fear as the celebrated detective's eyes drilled into him. "I… Yes, I see what you mean. I'd normally have come in to check on him before the service, but when I got here this morning, everything was open, and so I went to tend to other things."

"Other things?" I asked, hoping that this would be the key to the whole case. It would be a real coup to solve a murder within seconds of discovering the body.

"That's right. The guttering around the south transept has been leaking, and I finally had a chance to look at it."

Unimpressed by this line of questioning, Grandfather changed the topic. "Mr Thompkins, I'm afraid you'll have to tell the congregation that Baron Fane's funeral will not be taking place this morning." He bowed his head for a moment in reverence, though I wasn't certain which of the two men's deaths he was marking. "With that done, I'd be most grateful if you could call the police."

"Yes, m'lord. Course, m'lord." Though Grandfather was not a regular visitor to Condicote, everyone knew him. It was of great pride to the village that a local boy – my father, Walter Prentiss – had married Lord Edgington's own daughter, Lady Violet Cranley. Except for winning the ferret race at the Tatchester country fair for five years in a row, it was one of the few claims to fame that Condicote could make.

Slow, dependable Bob Thompkins shuffled from the vestry to do as my grandfather asked.

"Quick, Christopher," my mentor hissed once we could hear the verger's hushed voice addressing the crowd. "We must use this time to observe as much as we can. Try to remember the lessons I have imparted over these last few months. This is the perfect opportunity for you to put the theory into practice."

I tried to recall all that he had told me since school had finished and I had devoted my time to becoming a shrewd (or at least passable) detective. In my mind at that moment, I could see a notepad with several of the rules he had made me memorise like Bible verses. There were phrases such as…

We must forever imagine the unimaginable and consider the improbable.
Learn when to talk less if you hope to understand more.
And… **Never overplay your part.**

But I didn't see how any of these mottos would help me. I padded about the room to inspect a few dusty relics, and glance at the reverend's spare surplice and tippet. None of this helped me formulate a theory for why the man was dead, and so I went to the window to see what was happening outside the church.

"Christopher, what are you doing?" The real detective was not impressed.

"I'm having a look around, as you said."

He bit the inside of one cheek. "The body, Christopher. Perhaps you should start with the body."

"An excellent idea." I returned to my original position and did as he'd suggested.

He waited a few seconds before prompting me for my findings.

"Do you notice anything?"

"Do I!" I responded, whilst trying my darnedest to work out what it was I should have spotted. "Well, no, to be perfectly honest, I don't." Before he could sigh, or tut, or do both at the same time, I kept talking. "But that doesn't mean I won't. Now, first things first; he's dead."

"A stunning observation, my boy. I wait with bated breath to know what further details you will uncover."

I ignored him and moved on to a slightly subtler observation. "Strangled by the neck."

"As opposed to the feet? Very good, Christopher." He was in a particularly sarcastic mood and twirled his moustache between two fingers as he spoke.

"First, the killer nobbled the victim with a heavy object to the head, but I believe that it was the unwieldy length of rope that finished the job. I must say, though, it would have been extremely difficult to tie around the vicar's neck."

"Now we're getting somewhere!" He clapped his hands together but waited for me to reveal more.

"To me, that suggests that…"

"Yes?"

"It suggests that …" I thought I was about to give up, but a spark of brilliance glimmered in my brain. "It suggests that the killer was a man of some strength."

"Man or woman, you mean? Don't forget that I have in my employ two women who could be national arm-wrestling champions if they put their brawn to it. But otherwise, you have made some truly worthy observations, and I applaud your effort." I could tell from the way he said this final word that my *effort* still wasn't quite good enough. "However, you have missed a key fact."

I straightened up from my study and looked him over. "Oh yes, and what is that?"

"The key fact you have missed is that the dead man who was struck with a heavy object then strangled with an unwieldy rope is holding… a key."

"So he is!" I can't tell you how excited this made me. Of course, I should have noticed such a significant piece of evidence myself, but it unlocked so many wonderful possibilities that I couldn't help but be excited. "What a mystery this presents. Who can possibly say what doors that key will open." I examined the small silver point that was sticking up between the cadaver's clenched knuckles. "Perhaps there is a secret room here in the church which we will only discover by following a series of clues that are hidden in the remains of an ancient—"

"I'm sorry, Christopher, but I'll have to stop you there." Having done so, he pointed across the room to a small cupboard, the door of which was standing ajar. "Have you been reading adventure novels again? You must always remember that your imagination makes a proficient magnifying glass, but a terrible compass."

I had to wonder how this wisdom complemented his previous recommendation that **"We must forever imagine the unimaginable…"**

We heard Bob Thompkins' soft voice fall silent and the congregation bustling out of the church. To avoid alarming any of the parishioners, I felt that he must have fabricated a believable story for why the funeral could not take place. His work was soon undone, however, as he shouted, "Del! Hullo, P.C. Brigham? You'd better come in here. Looks like the reverend's been murdered."

A rash of surprised voices broke out, and he appeared a moment later to explain, "I called the police, as you asked."

The sound from the nave increased, and it was clear that the people of Condicote were unhappy to have had the wool pulled over their eyes.

"Is Oldfield really dead?" one man demanded.

"He's probably just been at the wine again," a woman said, and I thought I recognised Mrs Grout the grocer's voice. "We all know that the reverend is a man of both heavenly and earthly pleasures."

"Tell us the truth," Granny demanded.

I heard P.C. Brigham clear his throat to address the crowd. "I can't possibly tell you the truth if I don't know what it is now, can I? Please wait outside, and I will report back when I have something to tell. After all, I am a servant of the people, and that makes all o' you my bosses."

This seemed to placate the restless masses and, a moment later, the skinny constable appeared in the vestry. Whilst I had been listening to the goings on outside, Grandfather had continued his observation of the crime scene. I couldn't say what he had discovered, but he was certainly happy with his findings.

"You're looking for a thief," he declared before the officer could pass through the same emotions that we had all experienced.

"So 'e's dead then?" Brigham showed no great horror at this fact and deferred to Lord Edgington's greater experience in such matters. "Do you have any idea who mighta done it?"

"I just told you, man. He was killed by a thief." Grandfather could be terribly literal at times.

"Right you are. Now would you happen to know which thief, in particular, might be to blame?"

The constable, the verger and I waited to hear what the sleuth would reveal as Grandfather looked vexed with the lot of us.

"Perhaps I should start from the beginning." He ran one hand through his long silver hair before explaining what we'd clearly missed. "From various signs on the body, including skin tone, temperature and the level of flexibility in the dead man's limbs, I believe that the vicar was murdered at some point yesterday evening. In his hand you will find a small silver key which, it seems fair to assume, opened the aumbry on the wall. In my experience, such a cabinet would normally hold a ciborium or another religious artefact of some value."

We stared back at him, blank faced, and he paused to clarify something for the simpletons in his midst. "An aumbry is a box for storing precious objects within a church." When we continued to act as though we were making great efforts to decipher a foreign language, he released a long, tired breath. "And a ciborium is a tall, metal vessel with a lid. It is used for holding the host during a service."

"Any fool could work that out," the constable said, as though this were true.

"Simple," Bob Thompkins agreed.

Grandfather did not show his annoyance but, having spent more than fourteen seconds of my life with the man, I knew that he loathed wasting his precious time in such a manner.

"The aumbry is empty, which leads me to believe that Reverend Oldfield was murdered for its contents. If you can find the stolen property, there's a good chance the killer will be nearby."

The verger chewed his lip for a moment and, once my grandfather's words had been decoded, he posed a question. "This 'ciborium', would it happen to look like a big gold cup with a hat on the top?"

"Yes, that's the very thing."

Thompkins puffed up his chest. "Then I can confirm it is normally kept inside this here…" He searched for the word that Lord Edgington had used. "…box."

"Excellent work, Bob." The constable seemed more impressed by the verger's trivial observation than my grandfather's skills of deduction.

"Thank you, Del."

"However, there is a question which I think begs asking." The officer straightened his navy-blue uniform with a tug so that the brass buttons shone in the light that cut through the small window. "Is it not possible that we are looking for a bell-ringer? A murderous, thieving bell-ringer?"

The matchless Lord Edgington, who had worked with so many of the great detectives over the course of his forty-year career at Scotland Yard, apparently couldn't believe his ears. "A bell-ringer?"

"That's right." P.C. Brigham nodded, and the verger nudged him with an encouraging elbow.

"You know, I was wondering the very same thing."

"A bell-ringer?" my grandfather repeated in an incredulous tone, and I was extremely happy that I hadn't been the one to raise this suspicion.

"The very same." Brigham winked at Thompkins before explaining his flight of genius. "You see, the reverend was murdered with a bell rope. Seems to me that the likely culprit would be—"

"A bell-ringer?" The third time was the charm for the former superintendent, who now snapped out of his trance. "No, I have no reason to believe that the murderer is a bell-ringer, just as I have never considered a chef to be a likely suspect when investigating a stabbing. We are in a church, are we not? The killer could have taken a spare rope from the bell tower before coming into the vestry."

"Fair enough." Thompkins had a deep country accent and smelt of hay. "You gave it your best go, Del. You should be proud o' yourself."

"That is very kind of you to say, Bob." The two men nodded to one another before grandfather intervened.

I believe that he slowed his words down to make certain that his message would be understood. "As residents of the local area, could you possibly tell me whether any names come to mind when considering the handling of stolen goods?"

28

P.C. Brigham looked at Bob Thompkins, Bob Thompkins looked at P.C. Brigham and, at the exact same moment, they both said, "You mean Caswell and Alsop?"

Such was the unusual manner in which the two locals spoke that even my grandfather was confused. "I don't know, do I?"

It was Brigham's turn to offer an explanation. "Adam Caswell and Marcus Alsop. They're the only villains we have to put up with around here. Along with poor deceased Baron Fane, they were quite the little gang. Forever drinking themselves into a stupor and causing trouble. P'rhaps they decided to clear out of here now that their protector has croaked. P'rhaps they killed the vicar, made off with the loot, and are living a charmed life on the back of their ill-gotten gains, somewhere on the south coast."

I'd been to the south coast of England on several occasions, and it was hardly crowded with retired thieves. I suppose that a Tatchester bobby wasn't to know that, though.

"I'll need their full details, and I'd like you to commence the investigation by asking around the village to find out what both men were doing yesterday evening."

"Right you are, sir," the constable responded with a tip of his helmet. He hesitated for a moment, as if uncertain whether he should speak again, before deciding in the affirmative. "And should I get you a list of the local bell-ringers? Just to be on the safe side."

CHAPTER FOUR

"You know, my boy." Grandfather was all smiles as we left the church. "I really wasn't expecting much excitement on our sojourn to the country. This is all rather interesting, don't you think?"

"I'm not sure that's the word I would use." Considering the fifty-eight years that separated us, it was surprising how often I had to be the sensible one.

He laughed a single note. "I mean to say, it's a terrible situation, and I'm certain that the vicar will be greatly missed, but I haven't had a good murder to investigate for far too long."

It was a morning filled with confusion – which was nothing out of the ordinary for me. "But we solved a case just a few days ago. Have you forgotten that we spent Christmas running around after a killer rather than ripping open presents and swilling mulled wine?"

He wasn't paying attention as he looked at the lines of cottages that led up to the market square. Condicote had a timeless feel to it. It was all paved grey stone and winding streets, the kind of place that modern architects would baulk at, but which held all sorts of charm for a young man like myself with adventure on the brain.

You see, my grandfather had been right in his supposition, I had been reading a rather sensational novel – John Masefield's 'Sard Harker' to be precise – and it had turned my mind to the possibilities of travel, dangerous endeavours, and the pursuit of untold riches in foreign lands. I very much doubted I would find such things in a small English market town, though I could still dream.

"I'm sorry?" my companion asked, but we'd both forgotten what I'd said by this point, and he was soon focused on the case. "Yes, as I remarked, it's all very interesting; the vicar's death occurring so soon after Fane's. Not to mention the missing valuables, and the criminal associates of a local baron. What can you tell me about him?"

"Not much."

"Christopher, how many times must I tell you to use full sentences?"

As we passed the row of thatched houses, children, housewives and a few old gents peered out at us, whispering to one another as they recognised the famous detective.

"I can tell you that my grandmother really didn't like him," I replied, answering his first question rather than the grumpy sequel.

"I knew that much." He emitted another brief laugh. "Does she like anyone?"

"She likes you for some reason, though she tries not to show it." This fact had never surprised me, as my grandfather is almost impossible not to admire. "But she took against Fane when he was a young man. He was a bit of a Lord Byron, by her account. His despotic father died when he was barely of age. Fane inherited a fortune, married a rich American heiress and spent the last two decades frittering away every penny of their immense wealth."

"Fascinating."

It felt rather wonderful to know more than he did on the matter. "I saw him often over the years, and he certainly cut a dashing figure. He had an incredibly full beard and always wore tightly fitted tailcoats over his powerful frame. On his feet, he sported high boots, and he carried a riding crop for some reason. All in all, he seemed like the kind of chap who hoped someone would turn him into a hero in his own novel. Granny said that he was a rogue with the ladies and a wicked gambler. Granny's butler, Lambert, went even further."

"Excellent stuff!" He was clearly having a whale of a time, or at least a porpoise or two. "And you were wise to seek the opinion of a servant. They often know more about what goes on in places like this one than the heads of the town council. Now, what did Lambert say?"

"He claimed that Baron Stamford Fane had fallen into bad company and resorted to criminal means to cover his debts."

"So he was a robber baron!" Grandfather's smile only grew wider. "Extraordinary. And what sort of crimes were this nefarious, yet no doubt well-spoken, gang guilty of?"

I tried to recount the story I had heard, much as I might recite the plot of a good book. "Well, from what I understood, there were accusations of fraud, deception and even common theft."

Grandfather rubbed his hands together. Christmas clearly wasn't quite over for him. "How wonderful. As much as I love investigating a good murder, I do sometimes miss more common-or-garden rogues. When I was a young policeman working the rabbit warren of East London, I considered the criminals in those insalubrious neighbourhoods to be my equals in a complex and unwinnable game. Murder is an entirely different dilemma, and it requires a different approach."

"Couldn't the cases be connected? Isn't it possible that one of Fane's terrible associates killed him and made it look as though it was an accident before despatching the vicar?" Even as I suggested such a series of circumstances, they sounded quite outlandish.

He stopped just at the point where the simple cottages gave way to grand Tudor buildings, which were interspersed with stone fortifications of Norman design. "I am very happy that you would consider such links between the crimes, Christopher. It shows that you are putting that imagination of yours to good use. But we must remember what your grandmother told us. Fane's death has been investigated by Scotland Yard and the man they sent will have combed through every scrap of evidence. It has been determined that the brakes on the car were in good standing, and it sounds as though a number of reliable citizens here in Condicote bore witness to his intoxicated state. If the Yard is happy to say that Fane died a natural death, then we would need substantial evidence to undermine such a conclusion."

There was a serious, maybe even cautionary note which ran through this speech. It was not the first time that he'd lectured me on the unparalleled efficiency of his former employer, and I tried not to doubt him.

This older part of town – where the great black and white, half-timbered marketplace dominated the central square – was a hive of activity. Sellers were hawking their wares from the galleried building, and shopkeepers were re-opening their businesses after the excitement of the funeral that never was. Carts and rather shabby Austin motor cars thundered past us as I reflected on my task. I was used to crimes taking place in single houses, or small villages at a push, but the once-thriving market town was a new proposition.

"Where do we start?" Standing in the middle of the square, I felt a little out of my depth.

"It seems a simple enough case to me." Grandfather was typically imperious in his reply. "We're looking for information on two criminals who are known to be fond of a drink."

"The pub!" I couldn't resist a smile, as I'd become rather fond of such establishments.

"That's right, Christopher. Off we go!"

If there was one place in Condicote I did not mind being marched towards, it was The Drop of Dew Inn. It was housed on the other side of the market in another building dating back to Elizabethan times. To all appearances, Condicote must have been important back in those days, as the buildings were far more elaborate than in most English country towns. Even the pub had its share of grandeur. Its first-floor rooms overhung the pavement, and the neat, black and white façade was embellished with the coat of arms of some ancient family.

The sign above head height bore a painting of a water droplet that appeared to be glistening in the silvery moonlight. There was something rather magical about it, and I was eager to go into the pub not only to discover what food they served, but what mysteries the place held.

"We're looking for two men by the names of—" My grandfather was interrupted before he could finish his enquiry.

"Caswell and Alsop, no doubt." The woman serving was so short that her head was only just visible above the bar, and yet she was clearly not the sort of person to whom the customers would show disrespect. She was tiny but muscular, like a bantam fowl, and had a hard, narrow face which looked as though it had been compressed for some months in a metalworker's vice. "They're up in their rooms."

Grandfather may have wondered how the landlady knew our business so readily, but he never posed unnecessary questions. "You're very kind, madam. And may I further ask whether either of the men—"

"Left the pub between last night and this morning?" she guessed again. "Caswell did. Alsop was here with his strumpet."

Lord Edgington was quietly impressed by the woman's efficiency. I have no doubt that he wished all witnesses would provide us with the information we required so readily. "And you're certain that's the case? There is no way that Marcus Alsop could have slipped out of the inn without being seen?"

Instead of answering aloud, she pointed to the staircase that was in the corner of the small, comfortable parlour and then at her eyes.

"Surely you slept?" was my bewildered reply.

"Not last night, I didn't," she explained, just as a yawning hulk of a man appeared from a back room to begin his duties at the bar. "We've the only rooms for travellers to rent in a ten-mile radius, so there's always one of us here on duty. I took over at twelve midnight, and he'll do the same now."

She pointed one thumb at the man I could only assume was her husband. If my supposition were correct, they made an unusual couple. There must have been three feet between them – in height, I mean, not distance.

"And there's no back door or window through which he could have escaped?"

The pair of them rolled their eyes at me, but only the woman spoke. "He was here, I tell you. Ask his hussy if you don't believe me."

"That is just what we will do, madam." Grandfather bowed his head in thanks before realising what he had said. "Or rather, we will consult the lady in question." He bowed again and ushered me up the stairs.

"Alsop has the room at the end of the corridor," the landlady shouted after us. "You can't miss it."

CHAPTER FIVE

I would much rather have stayed down in the lounge in a deep armchair before the smouldering fire, but such pleasures were denied to me for the simple reason that we had a murder to investigate. You know, I sometimes wished I had a normal grandfather who was more interested in everyday concerns.

The staircase gave on to a dark corridor, and we followed the noise of a woman's gentle laughter to the door in question. Grandfather knocked but, instead of a "Come in," or perhaps a "Who's there?" we were greeted with silence.

To my surprise, a transformation came over my companion, and, before my eyes, he became a real policeman. "Alsop, you open this door this moment or I'll come back with five officers who are less gentle than I am. They'll knock it down and toss you into the street."

I could hear the sound of hurried movement from within the room and, after a few seconds, the door flew open.

"Who are you?" a surprisingly well-spoken chap of around twenty asked us.

"I am the Marquess of Edgington, and this is my grandson Christopher," grandfather responded, before following this with another of his favourite phrases. "Perhaps you've heard of me?" A hopeful expression occupied his face.

I think the fellow relaxed a little as he leaned back against the doorframe. "Heard of you? My mother talks of little else." I did not think much of this just then, but it would come back to me some time later. "What do you want with me?"

I looked past him into the messy bedroom, expecting to see the woman we had heard, but there was no one else there.

"We're investigating a murder, and I would like to know where you and your associate Adam Caswell were at eight o'clock last night."

Before he could answer, a winsome young woman popped up from behind the large mahogany bed. "A murder?" She sounded appropriately shocked. "Who's been killed?"

They kept their gaze fixed on the old detective, who was in no hurry to cut short their suspense.

"Reverend Oldfield," I answered when the silence was too long, even by Grandfather's standards. "We found him in the vestry this morning."

Grandfather did not seem too unhappy with me for giving away such a detail. "I notice that you chose not to attend Fane's funeral. I'd been led to believe you were close acquaintances."

"The funeral!" The young lady climbed out from her hiding place, her pretty face all the more amazed.

"Scarlet, we forgot the funeral!" her foppish friend replied.

The pair stared at one another for a moment before they both started laughing in one sudden burst of noise. Alsop had moved clear of the doorway, and I had a better view of the room. It certainly looked as though they had spent the night in there together. There were empty bottles of beer lying about the place, a half-finished game of draughts sat neglected on a small table, and there were papers covered in scrawled handwriting which were strewn about the floor.

"What time is it, anyway?" Alsop asked, but Grandfather pushed the chap further into the room.

"A man is dead and the two of you seem to find it funny."

"Stamford was a drunken fool, and he shouldn't have been driving," the young man retorted. "I told him as much before he drove off with a bottle of whisky under his arm."

"I'm not talking about Fane. I meant the vicar."

"Oh, yes, the vicar. I forgot about him."

He was dressed in red silk pyjamas, but his appearance until now had not concerned him. Upon noting our presence within his sanctuary, he became more self-conscious and reached for a dressing gown. His sweetheart, or whatever she might have called herself, was less worried about her appearance and jumped onto the bed covers to watch the proceedings from a better vantage point.

Grandfather needed no invitation and took a seat beside the unlit fireplace. "Young lady, would you mind telling me where this man was last night? And before you answer, I should let you know that I have no small amount of experience in detecting lies and liars."

"Leave her out of this," Alsop's temper flared. "It's me you should ask."

Grandfather ignored him. "Young lady?"

Still unruffled by the presence of the great man, she smiled sweetly and answered his question. "We've been here the whole night. And if you don't believe us, ask the old chap in the room next door. He was banging on the wall every five minutes to complain about the noise we were making."

Grandfather maintained just as friendly a manner. "You were having a party, I see."

She shrugged and turned her head to look at me. "Not a party, no. We were just... living our lives."

Her enthusiasm spread to her partner, who took this as his cue to fall onto the bed and wrap her in his arms. "That we were, my scarlet one! That we were."

They rolled about on the bed for a few seconds, and Marcus kissed her neck like a bee trying to access the nectar in a flower. I must admit that I felt my cheeks burn and had to look away. I wasn't used to such displays of affection. I once saw my mother take my father's hand whilst they were reading in our conservatory at Kilston Down. Father was so embarrassed that he couldn't look at me for a week.

Grandfather attempted to rein them in once more. "A man has been killed, and a valuable item from the church is missing. I would appreciate it if you could take this matter seriously."

The chap laughed at Grandfather's response and sat back against the headboard. "I see. Something has been stolen, and so we must be the culprits. Is that what you're implying?"

"I'm implying no such thing." Grandfather had met a more calculating foe than he might have expected and was clearly enjoying the challenge. "But I'll happily state it outright if you wish."

"You're fun!" Scarlet emitted a hoot of appreciation. "I've read plenty of stories about you, of course, but the papers always make you out to be a fusty old thing. You're not at all what I was expecting."

With this, she seized a pad of paper that was resting on a nearby stool and began scribbling with a pencil that had previously held her hair up on her head. As her auburn locks tumbled down around her shoulders, I couldn't help noticing how pretty she was. She had skin as pure as fresh snow and near-luminous blue eyes that glowed like the headlights on one of Grandfather's many cars. And yet, the force of her personality shone even more brightly than her beauty.

I didn't know these people from Adam and Eve, and yet, within a few minutes of meeting them, I hoped for nothing more than to join their little gang.

Grandfather had been examining our suspects. When he spoke again, he adopted a softer tone. "You have me at a disadvantage, madam. You appear to know plenty about me, and I haven't even learnt your full name."

At that moment, I wondered if it was possible for Scarlet to express any emotion other than happiness. Her face seemed to have been pre-formed into a smile, which only grew as she answered him. "My name is Emmeline Warwick. My friends call me Scarlet."

"But Emmeline has such a pretty sound to it." Grandfather seemed as sad about her choice of name as anything else that had happened that day. "Why would you go by anything else?"

She stopped writing and looked up at us. "My mother once told me I was a scarlet woman, and I rather liked the idea, so it stuck. I've barely spoken to her since and took it as a symbol of my independence. I believe you've met my brother Fabian in London? He chose a different path from mine, but we have both provided an abundance of shame for our dear, hardworking family."

We'd crossed paths with Fabian Warwick on one of our previous cases, and it was fair to say that he had scandalised London society with his behaviour. His sister's affair in a small, country hotel seemed exceedingly tame in comparison.

"And what about your friend Adam Caswell?" Grandfather was far better at concentrating on our investigations than me… Well, he was better at concentrating in general, actually. I was more of a dreamer than a doer. "We were told he would be here too."

"Adam!" Marcus Alsop yelled his associate's name from where he was sitting. "Adam, you lazy bear. Wake up!" All this achieved was a bang on the wall from a grumpy neighbour, but the debonair young chap was in no hurry to leave the room. "You know, we like to shock the locals here as much as possible, but we're really not the hellraisers everyone makes us out to be."

"Oh, yes?" Grandfather crossed one ankle over the other and awaited an explanation.

"Yes!" Marcus brought his fist down onto the bed as though squashing a bothersome fly. "We're not killers, and we're barely thieves – except for fun when I've had a little too much gin. What people here cannot comprehend is that we choose to live our lives in search of pleasure rather than allowing ourselves to be ruled by the drudgery of common existence."

Scarlet raised one half-moon eyebrow. "You know, that's rather a neat turn of phrase. Would you mind if I wrote it down?"

He waved a hand through the air in flamboyant acceptance. "The police have been after me ever since I moved here." His bad mood had dissipated like a cloud on a sunny day, and he began to laugh once more. "You know, that Brigham chap tried to have me up before the magistrate for stealing a flock of sheep recently."

"Had you stolen them?" Grandfather's impassive expression only increased the humour of his dry retort.

"I very much hadn't, and so I turned out my pockets and told him just that. I barely have room to fit Scarlet up here with all the books and papers she has, let alone a pack of woolly monsters."

"I admire your joie de vivre." Lord Edgington paused, and we all knew that a *but* would be just around the corner. "But it is a lot easier to have such an attitude when one comes from money. I can see that neither of you were short of silver spoons in your upbringing."

"Says the Lord-Lieutenant of Surrey, owner of one of the richest estates in the country and a man with a taste for expensive cars." Scarlet had a good snicker at Grandfather's hypocrisy.

"You really *have* read a lot about me." There was no question about it; he was impressed by her quick responses.

"I have indeed." Her defiant tone faded a little. "And I happen to know that, when you were young like us, you turned your back on your old-fashioned education, and sought something more nourishing for your soul. We've done quite the same thing as you."

Grandfather held a finger up to interrupt her. "I also turned my back on the fortune you were so quick to assign me. I became an officer and worked my way up through the police without my parents' connections or any helping hands. I only took on the wealth of the Cranley Hall estate when my brother died and there was no one else to look after it."

She leant forward as Marcus closed his eyes. He seemed quite happy to let her talk. "That's not so very different. All three of us have tried to become something more than what our parents prescribed. Mother wanted me to marry a doughy second-cousin with a farm in Hertfordshire, and I said no. I told her I wanted to see the world before I'm trapped into marriage. I want to be a writer."

If she hadn't dazzled me enough before this point, her final sentence could have been fashioned just for me. "Oh, how marvellous! What will you write? Who are your biggest influences?"

Grandfather looked at me as though my silence was preferable to such interruptions, but Scarlet answered all the same.

"I want to write something entirely new." Her sparkling blue eyes filled with hope as she looked up at the ceiling. "Something so modern that it seems as if it was written one hundred years from now. Something paradoxical and true."

"You sound like your brother," was all my grandfather would say and, though I longed to ask her a hundred more questions, I kept quiet.

"The point is…" Marcus's eyes clicked open in a rather startled manner. "…we aren't killers, and we had no interest in the vicar. I've said three words to the man in all the months we've been here, and each of them was 'Morning!'"

I believe it had become apparent to my more experienced colleague that we weren't learning anything useful, so it was fortuitous that, at this very moment, the door creaked open and a chap as wide as he was tall sidestepped into the room. I'm not exaggerating; he truly was the squarest fellow I'd ever seen. He was so broad that he had to angle his body to make his way through the meagre opening.

"We missed the funeral," he said as he eyed the unexpected visitors. "But you'll never guess what I got for us last night."

"Adam, this is Lord Edgington," Marcus interrupted before the slow, lumbering chap could say anything incriminating.

Apparently unaware of who my grandfather was, the oaf kept talking, "Hello, Lord Edgington, look what I've got." From behind his back he produced a rather elegant golden cup with a lid on the top and finely engraved scrollwork all over. I could only assume that this was the missing ciborium.

CHAPTER SIX

"Caswell, you total nincompoop." Marcus shot up from the bed to grab his simple-minded friend by the shoulders. "What on earth have you done?"

Adam Caswell glanced about the room again, perhaps re-evaluating exactly who the smartly dressed old man with the amethyst-topped cane, dove-grey top hat and matching morning suit might be.

"What... I... I haven't done nothing. I just..." He was so panicked by his friend's question that I was afraid he might go crashing through the window to escape. It was not an advisable route, seeing as we were some fifteen feet off ground level with only the hard stone road to break his fall.

"Don't you know who Lord Edgington is?" Marcus was dumbfounded. "The man's a detective."

"I've heard the name... I think. But I reckoned he was just a friend of Stamford's. How should I know he's a..." He didn't finish this sentence but dropped the cup to the floor and began to panic. "What have I done? What have I done?"

Grandfather didn't need to put any questions to the chap, as his friends were doing the job. Still with her pad and pencil in hand, Scarlet rushed over to speak to him. "The vicar's dead, Adam. Please tell us you didn't have anything to do with it?"

He froze to stare at them for a moment and could only summon one more word before he broke down in dolorous shrieks. "Blood!"

Grandfather rose from his chair to examine the ciborium and, sure enough, the once beautiful (now slightly dented) artefact was covered with dried blood. Scarlet showed almost as much emotion as the guilty giant. She collapsed back onto the bed and wouldn't rise again for some time.

"Tell the man what you did, or you'll hang." Marcus hadn't let go of his friend even as the huge fellow twisted about in distress. "It was an accident, wouldn't you say? You went to talk over your past sins with the good reverend and somehow hit him with that thing."

"It's a ciborium," Grandfather explained, though it really wasn't the moment to worry about vocabulary. "Sadly for Mr Caswell here, the vicar was subsequently strangled with a bell rope."

For all his agitation, Caswell would not deny the crime or offer any more information on what had occurred. I knew what came next and, sure enough, Grandfather gave me a swift flick of the eyes to despatch me downstairs. I bolted off along the corridor and took the stairs three at a time to launch myself at the bar, which was now manned by the tall landlord we'd seen before.

"Call the police! Immediately."

Swift to action, he nodded and ran to the front door. "Del, over here!" he yelled through it. "P.C. Brigham! Lord Edgington's boy says you're needed."

Things happened quickly after that. Scotland Yard was called in to examine the physical evidence of the crime. It was the first case in some time where I'd had the chance to see high-level police officers work their magic, and I must say it was terribly interesting. Normally, my grandfather and I had to be careful not to be seen to be interfering with an official police investigation, but with most of the work already done and the culprit caught, they were happy to have us at hand.

It certainly didn't hurt that Grandfather's old colleague from his days in the police, Chief Inspector Darrington, was in charge of the case. We had access to all the findings that were made that first day as Caswell was kept in a cell in Condicote police station.

"It's not looking good for the chap," the chief inspector confided in us once the vestry had been swept for clues and the suspect's room had been turned over by officers. "He's not the brightest star in the night sky and isn't doing himself any favours by keeping his mouth shut. I was willing to give him the benefit of the doubt, but he's got no real explanation for how he came by the ciborium."

Darrington was a serious, hardworking sort of fellow with a beautifully presented black suit and a military air. I'd only met him a few times, but he always looked as though he'd come from having the shiny metal buttons on his blazer polished before speaking to us.

"It's a sad case," my grandfather concurred as we sat in the Drop of Dew. "This Caswell fellow clearly doesn't understand the trouble he's in." The two men were sipping pints of bitter, whereas I was in seventh (or possibly even eighth) heaven to have a chicken pie and a glass of lemonade. Was there ever a meal so delicious? Ever a treat quite so sweet? Ever a—

"Christopher!" my mentor barked, and I stopped composing a poem to pies in my head and tried to concentrate on the discussion. "The chief inspector was asking whether you had any thoughts on the matter. Do you believe that Caswell is guilty?"

I almost choked on a chunk of potato and had to wash it down with a gulp of my drink before I could reply. "Oh, I… Yes, I'm afraid it seems that way. All the evidence points to the fact that he was involved, and we've found nothing to contradict the likely scenario."

"Which is?" Darrington asked, his tone and eyebrows rising in unison.

"That he killed the vicar in order to steal valuables from the church and sell them for cash. We heard that Caswell and Alsop have both had their brushes with the law. Does Caswell have any convictions for violence?"

I thought grandfather might contribute something at this point – or tell me I was asking irrelevant questions – but he placed his hand on his chin in reflection and looked just as interested to hear the answer as I was.

"Nothing like this, but he does have a colourful past." Darrington took a slug of beer and licked the ivory foam from his lips. "He comes from a good local family, but he's been in prison for theft before. There were no reports of any strangers in the village last night, either, and there's nothing to suggest anyone had a vendetta against the deceased. To be honest, it seems like a perfectly simple case."

"Exactly," I replied a little too zealously. "And that's what I don't like about it."

The two experienced detectives smiled at the innocent fool who was stuffing his face with pie.

"That's admirable that you would care so much, Christopher." Grandfather slowly closed and opened his eyes in approval. "I think perhaps I am to blame for your attitude, though. I have told you about so many complex and contradictory cases that, when an everyday sort of affair comes along, it's almost impossible to believe."

Darrington put his hands together and gave his own view of the situation. "The facts are clear. Caswell has no alibi for the whole of yesterday evening when the vicar was murdered. Furthermore, he was in possession of a valuable item that was stolen from the scene of the crime."

The three of us fell silent to watch the crackling log in the open fire. It provided the perfect accompaniment to help us think, but there were no two ways about it; Caswell was as guilty as any killer we'd encountered. And yet something still niggled at me.

"It doesn't make any sense. Killers don't loiter near the scene of the crime with their loot, waiting to be caught. If Caswell was guilty, he would have got out of Condicote, or at least hidden the evidence."

Darrington inhaled the heavily scented air and let it back out again in a long, slow breath. "He's not the usual sort of criminal you and your grandfather have to catch, Christopher."

A connection sparked in my brain then, and the way I'd been feeling made a touch more sense. "That's just the problem. If I were a killer, looking to cover up my crime, I know who I'd choose to take the blame. And it's working, too. Caswell has no defence and can't explain why he was carrying around a blood-stained relic."

"A ciborium isn't, by definition, a relic. In fact, it's really more of a—" Lord Edgington could see that neither of us was particularly worried about the correct ecclesiastical terminology and cut himself short.

Darrington knew something else that would only serve to condemn the suspect. "Several witnesses have come forward to say that the vicar went tearing through the village on his bicycle at seven thirty last night. He had visited some elderly parishioners in Yockwardine and was on his way back to St Bartholomew's. What's even more interesting for us, however, is the fact that Caswell had been walking out that way and was seen striding through the centre of town in the direction of the church a mere ten minutes later."

"So you think there was an altercation between the two of them?" Grandfather concluded, tapping his cheek as his colleague constructed a possible sequence of events.

"Precisely. It would make sense that Oldfield bumped into Caswell with his bicycle and the big lout wasn't happy about it. The vicar raced away, thinking he'd be safe once he reached the sanctuary of the church, but our culprit cares nothing for convention and thundered inside to strangle the clergyman to death."

"I'm sorry, but that doesn't convince me." I tried to believe his theory, but a spider's web of doubt had threaded through my brain, and I couldn't see it any other way.

Grandfather reached out to put one hand on my shoulder. "Chrissy, tell us what you concluded when we first found the vicar's body. Remind me exactly what you said."

"I said he was dead."

"Christopher!" This was not the first roll of the eyes he had made that day, and it would not be the last. "I was referring to what you said soon after that."

I needed a moment to remember. "I said that the killer was a man of some strength."

"That's the very thing." My heroic forebear clicked his fingers before underlining the fact I had hoped to ignore. "And who else in this town would have the physical power of a man like Adam Caswell?"

I didn't answer him because there was nothing left to say.

Darrington clearly felt sorry for me and tried once more to make the case for our only suspect's guilt. "I know it's sad to think of that rather cheerful monster going to the gallows, but I've met fellows like him before. His simple, smiling exterior is a façade. The vicar was running from something. Everyone in the village who saw him has attested to that. Mrs Ivy from the jeweller's even said that he had a look of fear in his eyes.

"There hasn't been a post-mortem, yet, but the doctor's initial findings match with your grandfather's idea that the vicar was murdered in the late evening, shortly after Caswell was seen walking towards the church. The fact is that all the clues we've discovered point to one man, and we'd be fools to overlook such a weight of evidence."

I had one more challenge left in me. "If Caswell went to St Bartholomew's to kill Reverend Oldfield, why did he steal the ciborium? Why would he keep hold of it? Surely even the simplest of men would know that such a connection to a crime would land him in gaol."

Darrington used a soft tone to try to convince me, as my grandfather remained quiet. "Because, dear boy, people like Adam Caswell don't think that far ahead. Of course some part of his brain knew that the stolen item could prove his guilt. What he failed to consider was that he was the first name on a very short list when we considered who might be responsible for such a theft."

I wanted to snap at his words; I wanted to find the single piece of evidence that everyone else had overlooked which would rule out the gentle giant's involvement, but I couldn't do it and so Grandfather took his turn.

"We saw the moment when the two ideas solidified in the killer's head. You were there when he realised where his actions would take him. He saw the blood on the ciborium and lost control because he knew he would hang for his crime. Until that moment, he'd been happy with himself. But on discovering that there were detectives speaking to his friends whilst he was sleeping off his misadventures, the truth exploded in his brain like a rocket on Guy Fawkes Night."

I had more questions and more doubts. I couldn't make sense of what Caswell had been doing between the time he supposedly murdered the vicar and four hours later when he returned to the inn. I couldn't see why a man with no record of violence would suddenly murder a well-known figure in his own village. But most of all, I couldn't quite understand why I cared so much.

Except... I could. It was because of Scarlet and Marcus. It was because of the expression I'd seen on their faces as the police led their friend away. I couldn't bear to see those vibrant characters reduced to such listless sorrow, and I wanted to believe that the wrong man had been arrested.

I could see that my grandfather was torn between the official conclusions of his colleague from Scotland Yard and my thoughts on the case, but the tower of evidence that the police had built meant nothing to me. I was certain that Adam Caswell wouldn't have killed another human being because, at the moment that P.C. Brigham clapped him in handcuffs, the look in Scarlet Warwick's eyes told me he was innocent.

CHAPTER SEVEN

We had an unexpectedly quiet New Year's Eve.

"This is still a celebration. We can still have fun." Mother exclaimed on several occasions, but it only reminded us of the dismal situation in which we found ourselves.

As the minutes ticked down to 1927, I looked back on my year and, instead of concentrating on the progress I'd made as a detective – and the fact I'd passed my school exams on my very first try – I could only remember the people we had lost. All that death! All those good souls who had met premature ends; it was far too sordid and sad.

Bizarrely, it was my ever-restrained father who made the difference. "Come along, you moping ninnies." He'd found a bottle of champagne in Granny's wine cellar and was determined to open it. "1927 will be an unforgettable year. Think of all the advances that will be made in aviation, medicine, and sanitation." I never said he was an inspirational speaker. He was just the type of man to reflect upon improvements in sewage treatment in a New Year's speech. "Imagine what is just around the corner!"

"More innovations in sanitation, perhaps?" My Grandfather could be an impertinent so-and-so.

"Among other things. But that's not all." Dear Papa was undeterred but waited for Todd to hand out seven champagne coupes that were filled to the brim with sparkling fizz. "Chrissy is following in his grandfather's footsteps. My business has been going from strength to strength, and dear Albert is soon to marry a charming young lady who already feels like a beloved member of our family."

Cassandra blushed at this. "Oh, Mr Prentiss, you are so kind. I really don't—"

"Observe, child!" Granny snapped before her son continued speaking.

"Wherever your wedding takes place, it will be a joy to behold. And so, I would like to raise a toast. To Albert and Cassandra. To the Prentiss-Cranley family. And to 1927!"

"To 1927!" the rest of us echoed, and we stood up to raise our glasses skyward before drinking. Even Delilah became excited and threaded her way between us as though she were playing a parlour game.

When we'd finished, I felt a familiar buzz, not just from the champagne, but the chatter of a happy family. Grandmother's meagre Christmas tree was still standing in the corner of her drawing room and, just for a moment, I had that inexplicable tingle that the season so often brings. It started at the back of my neck before dispersing through my veins like an electric shock.

"It's almost midnight." My brother pointed to the grandfather clock beside the door, and we formed a circle in preparation for the chimes. "Well, not quite yet. There are still twenty seconds to go."

I picked up a cushion to throw at him because he really was rather useless.

"I hope you're in good voice tonight, Grandfather," I told my favourite old man.

"Whenever am I not in—"

"Ten!" Albert shouted, and we all joined in as the second hand ticked towards a new day, a new year and whatever the future would hold for us. Sure enough, when we linked arms and sang Auld Lang Syne, I managed to forget about Reverend Oldfield and even Adam Caswell in his cold cell. We could hear fireworks in the field beyond the village and Albert, Cassandra, my parents and I ran to the top of the house to see those elegant bursts of colour. For a few minutes, as we marvelled at the instantaneous blooms of light, nothing else mattered in the world but the people I loved most.

I wished that the joy and optimism of that moment could have lasted a little while longer, but it was not to be. Our family returned to Surrey the next day, but Grandfather and I stayed behind for the inquest. Such affairs are normally brief, perfunctory things, and the local coroner had no interest in alternative theories as to what had really happened or potential holes in the evidence. He was there to establish an official record of the time and cause of death, the location of certain people at certain moments and the investigating officers' initial theories on what had taken place.

It was held in the Lock and Key – the larger of the two pubs in Condicote – and, to be perfectly honest, I've been to more formal children's parties. With his pint of bitter in hand, P.C. Brigham was called to speak first and gave a concise account of what we had discovered in the vestry.

Scarlet Warwick cried throughout the proceedings. Marcus was there to comfort her, but I suffered just as she did. It was a shock to see such a strong person reduced to emotional exhaustion and even worse to have to watch Adam Caswell listen so calmly with that sad half-smile on his face. He denied his part in the crime but could offer no evidence to prove his innocence or explain how the ciborium had come into his possession. His claim that it had fallen off the back of a car drew laughs from the excited audience, and Adam looked resigned to his fate.

With the news that the police from Scotland Yard had already arrested the suspect, the case was forwarded to the magistrate's court, who would inevitably pass it on to the Tatchester Assizes, just as soon as a High Court Judge was sitting there.

When Adam was led away by the police, Marcus and Scarlet were hounded from the town hall by a pair of journalists who had come up from London on the scent of a juicy tale. I waved as they passed, but they only caught a glimpse of me before disappearing outside. The room emptied far too quickly and then my grandfather and I were alone with nothing left to do but head back to my grandmother's house. The pair of us walked back despondently through the town and, if we hadn't promised Granny that we'd stay one last night in Condicote, I would have happily driven back to Surrey forthwith.

CHAPTER EIGHT

You might not have read it in any of the myriad newspaper articles that have celebrated his most famous cases, and it certainly won't be found in any book that the Metropolitan Police has produced for their new recruits, but my grandfather was a truly kind man.

"I don't see why we have to leave the house at this practically immoral hour," I complained when he woke me at six o'clock (in the morning!) on the day after the inquest.

"I've already told you, Christopher." Though I'd never liked being called Chrissy as a child, I'd actually become rather fond of my cheery diminutive. Whenever he used my full name these days, it set me on edge. "We have somewhere important to go. Now stop dilly-dallying and get ready."

Just to make sure that I did as instructed, he pulled off the bedsheets and the full chill of Granny's freezing house attacked me like a flight of spears.

As I was saying, my grandfather was a truly kind man, but he had an unusual way of showing it.

By the time I'd fallen from the granite-hard bed into some clean clothes and immersed my whole head in icy water to wake myself up, he had already eaten breakfast and was waiting at the door.

"Come, come, Chrissy. There's no time to eat."

I almost screamed. "Then why didn't you wake me earlier? Cook promised me black pudding for breakfast."

He was stepping across the threshold but stopped to look back at me. "Is that really what you would have wanted? If six o'clock is too early, I can only imagine how half-past five would have struck you."

He had me there. "Touché, Grandfather. But perhaps a sandwich could have been prepared for the journey?" My mouth was watering at the thought of a black pudding bap, but I pulled on my long woollen coat, took the scarves and hats that Todd had set out for me and dashed after the fleeing septuagenarian.

"It's just possible, Christopher, that I prefer the interior of my car the colour it is now. I'm not sure that brown sauce and grease stains are the right look for an Aston Martin." He was already sitting in the driver's seat, as the exceedingly modern engine in his sporty car didn't even need cranking.

I didn't answer. I just climbed into my usual spot, and my tummy rumbled like far-off thunder. I really should sew pastry pockets into my coat for such moments, or perhaps I could wear hats in order to conceal a few sandwiches up there.

I had no idea where we were going until he stopped the car in front of an intimidating stone building with an incredibly long façade. Tatchester Correctional Institute – or gaol, as any sane person would call it – was even more frightening than my grandmother's house.

"I had to trade in some favours to get us inside," my companion said as he hopped from the car. "Quick time, Chrissy. We haven't got all day."

I was still peering up at that luctiferous edifice and would require a few moments to appreciate the effort he'd gone to on my behalf. "You really are a very kind man," I shouted in the direction of the pillbox where he was already talking to a prison officer.

There are few places in my life that have caused me such agony. I felt like Odysseus descending into the underworld as we passed the first gate. At each stage of our journey through that inescapable labyrinth, we were handed from one sour-faced officer to another before finally reaching the corridor where remand prisoners were held.

"Five minutes. Room at the end," the rather rough attendant informed us. "Careful, mind. 'E's a big one. You don't wanna get too close."

We nodded our thanks and left him in his own secure cell to read a newspaper. Grandfather must have been to such places many times, and yet even he seemed depressed by the dim space. The men we passed showed little interest in us. They made me think of bodies with the souls removed. Some looked out through the slits of windows. Others lay on their bunks, staring at the ceiling, but there were no books for them to read – no activities to keep their minds alert – and the reality of incarceration became clear to me for the first time.

"Adam," I sang as we reached the barred cell at the end. There was no one to let us inside and anything we had to say to him would be conducted through the metal grill.

"How nice of you to visit," the big chap said, as though we had called by his mother's house to see him. "I wasn't expecting anyone today."

For all his slowness and limited vocabulary, he had a warm, neutral accent, which was quite different from most Condicote residents.

Showing no fear, Grandfather stepped closer to the bars. "Adam, I arranged for us to see you as I thought we should speak before you go any further down this treacherous road."

"That's nice. What would you like to talk about?"

"About you, Adam," I rushed to say. "You must tell us everything you know that could prove your innocence."

To my surprise, he seemed disappointed. It was as though he'd hoped we'd come for a chat about football or the weather. "It's too late for that. My solicitor told me not to get my hopes up for a lucky verdict." He smiled then, and it almost broke my heart. "But I spoke to my ma, and she said that hanging doesn't hurt so much these days. She says that the long drop finishes you off nice and quickly and, if I'm lucky, I'll get Thomas Pierrepoint. Everyone knows he's the swiftest executioner in Britain." He sounded like a young boy discussing his favourite sportsman.

"But you didn't do it, did you?" My words were a frantic supplication. "You didn't kill the vicar and so you shouldn't hang for it."

"Oh no, I didn't kill him. Why would I?"

Grandfather had fallen quiet, and I wondered whether he was reconsidering his conviction that the police had arrested the right man. Caswell was no monster; he was like a large docile animal that had wandered into the wrong habitat. The cell he was in looked barely big enough to hold the poor chap.

"So there must be something you can tell us that will help." I looked into his eyes and felt ever more convinced that he shouldn't be there. "Tell us what happened that day. Why were you out walking?"

He shrugged and turned away so that he could look at the tiny mirror on the wall. I doubt he could make out more than a quarter of his face in the smeared glass. "I was just walking. Scarlet and Marcus were busy, and so I went to see Ma and then kept on through the village. That's what I always do when everyone's busy. I like walking."

"Did you see the vicar on his bicycle?" Grandfather asked in a plangent tone.

"Oh, yes. He came clattering past on his bike. I was walking in the middle of the lane, and he almost hit me. I wondered what had got into him."

"Did he say anything?"

The prisoner had to think for a moment. "He said, 'Sorry'. I told him it didn't matter, and he sped off again. I thought he must have an appointment or something."

"And you didn't see him again after that?" Grandfather looked more interested now. It felt for the first time that he might be on Adam's side.

"No, I just kept walking."

A thought flashed into my mind in big letters like the sign above a Shaftesbury Avenue theatre. "What about another suspect? Did you see anyone on your walk who could have been responsible for the murder?"

He smiled his enormous smile. "I saw lots of people. There was Mrs Eileen Grout, the grocer, and Mayor Eric Hobson, the mayor. Oh, and Mrs Pauleen Stanley, the busybody, was leaving the church when I passed. She's never liked me, so I didn't say hello to her." I can't say I'd previously met anyone who insisted on using people's full names and their roles in the community.

"Excellent, Adam. That's very good. And can you think of any reason why one of them might have argued with the vicar?"

"No."

I wouldn't give up so easily. "Perhaps someone in the village argued with Reverend Oldfield, but things got out of hand, and so he murdered the man. All the killer had to do to shift the blame was steal the ciborium and make sure you found it. Don't you think that's possible?"

Instead of rising to the challenge, he just laughed at me. "In Condicote? Are you serious? There are no murderers in our little town. It's a kind, friendly sort of place."

"And yet someone was murdered, Adam!" I was practically shouting, which caused the man on duty to poke his head out of his room to check what was happening. "If you didn't do it, who killed the vicar?"

He had such a big heart that he managed to feel sorry for me at this moment. He came to the bars to put one giant hand through, and it instantly dwarfed mine. "That's a good question. To be honest, I hadn't thought about it, but someone must have done him in."

"Do you have any enemies?" Grandfather had started to pace in front of the cell, so at least I knew he was thinking. "Is there anyone who would have wished to make it look as though you were a killer?" I could see that this scenario appealed to him and so he asked a further question. "Isn't it possible that someone wanted to hurt you but, to hide their real motive, they planted evidence to suggest you were the culprit?"

"I suppose it is, but I get on well with everyone. P.C. Brigham can be a bit grumpy, but we still have a beer together in the Drop of Dew from time to time."

Apparently ignoring this response, Grandfather continued with his theory. "It's a rather clever stratagem – killing someone to see another man hanged. Murder by proxy, if you will. Perhaps…" His words faded out as he constructed a case in his head.

The eminent detective's supposition did not cheer Caswell. If anything, he seemed sadder than when we'd first arrived. "You don't need to worry about me. I've had a nice enough life, and I'm trying not to think about what'll happen after the trial. To be honest, I'd rather just remember the happy times. All the fun that me and Stamford used to get up to before he died. All the games that we played with Scarlet and Marcus. That's who I'll miss the most…" His whole jolly face had collapsed in sorrow. "…my friends."

Grandfather looked concerned as it became clear that the caged man in front of us would not reveal some hidden facet to the case. "I don't know whether you're protecting someone, or you don't realise the weight of the situation, but when the time comes to speak at the trial, you must defend yourself."

This fact only seemed to sadden him more. "I was holding the pretty cup that was used to bash the reverend over the head. Any jury will convict me; I don't stand a chance."

Grandfather seized the bars with both hands. "Then tell us how you came by the ciborium, and maybe we can–"

Adam crashed down on the low bunk behind him. "I tried to say it already and everyone laughed at me. I saw it drop out of a car and went to pick it up, but no one is going to believe that. Now that's enough. I don't want to talk about things that make me sad."

The old lord straightened his back and examined the man for a few seconds before replying in a calm voice. "Very well, Mr Caswell. You don't have to tell us the details, but I beg of you, tell your barrister everything. I have seen bleaker cases than your own come to good, and you mustn't give up hope."

Adam hesitated a moment before nodding, but it was hard to know whether he would take the advice. "Thank you, Lord Edgington." He rose once more, and it was like seeing a new mountain take shape. "If I was on that jury, I'd convict me of murder and send me to the gallows, but I still appreciate you both coming here."

Grandfather replied with a silent bow, just as the prison officer shouted down the corridor that our time was spent. We made our way back through the prison and, with every gate I passed, I breathed a little more easily. By the time I was outside again, it was as though I'd had an extra six hours sleep and eaten three breakfasts. Of course, that just made me feel more guilty for leaving Adam Caswell behind.

"What now?" I asked my grandfather when we were back in the car.

He didn't answer but kept his eyes fixed on the windscreen in front of us. Of all the places in the world I wished to visit, Lord Edgington's brain was surely the most fantastical. I could only imagine what wondrous landscapes that infinite space contained, and I hadn't a clue what he was thinking.

"What can we do now, Grandfather?"

"What can we do?" he said, coming back to reality. "If the man won't help himself, there's little hope for him."

"But you do believe that he's innocent, at least?" I was pleading with him to say yes as much as asking the question. "You see now that he couldn't have committed such a crime?"

He finally turned to me, and I knew before he said another word that I would only be disappointed. "What difference does it make what I believe if we've found no evidence to prove it? We looked over the crime scene several times. I've read the notes the police made and discussed the case with Scotland Yard. No matter how gentle a soul Caswell may possess, nothing can get him off the charges he faces. I'm sorry, my boy, but I don't know what else I can do."

I wanted to argue. I wanted to beg him to try harder and fashion an explanation for the impossible, as he had in so many of our prior investigations. Instead, he started the engine on his Aston Martin, and I shut my mouth and wouldn't open it again until we were back in Condicote.

CHAPTER NINE

We said farewell to my grandmother, who even managed to speak softly for once as she stood in front of The Manor, right where she'd welcomed us before the New Year. "I know this case has disturbed you, Christopher, but it's just the beginning. The trial will turn up unknown secrets upon which your grandfather here will have all sorts of interesting opinions."

"Thank you, Granny." I held out my hand to her, and she glanced at it for a moment before shaking it rather formally – she was not one for physical interaction. "That certainly gives me something to consider on the way home."

She winked at me then. I'd never seen her make such an intimate a gesture before, and I felt rather touched by her concern for me. Perhaps she wasn't such a cold-hearted devil after all. Perhaps she had a soft centre like so many of my favourite chocolates.

"Edgington." She nodded at him, and a stern expression passed over her face once more. "Make sure you don't crash on your way home. It would be a great tragedy to destroy such a wonderful car."

He laughed under his breath and bowed low like a Japanese servant in an adventure novel I'd recently read. "Thank you, Loelia." I sometimes forgot that my grandmother had a first name. "And you make sure that you don't choke on a chicken bone all alone in that immense house of yours with no one for company but the few disgruntled staff you pay."

"You are too kind!"

The two of them could have kept exchanging veiled insults all afternoon if I hadn't broken up the well-mannered fight. "Come along, Grandfather. It's potentially a long drive back to Surrey."

"I very much doubt it," he said with a roguish glint in his eye that told me I was in for a nerve-racking journey.

Todd and Halfpenny had prepared the cars before setting off for Cranley Hall. Delilah was waiting for us but would not meet my eye as I climbed into the passenger seat of Grandfather's Aston Martin Cloverleaf. Normally, she would have jumped in to squash me for several hours, but she was evidently furious at being left out of the investigation.

"I've already told you," Grandfather reminded her – he had a habit of speaking to our dear canine as though she were a person. "There are no dogs allowed in churches, prisons, or public inquests into a death. The case was resolved surprisingly swiftly, and it is not my fault that you had to stay at home."

She let out a song-like cry as she scurried over me into the dickey seat, and I wondered for the seven hundredth time whether she understood every word he said.

I had plenty of time to think on the way home, but I still couldn't say what it was about the vicar's murder that was different from all the others we'd investigated. Perhaps it was my first potential miscarriage of justice – the first case in which we had failed to prove beyond a shadow of a doubt who the murderer was.

It had been six months since I'd become my grandfather's full-time assistant. My schooling was a distant memory, and I was ready to grow up and become a man of the world. Surely, part of that ambition meant not falling to pieces at every dead body or perceived injustice we encountered.

"None of it makes any sense," I said aloud but hoped that my grandfather hadn't heard me over the sound of the wind attacking the car as we shot towards Gabbett's Cross.

"You're letting your emotions get the better of you, Christopher. The fact is that, if I'd carried every ounce of sorrow around with me through my career as a police officer, I'd never have been able to do my job."

I didn't respond at first but allowed this concept to sink slowly into me like ice through a drain. "That's not quite true. You did carry your failures around with you; you've told me so many times. The cases where you felt that things hadn't been resolved exactly as you wanted, or the killer avoided the punishment he deserved. You know the names without me having to remind you. There was John Fletcher Schoolcraft, Clementine de Paul, Morwenna Fairbright and any number of other examples. Those cases stayed with you for decades." It wasn't enough to say the word once, so I gave it a second go. "You spent decades of your life bearing that pain and, even now that we've finally solved them, they remain with you deep down. So you can deny it if you like, but I know you've felt the same way as I do right at this very moment."

My words blew stronger than the winter wind that rattled the windows and flapped at the thick leather roof. The temperature was diving again, and a sudden chill made me shiver as I awaited his response.

"You're right, of course." He spoke these four words and would need a minute of silence to conceive of any more. "My whole career was a copybook of failures and fears. My missteps made me a better detective because I wanted so desperately to avoid committing the same mistake twice. The difference between those names that stayed with me and Adam Caswell today is that those were real injustices and, as far as we know, this is just an unhappy ending. Caswell is a thief who saw an opportunity and took it. Perhaps he never intended to hurt Reverend Oldfield. Perhaps he was caught in the act and panicked as he did when he was arrested. But the point is that Caswell is guilty and will go on trial for his crimes."

Despite the speedometer on the dashboard approaching seventy miles an hour, it was as though everything had slowed down. The dark clouds overhead appeared to be glued in place in the sky. The other cars we passed barely moved, and the sheep and horses in the fields might just as well have been children's toys set up for a game.

"Where is your belief in me when I need it?" My anger peeked up above the surface, and I didn't recognise my own voice. "You say that I'm going to be a great detective like you but, on the first case we've come across when I have a real conviction about something, you say I'm being sentimental."

"The evidence—"

I couldn't look at him then and kept my eyes on the road ahead of us – just as I always wished he would. "Oh, yes, the evidence. I've heard all the evidence, and I still say there's something wrong here."

He called up another argument like the rear-guard in a battle. "Well, I have a story that you've never heard before." He paused so that his words would stay longer in my mind. "Sacheverell Briggs, how do you like that for a name?"

"I think it's perfectly stupid, and I'm glad that my parents had better taste than to call me Sacheverell!"

He showed no amusement at my impertinence but glanced at me through the side of one eye. "Sacheverell Briggs went missing in my first year as a police constable. He was a banker in the City of London and was known for carrying a bundle of notes with him wherever he went. Some people might say that he deserved whatever happened to him, but then they didn't know Sacheverell. He may have been filthy rich and a terrible fop, but he was one of the most generous men in the City. For all that he carried in his wallet or spent at his club, he matched in donations to help the less fortunate. He was a gentleman, but I can only assume that someone slit his throat and pushed him into Muswell Stream for the sake of the twenty pounds in his wallet."

He didn't need to emphasise how sad this story was; the silences that punctuated it did a good enough job. "That's all we found of him, you see? His empty wallet. He had no family, and his friends were strangely absent once he couldn't lend them any more money, so it was just me and a few of my colleagues at the memorial. We never found his killer, or even a clue as to who was responsible for his death. Sacheverell Briggs's life was worth the twenty pounds he had taken from his bank that afternoon, and the saddest part of it all is that lives have been bought and sold for far less."

"Then why are you telling me this story?" my voice was quieter, but I was still just as incensed. "What has some forgotten swell got to do with me?"

"We never found Sacheverell's killer, but it was not for want of trying. I spent years investigating his death. I questioned every contact that I made for the next decade, spent weeks of my free time trying to track down the faintest shred of evidence that might give me the answer which I so desperately sought. By the end of the first year, I couldn't remember what the dear man looked like, but I wouldn't give up hope. I was obsessed with the case because it was the very first one that was out of my grasp, and it galled me like little else I've known in life."

Whenever he stopped speaking, the rhythmic hum of the tyres beneath the car seemed to urge him to speak. "No matter what success I would find – for all the plaudits I won and fame I achieved – I would never forget Sacheverell Briggs." Mmm mmm mmm went the wheels on the road, practically begging him to continue. "I am the great Lord Edgington. The man who single-handedly secured the confession of the Dartford Butcher and unpicked the riddle of the disappearing Nichol Brothers. I am everything everyone says about me, and yet I never got over my very first failure, and I am certain that I never will."

CHAPTER TEN

Part Two – February 1927

Despite everything that happened, as the weeks passed, I managed to recover my good spirits. It certainly helped that I could return to my lessons with Grandfather at home in Cranley Hall. He took me through the notes of his old cases, and I learnt how he had infiltrated the infamous Hopps gang and picked out murderers from a room of six hundred people in the Opera Slaying of 1899.

His own stories were mirific, but if there was one thing in which Lord Edgington took pride, it was his ability to delegate. He called in his old friend from the Metropolitan Police each week, and so P.C. Simpkin taught me about his skills at researching, and how he could worm out relevant information from the great libraries that were dotted across the capital. Chief Inspector Darrington called by on Friday evenings – as long as there was a fine malt whisky open – and would reminisce with my grandfather on their time together on the force.

I sat in rapt silence as they talked, and I wasn't the only one who enjoyed these meetings. Todd, our chauffeur turned butler turned who knows what else by this point, was invited to listen after his lingering presence became so obvious that Grandfather could no longer ignore it. It was dear Todd who had fed my love of adventurous literature – in return, I'd lent him my favourite (infinitely bleak) Thomas Hardy novel but, for some reason, 'Tess of the D'Urbervilles' wasn't his cup of tea. Of course, my grandfather's stories from his days as an officer put even 'Sard Harker' to shame and, short of travelling to incredible lands in South America and fighting off satanic witch doctors, the real hero in my family had done it all.

Even as I enjoyed my training and worked as hard as I could to improve my abilities as a detective, it seemed as though my every move was made in semi-darkness. As though the light of the sun, moon and stars had been turned down by half. I knew what had caused it, of course. I hadn't forgotten Adam Caswell or his friends, and my dreams each night were haunted by the image of the vicar's pallid countenance.

I no longer talked about the possibility that the wrong man would hang for the crime but, outside of my lessons, all I could think about was the trial. My briefly sympathetic grandmother had told me that there was a long way still to go. She'd insisted that unexpected secrets would emerge and that the case had only just begun. This was something that hadn't occurred to me before, and I clung to the hope with both hands. The one idea that never entered my mind was that Caswell was guilty and, though I wouldn't share them with my grandfather, I spent many evenings in my room, scribbling notes that I prayed could save the accused.

It was almost March by the time the twin envelopes arrived at Cranley Hall. I had begun to wonder just how slowly the cogs of British justice would turn before the case could come to court.

"There are two letters this morning, m'lord," Todd came into the petit salon to announce.

We were not engaged in our usual lessons. At ten in the morning, I would normally have had my head down over a pile of books in the library, but Grandfather had decided I'd been studying too much recently and devised another activity.

"It's all in the wrist," he insisted as I prepared for my second attempt.

"The wrist," Todd explained, and made a swooshing motion through the air to encourage me.

I grasped the knife, closed one eye and, with the tip of my tongue between my teeth to keep steady, sighted the target at the far end of the room.

Grandfather counted down to my next throw. "Three, Two, One and…"

The blade went spinning out of my hand on a perfect line towards the bullseye before curving off at a truly inconceivable angle and somehow lodging itself in the ceiling.

"How is that possible? Are you playing a trick on me?"

The two inevitably superior knife throwers could not hide their amusement. "It's all in the wrist, Chrissy. How difficult is it to understand that?" This was not the first time my grandfather had offered such advice. It seemed that everything from fly-fishing to calligraphy required agile joints.

66

"And what if I don't have the type of wrists that are suitable for… anything? Am I doomed to spend my life as a clumsy oaf just because the bits between my hands and forearms aren't up to normal human standards?"

Grandfather looked puzzled as he attempted to work out how the knife had followed such a trajectory. "No, my boy. It's merely a question of practice. If you practise each skill we study, you will be a master in no time… Well, in some time, but not as long as you might think."

Lithe, sporty Todd cleared his throat and told me something that he presumably deemed encouraging. "I heard a supposition that, whatever you might want to do in life, be it learning the piano, painting or playing tennis, it takes a solid year to become truly great at it."

"Well, that's not too bad," I replied, thinking I could do an hour of tennis every week for twelve months and, come 1928, compete in the Wimbledon Championships.

Grandfather was standing beneath the still suspended knife and replied absentmindedly. "He doesn't mean the odd game of tennis here and there, Chrissy. He's talking about a solid year of time, most likely split over decades."

"That's impossible!" I had to swallow to even process such a thought. "There's not enough time in someone's life for such a thing, what with eating and sleeping and occasionally reading books."

It was at this moment that the knife dislodged itself and Grandfather stood aside just in time to avoid a nasty cut in the top of his skull.

"More to the point," I continued, "unless you plan for me to infiltrate a band of carnival performers, when would I ever need to throw a knife anyway?"

My teacher issued a stern tut. "Really Chrissy, you must know that every skill is worth having. That is why I've started knitting in my spare time. Who can say when a purl stitch might save a life?"

It was very difficult to answer such a question. Luckily, Todd intervened.

"M'lord?" He was still holding the silver tray with the two letters.

"Of course, Todd. My apologies." The old man walked over to take the proffered post. "And perhaps you could take a moment to teach Christopher here how to throw."

To my disappointment, Todd had nothing better to do and was soon showing off his circus skills. He launched three knives, one after another with alternate hands, so that they landed in a neat grouping in the centre of the target. I'm fairly certain he closed his eyes on the last throw.

"Who are you?" I heard myself whisper.

"You see now, Master Christopher?" He bowed a little to show that he was not just good at everything he tried, but humble with it. "It's all in the wrist."

I was still quite ignorant on the matter and was about to explain this fact when his employer sounded a note of alarm.

"What is it, Grandfather?" I was happy to truncate the morning's activity before Todd showed me up any further.

"It's my subpoena to appear in court as a witness in Adam Caswell's trial at the Tatchester Assizes."

"Isn't that what you were expecting?"

He didn't look away from the two envelopes and tapped the open letter against the palm of his hand. "Yes, but that's not what surprises me."

"What do you mean?" A hint of apprehension had entered my voice, and I moved around him to see what was written.

"There are two letters, Christopher. One for me and one for you."

I've never claimed to be the smartest boy in the British Isles, and it took me a good four seconds to realise what this meant. "Are you trying to tell me that—"

"The defence is calling you as a witness."

CHAPTER ELEVEN

Whenever I'd pictured the trial, it had been at the Old Bailey in London with thirty different barristers in black gowns and curly wigs. In the end, it wasn't nearly so grand and might as well have been held next door at the Tatchester cattle market. Perhaps that's not quite fair as there was the odd wig on display and both the prosecuting and defence barristers wore gowns, but the court was full of rowdy locals and, much like at the funeral-cum-crime-scene, the population of Condicote had turned up to spectate.

Admittedly, I wasn't there for the opening of the trial. In fact, I wasn't allowed in court until I'd given evidence, but luckily, my mother was there in my place. She would fill me in on all the details once I'd done my bit and, I must say, her attention to detail was such that I felt I had been in there with her.

I believe that the proceedings unfolded in the following fashion.

"You are here to determine the guilt of Mr Adam Caswell," the rather angular prosecutor began. His nose, chin, elbows and even his ears looked as though they had been moulded to the exact same pointy angle. "By calling a series of witnesses, I will set out to prove that the man you see standing in the dock, flanked by two officers of the law, was responsible for the death of Reverend Adolphus Oldfield. By the time that you gentlemen of the jury leave this trial, there will be no doubt that Adam Caswell slew a man of the cloth in order to steal a valuable sacramental vessel from St Bartholomew's church in Condicote."

As he introduced the case, there was a dramatic and grave quality to everything he said, but then it was his opposing counterpart's turn to express the exact opposite.

"Through substantial witness testimony and various relevant artefacts the police have gathered, I intend to show that the crown's case in this matter is based on little more than circumstantial evidence. Adam Caswell is not a violent man. There was simply no reason for him to have suddenly decided to murder a fellow villager, let alone a beloved priest. It is my job to prove this assertion, and I am confident that the evidence will show that Mr Caswell is innocent."

Once the initial arguments had been presented, the prosecution had the first chance to call witnesses. The haughty fellow attempted to show that it was a cut-and-dry case of a violent thug praying on a small community in the hope of a quick profit. Mrs Ivy from the jewellers was called to explain what she'd seen on the night of the vicar's murder. Chief Inspector Darrington gave a dispassionate account of events on behalf of Scotland Yard, and various Condicote residents were called to describe their low opinion of the man in the dock. From what my mother told me, it was the evidence of the local G.P., Dr Beresford-Gray, that had the most impact. The sighs and grimaces from the jury when she described the wounds on the vicar's body left little room for positivity in Adam's camp. And, at the end of the first day, they exited the court feeling really very glum.

My turn came the following morning. I was dreading standing in front of the court, just as I would hate to tread the boards in a West End theatre. As witnesses, my grandfather and I were kept in a dull little room until it was our turn to give evidence. Luckily for me, I had another John Masefield book to pass the time, whereas Grandfather strode about impatiently. It was hard to know what he was thinking, but I could only conclude that he was still uncertain whether the man accused of Reverend Oldfield's murder deserved to stand trial.

As we killed time in this fashion, Adam Caswell was standing in the witness box. His barrister did his best to present his client in a positive light, but then the prosecution had the chance to undo that good work.

"You are pleading innocent to all charges, is that correct?"

"That's correct, m'lud." He smiled his childlike smile, as though happy he knew the answer.

In response, the learned gentleman, or whatever you're supposed to call him, produced a silent laugh. "You must address the judge as m'lud or Your Honour. I am merely a barrister, and you may call me sir."

Caswell looked a little out of sorts and shifted from foot to foot before replying. "Thank you, Sir Barrister."

This provoked some giggling from the audience, but it was still early in the proceedings, and the real laughter was yet to come.

"Tell me, Mr Caswell," his interrogator continued in a casual, airy voice, "what would you have done with the ciborium that was stolen from St Bartholomew's if you hadn't been arrested?"

"I would have sold it." The supposed killer's amicable nature was irrepressible, and he grinned once more.

"So you admit that you stole the item in question?" He pointed to the still blood-speckled artefact that was on display on a platform in the centre of the court.

"No, I didn't say that." He turned to the judge to plead his case. "I didn't say that, m'lud. Sir Barrister is putting words in my mouth."

"You're quite right, Mr Caswell," the fluffy-haired judge responded. "Mr Appleby, please be more careful with the way in which you construct your questions."

It gave my mother great comfort to see the judge take Caswell's side in the matter and, as she later described these events, she still maintained some hope that he would finish the trial a free man.

"Of course, m'lud." The smarmy prosecutor turned over a paper on the lectern in front of him as though he wished to start his questioning afresh. "Perhaps you could tell us how you came to be in possession of a stolen sacramental vessel that was covered in the blood of a recently slain clergyman."

"Someone threw it in front of me." I don't think he was intending to be funny, but some of Adam's responses make the audience snicker. "No, really. I was walking back through the village at about midnight and this thing came flying out of a passing car."

"How interesting. Could you perhaps describe the vehicle?" The barrister would occasionally send glances in the jury's direction to show how much he doubted the suspect's version of events.

"It was big… and black."

"I see. So, what you're saying is that someone in a *big black car* threw a precious object at you that had recently been used to knock a man unconscious before he was strangled to death? That sounds perfectly plausible. Please continue."

The more sarcastic that toad of a man became, the more panicked Caswell's voice grew. "I'm telling the truth. I went for a walk up to King Arthur's Camp. Whenever it's a nice clear night, I walk across Bottler's Down, and right up to Seven Barrows. You can see for miles up there and all the stars in the heavens."

"Oh, I see. You're something of an astronomer. Could you tell us which constellations you saw that night? Or perhaps you spotted one of the planets. Such information could help establish your alibi."

Caswell rolled up his fingers into a fist. The man was trying to make him angry and, for a moment, it seemed it might work. To my mother's surprise (remember I wasn't actually present for any of this but am repeating her crystal-clear impression of events), instead of snapping or throwing an angry response across the room, the giant calmed himself by taking a deep breath. "I don't know the names of any stars. I just know that they're pretty, and so I go up onto that hill once a week to look at them."

The case was a pendulum; there was a constant fluctuation between who had the upper hand. Just then, it was obvious that the simple man in the dock was at a disadvantage to the slippery gownsman.

"Very well, so you climbed up to King Arthur's Camp. But you started your walk on the other side of town entirely. Why was that? Why were you wandering the village from one side to the other with no apparent purpose?"

"I'd gone to see my ma," Caswell announced with great pride, before remembering a mitigating factor. "Only she said my boots were too dirty, and she didn't want me in the house."

"I see. So you're saying that even your mother could not bear to have you on the premises."

Caswell's defence barrister stood up to complain, but his colleague waved his hand in apology and asked another question.

"Tell me, Mr Caswell. Did you go past the church on this walk of yours?"

"Yes."

"And did you happen to see if there were any lights on inside?"

Adam raised one finger to his chin to have a think. "I'd say so. Yes, there must have been… in the little back room where the priest gets changed."

"Are you a church-going man?"

He looked up at the balcony at this moment and something there gave him the confidence he needed to answer. "Not regularly."

"You mean you do go to church, but not every week?"

"I… Well, no. I haven't been since I was nine. The vicar who was there when I was a boy didn't like me. He used to tell me off for singing too loudly."

"How interesting." It was Mr Appleby's turn for a nice melodramatic pause. "But if you haven't been into that building since you were a child, how would you know in which room the light was illuminated?"

Caswell began to breathe noisily in and out as he looked for a way to keep calm. "He's twisting everything. I don't know how he does it, but he's making me look guilty when I'm not."

"You must answer the question, Mr Caswell." The judge didn't have favourites after all. He was just doing his job and, at that moment, it was his job to push the defendant for a response.

"I can't answer. I can't think." The enormous chap hunched his shoulders and peered around like a wild elephant that was trapped in a snare.

The prosecution saw that this was the moment to attack, and his words fired across the court. "I put it to you that you knew which light was on because you slipped inside to murder Reverend Oldfield. I say that you planned out exactly what you wanted to do, had probably visited the church on various occasions to look for valuables, and thought you could get away with murder."

The accused looked up at the public balcony and a deep wail broke from him. It was the sound of a wounded soul – the unbearable moan of an animal with no hope left for its survival. The judge peered about, perhaps searching for keepers to sedate the panicked beast, but no one would come. And, in time, Adam collapsed on to the railing in passive submission.

CHAPTER TWELVE

After a short break for tea and such, it was time for me to go into the witness box. My mother, father and even my grandmother had come for support and, when I was called to give evidence, I was grateful for their presence in the lower gallery.

"Might you say that, by this stage in your life, you are quite knowledgeable about crime and criminals?" the defence barrister enquired once I had confirmed my name, and the formalities were out of the way.

I wished that my grandfather was there. I felt far more capable when he was at my side and was so nervous that I had a good stutter before each response. "I… Well, I… Ooh, that's a tough one." Predictably enough, this brought a roar of laughter from the public and a bang of the gavel from the judge.

"You will answer the questions put to you, please, Mr Prentiss." He was an old chap with a lazy eye and a tendency to spit. I thought I'd better do as he said, if only to avoid a drenching.

"I…" I began again. "No, I wouldn't call myself particularly knowledgeable on any specific subject."

"Oh?" The pink-faced defence barrister wore a confused frown. He rather reminded me of a clown act I'd seen at the Hackney Empire. "You have spent the last two years of your life investigating murders, have you not?"

"Yes, but I've spent the last five years trying to identify the birds in our garden, and I still can't tell a Dartford warbler from a crested lark."

This really got the public going but, instead of banging down his toy hammer, the judge looked puzzled. "They're totally different colours, boy. And doesn't the crest give it away?"

"You'd think that, wouldn't you?" I replied, happy to have found another bird lover. "Perhaps it's the pressure."

"The pressure?" What's a word for *even more puzzled?* As that's the expression the Honourable Mr Justice Manford wore at that moment.

"Yes, you know. You spot a bird and you've only a few seconds to take in all the details before it flits off again. I get quite panicked and scribble down in my notebook the first name that pops into my head.

I once mistook a greenfinch for a heron."

The crowd were having a lovely afternoon out, and it was a shame there were no ushers walking around the public galleries selling cigarettes and mint bulls' eyes.

"Order!" the judge finally proclaimed. "Order!"

"Perhaps we could leave ornithological discussion for another time and get back to the main topic of a man's senseless murder, m'lud?" The prosecuting barrister's supercilious manner was even more apparent when he was not the focus of attention.

"Yes, indeed. You may answer the original question, Mr Prentiss."

"Thank you, m'lud." I bowed my head politely. "Could you possibly remind me what that was?"

Even the defence was losing his patience now. "Knowledgeable, boy. Do you consider yourself knowledgeable on the matter at hand?"

"Oh, no. Not at all. You must be thinking of my grandfather."

There was howling laughter, and several members of the audience beat their feet on the stalls in appreciation. Even the accused had tears in his eyes and a smile on his face, so at least I'd brightened his day a little. I never intended to make a fool of myself, but it was just like when I was birdwatching. My brain, mouth and sometimes even my hands failed to work in unison and the wrong words popped out of me.

"Ah yes." My questioner was on firmer footing now and pursed his lips as he pushed on with the next question. "That will be the illustrious Lord Edgington, former superintendent of the Metropolitan Police, and one of Britain's most respected detectives."

"The very same," I replied, as it seemed he expected an answer.

"And would you say that your esteemed, not to mention highly experienced grandfather has imparted some of his immense wisdom in the time that he has been training you?"

I had to think about this one. "Well, he's certainly tried. You'd have to ask him if he has succeeded. He's here on the premises, you know?"

The defence barrister cleared his throat. He already seemed a little tired. "Very well, but it is safe to say that you have learnt a little of how murderers think and what to look out for when investigating such a crime."

"Objection, m'lud." The arrogant prosecutor shot to his feet. "I'm sure that my learned friend is aware that he is leading the witness."

"Quite right, Mr Appleby," the judge chimed in response, and the chap representing Adam Caswell had to rephrase his enquiry.

"Do you think you might possess some insight into how the mind of a murderer works, Mr Prentiss?"

I considered his point for a few moments. "I... Yes, I think that is fair to say. I have come very close to identifying a killer on a number of occasions. Unless my grandfather was only saying that so that I didn't feel bad."

I could see that the defence was becoming rather vexed by my responses, but it took me until this moment to realise why; I really wasn't helping.

"How many murders would you say you have investigated?"

I had a quick think. "One, two, three... I'm sorry, do victims killed by the same murderer count as one or multiple kills?"

He closed his eyes and held his hands to his temples. "Whatever you deem best."

"Eight, nine, ten." I'd run out of fingers and had to do some working out in my head. "Gosh, I'm up to eighteen already. How remarkable."

He finally had something from which to launch an argument and let out a sigh of relief. "That's eighteen murders you've investigated in a little under... what... two years?"

"Correct. Though I must admit, I forgot one that occurred in Suffolk. It was wrapped up in the space of a morning, so it was easy to overlook. My grandfather and I have investigated nineteen murders since June 1925."

"Nineteen murders!" His wig wobbled as he marvelled at this total. I was a little impressed myself. "That is a remarkable amount of experience you have accumulated in a comparatively short time. I honestly can't imagine that there are many young men your age with such a breadth of knowledge on the topic."

I'd finally located Marcus on the public balcony. He was clinging to the bronze railing and biting his lip as he awaited my response. There was no sign of Scarlet, and so I could only imagine she would be called as a witness at some point. I didn't want to let them down and tried my best to stop spouting nonsense and actually say something that would help their poor friend.

"It is quite possible."

"Thank you, Mr Prentiss." The barrister released a sigh of relief that I was finally cooperating. "And so, taking into account this range of knowledge, may I ask whether you have met another killer who in any way resembled Adam Caswell?"

"I have not."

"In what sense is he different from those you have encountered? Is it a question of intelligence?"

"Not at all." I was quick with my answer, as I didn't like the big chap in the dock to think I was accusing him of being a dunce. I've been called such things any number of times and it is not a pleasant experience. "I've known brilliantly clever killers and total buffoons."

"Then what is it about Mr Caswell that you found so unusual?"

I hesitated once more, as what I wanted to say was difficult to express. "He seems very gentle to me. I know there is nothing definitive in what I'm saying, but I genuinely don't believe that he is to blame for the vicar's death."

A sudden raised fist on the balcony told me that Marcus was happy with my reply.

"Objection, m'lud," the prosecutor popped up like a parrot on a pirate's shoulder to complain. "This is mere supposition and thus inadmissible in court."

Caswell's barrister would not back down so easily. "I believe this exceptional young man's perspective may shine a light on the character of the defendant, m'lud."

The judge tapped his fingers on his desk to suggest that he agreed. "I'll allow it, but please stick to facts, Mr Prentiss, not vague presentiments."

The barrister nodded his thanks and asked me another question. "Was there something in particular that made you come to such a conclusion?"

"There was." I had found my voice now, and I was determined not to come across as a silly boy playing a game. "I was present when Adam Caswell realised that he would be arrested for the crime."

"Could you tell us exactly what you saw?"

"He had come to show his friends the ciborium, which you can see on the platform below his lordship."

"The same item that he claims, under oath, was thrown at him in the street in Condicote some short hours after the vicar was murdered?"

"That's right. My grandfather and I were in the hotel room of his two close friends, Marcus Alsop and Emmeline Warwick, and he was very happy with his find. There was no sense, in my mind at least, that he believed there to be any connection between the ciborium and a violent crime. I believe that, had he known of such a link, he would not have shared the information with his companions, let alone spoken of it in front of two strangers."

I was feeling more confident and had no wish to stop talking. "Despite their ill repute in the village of Condicote, the three friends are not members of a vicious gang, nor do they have any convictions between them for anything more than youthful misdemeanours." I hoped this was more or less true.

"What was your impression of Mr Caswell at that moment?"

I cast my mind back to the few minutes when I became so certain that the defendant was not the killer. "It is difficult to say." I had been considering this very question for weeks and knew that thinking about it any longer wouldn't help. Instead, I turned my brain off and just spoke. "I believe he thought that he'd backed a winning horse."

"That he had enjoyed, if you will, a stroke of luck?" the barrister clarified.

"Yes, that's exactly it. Caswell hadn't come to tell his friends of the brutal act he'd committed. He was there to reveal that the wolf would be off his back for a few months as his ship had come in at last."

The judge cleared his throat and removed his spectacles to peer down at me. "Mr Prentiss, perhaps you could avoid quite so many metaphors, and speak in plain English."

The interruption had not distracted me and the words I needed came to my lips. "Adam Caswell is no killer, I'm certain of it. The only thing that makes sense is that the real murderer went motoring through the village, and the plunder was thrown from the car to make it look as though Mr Caswell was guilty. I refuse to believe that he is to blame for this terrible crime."

CHAPTER THIRTEEN

I knew why the defence had placed me – the idiot grandson of a great detective – at the centre of their argument. They must have heard from Chief Inspector Darrington that I was the only person without a connection to Adam Caswell who believed him innocent. Evidently, the fact I was their best hope of getting him acquitted did not bode well for his chances.

For all my fear when getting up on that stand, for all my apprehension and the litany of faux pas I'd made, seeing the look on Marcus's face made everything worthwhile. He knew I was on his side, even if no one else was, and I liked to think that Adam did, too. Of course, that didn't make it any more pleasant to be cross-examined by that odious prosecutor. He managed to make me look like a loon without a jot of sense in my head – which I suppose was fair enough.

When he'd finished with me, I stumbled from the box to my mother's comforting embrace. Thank goodness it was time for lunch. I might have collapsed where I stood otherwise. After a healthy selection of sandwiches and cakes in a nearby cafeteria, we returned to court, and the day was rounded off with Grandfather's testimony.

He showed no enthusiasm for his task and delivered the facts of the case in a concise and sober monotone. Neither of the barristers were able to twist his words to their needs, and I think the defence wished that he'd called P.C. Brigham to testify before Lord Edgington. The man was impervious to all attempts at manipulation.

We stayed at my grandmother's house that night, and no one was in the mood for dinner, cards or even dessert. Well, I forced myself to eat a little Tarte Tatin, and it was jolly good indeed. Caramelised apples baked in the oven on a pastry base with – my grandfather's cook's special touch – a crumble topping that brought everything together just perfectly. But, as I said, I really had no appetite and stopped after my third slice.

Perhaps the worst part of my companions' melancholy was that it was not for the man who was sleeping in a prison cell that night, but for me. I'm sure that, had I asked them, my family would have told me that I was the one they pitied. I was the naïve young idealist who believed that the undeniably guilty former-convict could conceivably be innocent. They felt sorry for me because they'd assumed I was cleverer than that.

When the morning came, they all put on brave faces for my benefit, but I wasn't quite so silly that I couldn't see through them. We trooped off to Tatchester in two of Grandfather's many Rolls Royces and took our places in the public gallery.

The day started with Scarlet giving evidence. She was mainly there as a character witness for the defence, and I was amazed just how closely her account of Adam's sweet nature chimed with my perception of him.

"Madam, how long have you known the accused?" the rather weaselly prosecutor asked when the time for cross-examination arrived.

"The best part of a year." It was clear that she would not be intimidated.

"And don't you think that is too short a length of time to know the true substance of a person?"

She folded her arms across the embroidered bodice of her smart black dress. "I certainly do not. How long did you know your wife before the two of you were married?"

Her comment initially drew no laughter from the public, but only because they were so eager to hear the squirming advocate's reply.

He looked at the judge, then back at Scarlet, before adjusting his wig and gingerly moving on to another question. "You cannot deny that Mr Caswell has a troubled past."

"That is true, but so has my boyfriend's uncle, and he's the Duke of Mayberry." She raised her voice to be heard over the raucous audience. "Good old Uncle Timmy was arrested for setting fire to his neighbour's rose garden. He was made to pay over one hundred pounds in damages."

The vivacious woman in the witness box gave a fiery return whenever the prosecutor attempted to undermine her. For every trap he set, she would tiptoe around it. For every verbal hand grenade he threw in her direction, she tossed it back before it could explode. I couldn't help wondering whether she should have been at the lectern defending Adam Caswell instead of the nervous, ruddy-cheeked man who was getting paid for the task.

To my pleasure and surprise, the defence's performance was

better than the day before. The barrister systematically dismantled the idea that Adam Caswell was a despicable criminal. What was most impressive about this was the way in which it was achieved.

"State your name, please."

"P.C. Derek Brigham of the Tatchester Constabulary, stationed at Condicote."

The clerk swore in the witness and the defence barrister started on his questioning once more. "How long have you known Adam Caswell?"

"Little Cassie?" Brigham had a very informal manner, even when in the witness box. "Well, I'd say I've known him half my life and longer. I used to shoot rabbits with his old man on the Fane estate when he were just a lad."

"Would you say that he has an aggressive temperament?"

The constable laughed at this. "Adam Caswell? Aggressive? Oh, no no no." He evidently caught the opposing barrister's dismayed expression and cleared his throat to amend his statement. "Which is to say that I didn't know him to be violent, but how can you ever really know a person these days? There was a fellow over in Newminster who married four different women within a year of one another."

Rather than cut the man short as I was expecting, Adam's barrister leaned casually over the lectern and encouraged him to talk. "Are you saying that Mr Caswell possesses a dark, hidden side to his personality, much like that disgraceful fellow in Newminster?"

Brigham lowered his voice a little as though he only wanted the defence to hear, "No chance. I will say it on record that Adam Caswell is no bigamist. He just doesn't have it in him. He's also never been married in the first place, so that would make it rather difficult."

The prosecution had heard enough not only of this diversion from the facts, but of the audience's amusement and rose to complain. "May I enquire as to the relevance of a bigamist in Newminster, m'lud?"

Before the judge could uphold the unspoken objection, the defence raised his hand in apology. "Perhaps more pertinently, speaking as respected member of Condicote society, would your prior knowledge of the defendant suggest that he was capable of violent behaviour?"

"No, of course it—" Brigham stopped himself once more. "Which is to say that the evidence certainly points to his involvement in the crime."

"I have no further questions for this witness, m'lud."

After Brigham's testimony, there came a warden from the prison where Caswell had been incarcerated when he was an adolescent. What I hadn't known before this was that the defendant's only prior conviction was for the terrifying crime of poaching rabbits on the estate of Stamford Fane's deceased father – a crime to which P.C. Brigham had recently confessed, under oath, in front of the whole court. The warden also testified to the fact that Caswell had been a model prisoner and developed quite the talent for woodwork whilst incarcerated. He finished this character assessment by wishing that all prisoners could be so well-mannered as Adam Gavin Caswell, which very much irritated the opposing barrister, who would subsequently forgo the opportunity to cross-examine the witness.

The morning proceeded in this manner with no clear blows landed to prove that Adam was anything more than a victim of circumstance. I noticed that the mood in the galleries improved as the day rolled towards its conclusion. When the barristers had made their closing submissions, and the time came for the jury to retire, there was the feeling of a public holiday. We retired for lunch in high spirits, and I think that even those amongst us who had been certain of a conviction – and certain that he deserved one – were beginning to question the facts.

My hopes were buoyed further when a clerk ran to the café opposite the court to announce that the jury had reached a verdict in record time. We stuffed the last of our sausage rolls into our mouths – well, I did, the others perhaps refrained – and sped back to our seats just as the foreman was leading those worthy members of the jury to their benches beside the judge.

"Have you reached a verdict?" the clerk of the court enquired.

"We have, m'lud." The foreman was a nondescript fellow of no great height or voice, and I had to strain to hear him.

"On the charge of the theft of a golden ciborium from St Bartholomew's church, Condicote, how do you find the defendant?"

There was a pause of a few moments before the foreman announced the verdict. I had to wonder whether someone had told him to do it in just such a way, or he had seen legal dramas at the theatre and wished to inject the same level of tension.

"Guilty, m'lud."

This was when my stomach felt as though it had disappeared,

leaving nothing but a crater in its place. And yet I held out hope that, through some unexpected loophole that a simpleton like me could never fathom, it was still possible for the jury to find Adam guilty of the lesser crime without blaming him for the vicar's death.

"And on the charge of murder?"

The judge had lost all his jolly charm and kept the foreman locked in his vision as the clerk asked this most terrible of questions.

"Guilty, m'lud."

Cries went up from the gallery above us, and I couldn't see who had uttered them, but I felt sure that Scarlet had broken down in tears. I looked at the supposed killer in the dock, and there was nothing but fear on his broad face. He searched the audience for his friends or perhaps even his mother. He needed someone to tell him everything would be all right, but his suffering was only about to get worse.

The judge leaned back to look for something on a shelf within the wooden box in which he was ensconced. As he pulled it from its hiding place, a flash of black material caused my grandmother to gasp and the inevitable was confirmed.

"Adam Gavin Caswell." The judge spoke the words as though each one was a despicable insult. The cap he had donned over his wig barely fitted him, but it was no less macabre for its proportions. The matching black gloves made it look as though he were the killer. "The sentence of this court is that you will be taken from here to the place from whence you came and there be kept in close confinement until three weeks from now and, upon that day, be taken to the place of execution and there hanged by the neck until you are dead." The words roared out of him, but he saved his most bitter tone for his final statement. "And may God have mercy upon your soul."

CHAPTER FOURTEEN

"I'll fight this!" Marcus declared on the steps up to the court. "I'll fight this with every breath in my body and every ounce of strength I possess."

Scarlet put one arm around him for support. "That's right. We'll appeal. There must be a way to do that, don't you think, Lord Edgington?"

Grandfather had been in a wordless state since the verdict had been read, which only complemented the surly nature he'd displayed throughout the trial.

"You can try. It might extend his life for a month or two, but without fresh evidence to prove his innocence, Caswell will hang."

Marcus stepped closer and his paramour's hand fell from his shoulder. "It's an injustice, pure and simple. Adam is a cat's-paw in all of this. The prosecution had no real evidence but for the ciborium, and I believe my friend when he says he found it in the street."

"He said that someone threw it at him," I clarified but, for the burning look I received, I wished I'd kept quiet.

"Whatever happened, it doesn't make him the killer." He couldn't stand still and turned left and right, whilst moving up the steps to expend his nervous energy. He was dressed in typically fashionable attire – his suit all sharp lines with black binding around the lapels – and yet there was something different about him that day. I believed he would have called off his rebellious way of life if it meant he could save his friend.

"Of course it doesn't." I could see how desperate Scarlet was to set his mind at ease. "And that's why we'll investigate ourselves if we have to. We'll find the evidence to overturn his conviction. I promise we will."

Marcus made no response to this but turned to my grandfather. "Will you take another look at the case, Lord Edgington?"

"If I thought it would do you any good, I would be happy to try. But what possible grounds could you put forward to challenge the verdict?"

He looked lost then, and his cheeks swelled before he replied. "What about clemency?"

"It's too late for that. The sentence has already been handed down and short of the Home Secretary coming to your rescue, there's nothing you can do."

"But if we go ahead with the appeal, isn't there some allowance given for people like Adam? He's no genius. The only reason I know him is because Stamford could twist and manipulate the poor man to do whatever he wanted. Isn't there a legal argument for when a person lacks the capacity to make the right judgements for himself?"

"You're referring to diminished responsibility, but such considerations hold no weight in English law. Adam pleaded innocent and has proved himself capable of standing trial. Such an argument would get you nowhere."

This wasn't enough for Marcus, and he pushed for more. "My mother has money. She can pay you. I don't always go running to her when I'm short of a few bob, but this is different. If you knew Adam the way we do, you'd realise that he couldn't be responsible for such a wicked crime."

I must admit that, in the very first moments I'd met the man, Marcus had seemed something of a fop. With his long sideburns, cut to violent points upon his cheeks, and his carefully coiffed hair, he was the very picture of a dandy, and yet there was more to him than met the eye.

"It's not about money," Grandfather insisted. "I'm seventy-six years old with a long list of things I'd still like to do with my life that I'm forever neglecting. If I were to chase after every lost cause, my skills with a paint brush and fishing rod would never improve."

Marcus had to take a step back to make sense of this. "So you're putting your amateur interests ahead of an innocent man's life? I know you used to be a policeman, but I really thought better of you." The tails of his coat caught the air as he and Scarlet spun away in the direction of the court. "Good afternoon to you, Lord Edgington."

"*Alsop...*" my companion mumbled to himself once they'd gone. "I should have known."

"Is that really the end, Grandfather?" I asked as the prosecutor appeared on the steps and shook hands with several Condicote residents. Mayor Hobson looked particularly happy that the case had concluded, and the lady doctor who had given evidence for the prosecution lingered nervously in the background.

"What else would you have me do, boy?" Grandfather was

watching the scene too. "We spoke to Caswell, and he offered us nothing. I've analysed every fact of the case, and I'm still at a loss to explain who else could be guilty of the crime. Dead vicars and religious objects falling from the sky—"

"From a passing car," I corrected him.

"Fine, from a passing car then… but it still sounds like fantasy to me." The volume of his voice dropped a few decibels. "I'm sorry, Chrissy. I genuinely am. But just because a suspect seems harmless, that doesn't make it true. During my career, I met hundreds of men who came across as savages but were as soft as dandelion clocks. Perhaps what we have here is the opposite. Perhaps, through stunted development or a basic lack of morality, his outward personality hides his violent instincts. Perhaps, like a wolf that feels threatened, he lashed out at Reverend Oldfield with the ciborium and then finished the job with the rope."

When I didn't answer, he became more persistent. "We've considered countless scenarios, and they all got us nowhere. I'm afraid that the case is closed."

I was still looking at the smug expression on the prosecutor's face. His opposing colleague had joined him by this point, and I was shocked to see them shake hands and smile. Neither of them would remember Adam Caswell. He was less than a footnote in their careers. They would go back to their chambers and move on to the next case. The defence would hope for better luck next time, and the prosecution would tell everyone of his red-letter day. But when the week was out, the only people still thinking about the man who'd been condemned to death would be the friends who had never given up on him.

CHAPTER FIFTEEN

Part Three – April 1927

The weather was all muddled that year. We had sunshine throughout March and the coldest April I can remember. At the beginning of the month, the snow returned to colour England entirely the wrong shade. In place of green buds springing from the soft earth, and the purples, yellows and blues of early wildflowers, we had blizzards and high drifts.

It felt as though we had travelled back in time to the dead of winter. Although I love building snowmen and having snowball fights as much as the next… near fully grown man, I could not find my usual joy in the frosty weather. Delilah must have agreed on this point as, just like me, she stayed indoors as much as was humanly – or, indeed, caninely – possible. Warm blankets, roaring fires and hot drinks were what I needed, and I was certainly in no mood to go trekking off on another chilly adventure with my grandfather.

Of course, as Robert Burns said, "The best laid plans of mice and men often go awry," and I imagine I fall somewhere between those species. The bad omens first arose when the ordinarily sociable Lord Edgington claimed to have no time for our lessons and was cold and imperious whenever anyone addressed him.

"It's not normal, Cook," I told our dear domestic in her roomy kitchen on the third afternoon of his unsociable behaviour.

She stopped rolling the pastry that she was preparing and looked at me with a frown. "Don't fret, Master Christopher. If you're imagining he'll go back to the dark days when he spent all that time in his room and cut himself off even from his closest friends, there's no need to worry."

I had to gasp for air. "I wasn't before, but I certainly am now!" I went to sit down at the table where our footman, Halfpenny, was trying not to slurp from a bowl of minestrone soup.

"Really, sir, there is no need for concern." His attempts at reassurance were rarely reassuring, and I braced myself for more dark thoughts. "I remember what Lord Edgington was like after your grandmother died, and it bears no connection with his behaviour this week."

He had another spoonful and realised that what he had said was not quite true. "Except for his belligerent mood, the inability to look anyone in the eye and his limited appetite, there is no connection whatsoever between the ten years he spent as a recluse in his own house and now."

"Halfpenny?"

"Yes, sir?"

"You're really not helping."

"Very good, sir."

My head crashed down onto the table in front of me, and I was about to have a good old moan when one of the bells on the panel above the door started ringing.

Our footman wiped his mouth on a tea towel – well, that's what it sounded like at least – and rose to hobble off through the house.

"Who can that be? His Lordship isn't expecting anyone as far as I know." Halfpenny was approximately the same age as my grandfather but four times as creaky. I swear that, if you listened carefully, you could hear that his joints needed oiling.

I looked up at the bells and realised why he was confused. The caller was not at the tradesmen's entrance, as was normal with all the comings and goings of such a large estate, but the front door. No one ever rang at the main entrance. We either knew people were coming and sent out a welcome party, or they had no business calling at the front of the house and rang for a servant.

Just as perplexed as our footman, Delilah and I went to see what was happening. The problem with living in a house the size of a large village is that answering the door robs all tension from a story. I would like to tell you that I zipped along that hallway to discover who had come a calling, but it took for ever. By the time I'd made it upstairs to traverse the interminable west wing corridor, I felt like going back to the kitchen for a sit down. Some minutes later – having long since passed Halfpenny – I'd walked through the front parlour and, with a bit of a heave, pulled open the immense wooden door which was surely designed on the off-chance that giants existed and would be coming for tea one day.

Standing on our equally oversized front doorstep was not a giant but a woman in a particularly large hat. It had a series of feathers from various tropical birds lodged in the top – at a guess I would say they were peacock, macaw and ostrich feathers but, knowing my luck, they were probably not. She stood there in a thin, gauzy dress and matching bolero, as though the mercury on the thermometer hadn't recently given up even trying to assess how cold it was.

"You must be the grandson," she said as I stood there gawping.

"I must be," I replied. "Or rather, yes, I am."

She stepped to one side so that the low sun no longer framed her, and I could see her face more clearly. She had an aristocratic bearing – like most people who visited my grandfather, in fact. At a guess, I would have said she was around fifty, and I half expected to remember her from some long-past family party.

"I'm dreadfully sorry." In case this sentence doesn't prove it, I should probably mention that she was extremely well spoken. "I haven't introduced myself. My name is Lady Alsop, and I'd like to speak to Lord Edgington."

Each word she said was pronounced with the utmost care, as though they were grapes picked from a vine. There was a reticence to her that I found intriguing and, though she did not and would not smile, she gave off an endearing warmth. In that respect, at least, she was a little like my mother – and nothing like my grandmother!

Instead of being the polite, well-mannered boy that my parents had always hoped I would become, I continued to stare at her.

"May I come in?" She pursed her deep red lips hopefully, and I opened the door a fraction wider to let her pass.

"Of course you may. Please…" I signalled the way with my hand, just as Halfpenny arrived, out of puff.

"Not to worry, old chap," I told him as Lady Alsop jaunted off along the corridor. "You have a sit down. I'll see to our guest."

He would have expressed his thanks, but he was still catching his breath. I accelerated to catch the new arrival and realised that I might have committed a faux pas by inviting her into Grandfather's house at a time when he wasn't seeing anyone.

"Are you one of Lord Edgington's old friends?" I asked, to know what sort of reception we were likely to get once we reached the library.

"Not exactly, but we have crossed paths over the years." From the way she said this, I wondered whether it was not just their paths that had crossed but their swords, too.

"How nice," I responded, as what else can one reply to such a vague statement? "I've met him many times myself." Well, obviously that's not the thing to say, but it was out of my mouth, and there was nothing I could do about it. "I know him really rather well."

She turned to look at me as we walked. I imagine she was trying to understand whether I was as much of an idiot as I sounded. "You're witty, Christopher Prentiss. I wasn't expecting that." If this was true, she certainly didn't show it and maintained the straight line of her lips all the way to our destination.

"Here we are." I raced a few steps ahead of her and knocked on the door before she could catch up, (just in case my grandfather shouted something rude). Luckily, it was almost lunchtime, and he was expecting a maid with his tray. I thought he might call for us to enter, but a few seconds went past and there wasn't a sound.

My mind ran with lurid possibilities. He was evidently dead from a falling book from one of his ridiculously high shelves. Or perhaps he'd simply consumed too much knowledge and his brain had exploded. My brother had once told me that such things could happen and, now that I say it, I do realise he was pulling my leg.

"He must be… busy."

Lady Alsop allowed a bewildered expression to trouble her features for a moment, but then dismissed it with a shrug. The one advantage I have over ordinary idiots is that, as I am the grandson of a lord, people sometimes mistake my foolishness for eccentricity. It has saved me on any number of occasions.

"Perhaps we should—" I began, just as the door creaked open and Grandfather appeared.

Dressed as elegantly as ever, he froze for a few seconds to take in the visitor, then turned and walked back into the library. Perhaps now you see why people think *I* must be eccentric.

"You can't get away that easily, Edgington." Lady Alsop raced after him. "I won't go until you do what I asked in my letter."

He had made it to the end of the room to place the desk between himself and his pursuer. The floor was covered with books, papers and a large map of the world, but this was not out of the ordinary.

"Madam, I believe you have had my answer, and I would ask you to leave."

94

She was suddenly more emotional, more aggressive. "Your answer wasn't good enough."

Ignoring her response, he turned to me to make an entreaty. "Christopher, you must believe me; this woman has no place here. If she will not leave of her own accord, please ring to have her escorted from the property."

I was standing next to the panel of buttons that would call Todd in the garage or a maid from the kitchen but, for some reason, I felt I should give our visitor the benefit of the doubt.

"Perhaps it would be polite to hear what Lady Alsop has to say."

"You're a wise boy, Christopher. I knew it the moment you opened the door to me." She had come to a stop somewhere around Iran if my geography was correct, and she had at least managed to fix the old detective with her eyes, if not her hands.

Her words seemed to placate my grandfather a little. "Of course he's wise; he's my grandson." He tugged on his red velvet smoking jacket with its black braiding, much as a Hussar general would straighten his uniform. "If he tries to convince you that he's a thickhead, don't listen to a word he says. He's been trying that ruse on me for some time, and I haven't fallen for it yet."

Lady Alsop began to stroll about on the map, and I finally realised something. "You're Marcus's mother, aren't you?"

Grandfather answered on her behalf. "See, he's a genius. All he required was your surname and several minutes to work out exactly who you are."

I ignored his flippant remark and asked another question. "In which case, why won't you talk to Marcus's mother?"

"Because he's scared of me." Her voice surged up and died back down like a wave breaking against a cliff. "And three days ago, I wrote to tell him that my son had been murdered."

CHAPTER SIXTEEN

Grandfather froze once more. His hands were flat on his cluttered desk, and his hair had fallen across his face. When he remained silent, Lady Alsop stamped one foot on Australia.

"Excuse me," he finally reacted, "but that's an antique map over which you're marching roughshod. I'd rather you didn't—"

"So you care about an old piece of paper but not my poor boy?"

I was trying to make sense of all that had occurred in the last ninety seconds, but her revelation had made everything more difficult. "Marcus is dead?" I had to ask, just in case she was referring to a different son.

"That's right. Four nights ago."

"In Condicote?"

"That's correct." Despite the tornado upon which she'd blown into the room, her speech was more controlled now. "I sent your grandfather a telegram as soon as the police contacted me. And I followed that with a letter the following day."

I looked between the pair of them, unsure what to believe. "Grandfather, why wouldn't you want to help this lady?"

"A guilty conscience," the forceful woman exclaimed as she took a step closer through the Pacific Ocean.

"My conscience is clear, Beulah. Your husband's behaviour was none of my concern. I barely knew the man."

"Could someone please explain what happened between you?" With all the books, carpets and soft furnishings in my grandfather's favourite retreat, my words failed to echo about the place dramatically, but they did the job I required.

"No," he grumbled, as she yelled, "Yes!"

She stepped off the Earth completely and went to sit down in a leather armchair beneath an art nouveau standing lamp in the shape of an immense hissing snake. "Your grandfather helped my now deceased husband to mess about with another woman."

"No, I did not." Fearing the damage she could do to his reputation more than his person, Grandfather shot around the table to address me directly. "Lord Alsop was a member of my club, and I happened to be in town one night when he was off frolicking with his mistress. He took me for a reliable sort and used me as an alibi without my knowledge. There's nothing more to it than that."

Lady Alsop relaxed into her chair so that her head was supported by its high back. "That may be, but you never contradicted him. You could have told me he was lying. Months passed before I found out the truth. Everyone in London knew of his dalliance, and neither you nor my supposed friends told me a thing."

"At which point she got old Bertrand drunk on his favourite bottle of Rémy Martin—"

"How do you know what I gave him?" This, in particular, seemed to pique Lady Alsop, and she sat up straighter.

"I have my sources!" It was a real tennis match and, with Grandfather in charge of the point, he turned back to me. "She got him drunk and cut off all his hair."

Rather than show contrition, our guest wore a proud grin. "That's right, but perhaps your sources didn't inform you of what happened next. When my dear husband woke up, I told him that if he ever put it about again, it wouldn't be just his hair that I'd trim."

"Proving, once and for all, that you are not the sort of person I wish to entertain in my library." He pulled his hands through his mane and needed a moment to calm down before he could say anything more. "Worse than anything, however, is the way you treated me."

Lady Alsop leant in my direction and, in a whispered aside, explained, "In case you were wondering, Bertrand was as true a husband as any from that day forth. We were married for another twenty years, and he died of a heart attack in our matrimonial bed… as opposed to some trollop's."

"Now do you see why I don't want this woman in my house, Christopher?" With his calm demeanour restored, Grandfather had come to a rest on the edge of his desk.

"No, not really."

"She threatened to do the same thing to me. And I don't know if you realise, but I happen to like my silvery tresses exactly where they are." He turned to glance at his reflection in the window. "Not all men my age are fortunate enough to have a full head of hair, and I'm rather attached to mine."

"Then let us call a truce." There was a tone of contrition in her voice. "You are no Samson, and I am not Delilah."

At this, our dog raised her head to see if anyone would offer her some food. Out of luck, she went back to sleep among three piles of books which formed a sort of highbrow kennel.

Grandfather made no response to the pact but kept his eyes fixed on the window to stare out across the snowy lawns of the estate.

This did nothing to dissuade Lady Alsop from her mission. "I'm still here, Edgington. I can wait as long as it takes."

"Not if I deprive you of nourishment, you can't." He sounded like a brattish schoolboy, and she scoffed at his poorly conceived gambit.

"You are a gentleman if nothing else. The rules of etiquette are so ingrained within you that I'm surprised you haven't already offered me tea and cake."

"Beshrew this ridiculous country!" He clapped his hands in lamentation. "I am a slave to my own good manners."

"I'd quite like some tea and cake," I said, but they were squabbling again and wouldn't listen.

"I'm only here because I believe you can help find Marcus's killer."

"I'm not a monster," he replied, his eyes once more on the intruder. "When I received your telegram, I had a colleague look into the details of your son's death, and he informed me that it was reported as a suicide. Although I have no doubt that the loss will be deeply felt, I can do nothing more to help you."

"I do not believe for one moment that my son could have killed himself." Her words became a wail, and she surged from her seat. "Surely you more than anyone can sympathise with the pain I have endured. Surely you know that I will do whatever it takes to see justice prevail."

He froze for the third and final time, and I was worried that he would become stuck like that. Perhaps the cold weather had got into his veins. Cranley Hall is bigger than a cathedral and near impossible to heat, even with all the fires blazing. I wondered again whether, like metal left out in the rain, a man gets to a certain age at which he simply corrodes. Yes, it was a silly thought and, no, Grandfather did not stay in that position for much longer.

"I'm sorry, Lady Alsop." The affront he had suffered was clearly forgotten, and he allowed a glimpse at the well of compassion that informed all he did. "I have nothing but sympathy for you. Despite his supposed ill-repute, Marcus struck me as a man of great principle. The world is worse off without him."

I watched her anger fade. In its place, sorrow rose to the surface, and she began to cry.

"I'll ring for that tea," I said, as my mother had taught me just how therapeutic a warm drink can be for the nerves.

Grandfather bit his lip as our visitor stood in the middle of the library with great salty drops falling from her to the carpet of books at her feet. As he was a born Victorian, I thought he might offer her a clean handkerchief or perhaps some smelling salts to bring her back to her senses. To my surprise, he picked his way through the debris and placed one hand on her arm.

"I feel your pain, Beulah. I honestly do. We parents shouldn't have to live through such torment. It goes against nature. Humans are built with just enough resilience to tolerate the passing of older generations, but nothing can prepare us for the loss of a child."

He did have a handkerchief for her and, when she finally broke away, he presented it with a downturned glance. She dabbed her eyes but still wouldn't say anything, so he conceded defeat.

"If you genuinely believe that Marcus was murdered, Christopher and I will return to Condicote to investigate." I believe he wished to release a sigh then, but that would have been terribly rude. "We will do everything we can to bring your son's killer to justice."

CHAPTER SEVENTEEN

By the time our maid Alice had appeared with tea and a selection of cakes, we had pulled three armchairs up to the fire, and I'd learnt a little more about the Alsop family.

"Marcus was always a headstrong boy. As a child, he knew exactly what he wanted to do in life, but his father and I told him that things weren't as simple as he wished to believe. We pushed him towards a career in the navy and, on the day he was to receive a commission, he ran away."

Much of what Lady Alsop said that morning was marked by fitful sobs. She would often find the strength to explain some sad point before crying at the seemingly insignificant moments. It was our job as detectives to suspect the motivation and involvement of every person we encountered, but there was no doubt that her grief was genuine.

"He was friends with Baron Fane and wasted his days away with that awful man. That's something else for which I blame my husband. The three of them had gone on fishing trips together when Marcus was young and, when Bertrand died, Stamford decided to treat my boy as something of a son. Of course, the baron had as much paternal instinct as a boa constrictor, and he led him to ruin."

"We were told that Fane was a gambler," Grandfather said when she fell quiet again. "From all that we heard of him in Condicote, there were few who mourned his passing."

"I certainly wasn't one of them." Her cobalt eyes swooped around the room as though in search of something. "In fact, I prayed for his removal from Marcus's life. That man was a parasite. He acted as though he were a benevolent playboy, when in reality he drained the life from everyone he met. A year after he left home, Marcus had gone through half of his inheritance."

"Do you know on what, exactly, your son spent his money?"

"On funding that man's existence, of course. He admitted as much when he came to see me about the appeal that he and that woman were mounting for the halfwit who murdered the vicar. Marcus said that Fane had borrowed ten thousand pounds from him against the value of his estate. After the man was dead, my son didn't have the heart to throw the baroness out of Seekings House, and so he came to me for help."

"When was this?" Grandfather needed no pen and paper; he kept a note of every last detail in a unique and infallible filing system in his brain.

"Shortly after the trial."

"And so you gave him the money?"

She seemed a little shy then. "I always found it hard to say no to my son. He insisted that it was a miscarriage of justice and believed he would find a flaw in the case. He'd already lodged the appeal but needed to pay for barristers and solicitors and who knows what else in order to continue with the process."

"Was that the last time you saw him?" I asked as Grandfather had fallen to pondering.

"Yes. But he telephoned me on the night before he died. He normally called me on Sundays. He could be rebellious and wilful, but he was still my good little man at heart." A sudden, stifled cry rent the room and her pain cut through me just as strongly as it did her. For all I'd seen over those last two years with my grandfather, it was impossible to appreciate what it meant to lose someone so precious.

"I'm sorry to hurry you, Beulah." Grandfather reached out one hand and placed it on the arm of her chair. "But if we're to make it to Condicote before dark, you must tell us all that you know."

She turned to me – perhaps in search of a substitute for her lost boy – and I tried to show her the sympathy she deserved.

"Marcus was enthusiastic on the telephone. He was certain that he was on the path to uncovering the killer. He told me that he'd asked you to look into the matter and that you'd refused—"

Grandfather clearly felt this needed explaining. "I regret my decision, of course I do. If I had known that anyone was still in danger, I would never have abandoned the investigation."

She was a forgiving woman not to have cut his hair off all those years ago and was quick to dismiss his fears now. "I don't blame you, Lord Edgington. The fact is that Marcus and his little friend evidently woke some beasts that they should have left sleeping." She took another noisy breath and found her thread again. "The day after we spoke on the telephone, I had a call from the police to tell me that he was dead. They found his body on a hill overlooking the village.

As you know, they claim it was suicide, but that's nonsense. Marcus would not have killed himself when his friend's life was still hanging in the balance."

This explained why I hadn't read anything about the case in the news. If the son of an aristocrat had been murdered, I would have expected a story on the front pages of The Times. A tortured young man taking his life didn't sell papers in the same way.

Grandfather had been stirring his cup of tea without drinking it for over a minute by now but stopped to pass comment. "You are not the first person who has told me that a member of her family would never have committed suicide, and I cannot promise that I will find the evidence to back up your claim." His sombre tone was soon eclipsed by a more positive attitude. "However, Christopher and I will leave no stone unturned. It is certainly hard to imagine that Marcus would have killed himself before exhausting the possibilities of his friend's appeal."

"That's not the only reason he couldn't have done it; he adored life far too much to throw it away. He was the most vibrant and capable young man I've ever met, and he would not have given up on his existence so easily."

It took him a moment to say it, but he found the right words to convince her. "I believe you, Beulah. I really do. We should leave as soon as possible, but is there anything else that you feel we should know?"

She searched her own mental notes for some significant fact, but there was nothing more to find. "I'm sad to say that I didn't know as much about my son's adult life as I would have liked. You will have to talk to Miss Warwick."

I noticed that, in a short time, she'd stopped referring to her son's girlfriend as "that woman" and perhaps even begun to entertain the idea that the "halfwit" wasn't guilty of murdering the vicar after all.

"You've met Scarlet?" I asked, excited to have news of her.

"Yes, she came to commiserate with me in my house in Yockwardine." Lady Alsop hesitated, and I could see the impact the brilliant young woman had made on her. "She was not as I'd imagined. In fact, she was even more convinced that Marcus had been murdered than I was. She really is rather special."

"Yes, I believe she is." Grandfather rose, and so I did the same. "You are welcome to stay here for as long as you need. I will tell my staff that they are to wait on you, but if we're to catch the killer before the trail goes cold, we must leave immediately."

"Thank you, Lord Edgington. I won't stay for long." Her transformation was complete, and she looked up at us with a serene glow. "I'm sorry for the way I behaved towards you in the past. Thank you for listening to me this morning. Thank you for believing me."

"It's a pleasure, madam." He bowed and kissed the woman's outstretched hand before leading me from the room. "I was afraid that might happen, Chrissy. I never can say no to an old foe."

"And yet, you say no to me all the time."

"Yes. Yes, I do." He cleared his throat as though wishing to turn the page on the experience. "We'll be travelling light to Condicote. Three cars maximum, and only the essentials on board. So, round up the staff, pack your bag, and meet me at the front of the house at record speed."

I did my best to accomplish this but, by the time everyone was ready, Lady Alsop had already left. I didn't blame her for staying in the warmth a little longer, or for enjoying a few of Cook's delicious homemade Garibaldi biscuits – speckled with sweet black raisins and adorned with glistening granules of sugar.

I really wasn't looking forward to another journey in the cold and found myself doubting whether we would even make it through the snow. The roads around Surrey were narrow and Grandfather's favourite Aston Martin would surely struggle. It was lucky, therefore, that Todd had prepared the Silver Ghost for us. Grandfather had four Rolls Royces. The new Phantom was perhaps the most impressive, but his *silver* Silver Ghost (as opposed to the incongruous blue one) was a thing of beauty. It certainly deserved its moniker, as there was something most otherworldly about it. It was the only car I knew that glided along like Charon's boat through the river Styx. Well, it normally did. We'd see how it handled all that snow.

Halfpenny would drive Cook in the Phantom, and Todd had picked out a Lagonda to travel in style with Delilah. There were hampers and crates of wine packed into the back of each car, and I had to wonder whether anyone had informed my grandmother we would be paying another visit.

"'Once more unto the breach, dear friends, once more,'" Grandfather recited as he rolled the car along the drive for the others to follow.

104

"That's stirring stuff, old chap." I tried to sound sincere. "But perhaps you could keep the car to a nice steady speed for once?"

He tilted his head from side to side as though weighing up the advantages of such an approach. Sadly, he plumped for the contrary and shouted another quote from some Shakespearean play I had never read.

"…when the blast of war blows in our ears,

Then imitate the action of the tiger."

The tyres spun on the frosty ground, and I hid behind my hands.

CHAPTER EIGHTEEN

Despite my grandfather's best efforts, the going was slow and, unlike almost any journey I could remember us taking, the other cars in our convoy stayed with us the whole way. I could only assume it was due to the extremes of emotion we had both witnessed that morning, but Grandfather remained quiet throughout.

I can't say I was a great deal more chipper myself. It was not just the news of Marcus's death, but the perplexing nature of all that we had lived through that year. We'd witnessed violence and murder before. I'd encountered some truly despicable killers and been happy to see them sentenced for their crimes, but there was something about this particular run of deaths that was especially hard to endure.

I could only conclude that it was the proximity to my father's ancestral home that was unsettling me. After all, murder was a Cranley family hobby, but the Prentisses had largely stayed out of such nastiness in the past. Perhaps it was that lack of containment that upset me; the feeling that this was no longer something my grandfather could control, as the violence had seeped out to the wider world. First the vicar had copped it and now poor Marcus: two people with no apparent connection beyond the village in which they lived. And then there was that loveable goliath Adam Caswell, awaiting his date with the hangman. It was all too much to bear.

By the time we reached Hope-under-Chesters, it was clear that we would need to stop for a break before pushing on towards Condicote. Grandfather was worried that the road would be closed over the Downs, but someone had been hard at work to keep the traffic flowing and we made it through. There was a viewpoint on the northern side of the Chester Hills and so my companion stopped to marvel at the white world before us.

"I have to tell you something, Christopher," my distinguished companion explained as I chomped on a Cornish pasty. "I'm sure that you have worked it out by now, but I would be a lesser man if I left it unsaid."

He was struggling to express himself. I hadn't a clue what he might want to say, so I just waited. He took a deep breath and, for a few seconds, I was terrified that he would reveal that he was gravely ill... or that my mother was... or perhaps I was somehow dying of a rare illness and no one had found the words to tell me. That obviously made no sense whatsoever as the last time I'd visited a doctor was four years earlier when Piggy Henderson let go of his cricket bat in a games lesson and it struck me square in the face. I'd fallen unconscious for a few minutes, but the hospital insisted there was no lasting damage.

Anyway, back to Grandfather's big speech. "Christopher," he began, "I have to confess that you were right."

To be quite honest, these words had a bigger impact on me than Piggy Henderson's cricket bat.

"I was *right?*" I believe I used a slightly disgusted tone, as though I disagreed with the very concept of such a thing.

"I should have listened to you. You showed such conviction in standing up for Adam Caswell, and I should have given more credence to your instincts."

I was seeing stars by now, and so I attempted to set the world back on its axis. "Oh, come along, Grandfather. You can't mean any of that. It's not my job to be right. If anything, it's my job to talk a lot of nonsense while you make good use of your time to find the killer. The only reason I believed in Adam Caswell was a silly sensation in the pit of my stomach that suggested he might be innocent. There was nothing scientific about it."

His eyes widened, and he seemed even more enthused. "That's just it, Christopher. Your inherent understanding of the case told you that we'd got the wrong man, and I wouldn't listen."

"But you hate all that sort of thing. You once told me that presentiments are handy excuses to do what one wanted in the first place."

I knew he loathed this word; his features squeezed together as he repeated it. "*Presentiments* are quite different from a good detective's instincts. Perhaps it's a fine line, but one is pure imagination, and the other relies upon a careful balance of evidence and forethought."

I leaned away from him towards the car window. "It doesn't make any sense, Grandfather. I can't be right. I just can't."

"I believe you are, my boy. If Marcus really was murdered, the only logical conclusion is that Adam Caswell is innocent."

I set down my pasty in shock. "The two things don't have to be mutually exclusive. Perhaps…" I couldn't think of an explanation because, as we've already established, I'm not generally very good at that sort of thing.

He grew a little more serious. "I trusted the Condicote police report into Marcus's death, when I should have come here to make certain that he hadn't been murdered. I could have let an innocent man go to the gallows and, instead of racing to correct my mistake, I attempted to hide from it. You would think that I would have learnt by now what a short-sighted approach that is."

I had thought a lot about the decade that he had been absent from my life. My grandmother was taken from us far too young, and her grieving husband's transformation from hero to hermit was difficult for everyone in my family to comprehend. And yet, nobody had spoken about it in the nearly two years since he'd come back to us.

"You know, Grandfather," I began, uncertain whether I would be able to broach the subject, "you rather scared me when you were so withdrawn this week. In fact, I was a little concerned that you'd fallen back into your old ways."

"You needn't have worried, boy. It's impossible to keep you out of any room in Cranley Hall for long. If it ever happens again, simply take me to task for my self-indulgence, and that should scare off any megrims forthwith."

This cheered me a touch, but there was more to lay bare. "As it looks as though we're both admitting things we wouldn't normally have the courage to say, I must tell you that I truly don't understand how the great Lord Edgington could have gone missing for so long."

He stared dead ahead at the snow-draped valley before us and the towns of Radsoe, Condicote and Yockwardine in the distance. At first, when he wouldn't answer, I was afraid that I'd said too much. Despite the affection we had for one another, he was still my elder, and I would never lose my fear that I was breaching certain invisible boundaries by talking to him so honestly. For most boys of my generation, grandparents were to be respected from a distance. My best friend once told me that he had never spoken directly to his grandfather. Marmaduke was so afraid of the thick belt with which the old man had blackened his son Horatio's derriere, that he never said a word to him.

"Your grandmother meant everything to me," my companion finally replied. "We were both sixty-five when she died, and the intoxicating flush of young love that we had once enjoyed may have gone, but it had been replaced by something so much stronger. She was the land upon which my life had been built and, without her there to support me, I was lost at sea."

I hated to witness such anguish in the resilient chap, but I didn't dare interrupt him.

"It was stupid of me to believe that the world had to stop when she was killed. I should have done what my family required. Not a day passes without my remembering what a mistake I made – how I failed to do my duty as a father and grandfather. But grief comes differently to each person, and I wanted to keep my suffering all to myself as though I had a sentence to serve."

He raised his chin to look at the sky where a few slushy flakes had started to fall. "That must be it. I'd sent hundreds of men to prison in my life, and this was my punishment. Not just your grandmother's death, but the solitude that came after." His troubled voice fell silent for a few moments and, when he spoke again, he was brighter. "But I served my time. That's the most important thing; I served my time and I'm back with you again. It's a blessing I never expected to enjoy."

Grandfather's hands were covered in fine lines like a creased newspaper. They were large and made my own look as though they belonged to a child's toy. This was a man raised at more than arm's length by his parents – a man who had grown up in a time when emotion and sentiment were considered entirely improper – and yet he took my hand and said something that I hadn't expected to hear.

"Thank you, Christopher." His thick thumb moved in a small, reassuring circle against my skin. "You released me from my prison, and it is our job to do the same for Adam Caswell."

He pulled away to wave to Todd and Halfpenny through the window and tell them that we were leaving. It had been a long time coming, but we were finally going back to Condicote to put things right.

CHAPTER NINETEEN

I could only conclude that my one remaining grandmother was growing soft in her old age, as she actually seemed happy to have us back with her. Well, either that or her sarcasm was too subtle for me to notice.

She even ventured out into the snow to greet us. "Oh, how wonderful. You brought your cook, footman and factotum. I'll have to give my own staff a holiday."

"It is very kind of you to welcome us at The Manor again, Loelia." Grandfather was on his best behaviour. "We will try not to get in your way."

"Nonsense." She was an absolute sunbeam for some reason. "It's a pleasure to have you here. I just hope you'll be able to clear up this nasty business with the murders." She spoke as though we were exterminators coming to deal with a mouse problem. "I think everyone in the village was content when it looked as though that simpleton was responsible. But we're all at a loss as to how yet another person could have been slaughtered."

"So you don't believe that Marcus's death was suicide?" I was frankly astonished that she would doubt the word of the local constabulary.

"Not for one moment. If you ask me, P.C. Brigham is saying that's what happened to ensure no one looks too closely at his past mistakes." She eyed my grandfather suspiciously at this moment, and I was certain she was considering his part in Caswell's conviction.

"Of course, the good thing about mistakes," he began in response, "is that we can learn so much from them."

Any warmth our host had shown us had vanished by this point. "That's all well and good as long as no one dies in the meantime." Her face was a picture of disapproval. "It's too late to do anything for the Alsop boy, and no one knows how long it will be before Adam Caswell finds himself up on the Tatchester gallows."

Grandfather was not one to show his irritation and smiled benevolently. "Then there's all the more reason for us to be quick about it."

"Now, I wouldn't say that either." Heaven forbid my grandmother should agree with anyone on a single point. "Too many people are prone to haste these days. No one has the time for good manners. Take our new vicar, the not so right Reverend Bodsworth. He came to introduce himself the week after he arrived in Condicote and barely had an hour to take tea."

"How you must have suffered." Grandfather made no attempt to hide his own hastiness.

Wrapped up warmly in spotted white, lynx fur, Granny kept nattering regardless.

"Perhaps Reverend Oldfield would never have died if people took a little more time over things. I still haven't heard any explanation for why he was in such a hurry in the first place. All those people in the village saw him rushing past on his bicycle before he was killed – he almost ran straight into Mrs Grout the grocer – but the only time I'd ever seen that man move at pace was when he was on his way to the public house for lunch."

Grandfather had spent this whole time trying to extricate himself from the conversation, whereas I was genuinely interested in what my grandmother had to say. There was something in the way she spoke about Marcus that told me she could be unexpectedly useful.

"Granny, do you know the Alsop family well?"

I had grown rather a lot recently so, in order to look down on me, she took an extra step up the grand stone staircase in front of The Manor – which some hardworking servant had evidently cleared of snow.

"Of course I do, boy. I know everyone in the Tatchester region. Well, everyone worth knowing at least."

"What do you think of his mother?"

She didn't need to consider the question, but looked off towards the village, as though offended by the mere mention of the woman. "She lives three whole miles away in Yockwardine, so I don't get to see her too often, but I must say she's a rather underwhelming character. Her husband was Viscount Tatchester, you know. But she has none of the poise for which one would hope from someone in her position."

Grandfather had apparently sensed that there was only one way out of this conversation: flattery! "Thank you, Loelia. You will definitely be the person to whom we must talk should we need to delve deeper into the underlying nature of your fellow villagers. You may turn out to be an essential witness."

112

"One does what one can." Perhaps it was just the cold air making her cheeks rosy, but I was sure that she blushed a little. "Now, I won't delay you any longer. You have a killer to apprehend after all." As though we were the ones who had been bending her ear, she took on a harried expression and turned towards the house.

The sun would soon be setting over the hills, and I doubted we would be able to do much poking about until the morning. Of course, my mentor had other ideas and, once Todd and Halfpenny had unloaded the luggage, and Cook had escaped to the kitchen to see her opposite number, it was time to head into town.

"Will you be walking, m'lord?" our chauffeur enquired.

"Not today, Todd. In fact, I'd like you to drive me in the Phantom. I intend to make an impression this afternoon in the hope it will dissuade anyone from following in the killer's footsteps. There are only so many times one wishes to visit this part of the country in such poor weather."

Todd was always happy to come along on our investigations and, still wearing his deep green livery and cap, he ran to make the car ready whilst we bade Granny farewell.

It was strange to be back there. Unlike many killers, I rarely return to the scenes of the crimes we have investigated, and there was something uncanny about driving past the church and on towards the high street. St Bartholomew's looked majestic with a patch of vibrant blue sky behind it and the sun illuminating the clouds like the letters of a mediaeval manuscript. Its Norman clock tower and sandstone masonry really did make the church stand out and, aside from the recent rise in violent crime in the area, Albert and Cassandra couldn't have chosen a nicer spot in which to wed.

There was snow atop every tombstone and coating the branches of the lime trees. Children from the village had even built a snowman with a dog collar made from a piece of cardboard and a sculpted surplice. Some savage had come along and placed a noose around the poor chap's neck, and I could only imagine how Reverend Oldfield's replacement would feel about such a graphic reminder of his predecessor's demise.

There was no sign of life in the graveyard, and so we drove on to the village. If it had been my grandfather's intention to leave an impression on Condicote, our arrival that afternoon certainly did the trick. It's hard to know whether it was the large, glossy and frankly funereal car, rolling slowly along the high street, or the presence of the one-time bloodhound of Scotland Yard seated in the rear, but everyone in town stopped to watch us pass.

We saw P.C. Brigham, who was lending Bob Thompkins a hand to clear the pavements of snow. Dr Beresford-Gray stood rocking on her heels on the front step of her surgery as Todd drove slowly past. Her head didn't move, but her eyes definitely followed us.

I recognised several other members of the parish I had met over the years, too. The organist from St Bartholomew's, Mrs Stanley, was buying a suspiciously large sack of carrots in the market. Mayor Hobson stood in the middle of the town square like a preacher without a soapbox, and a well-dressed woman in a fox stole and expensive cashmere coat was the only person there to hear whatever he had to say. I didn't get a good look at her face but, from her glamorous attire, I was fairly certain she was Stamford Fane's widow.

This was Grandfather's attempt to stir up the hornet's nest and, if the killer was there in the square, I had no doubt that he would be in abject fear to witness the great detective's return. Perhaps that should be the first criterion when searching for our culprit: he can't possibly have known that Lord Edgington would be in town when the vicar was killed. Either that, or he was a terrible fool to try his luck against the man who brought the Ealing Strangler to justice. He didn't stand a chance against my grandfather (and me).

The one problem with this powerful entrance was that, once we had driven the length of the village, we had to turn around and go back the other way. It was certainly less dramatic when we reappeared a few minutes later, and Todd had to look for a spot to park.

"Whom should we interview first, Grandfather?" I asked once we were out of our sparkling vehicle and the cold was nipping at every exposed inch of my skin.

I had hoped that the villagers would still be watching us with apprehension plain on their trembling faces but, to be perfectly honest, they'd gone back to their normal lives.

"I would have said that was obvious, Chrissy."

I nodded and summoned the name that was evidently on the tip of both our tongues.

I said, "Scarlet Warwick," just as he said, "Mrs Grout the grocer."

CHAPTER TWENTY

"Wait…" I was a good bit puzzled by this. "Why would we talk to Mrs Grout?"

Grandfather had already started the trek through near-freezing slush towards the large, bright grocery shop on the corner of the square. "Keep up, Chrissy," he said, to chastise my sluggish brain, before adding, "And keep up!" to correct my sluggish pace. "Your grandmother told us that the vicar almost collided with Mrs Eileen Grout on his final journey through town. However, she was not called as a witness at Adam Caswell's trial, which may suggest that she saw something which did not align with P.C. Brigham's assumptions about the case." He paused to peer about the square before pointing at a shop on the far side. "Instead, Mrs Ivy the jeweller was called before the court and claimed to have seen the fear on the reverend's face. She must have incredibly good eyesight to have made out such a feature from a distance of eighty feet."

"You're absolutely right!" This was hardly the bravest statement I'd ever made, but I had my reasons for agreeing with him. "Reverend Oldfield was in a hurry to get to his destination – or perhaps away from where he'd been. It's weighed on my mind ever since the trial. No one has given us a good idea of what the vicar saw before he was murdered."

"Precisely. I should admit that even I came to a lazy conclusion on the matter." He should have, but he didn't. "It was easy to ignore such a minor consideration when so much of the evidence pointed to one suspect, but I was remiss in my duties, and it is surely the key question we must answer."

We had reached the general shop by now and, with this statement made, he pushed open the door and entered.

"Mrs Grout, I presume?" Grandfather asked in an intimidating voice. He didn't normally go in for such obvious tactics with our witnesses, but I could see that he was determined to make up for his prior mistakes.

"Nah, I'm Sally Biggins," the squat, rather hairy woman answered. "I'll get Eileen for ya if I have to." She did not wait for an answer but stomped off through a door behind the counter.

I spent the thirty seconds that we were alone there laughing at my grandfather. He did not appreciate it, and his steely gaze travelled around the shop as I guffawed.

It was an impressive little place. A long, glass counter displayed fresh goods of all kinds from cheese to chewy sweets. On the floor just in front were twenty huge, open sacks containing pulses, beans and nuts of every shape and colour. The walls were covered with busy shelves, and I couldn't think of a single ingredient that 'Grout's Grocery' didn't stock.

"Lord Edgington, I presume?" the shopkeeper barked as she appeared from the back room.

It was immediately apparent that he would have his work cut out if he had any intention of intimidating such a person. Eileen Grout had skin as rough as an un-scrubbed potato and frizzy black hair like a scouring pad. She had thick, muscular arms with a band of black cotton over either one, like the rings of metal on a beer barrel. If either of us had hoped we could exclude the women of Condicote from our inquiries on the grounds that they wouldn't have the strength to kill the vicar, we would have to think again.

"What can I do for you?" She had the look of a woman preparing for an arm-wrestling competition as she leaned closer to the counter and her eyes became two narrow slits in the middle of her face.

Taking a moment to adjust his approach, the lead detective was suddenly all charm. "I'd like five pounds of your most expensive—"

I had to interrupt him then, as the last time he'd tried to buy his way into our witness's confidences, it had been something of a failure – and I had been required to carry his purchases.

"Oh, very well." He sighed and started again. "Dear Mrs Grout, I have been reliably informed that it was you and you alone who spoke to the vicar on the night that he died?"

She didn't know what to make of this, and her cheeks pulled into her mouth. There was something terribly pug-doggish about her. She simply had more skin on her face than most people, and her jowls were remarkably expressive. "So you reckons there's a connection between the killings then, does you?"

"What a quick mind you have, madam." He stood back to admire the undiscovered genius in our midst. "Truly, I've had assistants who would have failed to reach a conclusion so swiftly." I had to hope he wasn't referring to me. "You are just the kind of person I will need on my side if we are to crack this case open and identify the culprit."

He was beginning to sound like the Peter Pan I'd once seen in a pantomime, and it really wasn't his best performance. Of course, that isn't to say that he didn't know what he was doing. Big, fierce Eileen Grout was taken in by every last word he uttered.

"Whatever you need, Lord Edgington!" She was so excited she could barely speak. "I never thought my day of service would arrive. Some men join the army. Some women serve as nurses in wartime but, by working away here in the grocer's, I thought I'd missed my chance." Starry-eyed, she looked at my grandfather head-on and said, "I'll do whatever I can."

I think that my companion was a little disappointed at just how easy his task had been. "Very good, Eileen. To begin with, all I require is your account of the last time you saw Reverend Oldfield on the night that he was murdered."

She straightened her posture, as though addressed by a superior officer. "I was outside the shop tending to the veg boxes, you see? I saw the vicar crossing the village in a state of some agitation." Her voice had become more formal and her phrasing more precise. "It's hard to say exactly how I could tell that was the case just by the way he was riding his bike. I think he musta been swaying side to side, or something like that. Well, anyway, he was so upset he almost veered off the road and into my shop.

"So I says, 'Everything all right, Vicar?'

"And he says, 'I'm sorry, Mrs Grout, but I can't talk. I've just seen something utterly…' and then he stops himself like he couldn't put his finger on what it was he'd seen, and he says, 'I really must be going. Good afternoon to you.' And he raced off again."

"How curious," Grandfather replied. "And did you inform P.C. Brigham of what happened?"

"'Course I did." Grout's voice fell a little just then. "I had hoped I might be called to testify, but it weren't to be."

Her inquisitor sent a meaningful glance in my direction as our suspicions about the constable seemed to have proved correct.

"I told Brigham that the vicar looked like he'd seen a goat, and he said that was very interesting, but it didn't go any further."

Wise old Lord Edgington always left it to me to ask the silly questions. "I'm sorry. A goat? Don't you mean a ghost?"

"A ghost?" she repeated, as though I were the one talking nonsense. "There's no such thing as ghosts, lad! But Mrs McGregor's goat gets out of his paddock sometimes and causes all sorts of havoc in the village. It is not a welcome sight to find him in your garden of a morning. I can tell you that for nothing!"

Grandfather teased the conversation back towards sanity. "I have no doubt that is true, madam. Now, as for the evening in question. Once the vicar had ridden away, did you notice anything else that was unusual?"

"Unusual?" She thought about this for a moment. "That would depend on your definition of the word. I found it strange that the mayor walked his dog Henry round and around and around the square, as he normally takes him out to the hill behind Mrs Stanley's house. He went round three times at least. I know because I counted."

"Fascinating, Madam. That is truly fascinating." I have no idea how my grandfather could make such statements with a straight face. "However, I was more interested in any potential suspects who passed the shop."

"You mean Adam Caswell then? Well, when he walked past, he were doing something funny." She put one elbow on the counter and leaned closer. "He were whistling 'Yes! We Have No Bananas'. I've always found that song just hilarious." She laughed profusely to prove this point. "He even gave me a little wave as he wandered along the pavement."

"Yes, it is a witty song." Grandfather surely couldn't maintain his patience for much longer. "Now, was there anyone else who passed at that time?"

"Ooh, who might have come past after that?" She had another think. "Well, there were a few cars what passed. And, like I said, Mayor Hobson was there. But Henry the dog musta got tired as I didn't see them again after… let's say a quarter to eight."

"Very good. And apart from the people you have already mentioned, was there anyone else?"

"Anyone else?" She scratched her cheek. "Yes… Old Mickey Brown's cart rolled past full of turnips. But I can't say any other faces stood out to me. Should they have?"

Grandfather stifled a sigh. "Madam, you have been of the utmost help. I greatly appreciate your time, and I will be sure to keep you abreast of any important developments in the case."

She winked at him then. It didn't look as though he'd understood the gesture, and so she tapped her nose, too. "And I will be sure to inform you of any important developments I witness from this here shop."

With this nonsense resolved, we were free to go.

"That was a waste of time. We should have gone to see Miss Warwick first, just as I said." As we stepped out of the shop, there was the faintest hint of arrogance in my voice. "Aren't you going to tell me that I was right again? I could get used to this."

"Not at all, Christopher." He shook his head and tutted. "I will not say such a thing, as you are quite mistaken. Mrs Grout was the very person to shed light on the events leading up to Reverend Oldfield's murder."

"Oh, really?"

"Yes, really!" He tutted again for good measure. "She told us just what we needed to know."

"Which is?" I still didn't believe him.

"She essentially proved that Adam Caswell was not in a murderous rage as the prosecution at his trial chose to paint him. He was whistling a novelty song about bananas, of all things, and made no attempt to hide the fact he was walking towards the church. Had he planned to kill the vicar, it seems unlikely he would have waved at a gossipy shopkeeper."

"Oh, I—"

"Wait, there's more." Tut, tut, tut. "We now have a suspect, in the shape of P.C. Brigham, who we must assume withheld Mrs Grout's testimony. There was certainly no record of it in the police file I perused." I was about to speak, but he had more to say. "We also received first-hand testimony of the vicar's mental state as he cycled through the village."

"Yes, that is interesting. He was—"

"One moment, please Christopher. I haven't finished." Gosh, he was in a very tutty mood! "Remember the words that Reverend Oldfield spoke to Mrs Grout. He did not say he had seen *someone* – which would have fitted with my initial, admittedly flawed, hypothesis that Caswell was chasing him through the village. He said that he saw '…something utterly…'and then stopped."

I waited to be certain that he had finished speaking before adding a comment of my own. "Something utterly awful? Or something utterly extraordinary, perhaps? In everyday speech, there really aren't so many adjectives that we use with such an adverb."

"That's right. Utterly shocking, bizarre or terrifying: they are all very strong words, and it once more raises the question of exactly what the vicar saw that put him in such a…"

He was searching for the right word and so I attempted to help him. "Flurry-scurry?"

Generally preferring terms that were at least a century old, he found another option. "I was going to say he was in a twitteration, though I suppose your suggestion makes sense, too."

It wasn't quite as good a concession as him saying that I was right, but it would have to do.

"So what comes next? If you had any doubts left, it is surely now clear that Adam is innocent of any involvement in the vicar's murder. He was simply in the wrong place at the wrong time, but how can we find the evidence to prove it?"

A long black car drove along the high street as I asked this, and he waited until it had passed before providing an answer. "Next, we must speak to Scarlet Warwick."

CHAPTER TWENTY-ONE

Without another word – although I was tempted to tell him that he was copying my idea – we crossed the square towards the Drop of Dew Inn. The sun had set behind the row of shops on the western side of the market and the traders were packing their goods onto carts before shutting up for the night. Though it was a fairly small town by most standards, there was a buzz and bustle to Condicote that I found appealing. It was a shame that my grandfather and I couldn't go anywhere without someone being murdered. It would have been nice to explore a place, instead of always hunting for killers.

"Look there, Christopher." My esteemed companion held out his hand to stop me from crossing the road. "In the tearoom."

"You're right, Grandfather. It's Miss Warwick."

It's lucky that one of us was observant, as I would have walked right past and gone to the inn. Sitting at a table in the window of the A.B.C. teashop, Scarlet was looking at the papers that she had spread out in front of her. It had been over an hour since I'd eaten that delicious pie, and I was happy to enter any establishment that served food.

Grandfather, on the other hand, looked confused by the very concept of the place. He pushed the door open but stood back to let another customer exit. Even then, he stepped over the threshold with some trepidation. It was hard to know what had got into him.

"You came," Scarlet said, as though she'd been expecting us, and began to clear a spot at the round table. "It's a shame you took so long, but you're here now."

I sat down next to her, happy to be in the presence of that young spitfire once more. She veritably fizzed with energy, and I couldn't wait to hear her thoughts on all that had happened. However, there was something that I needed to say first.

"I'm so sorry about Marcus. I know we only met him on those two occasions, and in such sad circumstances, but he was an admirable chap."

She bit her pretty pink lip and stared up at the moulded ceiling of the café. "Yes, it's tragic. But I'm not allowing myself to think of all that until his killer is caught. And, before you ask, no, I don't believe that Marcus committed suicide. He was about to free Adam from certain death and there's no way on earth that he would have given up on such an important task."

I was expecting my grandfather to cut into the conversation with a pertinent question, but he didn't seem quite himself. He was peering about at the other tables, clearly still perplexed by this foreign environment. "I don't under..." he began, before turning his chair ninety degrees to get a better view of the place.

"Would you like something to drink, Lord Edgington? I bought some tea a little while ago, but it's gone quite cold."

"I don't under..." he said once more before finally revealing his quandary. "Why are there no waiters?"

Scarlet and I took no little amusement from his bemusement, and it fell to me to explain. "A.B.C. Tea shops are self-service cafeterias, Grandfather. You have to take a tray and go to the counter to choose what you want to eat and drink."

He shook his head in wonder. "How fascinating."

"Surely you encountered such places when you were a police officer?" Now Scarlet was the one who sounded surprised.

"I suppose they may have existed during the latter part of my career, but I certainly never ate in one. This is a real experience." Without further comment, he rose from his seat and gingerly picked up a tray from a stack beside the line of customers who were queuing to be served. He took each step in an experimental manner, as though uncertain whether he was doing it correctly. Quite out of place, he gratefully received the support of a fellow diner who ushered him forward to stand in line.

"Your grandfather is rather a strange man, don't you think?" Scarlet reflected.

"Oh, beyond a doubt. But then that tends to be the case with the peers I've met."

She nodded knowingly, and I felt she could have offered some evidence of her own to corroborate this idea. We would probably have discussed the investigation in which she'd engaged since her beloved's death, but we were both mesmerised by the eccentric old lord's behaviour.

As he approached the hot food counter where neat, white-aproned young ladies were ladling soup into bowls or handing over plates of savoury delicacies, he had the wide-eyed look of a child entering a toy shop. He shuffled along from counter to counter with the rest of the crowd, passing 'sweets', 'hot sweets', 'cold dishes' and 'toasted items'. The final stop was 'hot and cold drinks' before he was free to pay at the till. In the end, he had to call me for assistance, as he'd gained a second tray at some point, and each was laden.

"What did you buy?" Scarlet exclaimed as much as asked when we arrived at her table, and she had to remove the last of her papers.

"I'm not entirely sure." Grandfather still looked puzzled. "I chose anything that I hadn't eaten before. I recall beef rissoles, buttered milk loaf, rump steak pie, potted ham and tongue, lunch cake, empress cake and Lawn Tennis cake."

"You didn't scrimp on the cakes then," I felt compelled to remark.

He didn't seem offended by my impertinence, as he was already sitting down to consume one of the beef dishes... or it could have been potted ham and tongue. I have to say they all looked rather similar.

"Perhaps you'd like some help with the sweets." Scarlet didn't wait for an answer but swooped in to claim the lunch cake. I may be no expert when it comes to identifying birds, but I can tell the difference between an éclair and a strawberry shortcake sandwich from a mile away.

"Of course, my dear. Help yourself to whatever takes your fancy." He evidently noticed my apprehension as he soon added, "And you, Christopher. I have my work cut out with all this food."

"And with our case." Scarlet cleverly moved the conversation back to what really mattered. Before she could say anything more, the new vicar came into the café – perhaps this was a good thing, as her mouth was rather full. Daddy always told me to either talk or eat but never do both at the same time.

The full-faced cleric hung his hat and coat on a stand beside the door, then waved solemnly at his parishioners. He stopped when he saw us and looked as though he might introduce himself but joined the queue for food instead. There was something rather impressive about him. I don't think I'd ever met such a perfectly bald man in my life. His head was as shiny as a new farthing, and he wore thick glasses that made his eyes look bigger than his mouth. He did not seem the type to indulge in alcohol as his predecessor had, and this impression was strengthened by his election of tea and plain toast for sustenance.

"What do you make of the new arrival?" Grandfather whispered when the portly chap had sat down at a table some way into the long, narrow establishment.

"More or less what you would expect from a vicar." Scarlet dropped her voice to match him. "Though some folk in the pub are less than happy with his sermons. They're all hellfire and damnation. Not much in keeping with what the people around here like to think of as good living."

Grandfather had another question for her. "And your findings in the case of the two murders? Do you believe you've made any progress there?"

She set her wedge of cake down on its saucer. Just in case you're wondering, I had opted for the Empress cake. It was fluffy, light and delicious, and I would have to ask Cook to prepare me one at home.

Where was I? Ah, yes, Scarlet had set down her cake and seemed immediately composed. "I've certainly done what I can to continue Marcus's investigation. However, the only thing I would count as progress is seeing the real killer clapped in irons." She blew a rogue ringlet of hair from her face. "Where would you like me to start?"

The potted ham and tongue, or what have you, did not appear to agree with my grandfather and so he set it aside for a plate of grey balls of meat, which I took to be rissoles. I can't say they were particularly appealing. Of course, if Grandfather had somehow obtained access to my head at this moment he would have been saying, *focus on the case, Christopher, not the food.* To which I would have responded, *you shouldn't have bought so much food if you wanted me to think about anything else!*

"Start with Marcus's murder."

Scarlet flinched at this. "I'm glad you used that word, as there's no doubt in my mind that he was killed. For a start, this note was posted through the door of the Drop of Dew for me."

She rifled through her papers and came across a small envelope, no bigger than a booklet of stamps. She extracted a folded piece of paper and smoothed it out on a free spot on the table.

DARLING, I AM QUITE DISTRAUGHT. YOU WILL FIND ME AT KING ARTHUR'S CAMP WHENEVER YOU CAN SPARE A MOMENT TO RETRIEVE ME.

"How curious," I said, as there was definitely something unusual about the letter. "It doesn't sound particularly natural, does it?"

She snatched it back off the table. "Marcus never called me 'darling'. Not once in our time together. He detested such frivolous, sentimental language."

Grandfather had an explanation for everything, but even he could see the note was suspicious. "In such distressed states, men have been known to do stranger things. But it is another word in the note that alarms me. *Distraught* seems too perfect. It is as though its author wished to make it clear in just one word that this was a suicide note. The improbable capital letters make identifying the handwriting less simple, and talk of *finding* and *retrieving* is rather dehumanising, too. It already suggests that it would be a body you were collecting, not a living person."

"Exactly. And why would he have posted it through the letterbox at the inn? Marcus knew the owners well and could have left it at the bar for me, or even up in our room. The only reason someone would have posted a letter into an open establishment is to hide their identity."

"Was he seen in town at the time the note arrived?" I hesitated to ask this and felt sure that one of them would dismiss the question.

"Yes, what were Marcus's movements before the note was discovered?" Grandfather added, which I took as one point to me.

Scarlet's expressive features changed in phases. She had been cheery, then focussed and now moved on to glum. "It's impossible to say when it was posted into the Drop of Dew. According to Dr Beresford-Gray, by the time the landlord found it, Marcus was already dead. I'd been up to Tatchester to see Adam. I spoke to Marcus on the telephone at lunchtime and he told me he'd discovered something quite unbelievable. Typically for him, he refused to say what it was. I've no doubt that he had planned to reveal his discovery in dramatic fashion later that day. But that moment never came, and there was nothing on his body except for an empty wallet. I found that strange in itself, as he normally carried a fair few notes."

Grandfather would not focus on such details just yet and pushed her to continue. "Did you go up to King Arthur's Camp immediately after you were given the note?"

"No, I went to the police. I knew something wasn't right, and so I showed P.C. Brigham."

"I can only assume he dismissed your fears?" Grandfather was shaking his head even before he'd heard the answer.

"Very much so. He said he had to travel to Radsoe that afternoon. There were some escaped cows causing problems with traffic and, if he didn't go, he said that no one else would."

"I hope you didn't go up there in the snow all on your own?" I couldn't help but feel protective towards her, even though Scarlet would have done a much better job of looking after me than vice versa.

"The snow hadn't arrived then, actually, but no. I had to beg Mayor Hobson to drive me up there in his Crossley. It's a muddy path for the last part, but you can drive almost to the top of the hill."

"I don't suppose you noticed any extra footprints on that muddy path?" Grandfather asked.

"No, I wasn't thinking straight. I was worried about Marcus and not concerned with collecting evidence."

If that had been me, Grandfather would have criticised this failing. Perhaps he remembered how he had behaved after losing loved ones and stopped himself. "What did you find there?"

She didn't pause for breath or pour herself a fresh cup of tea before answering this most difficult of questions. She simply stared ahead and summoned an answer. "He was shot through the temple. The blood was still fresh on the ground and, when the doctor arrived, she said he couldn't have been dead for more than a couple of hours."

"There was a gun at the scene, obviously?"

It took me a moment to realise why this was obvious; evidently it wouldn't have looked like a suicide if the gun had been removed. "Obviously."

"Yes, a military pistol. There are so many of the damn things around these days that, with no serial number or affiliations, it's impossible to say to whom it belonged."

"Did Marcus fight in the war?" I asked, which was also a silly question as…

"He was too young. He would have turned twenty-one in June,

which makes his possession of a wartime pistol less likely."

"Indeed." I enjoyed making such empty interjections as they didn't influence the discussion in any way whatsoever but helped make me feel that I was part of the process.

Grandfather produced something more helpful. "Was there anything at the scene of the crime which could lead us to the killer?"

She'd had another bite of cake and needed to chew for a moment before swallowing. "Not a thing. But then, if I had murdered someone far away from civilisation with little chance of discovery, I would have taken the time to make sure there was no evidence left behind."

Grandfather seemed to have enjoyed the food he had been sampling and there were now two fewer rissoles on his plate. He dabbed his mouth with a paper serviette before answering. "There may not have been any physical evidence for you to find, but there are certain facts which stand out to me. For one thing, Marcus was killed at the spot where Adam Caswell claimed to have been when the vicar was murdered. On the face of things that would suggest that he was thinking of your incarcerated friend when he decided to end his life."

"I came to the same conclusion." I could see that Scarlet wished to put both her thoughts and the evidence in order, and she moved the dishes around on the tray as she spoke. "But if it wasn't suicide, it makes no sense. If he was so upset at the fate of our friend, why would he have taken his life before discovering the result of Adam's appeal which is due this week?"

This excited the old devil. "Precisely! The killer slipped up there. He really did."

"He chose that spot to make it look like suicide, but it had the opposite effect." She took a deep breath before delivering the key part of her theory. "And yet, it could suggest a further connection between the two killings. I can only conclude that Marcus was killed by the same person who was responsible for strangling Reverend Oldfield."

"Wait. That's not all." A significant point came to my mind at this moment. It had been so long since such a thing had occurred that I hardly believed it possible. "Might it not also be true that Marcus was killed because he'd discovered the culprit? The 'unbelievable' thing that he mentioned when you spoke on the telephone, perhaps it was the identity of the very man for whom we're searching."

CHAPTER TWENTY-TWO

My companions fell silent at this moment, and I took the opportunity to cast my gaze around the room, not just at the fixtures and fixings that made an A.B.C. Teashop so distinctive, but the people who were eating there. It was a busy little place for a small town, and half the village was present, chewing on brawn sandwiches and Bath buns. I hadn't noticed her before, but there was a familiar face a few tables away.

Sitting on her own was Dr Beresford-Gray, whom we had first seen testifying at Adam's trial. I had the definite feeling that she wanted to look at us but was stopping herself. Instead, she had fixed her eyes on a point in front of her and, even as she poured milk into her cup and stirred, she never moved them. It was as though she was frightened we might notice her – as though we were Medusas who would turn her to stone – and I couldn't understand why she would behave in such a way. I looked around the rest of the café in case I recognised any of the other villagers, but it was mainly cheery families and pairs of old ladies. Reverend Bodsworth had found a table for himself in the far corner but, even if he was as fierce in the pulpit as Scarlet had claimed, there was little else to inspire such terror in the doctor.

"I think we should take the time to look over the evidence that Marcus collected," my grandfather decided and immediately got to his feet.

"But you've hardly eaten anything," I said, looking at the selection of food still laid out on the table.

Grandfather sighed. "Are you suggesting you'd like to have something more?"

"Not at all." I have no doubt that this came as a shock to him. "I wouldn't want to spoil my dinner. I merely think you should be more careful in future with what you order. Wasting food ought to be a crime."

And, with that, I finished my last bite of cake, pushed my chair under the table, and left the restaurant. Of course, I couldn't be sure where we were headed and had to wait for my grandfather to traverse the square on the way to Scarlet's lodgings in the Drop of Dew. We received some wary looks from the departing market traders, and it was clear that my famous grandfather's presence in the town had been duly noted.

"You're back again then." I imagine that this was the spiky woman behind the bar's idea of a welcome. She must have swapped her shifts with her husband, as this was the first time I'd seen her on duty in the daytime.

"That we are, madam. And what a pleasure it is to see you once more." Grandfather was a charmer when he wanted to be. "May I ask whether you have any inkling as to who delivered the note to Miss Warwick on the day that Mr Alsop was murdered?"

"You're wasting your time." It was not the diminutive tough behind the bar who made this statement, but our companion, Scarlet. "I've already asked such questions. I'll show you now."

She gave the landlady a solemn nod and shot up the stairs. It appeared that she was still paying for a suite of rooms as, instead of taking us into the chamber where we'd first met her, we turned into the bedroom that Adam Caswell had previously occupied.

Any possessions he may have owned had been tidied away or perhaps given to his mother. In their place was what looked like the nerve centre of a police investigation. Piles of papers were stacked in the bay window overlooking the road, and others were pinned to the old wooden beams on the wall.

"You're right." Lord Edgington was evidently impressed by his fellow investigator's progress. "You have been busy."

I took a seat on the only free surface: an ottoman at the end of the bed.

Scarlet joined my grandfather to examine the notes. "Idle hands are the devil's playground. That's what my mother always told me. Though she also liked to claim that I should keep my hands unblemished so as not to be mistaken for a labourer, so she was a woman of some contradictions. Besides, Marcus did most of the work. I just made it presentable."

The more experienced detective was reading one of the pages that was pinned in plain view. "I suppose that these are your suspects?"

"That's right." Despite the suffering she had endured, Scarlet could not hide the pleasure she took in her role and rushed forward to explain her thinking. "I consider these five people to be the ones who would gain most from the deaths. You may notice that each of them sits on the town council."

Loelia Prentiss
Mayor Eric Hobson
Dr Beresford-Gray
P.C. Derek Brigham
Baroness Sorel Fane

I couldn't believe what I was seeing. "Loelia Prentiss? That's my grandmother!"

Scarlet seemed unmoved by my response. "Yes. Have you met her? She's a monster."

"Monster is a bit strong," I said before searching for a better word. "She might be something of a harridan, or perhaps a banshee, at a push, but I've never once considered her an out-and-out monster."

"Either way, she was no fan of Marcus, and truly despised Stamford, so she deserves her place on the list."

I thought I would lodge an appeal with the man in charge. I knew it wouldn't do me any good, but I felt oddly protective over even the less friendly members of my family and couldn't just ignore the accusation. "Grandfather, surely you don't think that Granny could be involved in any of this."

"Of course I don't," he said in a reassuring tone, before whispering quite the contrary to Scarlet. "Though that doesn't mean that Loelia lacks the savagery to smite her enemies like a vengeful god."

"You do realise that I can hear you."

He and Scarlet couldn't resist a conspiratorial giggle before he pretended to be serious and returned our attention to the list. "It's an interesting set of names, regardless. But one problem instantly comes to mind. How can you rule out everyone else in town?"

Scarlet's capacity to change between the light-hearted character that I'd met in that inn, months before, and the heartbroken woman searching for her lover's killer was impressive. "I can't entirely, but I think that each of these people had their reasons for wanting us out of the way."

"Us?" I asked. "Do you believe that you could be in danger, too?"

She considered the point. "I meant Marcus and his friends in general, as I'm not sure that I'm much of a threat to anyone. I've spent most of the last year since I moved to Condicote, writing in one of these rooms. After all, I was never invited to gamble with the men.

And I didn't go up to London to lose money in every Mayfair club that would allow them entry."

"Was that Marcus's pastime as much as Baron Fane's, then?" Grandfather was clearly intrigued by this point. "Gambling, I mean, not losing money."

Still with her eyes on the list, Scarlet perched on the side of the bed. "They certainly both enjoyed it, but Marcus wasn't nearly so accomplished as the good baron when it came to risking his fortune."

There was something important in all of this which I'd failed to consider. "Are you suggesting that Marcus's and the vicar's deaths could be connected to the baron's?"

It was grandfather who would answer my question. "The police said that he couldn't have been murdered. They examined the car in case the brakes had been cut, and Chief Inspector Darrington told me that the coroner had ruled out foul play."

Scarlet clucked her tongue. "It would make things simpler if someone had a hand in the Stamford's death, but I haven't found anything to suggest that was the case."

There was something in the way she spoke that caught my grandfather's attention. "In what way would it be simpler?"

"Oh, you know." She hesitated then, and I couldn't be sure why. "Stamford was very good at making enemies. I never understood why Adam and Marcus were so desperate to win his favour, but they both just adored him."

"Were you here at the inn on the day the baron died?"

"Yes, but I was writing for most of the day. Stamford could be entertaining company when he wished to be, but I never liked him when he was drunk. I was sitting in my window when he came back from a gambling trip to London in a foul mood. I don't know exactly what happened, but Marcus told me that his noble friend stormed into the bar, bought a bottle of whisky, and then went off again in a foul mood. I saw him get into his car and he could barely walk straight. He was swearing under his breath as he threw the bottle inside and sped off towards his house. They say he was dead a few minutes later."

"And that was around a week before the vicar was killed?" I asked, just to make certain I was keeping up with the facts.

"Something like that."

It was Grandfather's turn for a question. "Did you ever ask Marcus what he really thought of the baron?"

"I did, and he was fascinated by the man." It was clear that she was less enamoured of him. "Stamford had the ability to bend people to his will. For all the foes he had collected in this town, he had a good number of defenders. Mayor Hobson, in particular, would sing his praises to anyone who would listen. It can't just have been his title and money that people admired – after all, he hadn't a tosser to his kick by the time he died. Stamford was just one of those chaps who always got his own way."

"But I thought he was a villain through and through," I asked in surprise. "All I've heard of him my whole life is what a rotter the man was."

Scarlet wore a frown as though she pitied my naivety. "That may be true, but in my experience, villains can be an awful lot of fun. For all the scandal that Stamford inspired, there wasn't a man in this town who wouldn't sit downstairs in the bar with him, listening to the tall tales of his adventures."

Grandfather examined the list once more. "If the mayor was such an admirer of Baron Fane's, why do you consider him a suspect in Marcus's death?"

"Because they had a falling-out. It was over money, but I never discovered exactly what occurred. One day he came here to take tea with us and bask in the glow of Stamford Fane's brilliance, and the next they were bellowing at one another in the street. They seemed to have resolved their differences shortly before the accident, but who's to say the mayor wasn't putting on a show?"

He moved on to the next name. "The doctor examined the vicar's body, so anything that contradicts the initial findings that led to Adam's arrest could reflect badly upon her. Was that your thinking?"

"To a tee."

Grandfather pondered this for a few seconds before asking, "Would that really be enough for her to murder someone?"

"It's not just that." Scarlet seemed less sure of herself now. "Dr Beresford-Gray isn't from these parts. I know it can't be easy for a woman to do her job in a traditional town like this one, but she's done little to endear herself to the locals since she arrived. She's gone out of her way to join every committee going, but all she does when she gets up to speak is cause problems for everyone else. She apparently takes great pleasure in voting down every motion on the town council."

It was interesting to see Grandfather working with another assistant. I should probably have been jealous, but feeling anything except admiration for Scarlet was like taking issue with the stars in the night sky.

"As for P.C. Brigham," she continued, "it's hard to think of another job at which you can be so bad and not get the sack. He's the opposite of a good detective. He's a..." She searched for a handy metaphor, and so I made a suggestion to help.

"...bad detective?"

"Yes, that's it. He's entirely useless. He went along with the most obvious interpretation of Marcus's death because it was the easiest option. The man is a disgrace."

"That's not a reason to murder someone in itself, though." Grandfather tapped his cheek three times with his index finger. "However, it seems fair to conclude that P.C. Brigham's reputation was at stake. We already know that he concealed a witness's testimony and potentially ignored significant evidence. If Marcus discovered some damaging fact, Brigham would have wanted to keep it quiet."

He stepped to one side, as though hoping to see something new that he hadn't noticed before. In reality, of course, he wasn't looking at hard evidence, he was looking at five good guesses... well, four plus my grandmother. I saw the names and, to be quite honest, I was a little overwhelmed. It felt as though we'd arrived too late to put the pieces together and, even after all Marcus and Scarlet had done, we were still a long way from identifying the killer.

I know I complain about my grandfather stumbling across dead bodies wherever he goes, but it certainly makes things easier. Of the three recent deaths, we'd only been present for one of them. Even more puzzling was the fact that the first couldn't possibly be a murder, the second could only be a murder, and the third looked like a suicide but wasn't. It was all too much for me, and I longed for a lie-down.

"Which brings us to the final name on the list." He allowed the significance of this to sink in before going any further. "Stamford's widow, Baroness Sorel Fane."

"But, Grandfather, you said yourself that the baron couldn't have been murdered." It was my turn to be the voice of reason. "Aren't we trying too hard to find a connection which isn't there?"

"We're merely considering every possibility, Christopher."

The great detective looked at Scarlet and nodded for her to speak.

"The fact that Stamford's death was an accident doesn't contradict the possibility that he is the link between the other deaths." She seemed hesitant again and waited for another small gesture of encouragement from my grandfather. "I'm not saying that, because two people were murdered, he must have been, too. But it is conceivable that Marcus and the reverend were killed because Stamford was dead."

The old lord thought for a few seconds before responding. "Do you mean that his demise put an idea in the killer's head?"

"Perhaps. Or, with the baron out of the way, someone decided to get rid of Marcus and Adam, too. Condicote is an odd place. It's old-fashioned and rule-bound. You wouldn't believe the uproar that the arrival of a woman doctor had, let alone the taboo of Marcus and I running about the place together. I can't help thinking that all that scandal incinerated some loutish local's tiny mind."

I could see that grandfather wasn't convinced by this perfectly vague suggestion. "Fine, then who's the killer? Who would have wanted to get rid of you all?"

She took a deep breath before delivering her grand theory. "Of everyone I've considered, I believe that Baroness Fane is the most likely culprit. She never wanted us in Seekings House for one thing."

Grandfather had fallen silent and seemed content to reflect on the idea, which left me to ask the questions.

"That's hardly proof she's a killer. What else do you know about her?"

Scarlet's face relaxed into a smile. "After the inquest, she came into the bar when we were looking over the notes Marcus had made to prepare for Adam's trial. She stood staring at us for a moment, then simply exploded."

"What did she say?"

"It was strange and, even after she left, we didn't fully understand what had happened. She said that she blamed Marcus, Adam and me for her husband's death." Scarlet waited to see the reaction on our faces. "That's right. Even after he'd stolen from her, bankrupted the family and left the estate on the point of repossession, she said she still loved the incorrigible swine. She said that, even if we hadn't been behind the wheel of the car when he died, it was our fault for driving him to such debauchery."

CHAPTER TWENTY-THREE

There was no doubt that Scarlet had a wonderful brain, but it seemed that she'd devoted most of her time since her paramour had died to conjecture and speculation. In every motive she had identified, there was a singular factor missing; she was yet to gather any definitive evidence against the people on her list. Luckily for my poor granny, this proved just how haphazard Scarlet's approach to the investigation was. I had learnt enough from my grandfather's lessons to know that she would not be able to solve the murders without a little more method to her muddlement.

That evening, she led us through a series of gripping scenarios for why first the vicar and then Marcus had been killed. I felt like clapping after each one, but I could tell that they were just experiments for her. She was creating a compendium of stories rather than attempting to identify the chain of evidence that would save Adam from the gallows and lead us to the right culprit.

When the recital was over, we bade her goodnight – no wiser as to who had killed the two victims than we had been when we arrived. Grandfather and I walked in silence through the now quiet village. Mrs Grout had shut up the grocery shop. The market was deserted, and even the windows of the family homes that led away from the square were unlit.

"Do you think she has the right idea about her suspects?" I asked when ten minutes had passed without a word being spoken.

"I believe that Miss Warwick has an interesting view of the world around her." Such diplomatic language normally meant my companion was avoiding the question.

"That's not what I asked, and you know it. Truly, Grandfather, with your skills of evasion, you're wasted as a detective."

"Oh, yes?" I'd caught his attention.

"Yes, you should have become a politician."

He laughed at this, and I felt a little better about my failure to conceive of one likely suspect in the case.

"I'm sure I would have been just as wasted as a politician. What's the point of a job where you spend all day arguing and no one gets anything done?" I didn't have an answer to this, and so he switched back to our previous topic. "As for your question, the best answer I can give is both yes and no. While I don't believe that Scarlet or Marcus have cracked the case just yet, it was certainly worth our time to listen to what she had to say. And besides, being seen with her was another opportunity to ruffle some feathers in the village of Condicote." He produced a wicked laugh then. It was not the first time I'd noticed his penchant for stirring up trouble.

"So then, what next?"

"You mean, after you've eaten dinner?"

I may have been rubbing my tummy to soothe the growling beast within. "I am sorry. Was it so very obvious?"

"Just a little."

I stopped that singularly ravenous gesture and blushed as brightly as any robin. "So, what's next after dinner?"

"After dinner, comes bedtime."

I was frankly amazed. My mentor normally placed rest and refreshment below all other things. "Are you serious, Grandfather?"

"Quite serious, my boy. It's nine o'clock at night, and I have no intention of disturbing our suspects at this hour. Even murderers deserve some repose of an evening."

I hated to keep asking the same question, but I imagine that he read my mind, as he answered it without my uttering another word.

"And tomorrow will bring the perfect opportunity to observe key members of the community without anyone realising what we're doing."

"In the pub?" I suggested.

"Think again, Christopher." I did just that and, when nothing came to mind, he gave me a clue. "Tomorrow is Sunday."

"Fantastic." I waited a moment and then, just to be sure, asked, "You are suggesting that we attend the new vicar's service in St Bartholomew's, aren't you?"

"Yes, Christopher. That is exactly what I'm suggesting." He tittered behind his moustache. "Who knows? Perhaps a little of Reverend Bodsworth's Old Testament zealotry is just what we need to strike the fear of God into our culprit."

"As long as he doesn't give me nightmares." It was quite unnecessary to tell a personal anecdote at this moment, but that's exactly what I did.

"Our chaplain at school used to choose all the nastiest parts of the Bible to terrify us. I swear that he only read passages featuring some poor soul getting his divine comeuppance or a monster rising from the deep. Most boys complete their studies with a good general knowledge of the classic Bible stories – the Prodigal Son, Joseph and his fancy coat, that sort of thing. You can always spot an Oakton Academy alumnus, as we can recite The Book of Revelation by heart."

The dear old chap cleared his throat and proved my point.

"'And I looked, and behold a pale horse: and his name that sat on him was Death, and Hell followed with him.' Don't forget, Christopher; I, too, attended Oakton Academy. And I'm fairly certain that my chaplain back in the 1860s was much fiercer than the mollycoddlers you have today."

I gulped at the very thought of it. "You may be right." I kicked a pile of snow so that it turned into a fine mist and continued to recite the passage he had selected all the way home. "'And power was given unto them over the fourth part of the earth, to kill with sword, and with hunger, and with death, and with the beasts of the earth." Which, let's be honest, was not the cheeriest way for us to spend the journey.

I am happy to say that I did not suffer any apocalyptical nightmares that night. As far as I can remember, I dreamed sweet dreams of the sweet treats made by the sweet hand of our ever so sweet travelling cook, Henrietta. To be more specific, I pictured myself jumping into her apple charlotte. Can you imagine a more delicious swimming bath than one filled with sponge, stewed apples and custard?

The inhabitants of my grandmother's house got to church in time for the service the next morning, but the same cannot be said for many in the village. Granny took particular pleasure in listing those of her neighbours who had failed to make an appearance.

"Mr Bilson the chemist isn't here. Nor is Miss Julia Green, the old maid whom no one likes but we all tolerate. My good friend Sarah Cookson should be here by now, too. You know her, Christopher. She's the one with a hairy lip who put on all that weight after a trip to Blackpool last year. Emmeline Warwick – that terrible girl who seems to have a predilection for spending her days with the soon to be deceased – is also missing, and I noticed that our *lady* doctor turned up late." *Lady* doctors were another of my grandmother's pet aversions.

She went on like this for quite some time. The fact that we were standing at the front of the church, with a good forty or so of her neighbours within earshot, did nothing to dissuade her from making such statements (nor did it encourage her to lower her voice).

"My goodness! Who knew there were so many residents in Condicote in the first place?" Grandfather's eyes had glazed over in the middle of the extensive list. It was lucky that we were not relying on Granny to pick our suspects, as she would have surely found something bad to say about every last person in town.

Despite a few notable absences, it was still a wonderful opportunity to watch our suspects without their knowing. The aforementioned doctor looked just as nervous as she had in the café the night before. The mayor wore quite the least convincing smile I'd seen in some time, and there was no sign of the constable, so perhaps some animals had escaped from a farm somewhere, and he was hard at work. Just before the congregation rose for the opening hymn, Baroness Fane slipped into her usual seat, but I barely caught a glimpse of her through the crowd.

The organist flexed her fingers, and the soaring strains of England's greatest patriotic composition filled the air. Forgetting all about murder and treachery for a moment, I was moved by the uplifting music and the words of William Blake's rousing poem. It had been one of my favourite song to belt out in full voice when I was at school, and it almost made me feel nostalgic for assemblies, my old dormitory and…well… definitely not the school canteen.

The sparsely attended church came alive with the hymn, but I'll jump ahead to the best verse.

> **"Bring me my bow of burning gold:**
> **Bring me my arrows of desire:**
> **Bring me my spear: O clouds unfold!**
> **Bring me my chariot of fire."**

In my head, I sang like a tenor at the Royal Opera House – though, in the church, I sounded more like a tone-deaf cockerel who hadn't realised that no one wanted him to make so much noise. I was so hypnotised by my own performance that I'd forgotten to worry about whether yet another vicar was lying dead in the vestry at that moment. I was apparently the only worshipper who had achieved this feat, as a chatter of voices could be heard between each line.

When we finished the penultimate verse, there was still no sign of the celebrant.

"Not again," Granny complained, as though another murder in St Bartholomew's would be a terrible inconvenience.

We started the final stanza, but the intonation of the performance was not quite right. The end of each line went up as though it was a question, and we all wondered what had become of the recently arrived reverend.

"I will not cease from mental fight,
Nor shall my sword sleep in my hand
Till we have built Jerusalem
In England's green and pleasant land."

The song concluded, and Mrs Stanley allowed her organ to fall quiet. Even she was peering across the church to see whether the new vicar was still breathing. After a few seconds, there was a collective sigh as Reverend Bodsworth emerged from the vestry. It was immediately clear to all that, not only was he alive, the man was a real joker.

"It's a ghost!" some cheeky Jack declared, which earned him a few laughs.

"I'm not a ghost," the man with the surplice over his head snapped. "I'm stuck in this blasted thing." He waved his hand for assistance but, as he presumably couldn't see anything, he only caught the attention of a pillar. "Bob Thompkins? Is the verger here?"

Not the sharpest tool in an old, waterlogged shed, Bob would need a few moments to make sense of the issue before running over to help his boss with the garment. It was hard to say how the vicar had got stuck in a large, white sheet, but it certainly kept us entertained as we waited for the service to start. Thompkins attempted to yank the thing down, but the hidden priest's head was evidently larger than his predecessor's.

"I'll cut you free, Vicar!" the verger said, before running off in search of a pair of scissors.

If nothing else came to hand, there was always the knife from the statue of St Bartholomew the Apostle at the front of the church. Before I could suggest this, my grandfather strode forward and lifted the surplice so that it was no longer caught on Reverend Bodsworth's clothes. Just like that, his head popped through the opening, and he was free to do his job. There was a small round of applause, but the celebrant glared at his parishioners, and we all got the message to be quiet.

"I'm sorry for the delay," Bodsworth mumbled from in front of the altar. Clearly still unnerved by his mishap, he tripped over a shallow step and had to right himself by grasping hold of a tall wooden candlestick. "Oh…" There was a terrible moment when I truly thought he was going to say something unrepeatable, but he found the self-restraint for which priests are known and changed whatever word had nearly escaped him into "…fiddlesticks. Oh, fiddlesticks. What a day I'm having."

The laughter did not return, and there was a general feeling of wonder about the place as we imagined what embarrassment might come next. With a few deep breaths and a moment to collect his thoughts, further disaster was averted, and the service started in earnest.

Reverend Oldfield's replacement had an efficient, though hurried, air about him. He guided us towards the sacrament much as a librarian might give instructions for finding a book. His delivery had none of the fire I'd been expecting, but the sermon would soon make up for any shortcomings.

"Sin and retribution!" Having climbed the spiralling stairs to the pulpit, he began with these unhappy bedfellows, and things would only get more damnable from there. "The concept of sin and retribution makes up one of the cornerstones of our faith. And yet, too often, we forget that the latter cannot simply erase the former whenever we wish. God forgives, but he does so on his own terms. He differentiates between those who are truly ready to have their past misdeeds erased and those who will only go on to commit more wickedness."

He took off his glasses for a moment to rub his troubled eyes and, when he put them back on again, his stare was huge and frightening. The way he looked down on his congregation made me feel rather awful about myself.

When he said, "I see evil and impiety wherever I look," I could tell he was thinking of the time that I ate food from the school larder without permission. When he said, "Even with prayer and regular attendance at church, when the time comes to knock on heaven's gate, Saint Peter will be there to send the true sinners back the way they've come," my guilty conscience bellowed, *That's me! He's talking about me.*

"I must make particular mention of the great misfortune that has befallen this town and remind you that it is our job to question why such tragedy comes to pass. We have endured a murder, a suicide and a tragic accident, and we must look inside ourselves to understand why the Lord would have sent down such a punishment. We must strive to be better within and without, to achieve godliness in our own lives as our fallen brethren clearly failed to do."

I thought that spending two hours a week in silence memorising long passages of the Bible for thirteen years of my life had been a travail, but it couldn't hold a candle to the forty-five minutes to three decades that the good Reverend Bodsworth's morning service lasted. When the time came to approach the altar for communion, I was entirely convinced that I would turn to ash as soon as the wafer was in my hand and the wine touched my lips. I considered dousing myself in baptismal water just to make sure that I wasn't a demon.

Perhaps the clearest indication of the power his words had was the look on my grandmother's face. For the first time in my life, she looked… I hardly dare say it… she looked guilty. She held her hand up to her mouth to hide her shame, but I could still see it in her eyes. If a woman who had spent her life judging those around her could quiver before the message of the sermon, imagine how the killer must have been feeling.

I tried to catch Baroness Fane's expression on the other side of the church, but she was sitting in our row, and there were too many people in the way. Just behind her, though, Mayor Hobson looked aghast. I believe his lip was trembling, and I thought for a moment he might cry. That would have been an unusual sight, to see a grown man – and the mayor no less – burst into tears in front of everyone. Instead, his stiff upper lip prevailed. He screwed his mouth tightly shut and pulled himself together.

Dr Beresford-Gray's eyes were trained on the pulpit, and the one person who appeared unmoved by the fire and brimstone the priest was serving was Lord Edgington. Still very much a monarch with his sceptre, he sat with his arms folded, clutching his amethyst-topped cane in one hand. He showed no great reaction to the moralising sermon but smiled to himself when it concluded.

The atmosphere had changed in St Bartholomew's. There was a crispness in the air that could not be ascribed to the cold weather. When the time came to sing the next hymn, voices were flat and subdued. There was none of the normal fervour, and even the boisterous, outspoken farmers who sat on the back pew were strangely hushed.

The new vicar performed communion and concluded the service in that same slightly mechanical manner that I'd noticed before his sermon. It was as though he saved up his energy for the part which he loved best and performed the rest of his duties in the simplest way possible. It made me wonder why such a man would ever become a priest if his only wish was to shame his parishioners. When we filed out, he did not stand at the door to the church to bid us farewell but remained at the altar, surveying his domain.

"What an odd chap," Grandfather mumbled as we waited for our chance to leave.

"Priests often are," I replied. "My father says it's all that time they spend with their heads in books. Although, now that I say it out loud, I have a feeling he was criticising me more than the clergy."

He smiled a fraction before a new thought stifled his good cheer. "I do not hold with such demonization. There is nothing wrong with reading, despite what many parents say. We can learn so much from books. We can travel to far off countries and experience impossible adventures that our own plane of existence cannot offer."

This reminded me of the novel that I was just then embarking upon. John Masefield's wonderful 'ODTAA' was, like the previous book of his that I'd read, set in the fictional South American nation of Santa Barbara and depicted an ever-so-thrilling rebellion against a deranged despot. It was endless fun, and just the thing I would never experience in real life. The fact that my own existence was very much like something from the pages of a Dorothy L. Sayers mystery, did not change the fact that I longed to trek across mountainous regions or take to the open seas. And so, until someone offered to whisk me off on such an adventure, I would continue reading to my heart's content!

CHAPTER TWENTY-FOUR

"Lord Edgington." A woman's voice carried out of the church after us. "May I have a word?"

We stopped beneath the pointed arch of the clock tower and waited for Stamford Fane's widow to emerge from the shadows. Though we'd been in the same church countless times over the years, I'd never had a chance to see her at close quarters. She was a striking woman with dark eyebrows and darker eyes. Her long lashes batted as she got the measure of my grandfather and, just before she spoke again, I remembered my ever-disapproving grandmother telling me that she was not British, but, "of all things, American!"

"Lady Fane," my grandfather said warmly, and I wondered whether he'd done some clever calculations to realise who this woman was or perhaps I'd told him at some point and forgotten. "How may I be of assistance?"

Her eyes stayed fixed on my senior associate. "I thought that, as you'll probably be calling at Seekings House to talk to me at some point, I should extend the olive branch and invite you to tea this afternoon." She had a light, lilting accent that was more transatlantic than fully Yankee and it was clear that she had lived in Great Britain for some time.

"That is so very kind of you, madam. We happily accept your invitation." Grandfather tipped his hat. I sometimes wondered whether he was as easily charmed by pretty ladies as I was.

She wore a tight black skirt and jacket – "modern" mourning attire, my father would have called it, with a cynical shake of his head. I thought it very fetching and couldn't help admiring this singularly glamorous individual.

"Then I will see you both at three o'clock." She nodded politely and, with a brief glance in my direction, strolled through the graveyard towards the main road.

"It looks as though we have the chance to find out more about Stamford Fane sooner than I might have hoped," Grandfather drummed his fingers on the end of his cane and waited until there was no one left in view.

We were about to go when the vicar appeared in the vestibule. Much as he had in the café the day before, he looked as though he wanted to talk to us but changed his mind and set about closing the church.

"I beg your pardon, Reverend," Grandfather began, "but I must say how thoroughly engaging I found your sermon. It has been some time since I came across such an orator in the church. I hope your parishioners appreciate how lucky they are to have a true elocutionist in such a small town."

I could see that the old devil had got through the vicar's defences, and he stopped what he was doing to accept the compliment. "You are too kind, Mr…?"

"Not quite, I'm a lord." Whenever he got the chance to introduce himself to a soon-to-be-impressed stranger, there was a touch of smugness in my grandfather's voice. "I'm the Marquess of Edgington. Perhaps you've heard of me?"

The vicar was one of those types who are normally so uncomfortable in the skin they inhabit that they can never meet a person's gaze for more than half a second. But he was certainly staring at my grandfather just then.

"The detective?" he asked with a note of surprise in his sonorous voice. "How very exciting to have you here. Are you looking into the murders?"

Grandfather had replaced and removed his grey top hat twice already since leaving the service and now spun it around on his hand. "I am merely here to accompany my grandson on a visit to see his grandmother. However, if my services are required, I am always happy to offer them."

Reverend Bodsworth rubbed his eyes behind his thick-lensed glasses so that his meaty fingers momentarily grew larger. He was a big man with a substantial pot belly that was visible even through his vestments. "Marcus Alsop's death was a terrible shame. It's not the sort of welcome one expects when taking on a new parish." He crossed himself, thus betraying his high church leanings that were already apparent in the service.

"I'm sure it must have come as a shock. Especially considering the way that your predecessor met his end."

Grandfather was testing the man, but he showed no fear in his response.

"We are all but vessels on this earth and must go where we are sent." He closed his eyes as he spoke, perhaps tuning himself to his divine purpose. "As it says in Ecclesiastes, we must 'Fear God, and keep his commandments: for this is the whole duty of man'."

Grandfather nodded contemplatively. "Indeed. That's from Ecclesiastes…"

"12:13."

"Yes, of course. 12:13. One of my favourites." Grandfather's moustache wriggled, and I was certain this wasn't true.

The priest locked the door to the church and turned back to us with a more peaceable expression. "If there is anything I can do to assist you in your enquiries, Lord Edgington, you need only ask."

"That is very kind, Reverend. I may well take you up on the offer before long."

Reverend Bodsworth bowed his smooth, shiny head again and patiently waited for us to leave the churchyard.

"What a perfectly strange fellow for a perfectly strange town," I said once we were out on the pavement.

It had not snowed overnight, and a weak sun had emerged from the clouds to continue the slow thaw. I really do not understand weather in the slightest as surely, by April, that big ball of fire in the sky should have been capable of burning off a few white flakes, yet there was still an impressive bank of snow resting against the walls of the church.

"He would do just as well to make some exceptions for the uniqueness of each individual as spend his life preaching the perils of sin and damnation." My companion clearly didn't approve of that morning's sermon.

I was too distracted to notice that we were walking in the wrong direction. "Grandfather, don't you think it's possible that the fact the two murders happened so close together is just a coincidence? There could be two murderers… or perhaps Reverend Oldfield was killed for some reason that was personal to him, and then Marcus got too close to the culprit and so had to be silenced?"

"We certainly cannot rule out such possibilities." He pouted for a few seconds before forming the relevant question. "But why would anyone want to murder Reverend Oldfield in the first place?"

"Well… I don't actually know."

"And I don't blame you." He tapped his cane on the cobbles as he walked. "You have raised an interesting point, Christopher. I have been looking at this case from the perspective of Marcus and his friends, when it's quite possible that there is another unrelated reason for the first murder. And so, what can you tell me about the deceased incumbent?"

I had to think for a moment. "Well, he was unmarried, for one thing. He liked a drink and seemed to spend most of his free time fixing his bicycle."

"Were there any scandals concerning him? In my experience, vicars are just as susceptible to the wagging tongues of their parishioners as anyone else is."

"Not that I heard and, considering who my grandmother is, I would surely have known if he'd been sleeping with the mayor's wife or helping himself to money from the collection plate."

"Indeed, you would have." We walked in silence until another thought occurred to him. "What did your grandmother find so objectionable about him?"

"Let me think…" Granny had a rolling list of complaints about most of her fellow villagers. It was no simple task to recall them. "She claimed that he didn't keep his robes well pressed – that is something she simply cannot abide. He also once failed to open the church until twenty minutes before his Sunday evening service, and Granny always likes to get to church a half an hour early."

"I'm sorry to interrupt you, my boy, but perhaps I should have phrased my question differently. What did your grandmother find objectionable about him that could in any way influence a murder?"

"Oh… ummm… nothing, I don't think. He was a dreadfully normal chap. He did once fall asleep during a hymn, but Granny didn't seem to mind and thought it quite amusing. In fact, she rarely complained that he performed most morning services still reeling ripe from the night before."

"What on earth is 'reeling ripe'?" Grandfather enquired.

"Tap-shackled, bumpsy, tosticated, you know?"

He looked a little offended then. "I certainly don't know. And for the very last time, Christopher, please use full sentences."

"I'm trying to tell you that he would turn up to his services still squiffy. Reverend Oldfield was a notorious drinker."

"Why didn't you say that from the beginning?" He hadn't tutted at me for hours, and it was surely overdue. "Your grandmother certainly has a curious sort of morality. She hasn't the slightest issue with a drunken clergyman, so long as he's ironed his surplice."

It finally dawned on me that we'd passed the row of thatched cottages and were approaching the centre of the village. "Grandfather, it's almost ten o'clock and I haven't had any breakfast. Please tell me we're not embarking on a busy day of investigating. I don't think I can take it."

"You do put food above all other things, don't you, boy? If you were ever to start your own religion, your followers would pray to a chicken leg, and communion would be a five-course meal."

"As delightful as that sounds, I would never start my own religion as it would take too much time away from eating."

"Well, we're hardly voyaging into the wilds. There's bound to be something to eat."

"You'd think that, but this is Britain and today is Sunday." I attempted to maintain my jovial attitude and probably failed. "Pubs don't start serving until half-past twelve, and the only other place open today is the newsagent. I can't imagine that The Times or The Chronicle taste particularly nice."

"Do stop fussing. I promise we will be home for Cook's Sunday lunch."

"I'm not fussing. I'm merely aware that your priorities don't always align with my own." I begrudgingly accepted defeat. "Where are we off to first, anyway? A quick chat with the good lady doctor? Another call on Mrs Eileen Grout the grocer?"

"We're starting at the top. Two men have been murdered for something that I can only assume was more valuable than the church ciborium. I mean to say that I have every intention of talking to—"

"Mrs Stanley who plays the organ?"

He looked at me as though I was quite dim. "No, Christopher, not the church organist. We're going to pay a visit to—"

"The mayor, obviously. I was only joking about Mrs Stanley... Though, now that I come to think of it, I've always found her a suspicious character. She has a wicked look about her, as though she's plotting something."

Having momentarily made a good impression thanks to my ability to follow a simple conversation, I had disappointed him once more. "She's not plotting anything, Christopher. She has a lazy eye."

"Ah, that will explain it." I laughed sheepishly and changed the subject. "And here's the town hall. But is there anything to say that the mayor will be in his office?"

"Yes, I have discovered two small pieces of evidence which suggest we might be in luck." Grandfather pointed at the large, black Crossley motorcar that was parked in front of the building, then up at the first-floor window where Mayor Hobson was waving down to us.

CHAPTER TWENTY-FIVE

Condicote Town Hall was a curious building, that had presumably once been used as the town's almshouse. It had a wide frontage that gave onto the market hall. The foundations were no doubt many centuries old, and the facade was an unusual mix of styles. Traces of Norman architecture, in the stones at the bottom of the walls and the central gateway, made way for a Tudor influence in the black and white gables. Evidently, the owners had built over the original structure, adding and taking away parts over time like a child with a set of bricks.

We walked through the arched gateway and, instead of continuing to a large courtyard that was hemmed in on all sides by the complex of ancient buildings, I followed my grandfather up a narrow stone staircase.

"Gentlemen!" The mayor was evidently waiting for us and held his hands out in welcome. "It's a pleasure to see you both."

"We've come to talk to you about the murders of Reverend Oldfield and Marcus Alsop," Grandfather said to send the cheery chap's smile into hiding.

"Yes, of course." Still dressed in the plain black suit that he'd worn to church, the mayor pulled at his collar as though he were feeling rather warm. "Can I get you some tea? And perhaps a biscuit?"

"Or several?" I could have been a little subtler, but my stomach was already rumbling.

He rushed out of the office in order to obtain the refreshments, and Grandfather made a start on that day's stint of interfering.

"What quick thinking, Christopher. Getting him to leave the room so that we can look around was a masterstroke." He winked to show that he knew I'd only been thinking of my appetite, but I appreciated the joke.

Considering how grand the exterior of the building was, the mayor's office was fairly compact in its dimensions. A heavy desk took up most of the space, and the walls were hung with old tapestries that I could only assume had come with the building. There was a battle scene featuring round-head soldiers fighting foppish cavaliers, and another with the Spanish armada all aflame, but these artefacts were of no interest just then to my grandfather.

"Look at this, Chrissy." He had walked to the far corner and was peering down over a model in a glass case.

I went to see what he had found and was really rather taken with the dinky thing. "It's Condicote. You can see all the little houses." I pointed to the major features like a giant giving a tour of the town. There were two steep hills on either side, just like in real life, and the main strip of buildings in between. "There's Granny's house. How simply charming."

"Yes, isn't it just." He was evidently not as enthusiastic as I was. "But there's something you're missing. Something which doesn't quite match the village you have visited every year of your life."

I overlaid my own map of the place in my head with the scale version in front of me. My eyes travelled from one end of the town, through the market square and past the lines of houses, to the far end where Seekings House stood... Well, it normally stood there, but it appeared to have been replaced by a great number of smaller dwellings.

"How strange." I attempted to make sense of the error. "Perhaps it's artistic licence. Perhaps whoever created the neat little toy decided that Condicote would be better off with just the one manor house." A spark of brilliance came to me. "Oh, I've got it! Granny must have given money to the council to fund the construction of this model. She's always hated her manor not being the only one in town." The longer I talked, the more certain I was that I didn't know what I was saying. "I'm wrong, aren't I?"

"I'm afraid so. What we're looking at is a plan for—"

"What you're looking at is the future of Condicote." The mayor reappeared, carrying a large metal tray with sugar, milk, cups and the like. He placed it on his desk and hurried over to reveal the details of a project he was clearly very keen to see realised. "It started when the baron was still alive. He needed to unlock the capital from his land and, as we have been unable to grow as a village for over a century, this seemed like the obvious solution."

"You're going to demolish Seekings House?" I couldn't hide how tragic I found the idea. Not only was it a pretty building with a lot of history, I'd played in the woods there every summer as a boy and hated the thought that they could be chopped down and paved.

"There's no other option." His wide, blithesome face became serious. "This village was an important commercial centre in the eighteenth century. Every scrap of cloth that was sold in the Tatchester region was made here in Condicote. But because of two properties with large estates that trap in the village, we are stunted." He repeated the word with some irritation. "Stunted!"

"I can see it must be a sensitive topic," I said in a whisper as Mayor Hobson calmed himself down.

"Ooh, I think I hear the water boiling." Merry once more, he nipped from the room to make the tea.

"Grandfather?" I said once I was certain we would not be overheard.

"Yes, Chrissy?"

"I think we've found our murderer. The man's a loon."

He had no time to reply as our suspect had returned with a slightly smaller tray which held a teapot and a plate of biscuits. As far as I could tell, they were of the plain, Rich Tea variety. It was Hobson's choice; I would have to take what I got.

Once we were sitting down at the desk, and I had secured several sweet, crunchy discs for my own needs, Grandfather returned us to the previous discussion. "So, you say that Baron Fane was in agreement with your plan to knock down his ancestral home and construct a series of new houses in its place?"

The mayor blew on his tea. "Oh, very much so. Very much so, indeed. I don't think it is any secret that the Fanes were somewhat limited by their financial situation. This would have eased their worries and solved the biggest problem this town has faced since the wheat blight of 1874."

Even I could see that something didn't make sense about this supposedly simple plan. "But where would you get the money to build all those houses and reimburse Baron Fane for the land?"

The mayor took a meaningful bite of a biscuit himself then. It was a message; he was saying, *you're just a boy, you wouldn't understand.* Well, either that or he was peckish.

"We have the thirty thousand pounds required. The council will pay for one third, the bank another, and Baron Fane would have provided the rest in exchange for fifty per cent of the profits."

Grandfather nudged me to continue.

"So how could he have invested money in such a substantial development when he didn't have any?"

Mayor Hobson realised that he was cornered and began to bluster. "Now, now, young man. I don't think that's any of our business. The Fanes have a right to privacy over such matters. The baron told me that he had the funds required to see things to completion, and I took him on his word."

Grandfather made a dubious noise, which was a cross between a sigh and a groan. "And when was all this supposed to happen?"

The mayor's expression kept changing, but he had settled on a nervous grimace. "If everything had progressed on time, we would have cleared the woods on the Fane estate this month and knocked down the house by the end of the spring. I hoped to complete the sale of every last house by the summer of 1928." His speech was peppered with modern expressions, and he reminded me of the proud, ambitious money men who worked with my father in the city. The big difference was that he wasn't used to such scrutiny and was becoming more nervous with every question we asked.

"Will the project give you something of a windfall?" Grandfather injected a healthy dose of mistrust into his words.

"It will give my home village a windfall, but it will do much more besides." Returning to his sales patter, he seemed to relax a touch. "You see, this is only the first step. With the baron's estate redeveloped, all that land beyond can be used. Old Mrs McGregor's fields are barely fertile enough to grow weeds, but they'll make the perfect spot for a hospital or school. In twenty years' time, this village could be as big as Yockwardine…" His eyes were wide by now. "…or even Newminster! Can you imagine that?"

"Yes, it sounds wonderful." If you can imagine Grandfather's cynical tone, you will know just how perfectly he delivered this retort.

"And what about now?" I asked. "Does the baron's death change anything for your plans?"

He looked between us, uncertain where to set his gaze. "There's no reason why it should, as I've told the baroness on a number of occasions."

"That's right, we saw you talking to her in the square yesterday. Is there any chance that you were waiting for her there on the night that the vicar was murdered?"

Mayor Hobson was an emotional sponge and absorbed whatever we threw at him. He fiddled with his tie in an exaggerated manner, and

I wondered whether he wanted us to know how nervous the questions made him, or he was simply terrible at hiding his feelings.

"The vicar? What has the vicar's murder got to do with me?"

Grandfather leaned forward, his words suddenly more forceful. "That isn't what I asked. I asked whether you were waiting for Baroness Fane in the square on the night that Reverend Oldfield was murdered."

It took me a moment to realise why he'd asked this question, but then I remembered what Mrs Grout the grocer had told us. She said that the mayor had walked his dog around the square three times that night, though he normally took him out to the fields. I'd considered this detail entirely superfluous and cast it to the back of my mind, whereas my grandfather had carefully considered its implications and neatly stored it for future reference. I suppose that was what made him a great detective, and why I was still racing to catch up with him.

"I admit I've been nervous about the situation. After the baron died, I wasn't certain what would happen, and I couldn't just barge into Seekings House when his wife was in mourning."

"Did you manage to catch her that night?"

He looked away from his interrogator in the hope that I would be able to ease his distress. "No, I waved at her car, but she didn't stop. I was on the other side of the market when she passed, and she must not have seen me."

"Yes, that sounds quite plausible," Grandfather said, whilst somehow implying quite the opposite. "Or she didn't want to talk to you."

"Perhaps it was insensitive of me." He grew more circumspect. "I can't imagine that any widow is thinking about her finances mere days after her husband's death."

The pulsating muscle on Grandfather's temple suggested that he did not agree with this naïve statement. "And yet you say you have spoken to Baroness Fane on several occasions since then?"

"That's correct." He attempted to take another gulp of tea but was shaking so much that he ended up spilling it onto the blue and white willow-patterned saucer. "In fact, she spoke to me at the funeral to say that, as far as she was concerned, the construction could go ahead as planned."

This certainly undermined the idea that the baroness was in too much grief to deal with earthly matters.

"She spoke to you at her own husband's funeral?" I failed to hide my surprise.

"It was not a long conversation. She merely revealed that she was happy to invest in the development just as soon as the baron's life insurance was honoured."

"And she was the one who approached you to discuss the matter…" The silence that Grandfather inserted in the middle of this question was deafening. "…at her own husband's funeral?"

"Or perhaps I was the one who spoke to her. The details really aren't important. What matters is that she was in favour of Baron Fane's scheme."

It was my turn to attack the man's choice of vocabulary. "The scheme of which you were surely a co-author? I've always thought that schemes were an evil, manipulative sort of endeavour."

"I didn't mean it like that. I just meant a plan, a project, you know…" He was a wriggling fish, and we weren't about to let him off the hook until he'd told us what we needed to know. I was rather pleased with that metaphor until I remembered that fish can't talk.

Grandfather looked at me knowingly before replying. "So the project that will save the town and line the coffers of the council, not to mention restore the fortunes of Baroness Fane, is dependent upon the money from the life insurance policy of a man who recently died in a nasty accident?"

"I don't think… You haven't quite…" The mayor dug his nails into the desk and appeared to have become stuck. I assumed he would be able to produce some kind of response, but it was beyond him.

"Do you know what I think, Mr Mayor?" Grandfather pushed his cane forwards as though activating the lever on the Tatchester gallows. "I think that there's something strange happening here. I think that you know more than you're telling us and so, this afternoon, I'm going to pay Baroness Fane a visit to find out the truth. I have the distinct feeling that you won't come out of this very well."

Hobson pulled his hands back to latch onto the arms of his chair. "No, you don't need to say anything to her." He was speaking extremely fast. "I haven't done anything illegal. I just need the construction of the houses to go ahead. I've been promising change in this town since I was appointed three years ago. I swear I haven't done anything wrong; I just want Condicote to fulfil its potential."

"I see." That chameleon Lord Edgington fell quiet. "So what you're saying is that you were attempting to avert disappointment in order to hold on to your appointment."

Although it couldn't have been more than forty degrees outside, the man before us was visibly sweating. His reaction to our questioning was perhaps a touch out of proportion.

"Ye...yes, I think that's it." He evidently doubted whether this admission would save his skin or condemn him.

Grandfather was about to land the hammer blow that would shatter him entirely. "I must inform you that we are aware of a discrepancy in your story." Fine, it was an exceedingly well-mannered hammer blow but a hammer blow, nonetheless. "Miss Warwick informs us that you had an argument with Baron Fane shortly before he died."

"That was nothing." The teacup in his hand rattled on its saucer. "We solved the problem like gentlemen."

"I believe she said that you fell out over money."

Hobson suddenly spoke a lot faster. "Yes, that's right. It seemed at first that Fane wouldn't have access to the funds that we needed, but he borrowed it from someone and everything was fine."

"He borrowed ten thousand pounds from Marcus Alsop." I jumped in because I was really rather enjoying myself. "Is that why the poor chap was murdered?"

"Alsop? I never... I mean, I wouldn't." I doubt that even Mayor Hobson knew what he was denying by now.

"That's right, Marcus Alsop, the murdered son of Lord Bertrand Alsop – one of the wealthiest men in the region."

"Young Alsop was a thief and a troublemaker. He was forever crossing paths with P.C. Brigham. Whatever you've heard about him, that man was not to be—"

"You're talking rot." I was tempted to stand up to loom over him but didn't quite have the physique for such intimidation. "Marcus was a youthful gadabout, but he meant no harm. He certainly didn't deserve the sorry end he met."

I was surprised that the mayor hadn't exploded. I'd never seen such a guilty character. "He killed himself; that's got nothing to do with me. Anyone who knows anything about this town will tell you that I work my fingers to the marrow. I'm an honest man." In an attempt to convince himself of this fact, he repeated it for good measure. "I am an honest man."

"Then why are you not concerned that two people have been murdered?" My words were deadened by the tapestries on the wall, but they still had the impact I required. The mayor threw himself back in his seat and looked as though he would melt under the pressure.

"Tell us what you've really been up to around here." Instead of hurling this demand at him, as I had intended, it emerged in a whisper.

My grandfather held one hand out to stop me. "Very good, Christopher. I think we have taken up enough of the mayor's time." He rose and tucked his chair back under the desk. "My best wishes for your building project, Mayor Hobson. I hope everything goes to plan."

I couldn't understand this sudden retreat. It seemed that we'd found our culprit – the man was nearly in pieces, after all – and it made no sense to give up now.

Trusting my companion more than I trusted myself, I stood up to copy his polite gesture.

"Thank you for the biscuits, Mr Mayor." I even gave a small bow to show my appreciation. "Have a lovely day."

CHAPTER TWENTY-SIX

"We had him," I declared once we'd left the town hall and were back on our journey through town. "Why in heaven's name did we leave when we could have pushed him towards a confession?"

"Because it wouldn't have been true." Grandfather walked with small, precise steps, as though attempting to make the journey last as long as possible. "The man is in no state to be interviewed."

"Of course he isn't. He knows we're onto him and he's scared for his life."

"No, no, Christopher. You're quite mistaken." I don't know whether he intended to sound superior at such moments, but he certainly succeeded. "Think about what he actually told us."

I did just that and couldn't detect any problems with the evidence we'd gathered. "He's desperate to see Seekings House demolished and the land redeveloped. Without the Fanes or – far less likely – my grandmother selling their large estates, the village can't grow. The mayor knows that he'll lose his job if he doesn't deliver on the promises he made, and I think he would kill to achieve his goals."

"Fantastic work."

I wasn't falling for his trap and whistled a little tune as I waited for him to continue.

"You have conceived of a singularly creative narrative in which a mild-mannered bureaucrat would resort to murder in order to see a few houses built. Yes, that's rather compelling."

"I don't see why you're dismissing the possibility. He was a perfect wreck in there. I've never seen such a guilty chap. And don't forget, I've met quite a few murderers myself."

He nodded in contemplation. "That is true, Christopher. That is very true. However, there's one thing of which you're clearly unaware. Much as he told us, a man like Mayor Hobson will never have been accused of a crime before. He's lived a simple existence in a simple town. From his manner and accent, I'd say he was a man of humble upbringing, without a sophisticated education. His reaction to our questioning was not spurred by guilt but fear."

"Aren't the two normally connected?"

Grandfather pondered the point. "They can be. But tell me this; have you ever walked past a policeman and felt a frisson of unease? A feeling that you must do something to show the man that you're not the sort in whom he need take any interest?"

"Yes, I have!" I was frankly impressed at how well he knew me, or perhaps how well he knew human nature more generally. "It has happened to me in London on a number of occasions."

"And what do you do as a result?"

"I whistle!"

"You whistle?"

"That's right. You see, I get terribly nervous and don't want the chap to think badly of me, so I whistle and end up looking a great deal more suspicious than I otherwise would have."

"Of course you do, and you're not the only one." Grandfather seemed pleased at the result of his supposition. "If the police arrested every person who got in a stew when a bobby walked past, our prisons would be overflowing, and our streets would be empty. Perhaps it would help you to think that Mayor Hobson was simply whistling to us in that office. I doubt it was guilt that made him act in such a manner, but fear of being associated with these terrible crimes."

We walked a little longer before another question surfaced in my mind. "But how do you know the difference? How can you be sure he's not our man?"

"For one thing, we are yet to discover any evidence that implicates the mayor." I should have thought of this myself. "If we'd built a case against him, his fear and equivocation might have been warranted, but we've barely fashioned a motive, let alone proof of his involvement in the murders."

"Still…" I knew I was speaking without thinking but was curious what nonsense I might produce. "…he could have killed to keep the Seekings House development a secret. There are surely people in this village who would disapprove of such drastic change."

"Would that be the development of which he has a model in his office, and about which he readily told us with great pride?"

"The very same!" It took me mere seconds to realise my mistake. "Ah, I see what you mean."

"This, added to the fact that we cannot link either victim to the construction project, leads me to believe that the mayor is a less than helpful witness. It is not that he is hiding something, but that he simply doesn't know how to behave around detectives like us." It was nice of my grandfather to suggest I was in any way his equal. "However, there is an important conclusion you should be able to draw from his testimony."

We had come to a stop in the middle of the covered market hall. There were pigeons nesting in the roof of the building, but, except for us, they were the only visitors on a Sunday morning.

I tried to recall our interview. "I think we learnt a little more about Baron Fane, and it put me in mind of one scenario that we have not discussed."

"Oh, yes?" His right eyebrow shot higher.

"Isn't it possible that - although the police say that his car had not been sabotaged and the doctor's inspection returned no evidence of violence against his person – Stamford Fane committed suicide?"

He put one hand on my shoulder. "That is an interesting hypothesis, Christopher."

"Jolly good! Then I'll have to update my summary of the case; the baron's death could be a suicide that looks like an accident. Marcus was surely murdered but made to look as though he'd killed himself, and I think we're still confident that the vicar was slain outright."

"It is more than possible."

I didn't wait for him to explain my own explanation back to me but offered a little more evidence for my theory. "Marcus's mother told us that he lent Fane ten thousand pounds. That is the same amount that the baron needed for his share in the construction project. We also know that he had been to London gambling on the night before he died. It seems quite possible that he had lost the money he was planning to invest and realised that he was worth more dead than alive."

"Yes, I was a little surprised at just how much his insurance will pay, but it is not unheard of for rich men to purchase such policies."

"It seems a selfless, if rather gruesome, gesture," I mused. "Perhaps the baron was so ashamed of his behaviour that he couldn't face the consequences. We know that he was an unlucky punter and prone to losing large amounts. My father says that such men are just as sick as dying patients in a hospital; neither can do anything to save themselves from their maladies."

"And that is where your theory falters." He spoke with all the mystery he could muster. "Nothing we have heard about Baron Fane would suggest he was a man who displayed shame nor, for that matter, selflessness."

"So where does that leave us?"

He wiggled his fingers like a composer planning a new symphony. "The baron's death provided the money which this whole village needs. It's too perfect, too neat."

I still wasn't sure what he was suggesting. "And so?"

His eyes said *full sentences, Christopher,* but his mouth said. "And so we must reconsider the possibility that his death was no accident."

I was really quite speechless, though I somehow managed to say, "I thought that everything we've considered up to now was based on the understanding that there was nothing suspicious about the baron's demise."

He didn't look at me then but cast his gaze across the square. "It was, and now it isn't."

I was tempted to argue with him, but I knew there was no point. He would only find a slippery explanation for whatever I told him, probably including the phrase *It is the foremost rule in a detective's notebook...*

In the end, I didn't even have to say anything, and he fulfilled my expectations. "The foremost rule in a detective's notebook is that **nothing is certain until it is certain**." He seemed a little distracted as he spoke, and I soon realised why.

Across the square, Dr Beresford-Gray had emerged from her office. She caught sight of us and offered a hesitant wave, then immediately turned and disappeared back indoors. Under normal circumstances, I would have been highly suspicious of such behaviour but, after our meeting with the mayor, I was no longer sure of anything.

Grandfather hadn't taken his eyes from the doctor's surgery. "Of course, we still cannot say whether the two murders we are already investigating had anything to do with the building project at Seekings House or the death of Baron Fane."

He started walking and so I followed him with a potential solution. "I've been wondering about that, actually. Whether the baron was murdered or not, what if his death triggered the subsequent killings?"

I stopped talking, and so Grandfather intoned, "Continue," in a priest-like voice.

"Maybe the killer saw an opportunity to assume whatever power the baron had in the village and decided to take it. Maybe the vicar and Marcus were simply in his way and that's why they were murdered."

He took a few moments to ponder my suggestion as we approached the police station. "That, Christopher, is a scenario."

"I beg your pardon?"

"It is a scenario, Christopher," he repeated, no more helpfully.

"Yes, but is it a good or a bad one?"

He ran three fingers through his silver mane. "I cannot say either way, but I do think it would require a level of coincidence to be anything like the truth." I was still quite ignorant as to his feelings on the matter, but at least he kept talking. "One thing that is clear is the prevailing question to which we keep returning."

He gave me a moment to consider this, and I continued looking brainless.

"Before he was knocked unconscious and strangled with a bell rope, the vicar told Mrs Grout that he had seen something 'utterly' remarkable in some way. Months later, Marcus Alsop told his paramour Scarlet Warwick that he had 'discovered something quite unbelievable' and was swiftly murdered. To understand why the vicar was killed, we must discover what it was that he saw on his travels through the village. And what, for that matter, Marcus had learnt that someone would kill to keep a secret."

CHAPTER TWENTY-SEVEN

I obviously didn't have an answer to these questions and so we ducked into the police station to get out of the cold. I say "ducked" as it was a truly tiny building with a truly tiny front door. At least three centuries old, it had a white façade and miniature black-framed windows. Adding to the hotchpotch nature of the place, it also had a slanting thatched roof, which gave the impression that the building was caving in on itself. I found myself wondering whether the door had originally been much larger but had buckled under the pressure of the floor above it.

The interior was less distinctive and could have been any one of a hundred village police stations. The downstairs was made up of two featureless, white rooms, neither of which had much to say for themselves.

"Good morning, Lord Edgington, Master Prentiss." Old Derek Brigham was the only permanent representative of the Tatchester Constabulary based at Condicote and stood up from his desk as he welcomed us. He had a perfectly round face, two bulging eyes and just enough hair left to permit three long strands to flap about on his pate as he spoke.

I say he was old, but he couldn't have been much more than fifty. However, he was one of those people who had surely been handed a pipe and cardigan when he was just a boy. He had the air of a cheery codger, and I had to wonder why he'd gone into the police force as opposed to spending his days staring into a warm pint of ale in the pub, or slowly following a herd of sheep about the place.

"Good morning, P.C. Brigham." Naturally, Grandfather removed his hat. "We have some questions to put to you regarding the murder of Marcus Alsop."

"Murder is it now?" He emitted a short laugh. "Last I heard, the poor fellow shot himself."

"Then perhaps you have a problem with your hearing." Grandfather made no exceptions for those of limited intelligence – which is something I knew better than anyone. "Alsop was in the middle of trying to save his friend from the gallows. There is no way that he would have committed suicide before his task was complete. Furthermore, he was in good spirits just a short time before his death and—"

"What about the suicide note?" Brigham clearly considered this the knockout blow and couldn't hide a gleeful curl of the lips.

"…and the suicide note was delivered by an unseen hand, features language which did not match the man's own speech patterns and, as far as I know, has not been compared to any existing samples of his handwriting."

"I see." Brigham wasn't the type to beat a retreat, and he grinned even wider. "You're coming here to cause trouble. In which case, I don't care who you are. You could be the King of England as far as I'm concerned. I'll still arrest you the moment I catch you engaged in any stirring."

For once, I had a chance to be pernickety in response to an awkward suspect. "I believe you're referring to the King of the United Kingdom and the British Dominions, not England alone. And as for stirring, while the Marquess of Edgington may be particularly talented in that field, I do not believe it is an arrestable offence."

The man looked quite taken aback. "The point is…" He searched for the right way to continue this sentence. "The point is… Alsop ended his own life. I've seen no evidence to say that he were murdered and, if he were, I'd have seen the evidence." Content with this circular argument, he raised his chin.

"This isn't even your first mistake," I continued. "You withheld testimony of Mrs Grout that proved Adam Caswell was not in a murderous state of mind and that the vicar had seen something out of the ordinary."

He laughed as though I was quite the wit. "Oh, that's a good one. Withholding testimony, was I?" He spat disdainfully below the table, and I had to hope there was a bucket there to catch the expectoration. "Grouchy Grout the grocer is the biggest yapper in this town. It weren't that I withheld her testimony. I just found myself daydreaming as soon as she opened her big mouth, and so I never bothered writing it down."

Grandfather stepped in then, as we were clearly getting nowhere. "Was Scotland Yard informed of Marcus's death?"

"It weren't necessary. Suicides do not fall under their remit, and so we dealt with it here. Besides, I very much doubt that the dead man's family would have wanted them folks from London poking around. You know how those hacks from the press like to follow detectives about the place looking for stories. Alsop's face would have been all over the papers, and then where would we be?"

"It was Lady Alsop herself who asked us to come here." Grandfather put his weight on the high table and spoke more quietly. "What you are essentially saying is that there was no evidence to find, so you didn't look for any?"

"That's about the size of it." The constable apparently did not view this as a failing.

Grandfather realised that continuing this line of questioning would only provoke more empty answers. He looked at me with something approaching despair on his face, and I did what I could to resolve the stalemate.

"Presumably you think Marcus's death a suicide and are happy that Adam Caswell will be hanged for the murder of Reverend Oldfield?"

"I… yes. Yes, I do… And, yes. Yes, I am." I'd at least made the policeman consider his answer.

"And yet, during the trial, you painted 'Little Cassie' as a peaceful soul who was not given to violence."

Brigham looked at the door, perhaps hoping someone would arrive to save him from such questions. "He has a criminal record."

"For poaching rabbits, isn't that right?" I asked, only for him to fall into my screamingly obvious trap.

"That is correct. He was arrested on the Fane estate with a brace on his belt."

"How interesting. And how many rabbits did you bag that day?"

He leaned closer to let us in on the secret. "As it happens, I was fetching my fifth when the old Baron Fane – that's Stamford's father before he died – nabbed Cassie. So what I did, right… I hid in the bushes so that I didn't get…" The realisation finally dawned on him. "Ah… I see what you're saying."

Like an assistant preparing a body for surgery, I had done my part and stood aside to allow the specialist to wield his scalpel.

"You may think we are stirring, but we are only here to save an innocent man from the gallows and find out what really happened to the two victims. We have no interest in your past criminal activities on the Fane estate, nor do we wish to make a fool of you for the mistakes of which you are already guilty in this investigation. P.C. Brigham, you are the eyes and ears of this village, and we could use your help." Grandfather had insulted and complimented the man in quick succession, but it seemed to do the trick.

The constable put his hand to one ear and pulled on his substantial lobe as he replied. "My mother always said these big lugs would come in handy one day. Now, how can I be of service?"

Lord Edgington straightened up to his usual imperious height. "You can tell us what you know about the plan to expand the village across the Fane estate."

"That?" he asked with a hint of astonishment. "But there's nothing in that. The mayor brought the proposal before the town council, and we eventually agreed that it would go ahead."

"Yes, but what reaction did it provoke?" I could see that Grandfather considered this point significant. "Did everyone go along with the plan?"

"Everyone 'cept the lady doctor." It seemed a little unnecessary to describe Dr Beresford-Gray as 'the lady doctor' considering that she was the only doctor of any description within several miles. "But then, she's known for being disagreeable. I used to have some beautiful flower boxes out on the pavement there. She said they were a hazard and made me get rid of 'em."

"Then she presumably changed her mind about—"

"About my flowers?" His voice became rather squeaky. "Some chance!"

"About the development of the Fane estate!" Grandfather positively groaned.

Brigham flipped a long strand of hair back over his balding head before answering. "That she did. We require unanimous decisions for such votes here in Condicote and she stood in the way of everything." The hair immediately fell back to where it had been, and he folded his arms. "To be perfectly honest, gentlemen, I don't pay too much attention to what goes on in council meetings. Far too boring for my liking. You'd be better off talking to the mayor himself."

"And give the man a heart attack?" I replied. "I think not."

Grandfather looked disappointed to have learnt nothing more

of value and returned us to the murders. "What about local grudges against the two victims? Beyond the evidence, or lack of it, who do you think could be responsible for killing the two men?"

Brigham scoffed. "Are you really asking me which of the citizens in my own town is a secret killer? You might just as well ask how a telephone works or why Mrs Ivy from the jewellers always wears a blue hat on a Tuesday." I failed to see the connection, but he evidently believed it was transparent. "We're normal folk around here. We don't go in for murder."

"Come along, man. I don't expect you to put a sack over a suspect's head and drop him from the gibbet. I'm merely enquiring what your instinct tells you. You're an officer with a great deal of experience. Someone in your position will have built up a good understanding of human nature during your many years on the job." Grandfather really was a master at flattering our suspects without them realising it was a ploy.

"I suppose you could say I have a third eye for such things. A sixth sense for sniffing out the good from the bad." He stuck out his chest and swept the rogue lock into place once more. "Yes, I do have something of a keen-edged mind. I'll grant you that."

His eyes as wide and bright as newly minted half-crowns, Grandfather tossed his hat onto the desk. "Then whom have you noticed in Condicote with a streak of savagery? Whom have you spied with the capacity to do harm? If there are suspicions which you have held on to for many years but never uttered, now is the time to unburden yourself."

The constable no longer appeared worried that his own position in the community was at risk. No, he was looking at me as though I was the one who deserved pity. "Well, I wasn't going to mention it. After all, it's not the sort of thing I like to say out loud."

Grandfather was full of fire by now and would not let the man get away with obfuscation. "Come along, P.C. Brigham. I know you have an answer for us, so who will it be? When you heard that the vicar had been murdered, right here in this innocent town, which name entered your mind?"

He looked at me and frowned a little before admitting the truth. "Very well. It were Loelia Prentiss, the boy's grandmother."

CHAPTER TWENTY-EIGHT

"That was a waste of time." I marched out of the station in something of a huff. "The very idea of my grandmother's involvement in such a wicked endeavour is preposterous."

Grandfather wasn't paying any attention. He had come to a stop in front of the closed doctor's surgery and was attempting to peer in through a small hole in the shutters.

"I'm sorry?" he eventually responded when it was clear that there was nothing inside but darkness.

"Granny – there's no way she could be to blame."

"Well, I wouldn't say that."

"What a great comfort you are." I was frankly surprised that he could be so callous. "The woman has a good heart."

"Oh, yes. She has a fine heart. It would take three werewolves and a vampire to give Loelia enough of a shock to stop her throbber throbbing."

"That's not what I mean, and you know it." I was becoming surly. "Will you please say something in defence of your beloved grandson's very own grandmother?"

He turned back to me and at least considered my request. "Ummm… no. No, I won't. We must not rule out a suspect just because she has a connection to our family. Nor should we be so close-minded as to suggest that old women cannot be savage murderers. To be quite frank, Christopher, I thought better of you."

He sauntered off, but I couldn't move. "I'm no bigot. I was just trying to take up the cudgels for Granny."

"As you should, Christopher, but that will not erase her name from our list of suspects," He would clearly keep talking whether I was by his side or not, and so I ran to catch him. "A number of people have now put Loelia forward as a potential murderer, and we would be remiss in our duties if we ignored their suspicions."

"Wait one moment. Are you pulling my leg again?"

He turned his unshakeable gaze in my direction. "I can assure you that I am doing no such thing. Your grandmother disliked at least one of our victims, not to mention the man who is due to hang for the first crime. She is also one of the few people I have met in my life who makes no attempt to hide her misanthropic character. She positively glories in her ill opinion of those around her. Furthermore, she is fiercely intelligent and, were she to set her mind to murder, I think she would be rather good at it."

I was speechless. I often made the mistake of thinking that I knew how my grandfather will react in any given situation, but his attitude had left me quite thunderstruck. I barely spoke another word as we descended the high street in the direction of The Manor. I took this time to question everything I knew about the world (and also consider who else on Scarlet's list could be the culprit). We'd already interviewed the mayor and P.C. Brigham. Assuming we kept the appointment with Baroness Fane, that would only leave Dr Beresford-Gray to interrogate. One of these slippery individuals simply had to be to blame.

"The best way for me to prove my grandmother is no criminal," I said after we'd both been deep in thought for some minutes, "is to find the murderer."

"What a wonderful plan." He sounded quite sincere. I'm fairly certain that he wasn't.

"Have you noticed that, each time we have glimpsed the doctor today, she has looked quite terrified? When she saw us in the square, she immediately retreated into her surgery."

"I have, and she was similarly nervous in the tea-room yesterday evening. But remember what I told you about the way people behave around detectives."

"To begin with, I thought the same thing, but Dr Beresford-Gray is nothing like the mayor. She is a well-educated woman, who will have dealt with the police regularly through her work. Add that to the fact that, when we passed her surgery just now, it was as quiet as a mausoleum, and the whole situation looks rather strange. Wouldn't you say?"

"Circumstantially speaking, perhaps. But finding that a surgery is closed on a Sunday is hardly evidence that its owner is a criminal."

I could tell that I would not be able to convince him, so I gave up. "Never mind. Let's just get back to the house before we miss lunch. I've got my fingers crossed that Henrietta has made one of her famous roast dinners. It's about time I murdered some Yorkshire puddings drenched in gravy."

He frowned at my choice of words but walked a little faster than before. When we arrived at The Manor, Delilah was upset that we'd left her for so long. She was hiding in the shadows under an exceedingly gothic chest of drawers – all dark wood and haunted carved faces… The piece of furniture that is, not our golden retriever.

Grandfather was away with his thoughts in his head and walked straight past her, so I stopped to make a fuss of her on his behalf. "Believe me, girl. I know exactly how you feel."

I washed my hands and went looking for the others in the dining room. Delilah had followed me and found another shady spot in which she could hide (whilst simultaneously remaining quite visible). Much like me, she lived in hope of her owner one day feeling sorry for her.

I was surprised to discover two guests at the table who had not previously been announced.

"I invited the vicar to lunch," my grandmother explained, rather ignoring the more unexpected addition to our party. "Oh, and Miss Warwick barged in here claiming that I was to blame for the recent spate of murders."

"A claim by which I stand!" Busy buttering a bread roll, Scarlet was quite unconcerned by my grandmother's attack.

The large, graceless vicar appeared unnerved by whatever discussion had preceded our arrival. "I've done my best to play devil's advocate but…"

"But you weren't here when Reverend Oldfield was murdered, so your opinion is next to irrelevant." This was my grandmother's response, though it might just as well have come from the enterprising young woman sitting opposite her.

Grandfather apparently did not know how to handle the situation and sat at the head of the long table without saying a word. The grim space in which we were about to dine looked like a neglected state room from one of my favourite Dickens novels. Miss Havisham's crumbling home was the obvious example that sprang to mind, but it wouldn't have been out of place among the mix of magnificence and mire in Boffin's Bower from 'Our Mutual Friend'.

The table was laid as though for a grand banquet, with floral centrepieces and polished candelabras. And yet, the room was so drab and dingy that there was nothing to make the silver shine. It didn't help that every curtain in the house was drawn so that barely a beam of light could penetrate that gloomy abode.

"Your grandmother was just searching for an argument to prove that she had nothing to do with Marcus's death." Scarlet did not take her eyes off her chosen suspect as she fired this comment along the table.

"And Miss Warwick has helped herself to bread before the meal has even been served." Trust Granny to focus on such a minor issue.

Apparently feeling that he should offer an explanation of his own, the vicar leaned forward to peer around his host. "And I have been telling my fellow diners that arguing gets us nowhere. It is not God's plan for neighbours to turn against one another. As Jesus said in his sermon on the mount, 'Thou shalt love thy neighbour, and hate thine enemy.'"

No one paid him much attention as Scarlet stole the limelight once more. "It's rather rich for Lady Prentiss over there to lecture me on what's right and wrong – be it dining etiquette or general morality. After all, she is by far the most despised creature in the whole of Condicote."

I thought Granny would bristle at this, but she offered a beaming smile. "Do you really think so? Oh, how wonderful! I have surely outdone myself."

The three of them were soon shouting over one another.

"Speaking of bread, I'm reminded of the parable of the loaves and the fishes, when…"

"Not just despised for your superior attitude and intolerance but…"

"I do like to keep the plebeians at a distance, but to claim the prize of the most loathed villager in…"

Grandfather wouldn't say anything, and so it was down to me.

"Will you all, please, be quiet!" I bellowed out my plea just as Halfpenny came into the room pushing a trolley which bore five bowls of French onion soup, swimming with croutons and melted Comté cheese. I should have been more concerned about the various warring factions, but don't forget I'd only eaten two eggs, some biscuits and a few pieces of toast that morning. Whatever is the opposite of being 'as full as a tick', I was that!

Our footman had turned to ice. It was his natural instinct when faced with a situation to which he felt he should not be party.

It would require some prompting to reanimate him. "Serve the first course, please, Halfpenny," Grandfather muttered, and the wheels on the trolley started rolling again.

Todd was a far smoother character and, acting in his second (or perhaps third?) main job as reserve butler, he poured wine for everyone but me. I was happy with Cook's lemonade and glad to say that our staff knew my tastes rather well.

Once we were unavoidably slurping away at the soup, Grandfather dared speak at last.

"May I ask how it came to pass that the three of you are eating together?" Thanks to the way in which he gazed down at everyone from his perch at the head of the table, he looked like a golden eagle.

"I've already told you, Edgington. This girl barged into the house and demanded victuals."

"That's not true in the slightest!" Scarlet brought her fist down and accidentally sent a fork flying through the air. It narrowly missed the vicar's head and, with his usual subtlety, Todd went to retrieve it from the spot where it had become lodged in the wall.

"One at a time, please." Grandfather knew how to set practicable rules. "If what Loelia says is not true, Miss Warwick, can you tell us what really happened?"

Disturbed by the confrontation, Scarlet clutched her spoon like a dagger. "I came to the house in search of answers and, when I got here, that woman invited me to have lunch."

Granny let out a loud noise like a sneezing pig. "I was speaking in jest. I never expected you to take me up on the offer."

"Ladies, please!" The vicar raised his hand to speak but was soon overruled. "Perhaps we could—"

"No, we cannot!" This was the first thing upon which Scarlet and my grandmother agreed.

"Is this true, Loelia?" The detective in our midst was never off duty. "Did you do as Miss Warwick attests?"

Granny's head swayed from side to side as she sought an excuse. "I suppose the essential facts are correct, but I didn't imagine for one moment that she'd be so impertinent as to—"

"Thank you." Her interrogator bowed his head as he interrupted her. Before he could ask another question, there was some more slurping to endure. We were all trying to be polite, but it was quite the noisiest sort of soup to eat with any dignity. "And so, Miss Warwick, may I ask exactly why you came here today?"

"I told you. I wanted to put some questions to the lady of the house."

"What sort of questions did you have in mind?" I asked, as I was afraid they would start bickering again.

"I planned to ask her why she murdered the man I love."

"The cheek of the girl!" Granny had turned quite purple at this affront.

This exchange led to a few more hurled insults and accusations. The vicar had learnt that it was best to stay out of things. He had pushed his glasses down his nose and was rubbing his eyes as though the weight of the world was bearing down on him.

"A little propriety, please." Grandfather was losing his patience. "Why don't you tell us why you think Loelia could be to blame for Marcus's death?"

Scarlet took a bite of her bread roll. She ate with all the appetite of a homeless urchin, which made me like her even more.

"I remembered something he'd told me." Perhaps for my easily scandalised grandmother's sake, she had swallowed before answering. "On the night before he was killed, we were lying in bed together and he said that he'd bumped into Lady Prentiss in the street."

"You know full well, I bear no title, Miss Warwick." Granny turned away to watch the tiny flakes of snow falling outside as though the conversation was of no interest to her.

"So then why do you carry yourself with the airs and graces of a duchess?"

"Ladies, please!" Reverend Bodsworth looked quite shocked by the exchange but was silenced by the two pairs of eyes that now drilled through his skull – metaphorically speaking, at least.

Grandfather stepped in to keep the peace… also metaphorically. Actually, I'm going to assume everyone knows what a metaphor is and stop making such remarks. "Continue, Miss Warwick. You were about to tell us what Marcus had recounted on the eve of his murder."

"Yes. We were together in our room in the Drop of Dew, and he said that Loelia Prentiss had taken him to task in the middle of the street in front of half the village."

"I really don't recall any such thing." A serious look crossed dear

Granny's face. It was oddly out of character. Though something of a stick-in-the-mud, and critical to a tittle of those around her, she tended to present her barbs with a touch of dark humour.

Grandfather ignored her reaction and addressed Scarlet once more. "With what, in particular, did Loelia take umbrage?"

"Marcus said that she lost her head because he wouldn't just roll over and watch Adam hang."

"Piff-paff! I have such encounters with the imbeciles of this town on a nearly daily basis." She shook her head in distaste. "I can't possibly be expected to remember every last thing I say."

"This was only a few days ago, Granny," I reminded her. "How many arguments do you start in an average week?"

The unrelenting Lord Edgington focused his attention on Miss Warwick. "Loelia didn't like the fact that your paramour was investigating the vicar's death; is that what you mean?"

"Precisely." The more enthused Scarlet became, the faster she ate her soup. "She said that he should think of the town and not go ruffling feathers where it wasn't warranted."

"Is this true?" I was eager to hear the old lady's defence, even if my grandfather wasn't. "Did you really try to stop him overturning an injustice?"

She shook her head so swiftly back and forth that she looked like a feather-ruffled hen standing up to a fox. "I wouldn't put it that way, exactly. I—"

Scarlet had finished the last traces of soup, and I thought she might lick the bowl. "You said that he was entirely selfish in what he was doing."

"Fine!" Granny pushed her chair back to respond. "It's true. I accosted your poor friend. But I didn't mean any harm. And I was not afraid of him discovering the truth about Reverend Oldfield, if that's what you think."

"Oh, yes?" Ever so slowly, so that it looked as though a spell had been cast upon him, Grandfather finally turned to address our host. "Then what *were* you doing?"

The words got stuck in Granny's throat, and she couldn't produce one of her acerbic responses. "It's all so… It's just…"

"Answer the question, you terrible woman." Don't worry, it wasn't me saying this. It was Scarlet. Now that she had finished the first course, she was free to attack in earnest. "You found my friend's attachment to Stamford so repellent that you took against them long ago. It wouldn't surprise me for one moment if you killed the vicar to incriminate poor Adam and then murdered Marcus to complete the job."

When Granny didn't reply, Scarlet joined her on her feet. "I'm right, aren't I? This was all about Stamford Fane. Were you so disappointed to have missed your chance to inflict some pain on the man that you resorted to the next best thing by slaying his friends?"

"The rope!" I said, as I couldn't let my grandmother go undefended. "Granny couldn't possibly have the force to strangle the vicar with such a thick rope. You'd need to be as big as Reverend Bodsworth or the mayor to stand a chance."

Inevitably, Grandfather saw a flaw in my argument. "Perhaps by throwing it over a beam, even someone of limited strength could have killed the man."

The reverend, meanwhile, was almost choking to death on a chunk of bread (and my recent point of reference). "I'm no…" Cough, cough, splutter. "I'm no killer! I'm a man of the cloth." If he'd had any hairs on his head, I believe every last one of them would have fallen out in shock.

"Stay out of this, Reverend." Scarlet had more to say and pointed across the table at her foe. "You tried to warn Marcus off his investigation and, when he wouldn't listen, you murdered him."

"No!" Granny cried, and I'd never seen the prickly woman so distressed. "You're twisting what happened. I would never hurt another—"

"Why should we believe a word you say?"

My beleaguered grandmother looked first at her adversary and then at me but couldn't summon a word for either of us.

My grandfather would have to answer for her. "Because she was looking out for your interests."

"I beg your pardon?" Scarlet almost sounded offended, but my grandfather continued regardless.

"That's right, isn't it, Loelia?"

Granny was still in something of a daze. "I… yes. Yes, that's right." She glanced about the room and her search eventually came to a stop on the only truly neutral observer. "I never disliked Marcus and Adam the way I did that despicable man, Fane. I tried to warn them against spending time with him months ago, but Adam was too naïve and Marcus too arrogant. I was looking out for his interests, yet again, when I spoke to him last weekend. I was afraid of the scandals he might unearth."

This explanation still wasn't enough for Scarlet. "So you knew that Adam didn't kill the vicar, and yet you'd rather he hang than fight for his life."

"It's not that simple." Turning back to Scarlet, Granny pleaded for understanding. It was quite heartbreaking to see. "I realised that, if there is someone in this community who is savage enough to murder a vicar in such a manner, I could only imagine what he would do to the person who uncovered his identity. I was afraid for Marcus's life and rightly so."

"Then why didn't you say that?" Grandfather betrayed a previously hidden streak of anger. "Why didn't you talk to me before things could get worse?"

Granny collapsed into her seat. She was a shadow of the normally bold individual I knew so well. "Isn't it obvious?" Her words were barely audible. "I didn't want you or Christopher to come to harm."

The reverend, of all people, was the only one to show sympathy. He reached his hand out to her before changing his mind and lightly patting her shoulder.

A sudden tearful wail ripped through the room then, but it was not from my grandmother. Scarlet's nervous anger had been replaced by sorrow and the sudden burst of emotion left us all quite stunned until she explained what was wrong.

"I heard from Marcus's mother this morning. There was a letter from Marcus's solicitor waiting for her when she returned to her house yesterday. Adam's appeal has failed, and he'll be hanged in two days' time."

"Ladies and gentlemen, your second course today is roast guinea fowl in a prune sauce with an assortment of—" Halfpenny had returned with the freshly stocked trolley but froze in the entrance as he took in the troubled scene.

CHAPTER TWENTY-NINE

"Two days?" Grandfather sounded just as haunted as our new friend.

"That's enough time, isn't it?" I longed for a positive answer, but I knew he wouldn't sugar his language.

"There's no hope," Scarlet replied when my kindly forebear opted not to disappoint me. "That's why I came here. I was desperate to believe that Lady Prentiss was the killer, because I don't know who else could be to blame."

The vicar turned his sadly sympathetic face towards her, but there was nothing he could do to soothe her pain.

When he finally spoke again, Grandfather's voice was soft and serious. "Fear not, child. We will do everything we can to right this injustice. Two days is a long time in an investigation, and I will not give up hope just yet."

He was too far along the table to offer her his hand, and so I did it for him.

A tragic smile broke out on Scarlet's face, and she squeezed my fleshy mitt in her own delicate counterpart. "Thank you. All of you! I must seem like a true lunatic, but I appreciate everything you have done." She looked at my silent grandmother and, though she wouldn't say anything more, I could see how grateful she was to be there at the table, instead of alone in her room at the pub.

Grandfather clapped his hands together to reanimate his footman. "Halfpenny, you may serve the main course."

I know that I talk far too much about food and the joy of dining, but I genuinely believe in the power of a good meal. Henrietta's incredible roast dinner livened our spirits and, far from disheartening us, I felt that the news of Adam's increased peril might be just the thing to push us forward. In fact, I was rather sad when the meal was over, despite the fact I had just eaten an exquisite cabinet pudding.

What's cabinet pudding, you ask? Surely you'd rather I continued with the story and told you about our trip to see Baroness Fane than hear me waffling about dessert?

Oh, very well.

Cabinet pudding is an exquisite concoction. It is a steamed cake cooked in a mould, with crystallised fruits and rum-macerated raisins arranged in an artful pattern that is visible through the custard on the top of the dessert. If you ever have the chance to indulge in such a delight, I recommend it wholeheartedly, and if, on the contrary, you have no sweet tooth, I must apologise for wasting your time.

Either way, that delectable treat was just what we needed to rise from our feast with belief, self-confidence (and full bellies). We would find the killer, save Caswell from the gallows and make Condicote a safer place; I just knew it.

"What a strange state of affairs," Grandfather burbled to himself as we left the village in the direction of Seekings House. "I have a number of doubts after everything we have just witnessed, not least among them being why your grandmother would have gone out of her way to confront Marcus Alsop, when she had previously told us how little she thought of the chap."

It was snowing again, but it was not the pretty kind of snow with large flakes that dance to the ground like angels in semi-suspension. It was wet, sleety drizzle, and I couldn't wait to be back inside. Delilah had made a big fuss about coming out with us, though I could tell that she felt just the same as me. She stuck to Grandfather's side for warmth as we walked, but that did nothing to combat the cold wind that was whipping along the valley into our faces.

"I have a question." I didn't know how to respond to his point, so a question would have to do. "Is Granny more or less of a suspect now? I'm beyond the point of rejecting her guilt out of hand, but wish I knew what just happened."

"Quite." Grandfather really isn't much help at such moments. "This whole infernal case is beyond perplexing. My only hope is that Baroness Fane can fill in some of the holes in our understanding. As things stand, however, we have more holes than solid matter and, despite what I told Scarlet, it will take an immense effort and perhaps some luck to discover the truth in such a short time."

We turned off the village road to walk up the long drive to Seekings House. The Fane estate was an immense, wooded spit of land that stretched off along the narrow valley. I had explored the place many times as a child, and I was as fond of the rows of oaks that lined our path as I was of the shady pine groves and the pretty lake in the centre of the property. It was there that my father had once failed to teach my brother and me to light a fire on a swiftly abandoned camping trip. Ah, what happy memories.

"What other doubts did you have?"

Grandfather turned his eyebrows up at me before eventually realising what I meant. "Oh, I wondered why adventurous young people like Scarlet and Marcus would have stuck around in this provincial town. Such minor points may seem trivial, but you never know what could be significant in a case like this one."

With the snow still lying on the ground, the birds of the estate were in a real flap (if you'll excuse the pun). A small flock of what I took to be chaffinches were hopping about the place – though they might well have been crossbills or bullfinches for all I knew and, had you tried to convince me they were bats, I would probably have believed you.

"Why didn't we drive?" I asked after several minutes with my head down to keep the icy wind off my face. I was wearing a big blue duffel coat and three to five scarves, but they did little to protect me from the cold.

"And miss the chance to get some exercise? You do love to fuss, Christopher. Snow in April is never as bad as snow in January, and this winter paled in comparison to the great frost of eighteen seventy… something. I don't remember the exact year, but it was as cold as the arctic across Britain for months."

"I know, Grandfather. You've told me several times." I didn't look up at him, as I could barely move the muscles in my frozen body. "But that does nothing to warm me right now."

"1875! It was 1875!" He released a short laugh and ploughed onwards, his cane essential as he traversed a patch of ice. "This is nothing to get worked up about in the slightest."

We left the long avenue of trees and made it to the opening in front of the house. Seekings was a grand old place, with a broad, sandstone façade covered in windows. In keeping with its neighbouring village, the place was a mish-mash of styles. The white framed windows were decidedly neo-classical, with moulded pillar reliefs on either side of them, whereas the crenellations atop the building were far more mediaeval in appearance.

On the circular driveway, there was a car collection to rival my grandfather's. Lagondas, Rolls Royces, Daimlers and Talbots of every colour – from black to shining silver – were arranged in lines amongst piles of snow. One, in particular, caught my attention. The police had evidently towed home the Lanchester 40 that the Baron was driving when he died. Whatever colour it had been, it was ashen now – consumed by the flames that had killed him. The bonnet was a little dented, and all the glass had blown out. As we wandered past, I took a furtive glance inside, just to make sure that the body was no longer there. It wasn't, of course, and I felt rather silly for looking.

Thankfully, Baroness Fane had an attentive butler who opened the door to us as soon as we stepped beneath the immense canopy of the front loggia. "Lady Fane is waiting for you in the short gallery," the well-spoken relic at the door informed us as we trooped past.

We stood waiting for him to lead us through the plush property, as I, for one, hadn't a clue where the short gallery might be. In the meantime, a boy appeared with a towel to dry off Delilah and take her to the kitchen for some refreshments. If I'd known the options, I might have elected to join her.

Though seventy if he was a day, the lofty butler was not quite so creaky as our own footman, and we made good time on our way through the maze-like ground floor. I noticed that several of the salons and lounges that we passed had been stripped bare. There was a sparkling ballroom, with a glossy pine floor and an elegantly painted ceiling, which was entirely free from the sumptuous fabrics and furniture it would once have contained. A smoking room on the opposite side of the corridor was similarly empty, with little left inside but the odour of expensive cigars. Those rooms which were untouched still retained their stately charm, and I could better understand now why my grandmother had been so envious of the luxurious manor that Seekings would once have been.

The short gallery was located at the end of a burgundy corridor in the west wing of the building. Perhaps predictably, it was named for the glut of art upon its silk-papered walls. I got the impression that the gold-framed paintings were arranged by date, with the oldest at the very top of the high-ceilinged space. There was a distinct theme to the pictures on each wall and, facing us as we entered, was Baron Stamford Fane himself.

Surrounded by his ancestors from centuries past, his portrait was just above eye level and immediately caught my attention. I was struck by what an impressive figure the man cut. He seemed to fill the hunting attire he wore, much as hydrogen inflates a balloon. His tightly sutured jacket gave him the air of an army general, whereas his thick black beard and shoulder-length locks lent him a devilish air. In fact, I soon changed my mind. He wasn't a soldier or a demon; he was a pirate through and through – a loveable tyrant – and I felt I might well have set sail with him, had he asked me to join his crew.

I'd only caught glimpses of the man when he was alive but, with his bulging muscles and dark looks, he would definitely have been at home aboard a ship with the Jolly Roger flying. I found it unusual that, instead of peering out from the canvas like most portraits, the subject's gaze was held by something out of frame – as though he was far too busy to look at me. In this respect, at least, the artist had captured the baron's famously arrogant character.

For a moment, I wanted to address the two-dimensional representation, just as clairvoyants will commune with spirits. *Who killed you, and how did they do it?* I thought to ask him, but I doubt he would have replied.

Waiting calmly for us to notice her, there was someone who, in her own quiet way, might prove just as useful as the dead man. We were about to get some answers from Baroness Fane.

CHAPTER THIRTY

"Good afternoon, gentlemen." It was almost a surprise to hear that soft American voice. "It is a pleasure to welcome you to Seekings."

Baroness Sorel Fane was a queen in her neglected palace. Arranged on a heavy wooden throne that reminded me of the coronation chair at Westminster Abbey, all that she was missing was a crown. She had changed since we'd seen her in church, and, foregoing her mourning attire, her gauzy robes were suitably elaborate. A red dress with a decorously smocked decolletage made her look like an Italian duchess, and I had to wonder where her family had originated before travelling to America.

"It is very kind of you to invite us." Rising to the occasion, Grandfather offered an elaborate bow. I attempted to follow his example, but my effort looked more like a curtsey.

The butler took our coats and motioned to the two chairs opposite the baroness for us to be seated.

"I trust that your husband's death is becoming a little more bearable as time passes, madam." It seemed a strange point upon which to begin our meeting, but then Grandfather was a calculating so-and-so and always knew what to do.

"That is what they say," she replied, without explaining how she felt on the matter. "Time heals all wounds, isn't that it?"

"So true." Within the higher echelons of society, there is normally some degree of polite discourse to endure before any real conversation can take place. I don't know why we must waste our time with such formalities but, given the sensitive nature of our visit, it was hardly surprising that Grandfather would follow protocol.

"I have not been nearly so encumbered as many bereaved women. You see, my love for Stamford had long since diminished." That certainly brought the small talk to a swift conclusion! "I'm sure you'll have noted my dry eyes on the day of his funeral. Though my companions in church believed me to be in a state of shock, it is hard to mourn a man whom I largely detested."

"So true." Grandfather was clearly taken aback by her honesty.

I, meanwhile, was positively speechless. Her claims went against the story that Scarlet had told us of her run-in with the incensed baroness in the Drop of Dew Inn.

"Stamford died as he lived: foolishly." She spoke with real vim, her voice as sharp as any dagger. "He wasted his years on this earth running up debts he couldn't pay and squandering both his family's fortune and mine. I kept some funds hidden from him, but the majority of what I brought to the union only lasted a few years thanks to that dissolute wagerer." Having released this torrent of revulsion, she paused to breathe. "So yes, thank you, Lord Edgington. His passing has become quite bearable."

We had caught her in a lie. We'd only been there for a couple of minutes, and she was already fibbing. I was certain that my grandfather would have realised this, and so I kept my mouth shut for the time being.

A brief hush descended, but the room was not quite silent, as there was a strange noise coming from the shadowy corner between our host's chair and the window. It was a sort of purring sound, and I caught the flash of a small white point whipping through space.

"Do you like animals, Christopher?" the baroness enquired, as she scratched the cushioned arm of her chair with one nail.

I held my breath as, stepping into a patch of light, there appeared the largest, most unusual cat I had ever seen. It had tall, pointed ears with long black tufts on the top that made it look like a feline god from the hieroglyphs of an ancient pyramid. The creature rubbed its tan muzzle against the leg of its owner's chair and, though twice the size of most domestic moggies, it looked a friendly beast.

"This is my caracal, Sekhmet. Isn't she the most beautiful creature you've ever encountered? The ancient Egyptians used them for hunting and kept them like royals." Her fingers teased the cat's ears and, for a moment, I imagined that the pair of them were purring in unison. "Stamford killed Sekhmet's parents on a hunting trip. Their heads are on the wall of his study, but he saved their kitten to give to me."

I held out my hand to see whether the pretty creature would nuzzle it, but she went snarling forward and gave me a nasty scratch.

"Oh, I wouldn't do that," the baroness continued as I sucked on my wounded fingers. "Sekhmet is quite wild. She has bitten me on a number of occasions, but I adore her nonetheless."

She leant forward remarkably slowly to put her nose against the vicious feline's. There was a moment's impasse before the cat got bored and went to roll about in the sunshine.

"That is love." The good widow sat back up to look at my grandfather. "I love that creature despite all her faults, but Stamford didn't know the meaning of the word."

It was about time that Grandfather said something, but he apparently wasn't in the mood, so I thought I might as well waffle. "Are you a real American?"

"Third generation, born in Boston. Why d'you ask?"

"Oh, it's just that the last man I thought was an American turned out not to be." I cast my mind back to an earlier case. "Interesting chap, though. Went by the name of Chet Novicki. Do you know him?"

She laughed at me rather sweetly, and I still couldn't get any sense of who this woman was. "No, sorry, boy. There are a lot of Americans in the world and even more fake ones."

My prattling had apparently knocked Grandfather from his daze, and he engaged our witness once more.

"What was happening in your husband's life in the days before he died?"

She looked a little surprised that he would ask such a question but showed no reluctance to answer it. "If the truth be told, we had an argument on Christmas Eve, so he sped off to London to lose all his money."

"Was that the money he'd borrowed from Marcus Alsop?"

"Precisely. He'd convinced that poor boy to give him the capital that we needed to invest in the redevelopment of the estate, and then he lost it at the first available opportunity."

"Ten thousand pounds!?" I couldn't hide my shock. "He lost ten thousand pounds gambling?"

She shrugged as though this were a perfectly normal occurrence. "Yes, and a lot more before that."

"What, exactly, was the cause of your argument before he left for London?" Grandfather kept us on the right track.

"His inability to hold on to any money, of course – even the money we had borrowed to save us from ruin. It always amazed me that such a smart young man as Marcus could have been so easily manipulated by my selfish husband, but then I suppose he'd done the same to me."

"That is a point I have been pondering, madam." Grandfather looked up at the wall of pictures behind her, as though proving that he was capable of such reflection. "Why would Marcus have lent him so much money if he knew the man was prone to staking his life and livelihood on the outcome of a card game or the result of a boxing match?"

The caracal had come to a rest beside her owner's feet and was purring happily once more. "You clearly never met my husband, Lord Edgington. Stamford was what my people back home would call a confidence man." Her American accent became a little more pronounced as she uttered this term. She made it sound quite exotic. "He could trick anyone on this planet. For one thing, he convinced my parents that he'd be a good husband. But surely his greatest accomplishment was making the people of this town believe that he was anything more than a charlatan."

"So Marcus looked up to him?" Grandfather still hadn't grasped the relationship between the two men.

"More than that, Marcus loved him. He was convinced that Stamford Fane was as great a human being as he claimed. From the time that boy was eighteen, he'd come to hear Stamford's tales of travel and adventures throughout his unparalleled life. Of course, most of them were pure confections, but Marcus was under his spell. He didn't even notice the empty rooms where Stamford had sold furniture and family heirlooms to pay our bills. All he saw was my corrupt and dazzling husband."

"What about Adam Caswell?" I asked and was immediately transported back to that lonely cell we'd visited in Tatchester gaol. "Why did the baron have anything to do with him?"

Sorel Fane's hand moved to the side of her chair to fondle her pet's soft tail. "Adam was just the same. He thought that Stamford could do no wrong. Of course, Marcus should have known better, but Adam was easily conned. Stamford really only kept him around as an unpaid servant. He was forever sending the poor kid off on errands."

"Did you spend any great deal of time with the baron and his friends?" Grandfather put his hands together as though in prayer.

"Not if I could help it. The one advantage to my marriage was that I was afforded the independence that many women desire. Of course, there was never enough money for me to do anything with that independence, but it was still a better existence than most of my contemporaries ever achieve."

Lord Edgington evidently felt that he'd discovered all he could through that particular line of questioning and took us back to the beginning. "How did you learn of your husband's death?"

She needed a moment to recall. "I was here. P.C. Brigham came to tell me shortly after it had happened, and then a young fellow from Scotland Yard turned up the next day."

"And you were happy with the explanation that it was an accident?"

Once more imitating the animal in front of her, she narrowed her eyes. "I wasn't happy. I was over the moon." She couldn't resist a slight curl of the lips. "But if you're asking whether I believed their findings, then, yes. I'd told the fool a thousand times not to get in a car when he'd been drinking, but he never listened to a thing I said."

"The cars on the drive," Grandfather began, and I thought for a moment that I would have to endure a discussion of his favourite automobiles. "I take it they belonged to the baron?"

This was the first time that she'd looked less than comfortable answering one of Grandfather's questions. "They did, indeed. He sold his mother's jewellery and his great-grandfather's writing desk, but he would not be parted from the very objects that ended up killing him."

I cleared my throat and, in quite the most hesitant voice I could muster, asked a question that Grandfather had failed to put to her. "So… or, rather, when you say…" I stopped myself, took a deep breath and began again. "You honestly don't think there's any chance that the baron might have possibly crashed his Lanchester… on purpose?" I wasn't as nervous as I'd made myself sound, but I knew from experience how suspects reacted to my rather adorable lack of self-confidence.

"Suicide? Stamford thought too highly of himself to do such a thing." She let out a fluted laugh. "Do you know the story of Narcissus, Chrissy?"

I found her informality jarring but answered all the same. "I do. He was a Greek beauty who rejected all suitors and fell in love with his own reflection. He died from starvation, as he couldn't tear his eyes away from the pool in which he saw himself."

"Correct. Well, Stamford wouldn't have taken all that time to waste away. He'd have jumped right in for a kiss and drowned. My husband

191

had eyes for himself alone and was only interested in other people for the way in which they could serve him. He was the definition of what the French call *un nombriliste*."

I was tempted to ask for the definition of what the French call *un nombriliste,* but I'd played that game before and lost.

"So then you don't think it's a coincidence that, soon after losing the money he needed to save himself from penury, he wrapped his car around a tree?" I was suddenly more confident, and I could see the effect it had on her. It was a rather neat trick, if I do say so myself.

"Actually, it wasn't a tree that killed him. It was a lamppost near the road onto our estate. He must have been so spifflicated that he turned too early, that pie-eyed fool."

I got the impression that she was making a reference to her late husband's drunkenness, but I'd have to look up some of her Americanisms when I returned to Cranley Hall. I was fairly certain that Grandfather would have a book in his library for translating more unusual New World terminology.

Apparently realising that she hadn't answered my question, she added another carefully tailored response. "But no, boy, I don't find it strange that he died just after sending us both to hell. We were bankrupt, and he got drunk to forget all about it. Sadly for him, but happily for me, he also forgot that he couldn't drive a car when so far gone."

To interrupt this dramatic declaration, there was a loud knock on the door, and our three heads flicked in that direction.

CHAPTER THIRTY-ONE

The door creaked slowly open and there stood a maid who had come to clean. She was soon sent on her way, so that was anti-climactic.

"And now your troubles are behind you," Grandfather told the Widow Fane once we were alone again. He had a clever tactic of delivering perfectly suspicious comments in such a friendly voice that it was hard for our suspects to know what to make of him.

"That's right." Her tongue flicked between her lips like an adder's. "But if you've decided that I had something to do with his death, I can assure you that the insurance policy was an old one and nothing to do with me."

"It truly was a stroke of luck that the sum of money his death will bestow was the very same amount that you require for the project that will make you a fortune."

The baroness straightened her back and looked even more imperial in her elaborate chair. "It was about time that my luck changed, don't you think?" She puzzled over this for a moment. "Let me set your mind at ease. If I'd had any intention of killing my husband, I would have devised a far more violent end for him. It was all over too quickly, and Stamford did not receive the interminable suffering he deserved."

The muscles in his neck pulled taut, and he stared down his perfectly straight nose at her. "So, if you didn't do it, who else would have killed your husband and made it look like an accident?"

For a moment, I believe that even the caracal held her breath in anticipation of what might come next. I don't think that Grandfather expected an answer, and the baroness certainly wasn't about to provide one.

"As you have already mentioned, the police examined the site of the crash and concluded that there was no evidence of foul play."

"Yes. Yes, they did." Lord Edgington clapped his hands together. "Then it looks as though we should strike you from our list of suspects and move on to the next witness. Come along, Christopher. Off we go." The fact that he stayed exactly where he was told even someone of my limited intellect that this comment was a facetious one.

"There's no need for sarcasm." The baroness's beautifully dark eyes caught the light of the candle-adorned chandelier. There was a mischievousness in them that I rather admired. To be perfectly honest, I'd met so many women in the course of my short career as a detective that I didn't fall in love quite so often as before. It had been literally months since I'd last had my heart broken, but I couldn't ignore the fact that the baroness was different from most of the wives of nobility I'd met, and she was no less interesting for it.

"Very well." Grandfather cleared his throat – or at least pretended to do so. "Then what of the money that Marcus Alsop lent your husband? Did he not ask that you return it after the baron's death?"

"I told you." She was not intimidated in the slightest. "The boy would have done anything for Stamford and didn't even broach the topic."

This fitted with what Scarlet had told us, but it was hard to imagine him forgiving a ten-thousand-pound debt.

With his progress slow, Grandfather changed his technique. "You were right when you said that I never met your husband, and that is why I needed to speak to you." His demeanour softened as he tried to win her confidence. "You see, we must rule out any possible connection between the baron's death and the two murders, and I believe that you are the only person who is capable of doing so." He turned his head a fraction and allowed his smile to stretch across his face. "There must be something you know about him that no one else would."

This made her pause. It was not the sort of thing you would expect a former police officer to say. There was something imprecise and perhaps poetic about it.

The baroness threw her head back as if in challenge but answered all the same. "Stamford was charming. I know that might not sound like a secret, but it's why I fell in love with him. When he came to Boston to propose to me, I knew he was the most impressive man I'd ever met. He was a silver-tongued British lord, with dark Latin features, and I was instantly hypnotised by him."

She put her hand to her neatly piled hair to check that it was in place, as though just thinking of the baron could somehow compromise her careful presentation. "It was all a sham, of course. Behind his smooth manner was a frightened whelp. His parents didn't raise their son so much as spend the first eighteen years of his life terrifying him. They were fiercely strict and only let him out of the house to attend

194

church each morning. Stamford once told me that the only friend he was allowed as a child was the family Bible. It was hardly surprising that, as soon as his father died, he went off the rails."

Throughout the wicked things she told us about her deceased husband, there was a touch of amusement in her voice. It seemed that, even now, she couldn't disapprove of him entirely. "He went to the opposite extreme of all they had brought him up to believe. He took immense pleasure in debasing himself and, once we were married and my dowry was secured, he liked nothing more than to shock me with his tales of womanising and debauchery."

"He sounds like a perfectly horrible chap." My grandfather often enjoyed a spot of understatement.

"He was." She let out a slow, troubled breath. "And yet I could never truly blame him for what he'd become. For a long time, I actually believed he had good in him."

"Then what finally proved that wasn't the case?" Grandfather's question seemed to remain with us for a few moments, like a weight bearing down on our shoulders.

"Isn't that obvious?"

"I wouldn't have asked if it was."

She recovered her composure a little before speaking. "We were married for fifteen years, and, in that time, I saw him do any number of terrible things. I saw him use and swiftly lose all his friends so that the only people left were devotees like Adam and Marcus."

She held herself for a moment and had to breathe before her emotions could overtake her. "Stamford had no conscience, and that is why I cannot mourn his passing. The world is a happier place without him, and the only comfort I can extract from our time together is that I bore him no children to continue his family line." She glanced around the richly decorated room as though she hoped it would be the last time. "The sooner this estate is razed to the ground, the better off we all will be."

Whatever tension this discussion had sparked in her lingered for some time. The pair of them had become trapped like cats in a staring competition, so I decided to ask a question of my own. "Don't you think it's too much of a coincidence that Reverend Oldfield and Marcus Alsop were murdered so soon after your husband died?"

"No, I don't think so," was the simple answer that came back to me.

"Well, I do," I told her. "You must have considered the possibility that he was murdered. You must have some theory of your own for who could be responsible for the three deaths."

"I knew nothing of Stamford's affairs."

Grandfather was having none of it. "I'm sure you can do better than that, madam. You're evidently a woman with a fine head on your shoulders, and you know this village far better than either of us."

She let out a tired sigh. "In actual fact, I really don't have much to do with the people around here. I could make a stab in the dark for why such misfortune has befallen Condicote, but that is all any guess of mine would be."

Grandfather nodded as if to say, *very well, go ahead.*

"It's a funny place to live," she replied to take us off on a tangent. "This town is too small to be truly significant but has a wealthy past which it cannot forget. I think that seeps into the character of the locals, and they all believe they're too good to be ignored. Perhaps someone here decided to draw a little attention to the place and get this fine old village into the London papers."

"Killing for fame: what an interesting idea. I suppose that would explain a robbery that wasn't really a robbery." He tapped the side of his cheek as he considered the possibility.

The caracal stood up to bat at her owner's skirts with a careless paw.

"Perhaps I could imagine the mayor cooking up such a plan." The baroness had apparently lost interest in the conversation and watched the rapscallion feline. "Or maybe imperious Loelia Prentiss was tired of being the second most important lady in this town and decided to make a name for herself."

I would have interrupted to pooh-pooh the idea of my grandmother's involvement in any crime, but our witness spoke again.

"To be perfectly honest, I answered all these questions when Marcus called to see me last Sunday. Surely Miss Warwick will have explained my thoughts on these matters."

"Marcus was here?" Grandfather appeared surprised by this, but it did not strike me as strange that our deceased friend's investigation had led him to the same places we'd visited.

"Yes, of course. He cornered me in church and requested an

196

audience the evening before he was killed. I had assumed that anything you wished to discuss today would be informed by that meeting."

This minor revelation had made my grandfather rather excited. "This is fascinating. How did he act when he came here?"

"Well, he wasn't suicidal if that's what you're wondering." The baroness looked across the room to a small card table with two chairs set around it, and I had to imagine that this was where she had received him. "He was his usual bright and bold self."

"Did he have a clear idea who the killer was?"

"Not to my knowledge, but he was confident that he could work out what had happened. He said that the pieces of the puzzle were beginning to fall into place."

"And that was all he told you?"

"I'm afraid so." She looked a little sorry to not be more helpful. "But he was scribbling in a pad of paper the whole time he was here. I assumed Miss Warwick would have kept his notes."

This time, Grandfather really did get to his feet to leave. "Thank you, madam. You may have been more helpful than any of us yet know."

CHAPTER THIRTY-TWO

Grandfather paused our retreat to look at the burnt-out car in the drive. He scratched at the scorched chassis with his cane then shook his head before hurrying onwards. Delilah spent this time walking around in a circle to keep herself warm. It had been somewhat difficult to convince her to leave the cosy kitchen in Seekings House, and she was apparently anticipating the journey home even less than I was.

"The baroness was lying, Grandfather, and yet you didn't challenge her."

"I beg your pardon." He'd evidently been deep in cogitation when I put this to him.

"We know that Baroness Fane confronted Marcus and Scarlet at the Drop of Dew shortly after her husband died. She accused them of sharing the responsibility for Fane's death, which made Scarlet believe that the baroness was still in love with him."

"Your point being what exactly?"

"My point being that she was either acting that day or she was lying to us now. She claimed to despise her husband but bear no ill will towards his friends. Evidently, the baroness went to the pub to pretend that she loved her husband, and I think I know why."

"Oh, yes?"

He was forever telling me that I should learn to talk less and listen more, but I rather liked my new theory. "We know that no one tampered with the Lanchester that the baron was driving. What we cannot say is whether he was poisoned and that led to the crash." It was sterling detective work, and I was looking forward to the adulation he would shower upon me. "It would have been easy enough to do. The baron called into the Drop of Dew to buy a bottle of whisky. Perhaps the baroness paid the landlady to put something in it."

When no response came, my skin tingled, and it wasn't just from the cold.

"Don't you think that makes a lot of sense?" I persisted. "It would explain all the unlikely coincidences." As I spoke, the fog cleared, and everything fitted together. "The vicar must have got wind of what happened and so he was killed, too. Then, despite all she said, Marcus can't have been happy to be ten thousand pounds out of pocket. He came to Seekings to demand his money and was dead the next day."

"Christopher…" He stopped walking and Delilah circled us once more. "I'm so proud of you. You have presented an instinctive yet complete solution to the mystery before us."

I was almost too nervous to ask anything more. "And what would you say the chances are of it being… correct?"

He took a moment to carry out the calculations. "Forty to fifty per cent."

I believe that I raised my fist in celebration. This was a big improvement on my average.

"You are right in saying that the baron could have been poisoned. Though his crisply burnt body was inspected by the local doctor, I do not believe that a full post-mortem examination was undertaken. What you have overlooked, I'm afraid, is the timeline of events. First, it seems unlikely that the baron would have called Seekings House to say that he was on his way home via the inn where he would purchase a bottle of whisky. Therefore, the baroness couldn't have known his plan. And second, Scarlet told us that Baroness Fane went to see them after the inquest. At that stage, everyone had accepted the idea that the baron's death was an accident, and his wife had no reason to distance herself from the supposed crime."

I don't mind admitting that this sent a real jolt of disappointment through me, and I lashed out with a retort. "You still haven't explained why you chose not to confront her. You knew she was lying and yet you didn't say anything."

"It was a fine effort, Christopher. Keep thinking about it and maybe you'll get to a truly perfect solution before long."

He charged off once more through the freezing afternoon. Although it was only four o'clock, the clouds overhead were so dark that little light reached us. When we left the extensive front garden and entered the wooded drive, it was as dark as night.

He returned to his intense contemplation, and I knew he was not telling the whole truth. "Is there something else I'm missing, Grandfather?"

"It is quite possible."

"Very droll. You know exactly what I mean. Was there something in particular that the baroness revealed that has set you to walk so fast?"

"I don't know who the killer is, if that's what you're asking."

I must admit that I was confused how this could be deemed an answer to either of the questions I had asked. On the other hand, it was nice to glean this slight yet significant fact.

"Then what *do* you know? Something has put a bee in your bonnet, and there's normally a reason for you to behave in such an eccentric manner."

"Eccentric, eh?" He gave a brief, melodic laugh in order to confirm my remark. "I prefer to think of myself as a man with a mercurial personality who does not live by the outdated standards with which society regards one's age, sex and social standing."

His reply was so obtuse that I struggled to remember what it was we'd been discussing. "And I've no doubt that is just how everyone views you, Grandfather."

He was distracted by something and apparently hadn't heard my vague response to his perfectly vague comment.

"As it happens, there is one thing that strikes me as exceedingly odd." He shook the snow from his long hair much as our dog would. "We were invited to afternoon tea, and yet no tea was provided."

Now I knew something was wrong with him. "Surely that's the kind of thing about which I would normally complain. Or at least, about which you complain about me complaining."

He stopped in his tracks and slowly sank a little lower in the snow. "I have no idea to what you are referring."

"Then that makes two of us!" I'd meant this to be an insult at his expense, but I don't think it turned out that way. "Perhaps we should stop talking in riddles and say what we're really thinking."

He held his thickly gloved hand out for me to shake, and I did just that.

"It's a deal," we both said at the same time, before I added, "You go first."

"I was thinking that it is odd to invite guests to afternoon tea and not even offer a glass of water and a biscuit. It certainly gives the impression that she didn't want us to stay." He really was very excited and could hardly keep his thoughts on track. "But, more importantly, we now know that Marcus came here and the next day he was dead."

"Yes, but we might just as well say that he spoke to my grandmother and was soon murdered. It doesn't prove that Baroness Fane is to blame."

"No, of course it doesn't. That's not what I'm suggesting."

"So then, what?"

"The way I see it, he must have learnt something here which made him a threat to the killer. Or rather, the killer must have been afraid that was the case."

"If you're ruling out the baroness, we're left with the mayor, P.C. Brigham and the doctor. They were all involved in the plan to build on the Fane estate and could have killed to protect their reputations."

Instead of rebutting this claim, he displayed a troubled countenance and carried on towards the road. "How did you come to such a conclusion?"

"We know the mayor has staked everything on this project, and the only suggestion that he's not involved in the murders is your idea that he looked too guilty for that to be true. As for P.C. Brigham, he's been hostile and unhelpful, and I believe he has changed (or at least ignored) evidence in order to fit his theories and hide his own incompetence. He must realise that Adam isn't to blame for the vicar's murder. Perhaps he has even concluded that the baron's accident was no accident. Isn't it possible that Marcus coming to Seekings House was a step too far, and so our devoted local bobby took drastic action to prevent anyone finding out just how useless he is?"

"It's an interesting idea, but that wouldn't explain who killed the vicar in the first place. And what about the doctor? Have you any grand theory for how she might be involved?"

I had to reflect for a moment, as it was not an easy question to answer. "It's impossible to say, as we still haven't had the opportunity to speak to her. What we do know is that she opposed the development of this estate before suddenly changing her mind at the key moment and agreeing to the proposal."

His only reply was a nice noncommittal "Hmmm…" and so I kept talking.

"Or perhaps she hid the evidence of the baron's murder." I was rather impressed with myself again. "That's it! The baroness really did poison her husband, and she paid off the doctor to hide the evidence." He wore a pained expression, and my confidence drained away. "What have I done wrong now?"

He shook his head. "Nothing whatsoever. In fact, I'm rather impressed."

This was a real shock to me as I was back to believing that I was a true and unadulterated jobbernowl. "I must have said something ridiculous. Tell me what it was, or I'll be worrying about it all the way back to the village."

"Really, Christopher, you must have more faith in yourself. Your summary of the potential motives of three of our suspects was succinctly done, and you have given me something upon which to reflect."

I still didn't trust him. "But…?"

"There's no but." He was quite adamant. "You are in fine form, and it's most impressive to see."

"What about a *however* then?"

"I promise you Christopher. There are no buts, howevers, althoughs or despites. You're doing a marvellous job, and I commend you for it."

I might have blushed just then, not that anyone would have noticed with that wicked wind whipping my cheeks. I was feeling really quite jolly as I reached the road, only to realise that he hadn't actually answered my question.

"So what was it then?"

"What was what?"

I had to grind my teeth to stop from shouting, and I wondered whether we had fallen into some kind of farce. "What was it in our interview with Baroness Fane that has got you so agitated?"

"Any number of things." He was infuriatingly literal sometimes. "It was a remarkably enlightening interview, didn't you think?"

"I have no doubt." I fought the urge to gather a handful of snow and force it down the back of his neck. Instead, I took a calming breath and attempted to construct a question that even he couldn't avoid. "But what, in particular, did you hear in the discussion that made you want to rush from the house?"

"Ah, that's simple enough."

We were finally getting somewhere… until he noticed the lamppost into which the baron had crashed his car and stopped to examine it. "Hmmm…"

"Oh, not another *hmmm!*" I sounded a touch vexed.

"Look at that." He pointed to a scratch in the blackened lamppost. "You can see where the Lanchester made contact. The flames were as tall as I am."

"So that proves…"

"It proves that the baron's car hit this lamppost." He knelt down to look at the slight indentation from a different angle before nodding to himself and standing back up again. "As for the key piece of information that Baroness Fane provided, we now know that we are following a path taken by Marcus Alsop. The path that may well have got him killed."

I swallowed down my fear, as what else could I do? "And that's a good thing?"

"It is indeed." He clicked his heels together so that a puff of powdery snow took to the air. "Now, enough dawdling. It's cold, and I'd like to get inside."

Delilah took this as her sign to shoot off ahead of us, and I trundled along behind as best I could.

CHAPTER THIRTY-THREE

To save you from the next three minutes of frustration as we not only came close to losing our toes to frostbite, but I had to tolerate the few ambiguous statements that Grandfather saw fit to share, I will now jump ahead to our arrival in the village proper.

"…the upshot being that we must visit Emmeline Warwick in order to ascertain what her paramour discovered shortly before he was murdered."

As we were standing outside the Drop of Dew at this moment, it was hardly a surprise to hear this. Indeed, this was one fact about which I had left Seekings House feeling comparatively certain. What I didn't know was how Stamford Fane's death could have influenced that of the vicar or Marcus. Nor could I say how—

On second thoughts, things are complicated enough without more of my blithering. Here is a nice clear list of the queries that were ricocheting about the empty cavern in my head at that moment…

- **How did Baron Stamford Fane's death influence the subsequent murders?**

- **What did the vicar see that caused the killer to murder him in St Bartholomew's Church?**

- **Was it the same "quite unbelievable" thing of which Marcus had spoken in his final telephone call to Scarlet Warwick?**

- **Was the fact that the mayor had acted so guiltily, or that my grandmother had hidden her deeply held emotions on the case, enough to rule out one and incriminate the other?**

- **Was the doctor hiding from us out of guilt, or because she preferred to keep her Sundays free for doing jigsaw puzzles, tending to her garden and the like?**

- **Could P.C. Brigham's incompetence be a sufficient reason for him to go on a murderous rampage?**

- **Why and, most pertinently, when had Baroness Fane lied?**

- **Was there a really very obvious suspect we had failed to consider? The girls in the tea-rooms, perhaps, or maybe Mrs Stanley, the organist?**

There were surely far more doubts upon which I should have been musing. However, it wasn't just the answers I tended to lack, but the questions that might inspire them. One of my grandfather's favourite "foremost rules in a detective's notebook" – he promoted and demoted such maxims on a near daily basis – was the concept that, **in order to excel in our line of work, we must learn to ask the right questions**. This was something at which I was still a mere amateur, but he insisted I was improving all the time.

Whatever the reason, I entered the inn feeling less certain than I had in months. It wasn't merely that we had embarked upon the most taxing investigation in my short career, but that the witnesses were harder to read than a copy of 'Remembrance of Things Past' in the original French. Having said that, I tried to read the first volume of Proust's masterpiece in English, and it was almost as unfathomable. There was no plot whatsoever!

"Back again, are we?" the frankly rude landlady commented as we entered. She was just the type to sell a poisoned bottle of whisky, but I decided to keep this thought to myself.

"It would appear that we are," Grandfather said, whilst removing his gloves. His rabbit-felt top hat was covered in wet smudges from the snow and would require careful cleaning by our footman. "May I ask whether Miss Warwick is on the premises?"

The short, slightly hirsute woman did not respond verbally but pointed towards the lounge with a faint growl. Delilah took this as an instruction and scampered off to find a spot in front of the fire.

"You are too kind, madam," I said, proving that I could be just as insincere as the smooth-talking lord.

We continued on through the bar, where a few aged locals were busy staring into half empty pint glasses with forlorn looks on their faces. A much more cheerful sight would greet us in the neighbouring room. Scarlet had colonised the place and had gathered various chairs and low tables around her. The worn carpet, replete with the scent of spilt beer, wood smoke and tobacco, was covered in pages of scribbled notes, and the odd pile of books.

"I must be getting closer," she muttered to us without further ado, as though she'd been expecting us to arrive at that very moment. "I may have been mistaken when I blamed your grandmother for everything, Christopher, but the answer has to be here in Marcus's notes."

Grandfather wasn't one to stand on ceremony – unless the ceremony was one celebrating his myriad achievements. He carefully cleared a space on the chair beside her to see what she was examining.

"I have very much come to that same conclusion." The two fell silent for a few minutes to read, and I stood wondering what a place like the Drop of Dew might provide by way of afternoon tea. I could only imagine that it would amount to a tankard of lukewarm ale and very little else.

Scarlet became quite animated as she finished what she was reading and, for some curious reason, threw the pages into the air so that they floated to the ground like large, topical snowflakes. "What I don't understand is why Marcus wouldn't have simply told me what he had discovered on the telephone that afternoon. He could have spared us so much bother. It might even have saved his life."

Grandfather put a hand on her shoulder. "You must not trouble yourself with such unknowable details, my girl." The old chap was good at comforting our witnesses when required to do so. "The fact is that he didn't share his finding with anyone, but that doesn't mean we can't work out what it was."

Her tone instantly brightened. "You've discovered something important, haven't you?"

Perhaps sorry for her hostile welcome, the landlady appeared at this moment with three gigantic mugs of beer. "There ya go. Save ya getting up and coming to the bar." Her tone was as hostile as ever, but I wanted to believe there was a sense of atonement in the gesture. "I'll be watching you, mind. Make sure you don't leave without paying." Or perhaps not.

Once she had gone, my grandfather responded to Scarlet's question without the need for any clarification or even a demand that she rephrase the question. If only he could have exercised such flexibility with his grandson.

"I believe we have." He moved in closer to share the secret. "You see, we have just returned from a tete-a-tete with Baroness Sorel Fane. We learnt that Marcus had visited Seekings House on the day before he was murdered."

"I already knew that. What good does it do us?" There was something of the grumpy child about Scarlet that afternoon. She reminded me of my admittedly adult but still very juvenile brother, Albert. She folded her arms across her chest and waited for someone to say something that might cheer her.

"Have you read his notes from their meeting?" Grandfather still sounded optimistic.

"For all the good it's done me, yes. Marcus's handwriting is small and terribly smudged, but from what I can make out, he believed that the vicar's death was connected to the baron's plan to sell the Fane family estate."

"What did he make of the baroness?" I asked, as she was a puzzle I still hadn't solved. It wasn't every day I came across an elegant American lady with burning eyes and a pet African wild cat. I was torn between thinking her an angel of the highest order and a devil in disguise.

"Like all of us who spent time at Seekings House, he found her cold, conceited and really quite fascinating. Why do you ask?"

"Grandfather seems to think that she's given us the key to the whole case. Sadly, his elderly brain is faltering, and he cannot explain how or why."

It was Lord Edgington's turn to adopt a glum tone. "Very funny, Christopher. With jokes like that, you could abandon detective work and make a living on the stage."

"If I thought for one second that you would let me, I might well give it a go." I'd been stoking the fire as I spoke but now went to fetch a chair of my own.

Scarlet had handed my grandfather a few loose papers to read, and so he completely ignored me. I hadn't the faintest idea how she could know where anything was; the room looked as though someone had taken an axe to a small library, and the pages had gone spilling from the books.

"Is there anything which might enable us to solve the unsolvable?" I asked Scarlet while we waited for him to return to us.

"There is no such thing as an unsolvable case, Christopher," Grandfather intoned without looking up from the tightly scrawled text. "There are only inferior detectives."

"That sounds like me then," Scarlet confessed with a huff. "I've read every last word that he wrote and don't feel I know why anyone was killed."

Her failure rather heartened me. "I can certainly sympathise with you there. I rarely understand why people go about stabbing, shooting and strangling one another, even after Grandfather has explained the reason. It's not just the horrid violence of our cases that bothers me; murderers always insist on making everything as complicated as possible. I believe they're all quite barmy."

Despite her claim to the contrary, that capable young woman still had some interesting observations to make. "Marcus interviewed everyone in the town who was willing to talk to him. He uncovered plenty of minor secrets and seemed to believe he was on the right track, but he mainly focussed on who the vicar was and what he'd been doing here in Condicote."

"Why? Who was he then?" I had to ask. "That sounds like something we should have discovered by this stage in our investigation."

She briefly glanced towards the door through which we'd entered. "He was a drunk." It was another anti-climax.

"Oh, we knew that much. I thought you were about to tell me he was my grandmother's secret love child."

"That would have been interesting. Now, let me finish. Reverend Oldfield was a drunk but, as the vicar, he also held a seat on the town council. They would have needed everyone's vote to go ahead with the plans to knock down Seekings House and put up a swarm of new buildings. He would have been a soft touch."

"Surely that would be a good reason not to kill him. I can't imagine that the fellow who has replaced him will go along with things so quietly." I dropped my voice then, as it was a sorry confession I was about to make. "With all that apocalyptic preaching he favours, I find him rather frightening."

"Still, what if someone on the council did something illegal, which the original vicar discovered?" she asked, as though this could be the evidence we required.

"I'm sorry. That's a bit vague, even for me. Could you be more specific?"

One of the most admirable things about Scarlet Warwick was the passion that she could summon on just about any topic. "Bribery! Or perhaps even blackmail. Let's say that certain members of the council were paid to go along with the development. After the plan was agreed, they may have decided to tidy up a loose end by bumping off the vicar. When Marcus started rifling through their business, he had to go, too."

"Then what was his unbelievable discovery that he mentioned to you on the telephone that day?"

She was bursting with ideas, but when the time came to produce an answer to the most important question of all, nothing would emerge.

"I…" she began. "I… I really thought I had something, but it's like searching for a halfpenny coin on a misty day. Whenever I think I've caught a glimpse, the air changes, and I lose sight of it once more."

"That's exactly what it's like to spend time with my grandfather! It really is the most infuriating—" I had to cut this sentence short as Lord Edgington had finished reading Marcus's notes and was looking straight at me.

"Infuriating, am I?" He shook his head but said no more.

Scarlet moved from her Gainsborough armchair to look at the pages the old detective had been reading. "Marcus's account of his meeting with the baroness is hardly revelatory, is it?"

"It certainly doesn't seem to be." He took a moment to consider the papers in his hand. "The baroness was telling the truth when she told us that Marcus had asked many of the same questions that we had. He wanted to know more about her husband's past, but beyond Fane's profligacy and general brutishness, Marcus discovered very little. He doesn't seem to have connected the Seekings House construction to Reverend Oldfield in any substantial way. In fact, he was some distance behind our own investigation – which is to say, not very far at all."

Scarlet went to collapse in her previous spot. For each dead end we discovered, she became a little more dispirited. I was used to such moments, but they were clearly taking their toll on her. "We might as well declare it a lost cause. I've spent all week trying to make sense of what happened, but the truth is always out of sight."

Giving up was normally my favourite solution, but I couldn't say that we'd exhausted every avenue of investigation just yet.

Grandfather offered her a sympathetic smile. "When I was a superintendent in the Metropolitan Police, we occasionally solved crimes that had been open for years. One case I remember well was known as the Dalston Scrobbler. It started in March and wasn't solved until the following year."

I settled back in my chair to enjoy one of his stories but, when he said no more, I had to prompt him. "Oh, come along, Grandfather. You'll have to tell us who was scrobbled."

His moustache appeared to shrug somehow, and I could tell he was happy to recount one of his famous cases. "Children! There were children going missing all over London and it created the most terrible scandal. The newspapers were full of scare-lines claiming that no child was safe. They terrified the middle-classes, though in truth it was only children from poor families who were taken. We found no trace of any bodies and worked on the principle they were still alive somewhere.

"It became something of an obsession and, in time, I discovered the kidnapper's pattern. Each child was taken from a different district around the city, and the culprit was travelling around the centre like the hands of a clock. The one area he skipped was Dalston, and I had to believe there was a reason for it.

"I stationed men there undercover and, as the days passed, we noticed one man in particular who was acting strangely. He would go out in the middle of the night and leave bags of old clothes – mere rags really – far from his home. We didn't arrest him as we wanted to know for certain that he was our man. He seemed respectable enough in himself. He was married, and the couple had a thriving haberdashery shop in Hackney Wick. We didn't let him out of our sight for weeks, and then the time came. A child went missing in Battersea and it bore all the trademarks of the Scrobbler. The only problem was that our suspect was in a pub around the corner from his house at the time the child disappeared."

For a moment, his voice died away, and we were left with the sound of the smoking fire and the hubbub of voices from the bar.

Scarlet and I would not say another word until he spoke again.

"The disappearances didn't stop. Every few weeks, another child would go missing. I didn't give up on my suspect entirely, as we believed some of the clothes he'd discarded belonged to one of the scrobbled children. But every time there was a kidnapping, he'd be drinking alone in the Railway Tavern. I almost wondered whether he knew we were watching him and did it on purpose. In the end, I could stand it no more and went to the pub to talk to him. It turned out that he was a loquacious fellow after he'd had a few ales."

At this, Grandfather remembered the drink that the landlady had brought him and had a refreshing mouthful. I'd had a sniff of mine and decided it wasn't for me, but there was a rather stooped old lady on the other side of the fire who was most appreciative of a free libation.

"He told me of all his woes. His work, his wife, his cruel family. I almost felt sorry for the chap, but I felt even worse for the poor officers who'd spent two months following his every move. You see, I'd overlooked something incredibly simple that should have been obvious. I paid my bill in the pub that night and took the constable on duty over to Hackney to arrest our suspect's wife.

"She was a vicious, dangerous woman, and we had to call for reinforcements before we could arrest her. It turned out that she'd been kidnapping children and forcing them to work in the haberdashery business. She had ten of the poor blighters sewing away at all hours in the basement of their shop. The husband was not responsible for the kidnappings and, as far as I could tell, wanted nothing to do with his wife. He thanked me for stopping her and, the next time I saw him in the pub, he was the one buying the drinks."

"What a strange tale," I had to say. "Wasn't he an accessory to the crime? Shouldn't he have been in stir along with her?"

"In theory, perhaps, but he was the one feeding the children and keeping them safe from his monstrous wife. He believed that the common law concept of testimonial privilege prevented him from bearing witness against her, which is why he didn't tell the police. Every child that had been taken gave statements as to how well he'd treated them, and quite a few said that they were happier in that basement than they had been at home. The trial against him collapsed, and he was a free man. I believe he went on to employ several of the children in his shop."

Scarlet had looked puzzled for some time and now explained the reason. "I'm sorry. I've completely forgotten why you're telling us this?"

Grandfather had travelled back in time and needed a moment to hear her question. "I was trying to reassure you that a week is not long to investigate a crime. I'm sure you're doing very well as things stand, but the time has come to see what we can work out together."

CHAPTER THIRTY-FOUR

The evening passed quickly, and we ordered food from the bar to keep us going. We all read through Marcus's notes and attempted to make sense of the tragedies that had befallen the town. Between discussions, I consumed a chicken pie which was full of the most delicious gravy I'd eaten in… well, a little under six hours, if I'm honest, but it was still very tasty. I enjoy a mother-of-pearl-inlaid spoonful of caviar as much as the next fellow but give me a serving of freshly cooked nosh from a good honest public house, and I'm as happy as a prince.

"What was it that kept you here, Scarlet?" Grandfather asked during a break in our work. "Condicote does not seem like the place for an ambitious girl like you."

A small smile broke across her face. "I doubt you need me to tell you that, Lord Edgington. I came here for Marcus, and I stayed here for Marcus. For all that he rebelled against his family's way of doing things, he couldn't bring himself to desert his mother entirely, and so he moved a mere three miles away from her. I might have resisted provincial living at first, but I came to love the way of life here, just as he did."

She paused, and her eyes began to wander. "I may wish to write novels and change the world, but I see no problem in sparking a revolution from a small town near Tatchester. Every writer needs to start somewhere, and I find just as much to excite me in the characters who inhabit this curious place as I would in the centre of Paris or Rome."

"That is a noble statement." Grandfather closed his eyes in approval. Whenever he did this, he reminded me of an Indian mystic I had once seen on stage at the Holborn Empire. "I'm sure you must have extracted whole books' worth of inspiration from Baron Fane."

She looked up at the heavy wooden beams that held the floor above us. "I suppose you're right. He was fascinating and, unlike Marcus and Adam, every bit the rogue that many in Condicote believed him to be. But there was already something so theatrical about the man that, if I'd captured him in a novel, he would have seemed quite unrealistic."

Grandfather released a brief laugh. "I know exactly what you mean. I've met many such people myself."

I had also known such people and one of them was sitting there with us. I didn't say this out loud, of course. Instead, I raised a point that I'd been considering for some time.

"If we can't prove who the killer is, we must at least show that Adam Caswell is innocent. On the night the reverend was murdered, Adam didn't return here to the inn for several hours. Perhaps that in itself is enough to block the execution."

"In what sense?" Scarlet reengaged her investigative instincts.

"He wouldn't have murdered a man in order to steal from the church and then killed time doing nothing at the scene of the crime. The vicar was murdered at around eight o'clock, and yet the landlady said that Adam didn't return until midnight. There was absolutely no reason for him to linger there, and nowhere else to go on a cold Wednesday night in the winter."

Neither of them had an explanation for me, so I kept talking. "What of the black car he saw? Did the police investigate that? Perhaps the real killer waited for Adam to come down from his stargazing, tossed the ciborium onto the pavement and then raced off into the night. I noticed, for example that the mayor's Crossley 18/50 fits the description that Adam gave."

"P.C. Brigham wouldn't go looking for holes in a supposedly watertight case. And neither did I." Grandfather was reminded of his own failings at this moment. "I allowed the official version of events to cloud my instincts. I should have trusted the pair of you when you said that Adam couldn't be involved."

Scarlet wasn't to be distracted and returned to the point at hand. "I asked Brigham about the car, and he said there are a hundred black vehicles that pass through the town each week. He claimed that, without more details, it's like searching for a blade of grass in a meadow."

"Hmmm…" I was at it now.

"What is it, Christopher?" I believe my grandfather had enjoyed his beer a little too much, as he was ever so dramatic in his responses that evening.

"Oh, nothing. I just found it a surprisingly coherent simile. I didn't think that P.C. Brigham had it in him."

He'd lost his enthusiasm. "How very helpful."

Scarlet ignored the old man's grumpiness and presented another significant point. "The very fact that there was another murder in a small town whilst Adam was in prison is enough in my mind to prove his innocence. But it's not enough. To be certain that he doesn't hang, we have to find the real culprit and time is against us."

"It has to be someone on the local council," I decided, perhaps without the evidence to bolster such a claim. "Everything we've discovered takes us back to the plans for Seekings House."

Grandfather's thick golden wedding ring clicked against his tankard. "There is a high probability that Adam was the dupe selected to take the blame. The problem is that our killer is a mere shadow without a face to uncover. We normally come by a great number of suspects, and it is the motive that eludes us. Here in Condicote, we have the opposite problem. I believe that Marcus was murdered for investigating the vicar's death and that Reverend Oldfield himself had seen something he shouldn't have. Perhaps they both died to cover up the baron's murder, but we're still at a loss as to who could be responsible for any of it."

This was the problem we had to resolve that night. The conversation wandered from person to person and point to point. In time, with the sun long since set in the valley, and many of the Drop of Dew's patrons having already returned home for their supper, we turned our focus to the victims.

"Tell me about Marcus," Grandfather prompted. "I don't believe you explained how you first met."

I'm sure it was just my imagination, but Scarlet's eyes seemed to sparkle whenever she spoke of her fallen love. "We met in London a little over a year ago. It was Christmas, and I was visiting my brother, who took me to the Gargoyle Club to meet his glamorous friends. Baron Fane was there, holding court on the roof terrace, and I don't think that my brother appreciated someone else stealing the limelight. He soon disappeared – not giving a fig for his innocent little sister – but luckily Marcus found me."

She gazed down at her hands as she spoke. "Well, I say it was lucky but, in truth, he dragged me around to all sorts of sordid places. I remember that we went to an unlicensed beer house somewhere in the Isle of Dogs. By the end of the night, the baron was in such a state that we were sitting in the docks with the sun rising, surrounded by drunks and vagrants as he sang 'Rule, Britannia!' I wasn't worried about the danger or the grime or even the freezing cold. All I saw was Marcus Alsop."

She paused to savour the memory. "I didn't know that he was the son of a peer, or how much money he would have inherited when he turned twenty-one, but I knew he was quite magnetic. We'd talked the whole night through, and I'd barely paid attention to my surroundings for a second. I could have been to a Chinese opium den or on a cruise down the Nile, and I wouldn't have noticed anything but him. I knew that I was in love that very night. Perhaps even more surprising was that he felt the same way. He told me the next time we met and asked me to move here to be with him."

When I didn't know what to say on the matter, Grandfather spoke for the pair of us. "I'm sorry, Scarlet. I really am terribly sorry that Marcus died. From the way he reacted after his friend's trial, I could tell that he was a thoroughly principled young man."

I found my voice then. "He was just wonderful. It's not often that I've met anyone like Marcus and, from the moment he opened his room to us, I felt as though I was spending time with an old friend."

There was no doubt that her eyes were sparkling after this; they were awash with tears.

"I'm sorry, I didn't mean to upset you," I attempted to reassure her.

"You didn't." She put her hand on mine, and I felt the tiniest bit invincible. "It's lovely to hear anyone speak so fondly of him. It's a lot of fun being a pariah in a small town until, suddenly, it's not. But what you've both said was very kind."

"Perhaps it's time we returned to The Manor," Grandfather interjected before I could fall in love with yet another girl who would want nothing to do with me as soon as the investigation concluded. "I'll settle our bill." He rose and retreated to the bar.

I helped Scarlet gather her papers, while Delilah whimpered at the thought of going out into the cold. It seemed wrong that we had worked so hard without forming a clear resolution on the case, but at least we'd had a fine supper and managed to stay warm. By the standards of my grandfather's investigations, this was pure luxury.

I bid farewell to Scarlet and accompanied my mentor outside. The snow was still falling and the streetlights around the market square lent it a silvery quality. It was quite magical, in fact, as though God was distributing snowflakes like coins on Maundy Thursday.

The weather conditions were not the only thing that the bright lights illuminated. We could see the buildings along the main road quite clearly, and the doctor's surgery remained shuttered and dead. Grandfather stopped to look inside, but it was clearly a fruitless task, as the building was pitch black. I was about to tell him just this when the door gave way, and he stumbled over the front step.

Delilah knew to wait in the street as her master disappeared into the darkness. Even before he found the switch on the wall, I had a sense that something was wrong. The small surgery was flooded with a sudden burst of electric light, and our eyes jumped to the body of the one suspect to whom we hadn't had the chance to speak. Dr Beresford-Gray was lying on the floor beside her desk with a surgical tourniquet around her neck.

Lord Edgington walked into the room to look at her a little more closely. "I'm afraid she's quite—"

"Dead, Grandfather? Yes, obviously she is." I may have uttered a soft tut. "You don't have to say it every time we find a body."

"Oh… sorry."

CHAPTER THIRTY-FIVE

It would turn out to be a long night. I went in search of P.C. Brigham, who was dozing at his post in the station. I gave him his instructions to call Scotland Yard and, though he was clearly reluctant to involve them, he eventually did as requested.

"Are you sure she's even dead?" he complained as he waited to be connected.

"Quite sure. Her skin is grey, and she's not breathing. Lord Edgington thinks that she was murdered at some point this afternoon."

He showed little interest in this information but replied with the standard response that people make when they don't know how to comprehend such news. "Terrible business this is. What is the world coming to? I was talking to the doctor only this morning."

I didn't like to hazard a guess, and it was at that moment that the constable was connected to an officer at Scotland Yard. With his one important task achieved, he accompanied me to the scene of the crime.

I would probably have gone home and got some sleep, but Grandfather felt it was his job to stand guard over the cadaver until the real police arrived.

"If the Yard had been called in when Marcus was murdered, there might not have been another killing." I had not expected him to take such a tone with P.C. Brigham, but there was no restraining him in moments like this. "Your string of failures here is unprecedented, and I will be making a formal complaint against you to the Tatchester Constabulary."

"But…" I thought the man in the blue uniform might cry. "But I was just doing my job. I never…" This was as much as he could summon by way of a defence. "I'll wait outside for the moment, shall I?"

"No, you'll take my dog and make sure she's looked after in the station." This was perhaps a touch pushy on the old lord's part, but his flared nostrils and stormy expression told the constable it would be in his best interests not to argue.

"Have you found anything significant, Grandfather?" I asked when we were alone.

"I can see nothing that will tell us who killed her. Perhaps, with their scientific techniques, my former colleagues will be able to uncover a clue that we have failed to detect."

"Isn't it true, this time, that the killer would require some strength to have murdered the doctor?" I was certain this would play some part in leading us to the culprit, but my superior was unconvinced.

"He would require two hands, that's for certain, and perhaps we can rule out children under the age of twelve, but it would not take a strongman to strangle someone with such a rudimentary device. Any reasonably fit adult could have done it. I have to assume that the doctor was murdered from behind, which would have made fighting off her attacker more difficult."

"Why do you say that?" There was bound to be some evidence I had missed.

"Well, the absence of a struggle, primarily." He moved around the room to point out relevant details as he spoke. "From the look of things, I would say that the doctor opened the door to her killer, or perhaps it was unlocked, and he just strolled inside to carry out his task. If you look here on the floor…" He knelt to examine a series of black marks on the white and blue Spanish tiles. "…I think that this is where it happened."

"You mean to say that the marks were left by the soles of her shoes as she fought for breath?"

"Precisely. The more pressing question is whether she knew the killer or not. However, I believe the answer is fairly obvious. It is Sunday after all."

It took me a few seconds to realise what he was implying. "You're right, there are few people in the village, and outsiders would have been noticed even more readily than on a weekday."

"Exactly. On our walk from The Manor to Seekings House after lunch we wandered past any number of cottages with the owners sitting in their front rooms looking out at the street. It is quite the pinnacle of entertainment in Condicote in the winter, and I believe that one of them can be relied upon to tell us if any unknown figures made an appearance today."

"So, more evidence, but nothing to lead us to the murderer." I sounded (and indeed felt) a little morose. "I prefer our cases when they resemble detective stories."

He stopped his examination to look at me in something approaching horror. "What on earth do you mean?"

"You know," I insisted. "The type with suspicious champagne corks or monogrammed cufflinks planted on the body. In the books I've read, the killers always slip up somewhere along the line, but this fellow seems to be rather clever, don't you think?"

"Yes, he's far too clever, but we'll get him." He looked at the marks on the floor once more. "He should have stopped after the vicar. I doubt that it was his plan to keep killing, but the more he does it, the easier it will be to uncover the swine. Imagine that each murder is a point on a map. He's killed at least three times now, and we can triangulate exactly where he is."

"That's an awfully pretty turn of phrase, Grandfather. Unfortunately, it's not true. We don't have his co-ordinates. We have a series of victims. We're no closer to naming the culprit than we were an hour ago."

He stood up stiffly and went to look at the doctor's bookshelf. I'd already had a peek myself and there was nothing particularly interesting. There were books on anatomy and illness, but not a Dickens among them.

"You may be right, Christopher," he said with his back to me. "But although it feels that we are far from the truth, the answers may be contained in this very room."

I doubt that, I thought but didn't say. I was looking at a woman to whom I'd never said spoken. She had pale blonde hair, with streaks of grey showing through, and a thin, serious face. There was no fear in her expression, as literature had taught me to expect. Perhaps it was the effect of death on her muscles, but she looked perfectly calm.

"Christopher, we're miles from London and a detective won't be here for some hours. If you'd prefer to go home, I won't judge you for a second."

I did want to go home, but not to my grandmother's drafty old place, or even my grandfather's estate. I wished I could be transported to my family home at Kilston Down – to my childhood bedroom, where I still had a collection of soft toys and all the books I'd read aged four to eighteen. That was the only place that could offer much comfort at such a moment, but I knew where I was needed, and I'd made my choice.

"Thank you, Grandfather, but I'll stay. After all, the foremost rule in a detective's notebook is that **two pairs of eyes are better than one.**"

He turned from the bookshelf, looking a little surprised. "I don't remember telling you that. Although it is quite undebatable."

"You didn't. It's one of mine."

He clapped his hands together in celebration. "Wonderful stuff, Christopher. After all, the foremost rule in a detective's notebook is that **it is each detective's prerogative to establish his own foremost rule.**"

It was sometimes hard to know whether he was joking or serious. I had to conclude that *somewhere in the middle* was normally the answer.

"What shall we do until the detectives arrive?"

I was hoping he might suggest that we lock the surgery and return to the pub to warm up, but I would not be so lucky. We settled down on the floor between a filing cabinet and a cupboard stuffed with medical equipment. I was so bored within five minutes that I put my gloves back on and looked through the doctor's files.

"Gosh," I muttered to myself. "There's a farmer in the village who's allergic to the effluvium of new hay. He must spend his whole life around the stuff."

Grandfather took the file from my hand. "Yes, it's quite a common malady. They say that William IV was a sufferer."

"That is quite fascinating, but there is one thing I don't understand."

"Oh, yes? What's that?"

"I don't know what effluvium means."

He chuckled under his breath. "It means smell. Now those are private files, so stop spying on the villagers of Condicote and put them back where you found them."

I was about to do just this when I noticed Stamford Fane's name on a manilla folder. "I suppose that means you don't want to look at this, then?" I held it out, and he snatched it from my hand.

"What a surprise; Dr Beresford-Gray inspected the baron's body before the local coroner approved her findings."

"What's surprising about that?"

He viewed me through the side of one eye. "I was being sarcastic."

"Well, it didn't sound like it. You should make it clearer, like… 'what a *surprise*'!"

He ignored me and explained what he hadn't discovered. "There's nothing particularly revealing in the doctor's case notes. The baron was a heavy-set, comparatively healthy man who drank too much alcohol one day and got behind the wheel when he shouldn't have. The impact of the crash may have knocked him out, but the subsequent fire, which was exacerbated by the bottle of whisky he had just bought and the alcohol already in his body, certainly finished him off. There's nothing to say that his death coming so soon before the two murders wasn't just a coincidence."

"Didn't you once tell me that coincidences are a lazy detective's excuse not to do his job properly?"

"Happenstance then."

I had a better idea. "Even if the baron's death is exactly what it seemed, perhaps Fane owed money to someone other than Marcus and, when he was dead and couldn't pay, it set in motion the chain of events that led us here."

"So tell me the name of the killer?" Grandfather held me in his gaze. "Who can connect everything we've discovered – everything we know? Who is to blame for all this destruction?"

I had to think about this and, when it was apparent that I didn't have an answer, I turned back to the tall green cabinet. "This is the vicar's file. Perhaps we'll find what we need in here."

"Very well." He looked a little dubious but accepted the papers that I held out to him. "Reverend Oldfield was an alcoholic. He had the liver of an old man who'd spent his life working in a pickling plant." His tone suddenly became more urgent. "That must be the answer! Someone murdered the vicar to help him avoid the misery of a long, slow demise."

I wrinkled my nose. "Or perhaps not."

CHAPTER THIRTY-SIX

It was the middle of the night by the time the police arrived. Two detectives I had never met before turned up in a small Ford van. They were calm and professional; the sort of hardworking types that my grandfather had told me were lacking when he was a young officer, but which the Metropolitan Police now worked hard to attract. They analysed the crime scene with the clinical detachment required of their profession, though they were unable to discover anything that my grandfather had missed.

So that was that; another body in Condicote, another victim to add to our list. Grandfather, Delilah and I trudged back to my grandmother's house feeling thoroughly dejected. It was quite possible that we'd spotted the killer ten times that weekend and not put a name to his face. For all we knew, he could have been an old man staring out at us from one of the thatched cottages, or a drinker in the Drop of Dew.

I struggled to remember another case which had so defeated us. My grandfather's normally brilliant brain seemed dull, like the edge of a knife that has been used for too long. My brain, on the other hand, was more like a knife that someone had crafted out of butter. Granny had already gone to bed, and the only person still roaming the halls of The Manor was our footman, Halfpenny. It was a sorry homecoming, and I wished that the rest of my family had been there to commiserate with us.

"Don't be too hard on yourself, Chrissy. You've done your best today. Sometimes things simply do not finish the way we hope they will." We had come to a stop on the landing, and he looked at me in a sympathetic manner.

"There are now less than two days remaining to save Adam," was all I could think to say to that. "He'll hang first thing on Tuesday morning. It's not enough time."

He gulped for air before trying once more to encourage me. "We're not giving up just yet, boy. And there is another day ahead of us before we have to panic."

"Goodnight, grandfather," I mumbled, when no other words would come, and then turned towards my room in search of rest.

I'd hoped that my dreams that night would bring me comfort, but they were full of images that I would rather not have witnessed. I saw Marcus, full of life on the top of King Arthur's Camp, before a hooded killer raised a gun to the poor man's head and pulled the trigger. I saw that same devil wrap the rope around Reverend Oldfield's neck and then strangle the life out of Doctor Beresford-Gray. I saw flashes of Baron Fane, but I couldn't tell whether he was screaming as he suffered the same fate or laughing at the other victims' anguish.

I woke up in a sweat at a half-past five and wouldn't fall asleep again until the sun was rising. We had dealt with more savage killers. We had even encountered greater tragedies than this sequence of deaths. But I had never felt so depleted as I did when I forced myself from bed the next morning. So it came as some surprise that my grandfather was full of the joys of the spring that still hadn't arrived.

"Today is the day, Christopher." He swept into the breakfast room, his long grey coat billowing behind him, and his top hat and cane stowed beneath one arm.

"What have you possibly got to be so happy about?" this was my grandmother talking, but it could just as well have been me.

"Today is the day," he repeated. "I have no doubt about it. Today is the day we find the culprit and save Adam Caswell from his unjust sentence."

"Upon what, exactly, are you basing this assertion?" this was Granny again – I was busy chewing on a buttered crumpet and couldn't talk.

"My years of experience, high rate of success and a feeling in my bones."

Granny let out a squeak of disbelief. "That doesn't sound very scientific, Edgington. But best of luck to you." She almost sounded as though she didn't want us to solve the case, though perhaps this was her standard level of misanthropic pessimism.

"I appreciate your generous support, Loelia, but luck is not something upon which I tend to rely."

I spent the time they were exchanging pithy comments collecting food to take with me so that, when grandfather declared, *it's time to go, Christopher!* I would be ready.

"It's time to go, Christopher!" he instantly declared, and I was up on my feet in seconds (with a napkin full of goodies all wrapped up and ready to leave the house).

"Where are we heading?" I asked.

"I appreciate your spirit." He was full of positivity and squeezed my shoulder. "We're going up to King Arthur's Camp to have a look at the spot where Marcus was murdered."

I sat back down at the table and shuffled my chair in as far as it would go. "On second thoughts, I think I'd better stay here in case anyone from Scotland Yard should call."

"Nonsense, my boy. It is a crisp, sunny morning (not that you'd know it within this tenebrous mausoleum.)" He didn't actually say the second clause of this sentence, but he cleverly implied it with a grimace and a shudder. "It is the perfect moment for us to tackle the world."

I tipped my head back in defiance. "There's a foot of snow on the ground. It's below freezing point, and I've seen the slope up to King Arthur's Camp, and it is steep."

"You say that, Christopher, but…" Instead of finishing this thought, he strolled forward and attempted to pull my chair out from under the table.

"Oh no you don't!" I bellowed, but he wouldn't stop.

Suffice it to say that, two minutes later, I walked out of the house feeling very disappointed in my pathetically weak grip.

"Don't be so blue." He made no attempt to conceal his pride. "You're not the first young tearaway I've had to wrestle to my will. It's not a question of strength. The secret is that there's a muscle in your—"

"I'd rather we talked about the case, if that's all right with you." I used a formal tone, as I did not want to be reminded of my humiliation. Just imagine being overpowered by a seventy-six-year-old! The sheer embarrassment was too much to bear.

"Ah yes, the case." I believe he actually patted himself on the back at this moment, though he may have been removing an errant thread or a piece of fluff.

I was lost for words… except for the following ones. "It's come to you in your sleep, hasn't it? You know who the killer is."

Running between us, Delilah issued a doubtful bark. Her master frowned in that special way of his that I was fairly certain meant that he was smiling inside. "I cannot make any such claim just yet. I do not know the name of the killer, but I do believe that a picture is beginning to form." He touched his back again and… Yes! It was definitely a pat. That conceited Herbert!

We had left the main road and were following a fence that cut near vertically up the hillside.

"Are you going to tell me what you've realised, or do I have to guess?"

He was smiling away to himself, and I had begun to doubt that we were actually related. If I'd had one tenth of his self-assurance, I would have been able to talk to beautiful young ladies, successfully identify murderers and engage in witty banter. As it was, absolutely none of his confidence had been passed down to me.

"I haven't realised anything, Chrissy." Oh, joy! Another riddle for me to solve. It was Monday morning, and I didn't have the energy. "You have been the driving force behind our every triumph this week."

I would have told him how unexpected this was if I hadn't been pulling myself up the mountain hand over hand. Very well, it was a hill, but it felt more like the north face of the Eiger.

"I did what?" I'm not certain he could make sense of this, what with the deep breaths I had to take between words.

"You have inspired me, dear grandson. You have trained your finely honed analytical mind while I wallowed in my failures. Without your presence this weekend, I would have looked a fool."

I had to stop for a moment. The double blow of pure amazement and physical exhaustion really knocked the wind from my dangerously skinny body. "Are you sure you're thinking of the right person?"

He looked down at St Bartholomew's as though it were one of the Seven Wonders of the ancient world. "It would be difficult to mistake you for anyone else."

"Come along, then. Tell me what masterstroke I have delivered."

"It was last night, in the doctor's surgery." He moved off once more. "Not for the first time, you reminded me that I sometimes fail to examine our victims' backgrounds because I devote so much of my attention to our suspects. I admit that, though it is a minor failing, I am prone to overexcitement when on the hunt for a killer."

"That is most magnanimous of you." I had fallen some yards behind. The one advantage of having an impossibly youthful grandfather is that, much like one of those immense ice-breaking boats they send to the arctic circle, he was terribly good at clearing a path through the snow. Delilah kept running up and down the hill to show us how easy life can be if you happen to have four legs.

When we reached the top, I wasn't nearly so far behind the old chap as I'd expected. I got there less than a minute after him and would have patted myself on the back if I'd had any energy left.

"Isn't it wonderful?" he asked, noisily pulling the air in through his nostrils so that his nose pinched together. "The Tatchester region is an underrated jewel within Great Britain's sparkling crown."

The sun was low in the perfectly blue sky, but it was glorious to experience real sunshine after a day of foul weather. The warmth made me feel better about the possibility I had caught frostbite by climbing up there without adequate clothing. I was no Captain Scott and was wearing the brown leather shoes I'd previously worn with my school uniform.

"The snow is a kind of rebirth. It refreshes as it transforms." He sighed happily. "I don't believe I've ever fully appreciated that before."

What I couldn't appreciate was what we were doing up there at such an hour. I extracted my parcel of food from my duffel coat and had a quick marmalade sandwich as I sat on the bench where Marcus's body had presumably been found. Delilah perched beside me looking hungry, but I was no muggins and would not give in to her manipulation. Well, I would, but she only got one cinnamon pastry and a croissant out of me, though I could tell she wanted more.

"Why did we have to come all the way up here?" I asked, once my stomach was a little less furious. "We can't possibly find any clues with so much snow on the ground."

He shook his head, still smiling his over-the-top smile. "You missed the point, Christopher. We are not here to search for evidence. I am already satisfied with our perception of each crime, and we have even narrowed down our field of suspects to a few key names. The reason we are here is that it is the finest point in the valley from which to appreciate Condicote."

"I see," I replied before taking another bite. I didn't, of course, but it really was such a tasty sandwich that I didn't mind what he said. If only I'd had a nice thick Welsh quilt to keep me warm – and a change of socks – I would have had no complaints.

I stuffed the crusts into my mouth, brushed the crumbs from my clothes and went to see why he was making such a fuss.

CHAPTER THIRTY-SEVEN

King Arthur's Camp had once been a hill fort. It was a raised ring on the top of the highest mound in the valley and gave a perfect view of that white and pleasant land. I could just make out Tatchester, ten miles distant, with its impressive cathedral towering over the town.

The mound on which we stood would have been occupied in the time of King Arthur and right back to the days when Roman soldiers walked those ancient lands. Even without the incredible view, I loved the thought of all the history that had taken place there.

"What do you see, my boy?" Grandfather had shifted into a romantic frame of mind. "Can you not divine the majesty of God's hand in the undulation of this exquisite landscape?" He sounded like William Wordsworth, and I was afraid he might compose a poem or break into song.

"I can see St Bartholomew's and my grandmother's house," I answered, no doubt too literally for his liking. "Oh, and the land to the south belongs to my family, too."

"What about up to the north?" His questions were so full of enthusiasm that I wondered whether he'd forgotten the string of murders and the innocent man who was soon to hang.

"There are several rows of cottages around the market square, and the Fane estate is in the woods beyond."

"You're quite right." He was proud of me that morning and I really couldn't say why. "That is just what I hoped you would notice."

Perhaps he'd started the day with a nip of whisky to keep off the cold. Or perhaps... no, that's the only explanation that came to mind.

"It is just as the mayor told us," he finally explained. "The town is boxed in by the two large estates and the steep hills. A narrow valley is not the ideal place to build a village, but then whoever settled here in the days of yore wasn't to know that there would be a population boom a millennium later."

I laughed for his sake.

"The members of the town council are in a difficult position; that much is clear. They could never convince your grandmother to sell The Manor, which only leaves Seekings House and the estate around it. So when the baron died, a seismic disturbance occurred. The baroness could have made things difficult for everyone involved, though we have seen nothing to suggest that was the case. In fact, from all she told us, she is eager to leave Tatchester as soon as her dead husband's family home is turned to dust."

"Are you saying she's our killer?" I couldn't just let him ramble. "There is a quality to her which I found quite formidable. We know that she was hiding something and, on top of that, her cat gave me a nasty scratch."

With the sun streaming down to turn his white hair golden, Grandfather considered the probability of such a scenario. "She is certainly the person with the most to gain from the development. If whatever Marcus and the vicar discovered was related to the viability, or perhaps legality, of the project, then it would have made sense for her to kill to ensure its completion."

"And yet, you don't think she's to blame?"

"I still cannot say." He seemed distracted and closed his eyes in order to concentrate. "We are here to consider the different sequences of events that could have taken place. One thing that seems likely is that, of the five people on the council, at least Dr Beresford-Gray was paid or otherwise persuaded to change her vote. I believe that is why she hid from us each time we saw her this week, and perhaps even why she was murdered."

"Yes, that would make sense." I was finally entering into the game he had started. "If the whole thing was built on bribes and manipulation, there's a good chance that the doctor became scared. Perhaps she threatened to go to the police, but the killer got her before she could say anything."

Feeling the cold at last, he went for a stroll around the hill fort. Hunched down in a ball, with her scrounged breakfast scoffed, clever old Delilah stayed behind on the bench.

"The poor woman would have been terrified," Grandfather declared in full voice. "And so we must ask ourselves, if she was being bribed, who was paying her?"

"The baron, I suppose?"

"That was my first thought, too, but we know that Fane had to borrow from Marcus to invest in the project that would have saved him from bankruptcy. We also know that, as soon as he had money in his wallet, he would stake it on a game of chance. That was his addiction, much as Reverend Oldfield couldn't resist a glass of tipple."

"The mayor then?"

"That is possible. After all, we don't know whether the doctor's silence was bought with thirty pieces of silver or three hundred. Of course, the richest person in town is—"

"Granny." It felt as though I'd had to defend the woman a thousand times already. I wasn't sure I had it in me to do it again.

"That's correct."

"But why would she have gone to such lengths to support the development? She would have made her sworn enemy rich in the process."

"Yes, she hated Baron Fane. I know that, and I've only been to Condicote a few times before. However, what she disliked about him wasn't his scandalous behaviour, the company he kept, or the wicked deeds in which he indulged. As you yourself told me, it was the fact that he had a grander house than she did. Loelia hasn't spent a farthing on The Manor since your grandfather died twenty years ago. She is a true miser in every sense of the word. And yet—"

"Can you please stop this? We don't have time." Something came over me like a headache at this moment, and I couldn't listen to any more theories. For all the time I'd spent with the venerated Lord Edgington, for all the dangerous situations in which we'd found ourselves, I'd rarely felt so hopeless as I did in that moment. "We can go on imagining plausible scenarios until Adam hangs, but it's not going to get us any closer to the killer because we're chasing a ghost."

I raised my voice as another wave of panic passed through me. "We've gone around in circles a hundred times. We've stated all the ways in which our few remaining suspects could be to blame for the murders, and then listed the evidence that proves they are not. I'm tired of trying and failing, but you're acting as though life is roses all the way."

"I don't know what you mean, boy." Rather than attempting to understand me, he became firm and formal. "There's certainly no reason to overreact."

I couldn't stay there any longer and marched back to the viewpoint to sit on the bench with Delilah. I didn't blame her for avoiding the snow. That stuff was terribly cold.

Grandfather soon caught up with me. He patted the placid beast affectionately and waited for me to calm myself. "You seem a touch out of heart, boy. Is everything all right?"

"All right? It's better than all right." The fitful murmur in which I spoke told him all he needed to know. "Everything is fantastic."

"There is no reason to be so defeatist. We may not have determined the full story, but we soon will." For once, his enthusiasm was less than infectious.

"That's easy to say, but the only people who would have had any interest in killing the unlucky victims are my septuagenarian grandmother, a baroness whose glamorous presence in the village stands out like an elephant in a swimming pool, a mayor who is so scared of our investigation that he can't speak to you without incriminating himself, and a policeman with the deductive skills of a blind, hairless, newborn bunny rabbit."

He could see how desperate I was becoming and spoke more softly. "That may be true, but we've faced such odds before and prevailed."

"You're not listening," was the only response I could summon as I turned away from him to look across the village. Delilah apparently understood the situation better than her master and pushed her head under my arm in sympathy.

"You must believe in yourself, Christopher. All the way through this investigation, you've evaluated the suspects correctly. On several occasions now, you've had to convince me of the truth when I refused to see it, and I'm sorry that I didn't believe you from the beginning."

I looked at him again and tried to explain the division between us. "You don't understand what I'm saying. For all your positivity, you can't change the fact that we haven't a clue which of our suspects is the culprit." I paused in the hope he'd finally listen. "Perhaps we've finally found a competent murderer, and this will be the case that defeats us."

"It's natural to doubt yourself. I was just like you when I was young." He continued with the same oblivious attitude, and it only made me more frustrated.

"No, you're wrong. I know what I'm capable of these days. But we've met so many competent people that it's hard for me to believe I should be the one at your side. Miss Warwick would make a wonderful assistant. Great Caesar! Even Granny could do better than me. And that is why the two of us together simply cannot solve this case."

This was what made him sit back on that bench and study me as he would one of our suspects. This was the moment when he realised what I was trying to say.

"If that is the case, then I have two things to tell you." He took his time discharging a long, steady breath before taking in another to replace it. "First, congratulations are in order. I'm happy to hear that you can see where your strengths lie without me telling you. And second, you are wrong. We are standing on the precipice of a great discovery. We may have collected all the evidence we require without identifying the savage behind the murders, but that just makes me more certain that we will catch him today."

I wanted to believe him, I really did, but I was tired of bashing my head against a brick wall (and perhaps a little cranky from lack of sleep).

"No more negativity," he said and, after almost two years working alongside one another, I finally had him.

"Grandfather, if you're going to be so bossy, could you please speak in full sentences? It is an Englishman's duty to use correct grammar."

"My goodness, you're right." He looked truly horrified. "I don't know what I was thinking... you've had more of an impact upon me than I realised."

He'd made me smile. "Your secret is safe with me. I won't tell a soul."

Delilah gave a happy bark, and her owner ruffled the hair under her chin. "We know you won't tell anyone, girl. The chance would be a fine thing."

I stood up to hold out my double-gloved hand to him. "Come on, old fellow. We don't want you to fall over in the snow."

"You insolent tyke." He accepted my offer, nonetheless. "The only way you can make amends is by forgetting all your pessimism and looking at the case with fresh eyes."

We began the far more relaxing return leg of the journey, and Delilah descended from the bench to rocket down the hill. I tried to refuse his request, but I could never stay angry with him for long.

"Very well, then. I've changed my mind. The only people who could be the killer are Baroness Fane and my grandmother."

"What a fascinating proposition!" Grandfather was quite as buoyant as his dog just then. "And what makes you say such a thing?"

"It's simple. For all that the London papers love to focus on the degeneracy of the working classes, as far as I can see, it's the aristocracy who are forever killing one another. Just think of the number of demented dukes and viperous viscounts we've encountered. This isn't even our first case that began with the untimely death of a baron in an automobile."

"You may have a point, my boy." He turned over my idea for a moment before developing a more serious mien. "Actually, you *may* have a point." The closer we got to the bottom of the hill, the more enthusiastic he became. "You're a genius, Christopher. An unmitigated genius. You will surely get a knighthood for this."

"I have no idea why, but I accept the compliment."

"Well, perhaps not a knighthood then," he corrected himself. "But a commendation of some sort. Or a mention in the newspaper. And if not, you at least deserve my humble thanks."

"Grandfather, what are you twaddling about now?"

He straightened up and feigned insult. "I am a Marquess, boy: a peer of the realm. You may accuse me of any number of sins, but Marquesses never twaddle."

"Fine, then what did I say that was so clever?"

He stopped and placed both hands on my shoulders. "You reminded me that no investigation occurs within a vacuum. I should have thought back to our past cases to solve this one. I've overlooked a very basic principle, but I finally see everything as it really is. And that is thanks to you."

"Then you're very welcome." I must admit, I was feeling rather proud of myself. "Now, perhaps we can go back to Grandma's house for a little more breakfast. I gave Delilah more of my pastries than I'd intended."

"Breakfast?" The tone of his voice jumped several notes higher. "How can you be thinking about food at a time like this? We must gather the suspects, talk to the police, and confirm that every piece of evidence we've acquired fits with our new theory."

"I beg your pardon, do you mean to say that—"

"Yes, that's exactly what I mean." I didn't know what he meant by saying that this was what he meant, as I hadn't finished saying what *I* meant. "I told you it wouldn't be long before we reached a turning point. You've done it, Chrissy. You've solved the case."

CHAPTER THIRTY-EIGHT

There were more than a few tasks to complete that morning before we could tie together all the loose ends, and the first was achieved before we'd even made it to town. We caught sight of Reverend Bodsworth, who was passing on his predecessor's bike as Grandfather called to him.

"One moment, please, reverend." We accelerated a little and, by the time we had reached the churchyard, Grandfather was pretending to be out of breath. "I'm so sorry to delay you. I just have one simple question to ask."

The thick-set priest looked curious and stepped off the bicycle. "Oh, yes? How can I help you, Lord Edgington?"

"I was wondering about Reverend Oldfield."

"Ahh, yes. A terrible business. I only met the man a few times before I moved here, but have heard that he was much loved in these parts."

"I have no doubt he was. However, I have a question about the direction from which he came on the night he was murdered. Was it in Yockwardine that he'd been visiting his flock?"

"Let me think now. I follow the same route myself." He paused, as though determined to be as accurate as possible. "I believe that he died on a Thursday, and so he would have taken the road to Radsoe before going on a loop through Newminster and coming back via... Yes, he'd have returned to the village on the Yockwardine road."

"Just as I thought. That is most helpful." Grandfather bowed his head. I noticed that he had an innate respect for the clergy that he didn't always show everyday folk.

"You are most welcome." A pall came over the vicar's face, and I could tell he felt guilty for being so blithe. "I'm afraid I must hurry. I need to be back here for a service at noon. There is no rest for the wicked." Such an expression is normally delivered with a frisson of irony, but there was none of that from Reverend Bodsworth. His face sombre, he climbed back on the bicycle and rode away.

"What a dry chap he is," I commented once he had passed Grandmother's house. "The village was better off with Reverend Oldfield than that cold fish."

Grandfather seemed less perturbed by his behaviour. "I agree.

There is a tendency in certain clergyman to look at the world through dark lenses. Let us hope it is just the pressure of his new role or the gloom of his predecessor's death that has made him that way."

"Imagine him conducting Albert and Cassandra's wedding? It would be enough to put me off marriage for life!"

Grandfather clipped me fondly around the back of the neck and we went to look for the detectives from Scotland Yard. Delilah was clearly excited by my discovery – the details of which I wasn't fully aware – and skipped alongside us all the way. And yes, dogs can skip. I saw it with my own two eyes.

My esteemed mentor still refused to explain the grand revelation I had inspired. "You have all the information you need to solve this case, Christopher. I will not patronise you by explaining any further."

"But I'd like to be patronised," I insisted. "I really don't mind in the slightest."

He stopped talking, and I knew there was no sense in trying to convince him. We found the two detectives from the night before asleep in their van outside the doctor's surgery. My grandfather didn't object to them getting a little rest, but their superior officer had just arrived and looked particularly put out at what he saw.

"You should be taking turns to guard the scene of the crime!" Chief Inspector Darrington barked through the window to wake them up. "Do not besmirch the good name of the Metropolitan Police by falling asleep in public."

"Yes, sir. Sorry, sir," they replied in short, clipped phrases, apparently intimidated by the stern inspector.

Darrington had something of a smirk on his face as he led us towards the Drop of Dew. "Can you tell me what's been going on in this town? It seems it has become a hotbed of criminal activity. I certainly never expected to be called out to a Tatchester village twice in quick succession."

"It should have been three times, in fact. Marcus Alsop, who became Viscount Tatchester on his father's death, was killed here a week ago." Grandfather was surely about to commence a long, twisting explanation of all we had investigated when he took pity on me. "Christopher, you might just as well go home and get some rest. Darrington and I will go over the evidence that we've accumulated, and then we'll gather the various players in St Bartholomew's at one o'clock. How does that sound?"

I couldn't quite believe he was being so thoughtful. "Oh, if I must. I look forward to seeing you a little later." I tipped my imaginary cap to them, which reminded me just how cold my head was and that I really must wear a hat in such weather.

Having travelled through a great range of emotions that morning – not least despair at the thought of Adam's fate the following day – I was in a sanguine mood as I passed back through the village. In the marketplace, fruiterers and butchers were calling to customers to buy their goods. Mrs Eileen Grout's shop was open once more, and there were boxes of produce on sale in the street outside. I had no doubt that the horrifically violent crimes were on every villager's lips, but it felt as though life had returned to normal.

Even if I hadn't been the one to identify the killer, per se, I felt happy to have been a cog in an ever-so-effective machine. Well, I did for a minute or two as I strolled along the road, but then I was struck by a sudden revelation.

This was all a test. Grandfather hadn't let me go wandering back to Granny's house to rest and enjoy a spot of elevenses. He'd left me alone with my thoughts so that I would reflect upon my shortcomings.

And what thoughts they were.

If the chasm in my head was a graveyard, then every element of the case had transformed into a tombstone. Mayor Eric Hobson's name was the first I noticed, but he did not seem significant enough in all that had occurred to be the killer. I remembered my theory that the crimes had been committed by an aristocrat, and my grandmother's headstone loomed over me. Was she really as cold hearted as she wanted everyone to believe, or was she merely entangled in a sad case that held no real connection to our family?

I spotted the other names we'd considered. Useless P.C. Brigham. Cunning Baroness Sorel Fane. Dead Dr Beresford-Gray – it seemed safe to rule out her involvement, at least. We normally had a larger pool of suspects from which to draw, and so I cast my net wider. Bob Thompkins was the verger at St Bartholomew's. He could have held a grudge against Reverend Oldfield that we'd never discovered. And Eileen Grout the grocer was… she had… I believe that… Fine, we hadn't come across anything to suggest she was involved in the murders. But who was to say we'd done a good enough job? I was willing to accept my incompetence if it helped explain the baffling events that had taken place in that normally sedate town.

"Good morning, Master Christopher," Halfpenny intoned when he opened the door to The Manor. Granny had been true to her word and given her staff a holiday to save money. "I trust you are having a pleasant day."

"No, I most certainly am not," I grumbled. "Grandfather is inside my head poking my brain with his clever stratagems, and I can no longer think straight. I spent the last five minutes imagining that I was walking around an imaginary graveyard."

"Very good, Master Christopher." This was clearly no surprise to the old footman who stepped neatly aside for me to thunder past.

I would have had a nap, but I was too restless. I would have played with Delilah, but she'd stayed behind in the town. I might at least have stuffed myself with food, but I felt oddly full. This was one conundrum that my training to be a better detective had not covered; I was at a loose end.

All I could do with my supposedly free time was sit on the bed in my drab room and look out at the church beyond Granny's garden. It was still just as handsome a building as when we'd arrived before New Year's Eve. It still looked charming in the slowly melting snow, but there was something tainted about it – something no longer quite right.

Grandfather insisted that I had all the information I required to unlock the case and identify the degenerate who had ended the lives of all those people. The answer had come to him when I'd talked about a previous case we'd investigated the year before. Both had been sparked by the discovery of a dead baron in an automobile accident, but I couldn't see what else they had in common. We were far away from the bustle and busyness of the capital, for one thing, and I still didn't know whether Baron Fane had been murdered.

It was tempting to believe that Grandfather had set one of his usual mental traps for me, and yet I knew that he was eager for me to solve the case on my own. So, what was I missing?

I thought back to the vestry, where we'd found Reverend Oldfield. I could picture the blood on his head and the thick rope still tied around his neck. I thought about that bright spark Marcus, and the way that he and Scarlet had suffered when their friend was sentenced to death. I imagined poor Adam Caswell in his hard, cold cell, where he would spend his last night on Earth before his unjust, final punishment.

That was the motivation I needed. That was the image that finally got my brain to stop jumping about from one half-hearted conclusion to the next and apply some of the lessons that Grandfather had taught me. I was viewing everything too narrowly – considering the same evidence again and again and only pondering how it could incriminate our small group of suspects. I had to look at the case in a different light, and so I went back to the beginning and tried again.

It felt as though I'd only been in my room for a few minutes when the bell on the church rang for one o'clock. The little machine in my head, which is sometimes slow to get started, had been going like the blazes. I could feel it throbbing, like an overworked muscle. But none of that mattered because I could see everything more clearly now. I had finally discovered the missing element that Grandfather had identified.

And did I know who the killer was?

Ummm... I was fairly confident, and there was really only one way to know for certain.

CHAPTER THIRTY-NINE

By the time I got to St Bartholomew's, the place was rather lively. Grandfather was having a word with Reverend Bodsworth, who did not approve of his house of God being used for earthly concerns but eventually put aside his reservations and returned to his office at the back of the church.

Scarlet was sitting in the front pew, looking despondent. I wondered whether Lord Edgington had told her of his plans, or she was simply reflecting on her loss in that quiet refuge. Most of our suspects had made it in time, too – though Grandfather's raised eyebrows told me that he considered me to be unforgivably tardy.

The mayor was hiding behind a pillar, as though that could save him from a lengthy sentence for his crimes (if he'd committed any, that is). P.C. Brigham was looking very sorry for himself, whilst simultaneously watching over the proceedings as if he were the one in charge. Delilah was a sleepy doormat at the back of the church and, true to form, my grandmother wore an expression which suggested the whole ridiculous event was beneath her.

"Are we missing anyone?" Chief Inspector Darrington enquired when I sat down next to Scarlet and took her hand.

Grandfather stood in the aisle before the apse and waited a few seconds before a well-dressed woman in a short black veil appeared in the doorway. I would have guessed he was clairvoyant, but I think that a more obvious explanation was that he'd heard the baroness's elegant black Daimler come to a stop outside. I thought it odd that she should be dressed in full mourning attire, having opted for more modern clothes until now. She was so very stylish, of course, that she made the long Victorian dress look impossibly chic.

"There are still a few more people to come, but they will be here soon enough." Grandfather smiled at the suspects, and I knew it was time to begin. "I have called you all here today to reveal why several members of this community were murdered."

The audience was rather too spaced out around the church to create much of a mumble of excitement, and so I added a, "Gosh, no! Really?" to make Grandfather feel better about the hushed response.

He did not appreciate the gesture and furrowed his brow.

"It has been a harrowing case for everyone involved." His voice was suitably solemn for the occasion, and it occurred to me that he would have made a rather good orator in the pulpit. "This village has lost its vicar and doctor. A young couple have been torn apart, and an innocent man has come within a day of his execution."

Perhaps it was just a coincidence, but I liked to think that Grandfather had timed this moment to perfection; it was just then that the two detectives from Scotland Yard escorted Adam Caswell into the room. Grandfather had evidently had to pull some strings to arrange it, but there he was, and he'd never looked happier. He was in irons, – his conviction still standing for the moment – but I was positive that it would only be a matter of time before his name was cleared.

Scarlet caught sight of her friend and ran the length of the church to embrace him. The big man did what he could to return the gesture, even with the shackles on his wrists. Lord Edgington was happy to wait, and once the pair had taken their places alongside me, his speech began again.

"Several people in this village have been killed for the sake of one of the emptiest, most intangible substances in the world." I would have guessed *dust*, but he went with "Money" and then peered around the nave to direct his judgement at all present. Such was the force of his icy stare that, for a moment as it passed across me, I wondered whether I myself was a suspect.

"One death occurred in this very church on the thirtieth of December. Reverend Adolphus Oldfield was attacked by the killer, with a valuable ciborium that was subsequently removed from the church. Unconscious, he was strangled to death with a spare rope from the bell tower. No one reported any disturbance, and there were no definite sightings of the person who committed this despicable act. However, certain villagers spotted Adam Caswell walking through the village at around the time of death before he returned to his lodgings at the Drop of Dew inn several hours later.

"Mrs Eileen Grout, the proprietor of Grout's Grocery, remembers just how anxious the vicar was that night. Shortly before Mr Caswell passed her shop, the vicar came shooting through the village on his bicycle and almost crashed into her. She recalls that he was in a state of some agitation and—"

"That he was, m'lord," Mrs Grout interrupted. She was sitting in the right-hand gallery, and I hadn't noticed her before. "He was in a sorry way, so I says to him, I says, 'Everything all right, Vicar?'"

"And he says, 'I'm sorry Mrs Grout, but I can't talk. I've just seen something utterly…' Just like that, it was. Coming to a conclusion all of a sudden. I thought perhaps he was scared to say what it was he'd seen. But anyway, he says, 'I really must be going. Good evening to you.' And then he races off again." Her face turned solemn at this moment, and she stood up from her seat to walk slowly forward. "Half an hour later, he was dead."

A shudder passed over the audience at this point. Standing next to the muscular woman as though he were her assistant, Grandfather appeared disappointed not to have evoked such a reaction himself.

"Thank you for your contribution, Mrs Grout."

"Any time, m'lord. As I told you when you came into my shop, Eileen Grout is always at the ready to do her bit."

Grandfather nodded his appreciation and, when she didn't get the hint, he gently guided her towards the nearest pew.

"Thanks to Mrs Grout's invaluable help, we had an important clue to suggest that Caswell was not our culprit. The vicar said that he had "seen something utterly…" Although he didn't finish that sentence with an adjective, it is fair to assume whatever it was had left quite the impact upon him. The idea put forward in Adam Caswell's trial that he had been involved in an altercation with the vicar was greatly undermined, not least because, when Mrs Grout saw Mr Caswell a few minutes later, he was not in the murderous rage that—."

"That's right, he were whistling!" Grout the grocer popped back up to reveal. "I'll never forget what the song was because I've always found it hilarious. It was 'Yes! We Have No Bananas'"

"I do like that one," cheery Adam whispered to Scarlet, by which time Mrs Grout had started a recital of her own.

"Yes, we have no—"

"Thank you, Mrs Grout." Grandfather was becoming impatient. "That will be all for now."

She jutted out her chin in disappointment and sat down a few spaces along from the grieving widow. I'd been watching Baroness

Fane whenever I dared a glance in her direction. She had sat through the admittedly far from revelatory introduction to Lord Edgington's presentation with quiet interest.

"Furthermore, as my capable grandson recently brought to my attention, the vicar was killed in the evening, but it was not until midnight that Adam Caswell returned from stargazing on the top of King Arthur's Camp. He walked along the high street and, halfway home to the Drop of Dew, a large, black car drove past him and the ciborium that had been stolen from this very church was thrown out. It would seem, therefore, that whoever killed the vicar planned to incriminate Mr Caswell and send him to the gallows in his place."

I felt I should add something at this point that I hadn't considered before. "It would also suggest that the killer knew Adam well if he was able to anticipate when he would be coming down from the camp." I didn't stand up, and I believe that he appreciated this.

"As I've already mentioned, my grandson is quite the assistant." He paused then and walked to the altar as though he wished to say a short prayer. "The result remains the same; Caswell was arrested for the vicar's murder. His case was heard at the Tatchester Assizes, and he was sentenced to death for a crime that he did not commit. I'm happy to say that his punishment has not yet been visited."

Adam let out an ever-so-quiet sigh of relief before Grandfather continued.

"The trial was a sham, and I don't think that either side gave the defendant any hope of acquittal. Mrs Grout was not called as a witness and, though it was inadvertently proved that Caswell was no greater a criminal than P.C. Brigham, the defendant's barrister failed to underline this key point."

Brigham looked like a kettle in a fire, and I wondered what it would take to make him blow his top.

"In the eyes of the public," Grandfather continued, "justice had been served. The story would have finished there if it hadn't been for Caswell's loyal friend, Marcus Alsop. From the moment the sentence was delivered in court, Marcus committed himself to overturning the verdict. He launched an appeal and returned to Condicote to interrogate half the village. I have read through the notes he made and, while he did not transcribe anything that could have brought about an acquittal, he was certainly on the right track."

He paused for a moment to allow the audience to digest the first part of his explanation. "On the day he was murdered, Marcus told Miss Warwick that he had 'discovered something quite unbelievable.' A few hours later, he was dead. There is no longer any doubt in my mind that what the vicar and Mr Alsop saw was the very same thing. Each was killed for getting too close to a secret that they should never have discovered."

There were a few nervous glances at this moment. P.C. Brigham looked at the mayor, but, still on his feet by the foremost pillar, Eric Hobson kept his eyes dead ahead. My granny must have been just as interested in their reactions, as her gaze darted back and forth between the other suspects.

"Until this morning, I could find no connection between the deaths, but I knew there had to be one." Grandfather's booming voice filled that elegant building and its resonance echoed back to us. "Just like Reverend Oldfield and Marcus Alsop, yesterday in her surgery in the centre of town, as the good citizens of Condicote ate their Sunday lunch, Dr Beresford-Gray was murdered to hide that same secret."

I was tempted to contribute something more, but was only about ninety-five per cent sure of myself and didn't want to look a fool in front of everyone. I mean, I *was* fairly certain; ninety-five per cent is a good deal higher than when I have to choose which cakes to eat or what books to read – two of surely the most difficult decisions known to man. I was really very positive, in fact, and—

"It was more than just a secret." I shot to my feet before I could doubt myself. "I would say it was something of a conspiracy."

Grandfather received my presence with remarkable grace. "That is quite true. A conspiracy in which several people in this room were involved and to which others were privy. A conspiracy that goes all the way back to the death of Baron Stamford Fane."

CHAPTER FORTY

We really should have invited more people, or at least congregated in a smaller room. Charles Dickens wouldn't have put up with such an unresponsive audience when reading his wondrous tales, and my grandfather should have expected better. The suspects couldn't have looked more blasé if they'd tried… which, I suppose, is exactly what they were doing. A grandfather and grandson crime-solving duo had just delivered an absolute thunderclap of a revelation, and the most we'd got from anyone was a yawn from Granny and an excited sort of humming noise from Mrs Grout.

I sometimes wonder whether all this detective business is worth the effort.

Grandfather wouldn't dwell on such disappointment but soon continued the narrative. "Baron Fane has cast his shadow over this investigation, though the fatal car crash near his estate occurred several days before Reverend Oldfield was murdered."

I had already noticed that my grandfather had gone to great pains to avoid giving too much away about the nature of the baron's death, but he was getting to the best part, and I listened just as attentively as the suspects.

"From everything that I have heard about him, however, he was not the sort of man to go quietly, even unto death. It will come as no surprise to anyone here that his plans for the use of his ancestral home at Seekings House sent ripples through the community of Condicote."

If this was going to be a proper double act – and I had any hope of avoiding the role of ventriloquist's dummy – I felt I should be more than a silent partner. "With the co-operation of the town council, the baron wanted to sell his estate and enable the expansion of the village beyond its current well-defined boundaries. He hoped to make a fortune developing the substantial tract of land."

I had a quick peek at Grandfather to make sure I wasn't talking nonsense, but he seemed happy to let me speak. "Of course the development would require a large amount of capital – capital that, as a prolific yet luckless bettor, Baron Fane couldn't retain long enough to invest. He borrowed the ten thousand pounds he required from his friend Marcus Alsop but swiftly lost it on a debauched gambling trip to London over Christmas."

If I was the 'straight man' in this curious stage combo – the one who would set up the jokes for my comedy partner to finish – then Grandfather knew just how to keep our audience entertained. "Money was not the only problem for the Fanes. The project could not go ahead without the agreement of every last member of the town council. No doubt to their surprise, Loelia Prentiss was an ardent supporter of the demolition of Seekings House, even if it made her nemesis richer than he'd ever been. But difficulties arose with a more recent arrival to the village, in the shape of Dr Beresford-Gray. She'd made a name for herself as a contrarian and opposed the plans to develop the woods around Seekings House." Grandfather often employed a pregnant pause before the allegation of some wrongdoing, and this one went long past term. "The doctor's sudden change of heart suggested her palms had been liberally greased."

He motioned for me to take over the telling, so it was a good thing I knew what came next. "This raised the question of whether the various murders were committed in order to cover up the corrupt process through which the development had been agreed."

My grandmother decided that this was the moment for a cynical burst of laughter. "How ridiculous. I could have told you that wasn't the case. No one in Condicote would resort to homicide in order to conceal a spot of back-scratching. That's just the way business is done around here. It always has been."

"Thank you so much for your help, Granny." She surely recognised the sarcasm in my voice as she rarely spoke a word without a substantial lacquering of the stuff.

The mayor looked less confident and pressed his tie against his chest as though he were afraid it might fly away. The baroness maintained her neutral expression, while P.C. Brigham risked a glance at the other members of the council before his eyes travelled back to Lord Edgington.

The man of the hour seized the story once more... Sorry, if that isn't clear, I'm referring to myself. "The bribe that was paid to the good lady doctor may have contributed to her death, but it was not the primary motive. Of everyone in the village, she was one of very few people who knew the secret that led to the demise of both Reverend Oldfield and Marcus Alsop."

I have, no doubt, criticised my grandfather in the past for prolonging revelations at such moments but, up there in front of our nervous audience, it was hard to resist making them wait. "A secret for which it was worth killing. A secret which—"

"It's not what you think!" the mayor yelled, his calm finally breaking. "I won't go to prison, I just won't!"

With this, he skittered along the aisle, but Chief Inspector Darrington made sure that he didn't get very far. He projected his leg from the end of his pew, and Mayor Hobson went tripping over it.

Grandfather walked slowly along to him and offered the poor, terrified chap a helping hand. "Mayor Hobson," he began, and then sought a softer tone. "Eric, you must learn to control your fear. I'm not about to arrest you, and I doubt that anyone here believes that you are the killer."

Lord Edgington winked at our suspect, and I couldn't tell if he was saying, *there there, old fellow. Everything's going to be fine.* Or it was more of a, *they might not think you're the one, but I know the truth.*

Grandfather sat the jittering creature beside the chief inspector – in case the mayor decided to make another run for it – and then returned to the front of the church to take over the explanation. I think he might have needed a moment to recall whereabouts we were in the story.

"Stamford Fane never got to sell Seekings House and so his wife, Baroness Sorel Fane, was left in charge of the project. However, it wasn't until today that I understood how the crash related to the other murders. We knew from the police that no one had tampered with the baron's car, but did that really mean his death was an accident?" His question surely flapped around the heads of every person present like a pigeon trapped in a bell tower.

"The key to this whole sad mystery only became apparent this morning when my grandson, in a display of his impressive observational and deductive faculties…" Admittedly, his compliments were becoming embarrassing by this stage. "…realised that this case bore certain similarities to another that we had investigated in London last year. A case in which a man named Baron Pritt died in suspicious circumstances behind the wheel of an automobile – though that man was driving a Bentley Blue Label tourer, whereas Baron Fane drove a Lanchester 40."

I have no doubt that the suspects assumed that the details of the vehicles involved would turn out to be extremely important to determining who was responsible for the murders. They were wrong. They were mentioned simply because my grandfather could not resist the opportunity to talk about cars.

"Before this watershed, we were left picking over scraps. We knew that Baroness Fane had no love for her deceased husband and yet she had made a declaration to the contrary in a very public manner weeks after his death. If Stamford Fane really had been murdered, as his heir and the person who would reap the most rewards from the sale of the estate, his wife was the obvious suspect."

I believe that Granny uttered a soft huff of disappointment that this title did not belong to her.

"The large, black Daimler that we saw parked on the driveway at Seekings House could have been the one which passed Adam Caswell on the night of the vicar's death. This was not enough to prove her guilt, nor was the fact that Marcus Alsop had visited her just one day before he died, and so I looked for another motive." He was a clever old goat and had dismissed certain theories but not the possibility of the baroness's part in the affair.

"Mayor Hobson – as we all witnessed just a few moments ago – had the look of a guilty man, but not the motivation. He needed the development of the Fane estate to go ahead to ensure that his job was safe, but we found little proof that this was enough to drive him to murder. Equally, my dear grandson's grandmother was no admirer of the victims—"

"Or many other people in this village, I might add!" Granny sounded like a heckler in the dark of a West End variety show.

"As she has just reminded us, however, that was not out of the ordinary for her, and I never seriously imagined that Loelia Prentiss was the killer."

"You could have fooled me," I said under my breath, but the acoustics of the church carried my words about the place. To cover my embarrassment, I took control of the presentation and strolled towards the – metaphorically at least – distant constable. "There was one person in the village who would have had the opportunity to shape the case as he saw fit. A man who had already obstructed the fair process of Adam Caswell's trial by withholding Mrs Grout's testimony."

I was only a few feet away from him now, and my eyes were at the same height as his. "I'm talking about P.C. Derek Brigham…" The silence at that moment was more than just audible, it was tangible, as every last person waited to hear what came next. "But, as it turns out, he wasn't the killer either, and we were quite baffled as to how someone had been rushing around Condicote murdering so many people without being spotted."

I clapped my hands together in a somewhat definitive manner and turned to the bulk of the audience. "And that was that, I'm afraid. We'd worked our way through the suspects, couldn't figure out for one minute what secret the vicar and Marcus had discovered, and were well and truly flummoxed." It felt nice to know more than my audience, but then Grandfather always knew more than me.

"There was at least one more person whom we hadn't sufficiently examined, though," he gently informed me.

"Was there?"

He examined each suspect in turn before landing on someone quite unexpected. "Emmeline Warwick prefers to go by the name 'Scarlet'. I have never entirely trusted people who hide behind pseudonyms, and my guard was up from our first meeting."

"It was?" I was having trouble making sense of what he was saying as he strode to the centre of the church.

"No matter how much love a suspect professes for her deceased partner, it is never wise to dismiss the possibility that she was involved in his death."

"Oh, you're doing me now!" That brave young lady seemed to thrill in the experience. "How very exciting."

"There was nothing to say that the person who killed the vicar was the same person who murdered Marcus, though this was the only possibility Scarlet would entertain. She knew she had won the high opinion of my grandson, which made me wonder whether she could have plotted Marcus's death in the belief that her heartbroken act would trick us both."

Even if she'd initially enjoyed the attention, this accusation made her defensive. "Oh, come along now. Why would I have killed him?"

"Yes! Why would she have killed him?" My voice was quite hoarse, and I don't think anyone heard me.

"Perhaps for keeping you here in this provincial backwater?" Grandfather was quick with his reply. "You do not come from great wealth, and have little money of your own to support you. Marcus wouldn't leave Condicote despite your objections, and I can't imagine that a life in a small market town offers many delights for a woman of such high ambitions. Furthermore, Marcus's bereaved mother was the person who convinced me to come here to investigate her son's death. She told us just how fond she had already become of you and how certain you both were that Marcus had been murdered. I know that you have been in touch with her throughout our investigation. Perhaps you planned to charm some money from poor, grieving Lady Alsop and move somewhere more to your taste."

Pausing for the briefest of moments, my grandfather once again displayed his near psychic abilities. It was just then that Lady Alsop herself pushed open the heavy door in the south transept and came into the church. She stood for a moment in the aisle and then took a seat in the final row of pews without saying a word.

"I didn't kill anyone," Scarlet muttered, her eyes on the floor.

Grandfather had made the most of these interruptions to glide across the apse and look at her more closely. "When we first met, you told me that you knew all about me and my past cases. You said you'd read all you could."

"I devour newspapers, books and pamphlets on a daily basis. I read all I can about everything."

I thought this a jolly good counterargument, but Grandfather did not waver.

"You made sure that you were involved in our investigation every step of the way, and there's nothing to say that you gave us all of Marcus's notes from his own attempt to solve the vicar's murder. In fact, you provided much of the information upon which we based our case. You told us that you had spoken on the telephone to your lover hours before he died and that he had mentioned an incredible discovery that he would have to explain in person. Who's to say you didn't pluck that detail from the murder of Reverend Oldfield in order to create a link between the two crimes?"

It was quite heartbreaking to see that poor lady suffer after everything she had already experienced. Her normally lively expression had turned hard as Grandfather launched his final question at her.

"Who's to say that you weren't the shadowy figure he met up on King Arthur's Camp? The person who shot poor Marcus in the head."

"I am!" I stepped forward to exclaim. "Leave Scarlet alone. You know just as well as I do that she was not involved in any of the murders."

"Oh really, Christopher?" His stare had become more invasive, and I felt his eyes drilling into me. "And why's that?"

"Because the killer isn't Scarlet, or Adam for that matter. The killer isn't even in this building."

CHAPTER FORTY-ONE

I ignored the constellation of suspects and the guilty expressions they all wore. I ignored my grandmother's dubious glare and the rather smug look that Grandfather was giving me that said, *that's my assistant; I taught him all I know.* I paid no attention to the angry silence that beseeched me to close my mouth and never open it again. However, I couldn't overlook the sudden burst of laughter that came from Miss Warwick.

"I'm so sorry, Lord Edgington." She held her hand to her mouth to stifle the noise. "I know you told me to keep a straight face when you accused me, but it's more difficult than I imagined."

Remembering why we were there, her happy expression faded, and her laughter turned into a soft whimpering. Adam moved to comfort her, and I kept talking so as not to lose my nerve.

"It took me a little while longer than Britain's finest pensioner-detective, but I finally understood the case of the Condicote murders. Grandfather told me that I had all the information I needed to identify the killer, but that was easy for him to say, as he already knew the solution."

I was worried that I was spouting abstract inanities and paused to concentrate on what was important. "Baron Stamford Fane's body was burnt to a crisp when he crashed his car into a lamppost. As he had been seen getting into his Lanchester just minutes earlier, and it was widely known that he had been drinking, no post-mortem was required. With a little guidance from Dr Beresford-Gray, the coroner signed his death certificate without further inspection.

"P.C. Brigham did do one thing right in this investigation. He called Scotland Yard when the baron died, but they were only here to rule out murder. There was no suggestion that the brakes on Fane's car had been cut or evidence of any obvious wounds on his body beyond the disfiguring burns, and so the detective closed the case and returned to London."

Grandfather had taken a seat by the chancel to watch my performance. His willingness to let me deliver the final piece of the puzzle gave me a jolt of confidence, and I decided I'd kept my audience waiting long enough.

"If a more reliable medical examiner than Dr Beresford-Gray had inspected the burnt corpse, we would have known from the beginning whether or not the baron had been murdered. But someone had bribed or threatened her to falsify evidence, just as they had to make her change her position on the Seekings House development. You see…" Very well, I did leave them waiting just a little longer. "…an impartial doctor would have immediately noticed that the body in the burning car was not Stamford Fane's at all, as Baron Fane is still alive."

This would have been the perfect moment to revel in the slack jaws and wide eyes of my audience – or perhaps end a chapter in a mystery novel – but there was no time for such things and I laid out the case against the ghost that had been haunting us all year.

"Fane had spent Christmas in London, gambling away the ten thousand pounds that he had borrowed from Marcus Alsop. His friend had lent him the money required for the development that would have restored the fortunes, not just of the baron, but the very village in which I stand. Fane was, or perhaps I should say *is*, a sick man. The promise of riches from the investment wasn't nearly so appealing as the chance to place so much money on a bet, and he returned to Condicote bankrupt once more.

"What he did have, however, was a plan. In London, he was known to spend time with the very roughest elements of society. He'd surely convinced one of his vagabond friends to join him for a luxurious trip to his country pile, making sure to ply the man with plenty of liquor along the way. When they reached Condicote, he hid the sleeping man in the back of the car and made a scene at the Drop of Dew to make sure that everyone there knew he was far too drunk to drive. He even bought a bottle of whisky to explain the combustion that would soon engulf his vehicle.

"Two minutes down the road, out of sight of any witnesses, he drove the Lanchester into a lamppost. From the remains of the car we inspected, it was clear that the impact itself wouldn't have killed him, and he must have pulled his unlucky companion into the driving seat and lit the bottle of whisky that would destroy the evidence of his duplicity."

I stopped again for just a moment to enjoy the look of horror on Mayor Hobson's face. Granny was never going to be shocked by anything I said. Baroness Fane was as unreadable as ever, but Hobson was practically guaranteed to react.

"Having already persuaded Dr Beresford-Gray to agree to the building project, the baron knew he could convince her to deal with any irritating queries from the coroner and must have telephoned her before carrying out the plan."

Oops, I hadn't thought of this detail before, but I think it made sense. "No one would miss the poor sap he burnt to death and, if it hadn't been for the events that have taken place since, I doubt anyone would have questioned whether Fane really had died in the accident. His plan would have been pointless if he couldn't access the money from the insurance policy that he had taken out on his life some years earlier, and so his story didn't finish there."

Gosh, it's hard work doing my grandfather's part in an investigation! I had to pause just to catch my breath. When I spoke again, it was to ask the baroness a question. "Did you know from the beginning that your husband was alive?"

It was the first time I'd seen her look the slightest bit flustered. "I noticed that one of the cars went missing around the time of the accident. It was a black Riley – by far the simplest in his collection and the one to take if you didn't want to attract too much attention." She swallowed and added an important detail that she should probably have stated before. "I didn't know he'd killed anyone, and I certainly wasn't part of his wicked plan."

The way that she pronounced these last two words made me wonder whether she was telling the truth – whether she had ever told us the truth, or even knew what such a thing was.

"That doesn't change the fact that you could have told the police." Scarlet stood up to shout across the aisle, and I thought that Reverend Bodsworth might stick his head out of his office to hush us all. "You did nothing, and so more people had to die."

The baroness looked to my grandfather for support, but he was just a spectator now. "Stamford came to the house the following week and told me that, if I didn't use the money from his life insurance to invest in the development, he would murder me next. He said he would be watching my every move."

"Was that the night that the vicar was killed?" I asked.

The baroness opened her mouth to speak, but there was no real explanation for her actions, and so she nodded instead.

Before Scarlet could launch another shouted allegation, I continued the story. "That night, Reverend Oldfield had been on his rounds, visiting sickly parishioners from neighbouring villages. He started in Radsoe and went on a loop that would take him back through Yockwardine and past the Seekings House estate. Through sheer bad luck, he must have cycled past just as the baron was leaving, and so the clergyman's fate was sealed."

"Fane was a fool to come back here." Brigham spat the words across the front rows. "Someone was bound to recognise him."

"Perhaps," Grandfather finally contributed. "But as Christopher explained, it was the only way he could get the money. There is no point faking your own death if you can't capitalise on your demise." He held his hands up then to apologise. "Please, Chrissy, the floor is yours."

I must admit that such interruptions can really throw a young detective's concentration. It took me a moment to remember where we were in the ever-winding tale. "The baron is obviously a clever man. He needed to get rid of the vicar in a way that wouldn't direct unwanted attention towards his own death, and he had the perfect scapegoat in mind. He must have driven past Adam on his way here and known that he went up to King Arthur's Camp on clear nights. All that was left to do was steal something from St Bartholomew's and plant it on his trusting friend. Adam did not have the violent character that the prosecution in his trial painted, but the circumstantial evidence was enough for a jury to convict him."

"What about Marcus?" Scarlet asked, her voice breaking and the tears finally coming to her eyes, just as she had promised they would once the case was resolved. "Why was he killed?"

"The baron told his wife that he would be watching, but he wasn't just keeping an eye on her. I've no doubt he was checking on his fellow members of the town council and even his old friends when he could.

I looked at Scarlet and wished that I could make her pain disappear. This wasn't just a story for her; it was a wound that would never heal. The least I could do was explain what had really happened. "Lord Edgington found no reason to re-examine the vicar's death, so Marcus took it upon himself to save Adam from the gallows. He spoke to all the obvious people, just as we later would. He went to Seekings House and interviewed the baroness and, at some point in all of that, Stamford Fane became worried that his secret would be revealed. Perhaps Marcus discovered something that he shouldn't have, but I think a more likely scenario is that the baron simply told him he was still alive."

This triggered a brief laugh from Granny, but I wasn't joking. "I believe that is what Marcus had in mind when he spoke to Scarlet on the telephone on the day he died. Stamford Fane had approached him with a ridiculous explanation for his disappearance. He played on their friendship to lure poor Marcus up to King Arthur's Camp, and then shot him dead."

My words resounded like that fatal gunshot. They echoed about the church just as a strain of celestial music struck up from the back of the church. Every person there glanced around in wonder, attempting to make sense of what was clearly some kind of heavenly host that had descended to—

No, hang on a moment. Forget what I said. Mrs Stanley, the organist, had slipped into the building when I wasn't looking and was beginning her daily practice.

I ignored the fact that I had momentarily believed we were experiencing a divine intervention and moved on to the final details of the case. "With our arrival here in the village at the request of Marcus's mother, the pressure on Baron Fane was even greater. He knew that, if we spoke to the doctor, we'd see through her lies. Every time we caught a glimpse of her this week, she was clearly terrified. A wave in the street sent her retreating into her office in fear, and Fane couldn't take the risk that his scheme would unravel, so a fourth person had to die."

I took a moment to reflect on his wickedness (and make sure I hadn't miscounted). "An as yet unidentified drunk, Reverend Oldfield, Marcus Alsop and Dr Beresford-Gray were killed so that the baron could continue the life of luxury to which he was accustomed. This vile man would have got away with his crimes, but he tried to be too clever. You see, the previous case my grandfather investigated, when Baron Terrence Pritt died in his car, was covered extensively by the London press. In fact, we had to promise interviews to one of the papers just to get the information we needed to solve the case. I have no doubt that Baron Fane read those accounts and imagined a solution to his problems. He successfully faked his death but couldn't leave his life behind entirely if he wanted to reap the rewards."

My voice had fallen to a low, resonant tone as I delivered my final proclamation. "And now, no matter what happens, the detectives from Scotland Yard won't stop until Fane is behind bars where he belongs."

I was rather proud of myself as Mrs Stanley's music became more dramatic and my audience measured the impact of my words. It would have been the perfect moment to walk the length of the church, climb into the back of Todd's Rolls Royce and drive home to Cranley with the case closed. Sadly, my small audience had other ideas.

"Hold on," Lady Alsop said, projecting her voice from the back of the nave. "If that's the case, where is he now?"

"Oh. Ummm… I haven't really—"

P.C. Brigham had a criticism of his own. "Aye, and if he's been wandering 'bout the village murdering people, why 'in't anyone seen him?"

"Well…" I responded noncommittally as they fired more comments in my direction. "I'm not really sure that—"

"That's right. How did he get away with it for so long?"

"You don't know what you're talking about."

"Why don't you let the real detectives do their job?"

Grandfather rose from his seat to save me. "Ladies and gentlemen, this is a house of God. If we could have a little decorum, I will answer your questions." He waited until silence was ensured before continuing. "Although Christopher has made a valiant effort to explain the tragic events that have taken place, there is one key factor he has overlooked." Another pause, another scan of the room with his pale grey headlights. "There were not four murders, but five."

CHAPTER FORTY-TWO

"Before I reveal anything more, I must say that you are holding the boy up to unfair standards. He has been observing my investigations for less than two years and has spent a mere six months under my tutelage. Not only has he stood before you and explained several surprising facts that many more experienced detectives had failed to identify, he did so without stumbling or stuttering and I, for one, am terribly proud of him."

"Hear hear! The boy is a marvel in my book." Granny echoed and, to give her due praise, she had not been one of the troublemakers… for once.

I almost shouted, *Thank you, Granny dear!* But I thought that would have sounded a touch unprofessional, so I sat down beside Scarlet and Adam and waited to hear the end of the tale.

The mayor wasn't so patient and, his voice still full of panic, shouted, "Get on with it, Edgington. Is Fane still alive? Did he really murder all those people?"

Grandfather raised his hand for silence. "Christopher came very close to the truth."

"Is Fane still alive?" The mayor asked once more, but Lord Edgington paused for that deafening silence to swoop around the sacred chamber and bounce back to our ears.

"All in good time." There was a sigh from the mayor as Grandfather took up the threads of the story. "Christopher realised what I did – what I should have known from the beginning; the Fanes held the biggest stake in everything that has occurred in Condicote over the last year, and Stamford Fane is a high-stakes gambler. He must have known when he lost his money in London that there was no way back for him. Not only did he lack the capital to invest in the project that would have saved him, he now owed Marcus Alsop ten thousand pounds."

Grandfather was standing beside the macabre statue of St Bartholomew at the front of the church. The flayed martyr had a metal knife resting in one hand and a piece of his own skin in the other. His sombre expression was mirrored on the face of the great detective.

"And yet, his problems would only increase once we all thought him dead. He had to come back to see the baroness in order to make certain that she would go ahead with the development. As a result, the vicar saw him driving past and would be the next to die. Caswell went to prison in Fane's place before this horrific chain of events presented an unexpected opportunity."

Grandfather smiled at what was surely his favourite part of any case. "You see, Baron Fane was anxious as to what his wife would do with her inheritance but, as several of you have stated, he could hardly walk around Condicote to make sure everything was going to plan. And that was when the fifth murder took place." Instead of just telling us what he meant, Grandfather shouted for assistance. "Reverend Bodsworth, could you come here for a moment? I have another question for you about the word of Jesus."

There was the faint sound of a chair scraping over tiles. The door at the back of the church opened, and the clergyman appeared.

"Of course, Lord Edgington. How may I be of assistance?"

I stood beside my grandfather, trying to make sense of what the wily old fellow was doing.

"I believe you recited a line from the Gospel of Matthew at Sunday lunch at The Manor. I was wondering whether you could repeat it for everyone to hear."

The priest put his hand to his mouth as he cast his mind back. "From the Sermon on the Mount, you mean?"

"That's the one." Grandfather took a few steps down the aisle to address him. "It was along the lines of 'love thy neighbour'. You know the sort of thing."

Bodsworth adopted the oddly flat tone he used when reciting from the Bible. "'Thou shalt love thy neighbour, and hate thine enemy,' Matthew 5:43."

"That is the very one. Thank you so much." Lord Edgington turned as if to leave but had something more to say. "It's a little out of context, but an interesting quote, nonetheless."

"You're quite right. I may have—" the reverend began, but Grandfather had moved on to another point.

"You see, Stamford Fane was raised by strict parents who offered little but religious scripture in place of the care and affection a child needs to grow into a functioning member of society. He could pass himself off as a priest just as easily as I could now pretend to be a police officer."

There was murmuring now as several amazed members of the audience had to express their incredulity out loud. One or two even used language that should never be uttered in church, but Grandfather would not be distracted.

"The baron had spent his childhood inadvertently training for the role, but then his father died, and he rebelled against his callous upbringing. With Reverend Oldfield dead, all he had to do was intercept the new priest before anyone in town saw him. He cut off his beard and famous locks, allowed his bulky form the freedom of loose clothes – as opposed to the tightly fitted attire he previously sported – and wore thick glasses to disguise himself further."

Grandfather continued on his walk, just as I found myself rooted to the spot.

"But there were two things Fane could not hide. First, the glasses hurt his vision, and he was forever taking them off to rub his eyes. And second, his interpretation of the Bible was unorthodox, to say the least. He presented himself as a damnation-obsessed, Old-Testament cleric, who was happy to dish out blame to the people of Condicote. However, I've known few priests who could so manifestly misinterpret the words of Jesus Christ and the message of love he offered."

I was having a hard time listening by now, as I was staring at the rather tubby priest who was standing in the aisle at the back of the church. We were supposed to believe that this man was the handsome fellow who'd been captured so dramatically in the portrait at Seekings House. The man I'd seen many times in my life, striding about the village like a king among peasants. At first, I could see no connection between them, but then I caught a glimpse in the dark eyes that were magnified by his beer-bottle lenses, and I knew they were one and the same person.

Fane peered down at the floor, perhaps contemplating his impending journey to that subterranean realm, as Grandfather piled up the evidence against him.

"'Thou shalt love thy neighbour, and hate thine enemy,' is not an instruction, but a warning. In the very next line of Matthew 5, Jesus tells us his real feelings on the matter. 'I say unto you, Love your enemies, bless them that curse you, do good to them that hate you.'

For a priest to make such a basic error in his reading of the Gospel is unthinkable, but it wasn't until I realised that Fane was still alive that I even considered the possibility that Bodsworth was not the person he claimed to be."

As Grandfather addressed the killer who had hidden in that sanctuary for so long, the sun moved out from behind a cloud and illuminated the stained-glass window in the south transept. A warm red light flooded through it to the very spot where Lord Edgington was standing and, on the window itself, St Bartholomew appeared to smile at the proceedings. Although I'm fairly certain this was just my imagination.

"In your so-called sermons, you talked of nothing but sin and punishment." He directed his words at Fane alone, who seemed robbed of his usual arrogance. "You wanted the people of the village to feel shame for their slightest human instinct. You heaped guilt upon them, even as you committed that most wicked of crimes. But you are the one who now faces damnation, and Condicote will be a better place for your absence."

I expected shouts of anger for the five people he had killed. I expected Scarlet to run the length of the church and strike that despicable man for the suffering he had caused. Instead, Adam gave her his hand, and she sobbed quietly, without a glance back at the killer.

The baron opened his mouth to speak, but there was nothing left to say. He was more despicable than any man I'd met, and there was no excuse for his transgressions. He looked at his wife, who had risen to glare at him and, seeing no other hope, he turned to flee.

"Stop him!" the constable shouted ineffectually, but there was no one close enough to prevent his escape.

As Mrs Stanley brought one hand down on a particularly dramatic chord, I searched about for something to throw. I was still standing next to the statue of St Bartholomew and reached up to borrow his knife. Stamford Fane was almost at the door as the weapon went spinning out of my hand across the rows of pews. It had left my wrist at just the right angle and seemed to maintain its course almost preternaturally. All eyes were on the flying blade as it shot through space and the baron moved closer to freedom.

He was at the door and about to pull it open when the knife struck… a few feet away from him and clattered harmlessly to the floor. Fane's look of joy is something I will never forget as, in the very next moment, the old wooden portal flew open and bashed him on the nose. Bill Thompkins came into the church looking extremely apologetic indeed. It was a long story, though, and no one had time to fill in the details as the bloodied baron lay on the floor clutching his face.

Mrs Stanley had stopped playing the organ, and there was no fanfare to signal the end of the investigation. Chief Inspector Darrington fetched his subordinates from the churchyard, and they shackled Stamford Fane for his journey to Condicote Police Station. From there, he would spend several months in the prison in Tatchester and, when found guilty of his crimes, be sentenced to death.

No appeal was forthcoming.

CHAPTER FORTY-THREE

Part Four – Summer 1927

We would have plenty of adventures that year. There would be more puzzles to solve and blackguards to apprehend. Albert and Cassandra's wedding day was quickly approaching, too, but before all that, there was another day that seemed really very important at the time. To everyone's surprise, even my grandmother came up to London for the celebration.

"Oh dear, dear," she said, brushing an invisible stain from the really very smart black suit that Grandfather had bought me. "You've replaced all that puppy fat you used to have with something… well, I don't know what to make of you, Christopher. I can only think you've gone too far in the other direction."

Knowing by this stage in my life that there really was no pleasing her, I laughed. "It's a joy to see you, too, Granny."

In the intervening months, Grandfather had made some changes. Impressed with my work on the Fane case, he'd decided that I was ready for a more rigorous schedule of tuition. We'd spent every day working at some new skill that he insisted was vital if I was ever to become a "real detective" – though I can't say I ever took to knife throwing. I barely had time for breakfast most mornings and was so tired by the time it came for dinner that I often fell asleep on my side plate.

"Don't worry him so, Mother," my father chastised our beloved scold. "We're here to enjoy ourselves."

I had motored (slowly) up to town in the back of Daddy's Bentley. Albert and his bride-to-be were particularly excited at the prospect of a day trip to fashionable Soho and were marvelling at the high, white building beside which we had parked. The only person missing was Grandfather, and he was rarely late. Sure enough, as the bells of St Anne's Church tolled twelve noon, he pulled up alongside us in a shiny new automobile.

"Don't tell me you've bought another car," Mother complained as he jumped from the burgundy beast.

"It is not just another car, my dear. It's a Daimler 35/120 limousine." He was so excited that he could barely stand still. "It's 'The Car of Kings'! And that's not just a slogan. George V has twenty-two of them." He put his hand on the front headlight, the way a proud father might pat his son's blessed head. "I doubt I'll make it to that number, but you never know."

I could see that my mother was about to tell him off for even entertaining such an idea, and so I intervened. "Perhaps we should go inside. We don't want to miss the fun."

The one problem with our trip to the Gargoyle Club on Dean Street was that the tiny lift only fitted four people at a time. Albert and I took the stairs while the others went up in two small groups. By the time we were halfway up, my brother was quite out of breath.

"How much further, Chrissy?"

"We're practically there," I replied, before swiftly changing the topic. "So you're not getting married in Condicote in the end?"

"No, we had second thoughts." He sounded a little bashful. "We've decided that the church near Cassandra's family estate in Hinwick is just as pretty and a lot less... murder-y."

I couldn't help laughing at him. I'd rarely met such an unlucky fellow, but it was good to see that his future was bright. "I must say, I'm incredibly happy for the pair of you."

"I should think so, too." We'd almost made it to the right floor, and his breathing was a little ragged. "Imagine the best man not approving of my future bride. It just wouldn't do."

I was the one who had to stop then. "Best man? Albert, do you really mean it?"

He leaned on my shoulder, and I helped him up the final flight of stairs. "Who else could make as good a go of it as you will?"

My immediate thought was, *just about anyone,* but I was so moved by the gesture that I could do nothing but smile.

"Don't get soppy, now, Chrissy. That's my job."

With our arms over one another's shoulders, we stumbled towards the club. My grandfather had become a member the year before, and the doorman knew me by now and waved us inside. The function was being held in one of the rooms on the upper floor of the chic venue, and a lot of our old friends were already there, but there was one person in particular I was eager to see.

"Congratulations, Scarlet," I said, running up to kiss her on both cheeks – which may sound terribly French, but it was the done thing in those parts. "I couldn't be happier for you. I really couldn't."

"Thank you so much for coming, Chrissy." She took my hand, and we were both beaming as our exonerated associate joined us.

"Isn't she clever?" Adam said with that familiar grin across his huge, potato-y face. "I couldn't write a postcard if I tried, and she managed a whole book."

"I knew you could do it," I told her most sincerely, as a few other members of our party arrived.

"Miss Warwick?" My grandmother sent these words ahead of her, much as a ship will toot its horn to warn oncoming vessels. "A word, please."

As the two of them spoke, I looked at the table where copies of Scarlet's book were piled high. The cover image was of a Lanchester 40, wrapped around a lamppost. On the top, in a large, dramatic font, were the words 'Two Lords, a Vicar and the Blazing Car Mystery by Emmeline Warwick'. Though the book would not be released for some months, and she had only recently signed the contract with a publisher, it made me happy just to see the cover.

"You dropped your nickname?" I noted with some surprise.

"That's right. I thought Emmeline sounded more grown up. And it felt wrong to keep using it without Marcus here." Her voice wavered for a moment, but she fought off any emotion as Granny had something to say on the matter.

"You'll always be a scarlet woman to me, Miss Warwick." She had already obtained a cup of tea somehow and sipped it to punctuate her impish comment. "But, as I was saying, you must visit me the next time you come to Condicote. I do adore a good adversary and, with Fane gone, the village is rather quiet."

Scarlet was a perfect match for my cantankerous grandmother. "As long as I'm invited for Sunday lunch, it's a deal."

Granny did not show whether this pleased her or not. She simply nodded and coasted across the room to correct Cassandra's enunciation, posture, or perhaps the way she wore her hair. Granny was most demanding of new arrivals in the family. I can only imagine the torment that Mother went through before marrying my father.

"I suppose I just needed a story to write, and the rest came easily." Scarlet was staring at the printed dummies of her book with almost as much wonder as I had. "Do you know how your grandfather feels about his life being turned into fiction?"

"I doubt it's the first time." I looked across at the legendary Lord Edgington, who was entertaining a number of his fellow Gargoylians with tales of his brilliance. "But I think it's fair to say that he's enjoying the attention."

Todd had arrived at the club before us and was busy mixing cocktails for all present. "Do you fancy a Blue Blazer, Master Christopher?" He had a devilish note in his voice as he held a match over a metal tankard.

A second later, an eruption of flame rose into the air as whatever alcohol was inside caught fire. The normally reliable chap had apparently gone insane; he poured an arc of fire from one mug to another but managed to avoid burning his hands in the process.

"I thought it was rather appropriate, considering the name of Miss Warwick's book," he explained, and I was tempted to ask whether there was any lemonade available.

Adam was evidently impressed as he raced across to the bar to fetch us each a flaming mug. I wasn't certain how to drink my inferno, but luckily Todd recommended that I wait until the flames had died down before tasting it. Perhaps the most surprising thing of all, though, was just how appetising the warming libation was as it ran through me. Despite the presence of strong whisky and who knows what else, it was sweet and nutty, and brought back any number of cosy winter memories.

All in all, it was a marvellous celebration. Everyone was so proud of the new author, and Scarlet even read out the part of the story where Grandfather returned heroically to Condicote to save Aidan Cosbell (some of the names were changed) from the gallows.

You can imagine how happy this made the old chap. When it was almost time to go home, he escorted me to the terrace to enjoy the vista over the rooftops of London. I loved it up there and took in the view as though the city was still totally new and totally alien to me.

"As Johnson said, 'When a man is tired of London, he is tired of life; for there is in London all that life can afford,'" Grandfather quoted, and we breathed in the undoubtedly smog-filled air. "Having said that, I must admit I'm a little tired of London." The ends of his moustache were pointing downward, but it was hard to know what he was really thinking.

"You've spent a lot longer here than I have, Grandfather. Don't they also say that familiarity breeds contempt?"

"Which is all the more reason for a change of air." He was smoking a celebratory cigar and took such a long time over it that I had to ask him what he meant.

"Did you have a particular plan in mind?"

He always had something up his sleeve. "Christopher, I think it's time I left these shores."

"Well, there's always the Isle of Wight," I replied without thinking.

"Not the Isle of Wight, boy. Or any British island for that matter. I'm thinking of Egypt, Kenya, Belgium – far-away lands about which I have read so much but never seen."

"You mean to go abroad?"

"Yes, Chrissy. That is generally where one finds such countries."

My heart raced at the very thought of the adventures we could have. I'd always wanted to travel, but I imagined that we would have started somewhere less frightening – like Scotland, perhaps – before moving on to France and what-have-you. As much as those wild and distant destinations terrified me, that was nothing compared to the idea of Grandfather leaving me behind.

"Just think of it, Chrissy. Think of the thrill it will be to plan such a grand voyage. I'll have to buy new maps!" This in itself provided any amount of excitement.

"Sorry, Grandfather, but just to make sure that I understand. Do you mean for me to help you plan the journey, or would you also like me to accompany you?"

A jet of thick smoke projected into the London sky as though he were a chimney. "How could I possibly go anywhere without you? Where would the fun be in that?"

The proposal was so unexpected that I found myself looking for excuses not to go. "But Albert's getting married, and I promised the boys in Oxford I'd visit them again. And Marmaduke's got his first performance in the theatre soon, and—"

"I'm not suggesting we leave tomorrow," he interrupted. "I was thinking of next year maybe. We'll have to get Christmas out of the way…" (*And no doubt solve a murder in the process*, I thought but didn't say) "…and then we can set sail when we're good and ready."

"What about our family? What about Cranley Hall?" My voice was positively quavering.

"They'll all be here when we get back. But don't you agree that it's a wonderful idea? Think of the aeroplanes and ferries we'll take – the cruises down foreign rivers and the night trains across the continent. It's a dream come true for a young chap like you… and an old chap like me." His words tailed off and, when he spoke again, there was a hint of trepidation in his voice. "You will come, won't you?"

To be perfectly honest, I'd never been an adventurous sort of person. My idea of exotic was the time I thought I saw a hoopoe in the garden (it turned out to be an unusually tall jaybird). I couldn't comprehend the idea of leaving my family behind for any length of time. It was the kind of thing that another, far braver boy might do.

And so, looking at my grandfather's expectant visage, I said the only thing I could fathom.

"Of course I'll come. I wouldn't miss it for the world."

The End (For Now…)

Get another
LORD EDGINGTON ADVENTURE
absolutely **free**…

Download your free novella at
www.benedictbrown.net

"LORD EDGINGTON INVESTIGATES. . ."

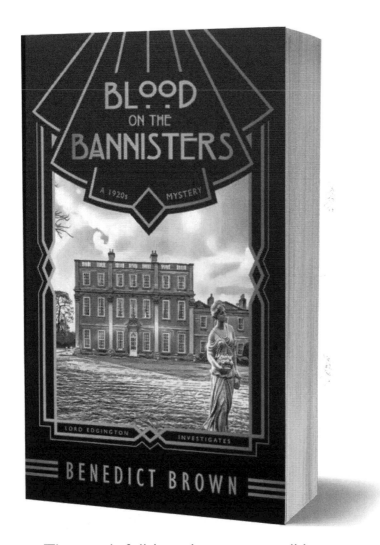

The tenth full-length mystery will be available in **June 2023** at amazon.

Sign up on my website to the readers' club to know when it goes on sale.

ABOUT THIS BOOK

I know I have some readers who (slightly strangely) prefer to read the back matter of the book before the novel itself, well, if that's you, let me just warn you that there are big spoilers for the story from this point on, so stop reading… here.

When I chose the title "What the Vicar Saw", I hadn't a clue what the vicar had seen, and so my first challenge was to come up with something original. I hope you all agree that was the case, but it was my wife, Marion, who came up with the idea. The suggestion she made put me in mind of a story I'd planned for some time, which was inspired by a real-life mystery. Right, final warning, the spoiler is coming… now.

In 1930, a bigamous belt salesman named Alfred Rouse enjoyed his life, travelling about the country hawking his wares and promising marriage and stability to the countless women he seduced. As his dependants began to add up – there was a woman as far away as Paris who demanded child support from him – Rouse sought a fresh start, took out a £1000 life insurance policy and hatched a cunning plan.

He befriended a down-on-his-luck drunk in a pub and arranged for them to travel together on Guy Fawkes Night, even going so far as to give the man a bottle of whisky to keep his passenger quiet on the way. Rouse knocked the man unconscious with a hammer and set fire to his car with the never-to-be-identified victim inside. Unluckily for the killer, he was no genius and was not only spotted walking away from the scene but was soon turned in to the police by the woman he was planning to marry next – who reported that he smelt of petrol and had singed eyebrows when he turned up at her house in Wales with a story about his car being stolen. After he was arrested on the lam in London, he told the police that he had given a hitchhiker a ride (and a cigar) then asked him to fill the petrol tank while he left the vehicle to relieve himself. This argument did not serve him well in court, and the legendary pathologist Sir Bernard Spilsbury was there to show that the car had been tampered with, the victim had been knocked unconscious, and the whole scene had been doused in petrol.

Three of Rouse's many wives and mistresses testified against him, and it took the jury just twenty-five minutes to find him guilty. Though an appeal *was* forthcoming, he was sentenced to death and, just before his hanging, Rouse sent a letter to the newspaper confessing to his crime. The victim was buried with a simple cross stating "In Memory of an Unknown Man. Died Nov. 6, 1930" in a church in Hardingstone, Northamptonshire, which, coincidentally, is just fifteen miles from the setting of the next Lord Edgington book, "Blood on the Bannisters".

It's surprising how often I find real-life examples of elements from my books that, at first sight, seem unrealistic. Even as I was writing this novel, there were two cases in the news of people attempting to murder their doppelgangers in order to fake their own deaths. With social media and the internet, it is now far easier to find people who look just like us, and it isn't just bigamous travelling salesmen from the 1930s who think they can get away with such audacious crimes.

The other twist that comes right at the end of the book is the kind of thing we could dismiss in mystery fiction as being unrealistic, but such things really do happen. A good example occurred to me when I came home from university for the first time in six months, then went straight up to London to meet my family at the theatre. There was my mum, dad and aunt, and I couldn't understand what Auntie Viv was doing with a rather dashing young man with long hair and a beard. It was only when my brother spoke that I recognised him – bear in mind this was before video calling took off, so I hadn't caught a glimpse of him since I left home. Dominic had grown a very long beard, his hair was in a pony tail for the first time and he'd got contact lenses, having worn glasses his whole life. It was one of the most uncanny moments I can remember.

A part of this story that is pure fiction, however, is the setting. Almost all the place names in this book are taken from the works of the former Poet Laureate, John Masefield. I am a huge fan of Masefield's enchanting children's books, 'The Midnight Folk' and 'The Box of Delights', and I've also enjoyed reading his poetry and adventure novels in preparation for writing this book. My love for Masefield started with the 1980s BBC TV adaptation of "The Box of Delights", which I watch every Christmas. Set in a very cosy-looking 1930s, complete with steam trains, snow drifts and plenty of magic, it's just about the most nostalgic show I've ever seen.

Masefield was a highly respected poet in his day and had the most extraordinary life, which I'll go into in the next chapter. He was born in Ledbury in Herefordshire, which he fictionalised as Condicote in several of his books, but he went on to travel the world. His children's and adventure novels feature recurring characters and places, and I love this intertextuality and decided that, rather than popping off to a famous beauty spot as they tend to, the Prentiss-Cranley clan could visit Masefield's imaginary village.

In my Condicote, I have used some of the features of Ledbury, such as the market hall and alms hospital, along with a few of the settings from the Box of Delights, like the Drop of Dew Inn and Seekings House. I also contacted the Society of Authors that manages Masefield's estate to check that I was actually allowed to borrow the names. So many thanks are due for their assistance.

This book felt different to the others in the series in a number of ways. First, it is a good bit longer than most, even after some careful trimming, but that was perhaps inevitable with the four-part structure the book has. In order to have a trial and miscarriage of justice, the timeline had to be convincingly long enough, and so I split the book into sections.

I later discovered that one of the first full-length detective novels – the incredibly successful "Trent's Last Case" by E. C. Bentley, which was published in 1913 – used a similar technique. Before that time, and perhaps due to the influence of short stories by the likes of Poe and Conan Doyle, it had not been common to write longer detective fiction. Bentley got around the difficulty of sustaining the tension in a 70,000-word novel, by splitting it into two parts and adding a healthy dose of humour. In the first part, the bumbling detective, Philip Trent, gets the wrong man before returning to the case years later in the second half of the book. Christie described the novel as "One of the three best detective stories ever written" and Dorothy L. Sayers considered it a "revolution" in the world of detective fiction. I haven't actually read it, but I intend to very soon!

Another way in which this book is different from its predecessors is that the trajectory of each section is more linear. My detectives normally bounce about the place like pinballs, but in this book, we gradually get to know the area, starting with The Manor and church in the south of the town and working our way north before finally getting a glimpse of Seekings House towards the end of the book. I think this suited the case that Chrissy and Lord Edgington must solve and highlighted the baroness's isolation from the rest of the villagers.

This is also the first book in which Chrissy finally solves the mystery – well, ninety per cent of it at least. I decided that I couldn't leave my readers hanging on any longer, especially as the next book is going to be focussed on Albert's wedding, and Chrissy might not have so much of the limelight. I hope he did a good job and that you all enjoy his progress.

If you loved the story and have the time, please write a review at Amazon. Most books get one review per thousand readers so I would be infinitely appreciative if you could help me out.

THE MOST INTERESTING THINGS I DISCOVERED WHEN RESEARCHING THIS BOOK...

Here we go, then. The last time I recorded one of these chapters for the audiobook, it turned into an eighteen-minute track. Let's see if we can be a little swifter this time around. (Another spoiler alert: we can't, it's a thousand words longer!)

Unlike my books which are set in real places, I couldn't rely on the history of the grand house on the cover for inspiration. The towns around Condicote are just as fictitious, and it's not even specified in which part of the country the story takes place – though it is definitely between two and seven hours' drive from Cranley Hall. This didn't stop me from imbuing the story with some of the incredible historical elements I discovered.

Even passing references in the book often require a fair chunk of time to research, and a good example of this is the reference to Muswell Stream, a hidden river in London. It's hard to imagine that my home city was ever anything but a giant slab of concrete, but like most places in Britain, it was once covered with rivers and marshes that have been tamed, drained and built over during the centuries of its existence. For Lord Edgington's anecdote about Sacheverell Briggs, I needed to find a piece of waterway which would have been open at the end of the nineteenth century but closed later on.

Muswell Stream was submerged in the twenties, but centuries earlier had belonged to the Bishop of London, and its springs were known for their healing qualities. A chapel to the Virgin Mary was built to mark them, and Malcolm IV of Scotland is said to have been healed there in the twelfth century. I love the idea of the hidden world beneath the capital and the many tributaries of the Thames still flowing in the darkness.

I needed to know something about British legal history to write this book, but thankfully my mum's cousin is a judge, so I didn't have to go too far down that rabbit hole. One of the first things he mentioned to me was the black cap that assize court judges would don before handing down the death penalty. They would also wear black gloves or, if no one was found guilty, white ones to mark the occasion.

I've already talked about the blazing car murder, but another true case that had an impact on this book was that of Derek Bentley. Bentley was involved in a robbery in (Izzy Palmer's favourite!) Croydon in 1952, along with another man who was under eighteen at the time. After Bentley was arrested, his accomplice shot a police officer just after Bentley is said to have told him "Let him have it". The prosecution claimed that this was an instruction to kill the policeman, but the defence argued that Bentley was telling his friend to hand over the weapon. Either way, Derek Bentley never fired a shot but, of the two men, he was the one sentenced to death.

Bentley had health and learning difficulties and was already in custody when the fatal bullet was fired. Though found guilty, the jury urged a softer sentence, but the government at the time found no grounds for leniency and Derek Bentley was hanged. The case caused a public outcry and led to a change in the law in Britain to give more weight to diminished responsibility. It was also a key case in the move to end capital punishment and, forty-five years after he was hanged, Bentley's conviction was overturned.

There was a film of the story made in the nineties, which I remember having a big impact on me. I think that, through the character of Adam Caswell in this book, I had the chance to right some wrongs. My research from the first half of the twentieth century and Victorian times is littered with cases of people who were put to death unjustly, and I'm glad to live in a continent (with the exception of Belarus!) where such irreversible miscarriages of justice can no longer take place.

The man in charge of Bentley's execution was Albert Pierrepoint, the most famous hangman of the twentieth century but, in the time of this book, Albert's uncle Thomas was plying his trade. In fact, the Pierrepoint family produced three of the most prolific executioners of the twentieth century, and Thomas is believed to have overseen the deaths of nearly three hundred people, including the blazing car murderer himself, Alfred Rouse, and the poisoner, Frederick Seddon –

whose conviction was sealed with the help of the forensic evidence of a young pathologist by the name of, you guessed it, Bernard Spilsbury. The Pierrepoints were known for their speed and efficiency, and Thomas's record was said to be sixty seconds from the cell to death. Which, now that I think about it, is really very grim.

Moving on to an entirely unrelated and far cheerier topic, let's talk about cakes! The Tarte Tatin that Chrissy forces himself to eat was the creation of two sisters who ran a hotel in the Loire Valley in the centre of France. The legend goes that Stéphanie Tatin was overworked in the kitchen of the restaurant one day and ended up caramelising the apples she was cooking. To save them, she stuck a layer of pastry on top and put the whole thing in the oven. Her accidental upside-down apple pastry was a big hit, and it was popularised in the twentieth century by famous French epicures and the world-renowned restaurant Maxim's. Though it has recently been transformed into a posh spa, you can still eat Tarte Tatin at Hotel Tatin where (I just checked) it is a whole €13 cheaper than at swanky Maxim's on Paris's Rue Royale.

I was curious about another sweet treat that Chrissy mentions, that of the Lawn Tennis cake. I found a mention of it on an old menu from an A.B.C. tearoom and wondered about its origin. I'm going to be honest, though I did find a recipe for it in one of Mrs Beeton's books, I never discovered how it got its name, but I was happily sidetracked by a related topic that was just as interesting. Lawn Tennis cake led me to the Wimbledon Championship and then to the American player Elizabeth Ryan.

Playing in the 1920s, Ryan won nineteen doubles titles – including a run of thirty-one consecutive wins with her main partner. She introduced a style of volleying which would influence greats like Margaret Court, Martina Navratilova and Billie Jean King. But what I found most incredible about this legend of the women's game was how she bowed out. In 1979, sixty-five years after winning her first title, she was watching the men's singles final in Wimbledon when she became ill and died a few hours later. She had held the record for the most Wimbledon titles for forty-five years and, the very next day after she died, Billy Jean King won her twentieth title and dethroned her. She really didn't want to see her record broken.

But that wasn't nearly enough time spent on the matter of food, so let's jump back to the café that Lord Edgington was so perplexed by. A.B.C. tearooms were the second most popular restaurants in Britain at the time – behind the Lyons brand equivalents. A.B.C. stood for the Aerated Bread Company, which had built its wealth through a revolutionary method of baking, created by a doctor named John Dauglish. He realised that, by introducing carbon dioxide into the dough instead of yeast, you could avoid the need for kneading and fermentation and speed up the baking process. He calculated that, if applied across the UK, this would save the British baking sector the equivalent of five hundred million pounds a year. His discovery would dominate bread for a century and on the back of his success, the company moved into other areas.

A.B.C. opened its first self-service cafes in the 1860s and, back then, it was nearly impossible for women to eat or drink in public without a male escort. The tearooms filled this gap, not least by providing women's toilets – which were not common in bars and pubs until nearly a century later – but also by offering secure and welcoming spaces where women could take refreshments. By the end of the century, they were even being recommended by the Congress of the International Council of Women as places where unescorted delegates could dine without fear of harassment, and they were often frequented by suffragettes.

I am not the first author to make use of an A.B.C. tearoom in fiction and, after I'd written the book, I discovered that Tommy Beresford eats eggs and bacon in one after escaping from a spy ring in Agatha Christie's 'The Secret Adversary'. They also make an appearance in books by some of my favourite authors like Virginia Woolf, W. Somerset Maugham, T. S. Eliot, A. A. Milne, Ruth Rendell, Graham Greene, P. G. Wodehouse, H. G. Wells and, would you believe it, one even pops up in Bram Stoker's "Dracula". What I can't say is whether the food they served was particularly tasty. Although around a million people a week drank tea in A.B.C. shops in the mid-1920s, George Orwell saw them as a sign of the creeping industrialisation of British food with, he claimed, everything they served coming out of a packet, tin or refrigerator.

Moving away from the high street to the backstreets, I had originally planned to have Baron Fane debasing himself in an east end opium den, but it turned out that such places weren't nearly so common as literature and television would have us believe. Though people in London to this day would be able to tell you about the district of Limehouse's connection to the drug, in reality, opium dens were not common, and the Chinese immigrant population was really very small compared to cities like New York and San Francisco. A few such dens may have existed in the middle of the Victorian era, but it seems they were mainly visited by Chinese sailors on shore leave and writers looking for material. Such locations feature in Dickens's "The Mystery of Edwin Drood" and Conan Doyle's "The Man with the Twisted Lip". Both writers are known to have taken a trip to Limehouse in search of the famed establishments, though what they did when they got there is less certain.

I'm sure I'm not the only author who, when writing quickly, creates fairly forgettable prose. As a result, when clattering out a few thousand words a day, every door will be *heavy*, every cottage *picturesque* and every doctor male and plump. Luckily, we have time to edit our work before readers get to see it and, after the first passing mention of her, Dr Beresford-Grey became a suspiciously nervous "lady doctor". Of course, this meant I had to check when female doctors were common in Britain, and I came across the stories of two amazing individuals. The case of James Barry is probably more famous, as it has been the subject of several books and plays. He was a highly successful and demanding military surgeon who improved the lives of the soldiers he treated for fifty years in the nineteenth century. It was only on his death that it was discovered that Barry was born a woman who had passed herself off as a man in order to work in medicine.

Even more significant to the history of the field, however, was Elizabeth Garrett Anderson, who was the first British woman to graduate as a doctor. She was only able to achieve this through perseverance, the fact she came from a comfortable background and a soon to be closed loophole. Showing academic promise from an early age, she started working as a nurse but was refused admission to the hospital's medical school. Thanks to her family's support, she was able to study privately and, in 1862, even managed to obtain a licence from the Society of Apothecaries to practise medicine – before they swiftly changed their rules to bar women.

Having the right qualifications did not mean she could get a job in the position she'd trained for, however. As no hospital would hire her, she opened her own practice and, in addition to seeing private patients, soon founded a facility to give poor women the chance to access medical care from a female practitioner. When the Sorbonne in Paris started admitting female students, she studied French and signed up for a medical degree, which she completed in 1870.

Throughout her career, she strived to advance medicine and give women opportunities in the field, whilst fighting against the common idea that employment could lead to women's brains becoming exhausted. She often beat a path as a test case for inclusion, only for the medical establishment to shut women out and, in 1873, became the first female member of the British Medical Association, nearly twenty years before women were widely admitted. The practice she established would expand to become a fully-fledged hospital for women and children, and she co-founded the London School of Medicine for Women with her colleague Sophia Jex-Blake, who was one of the very first women to qualify as a doctor through a British university – something that Garret herself had been prevented from achieving.

Along with her sister, Millicent, and daughter, Louisa, Garrett was active in the women's suffrage movement for much of her life. She would also become the first female mayor in Britain, and the school she established trained thousands of women to become doctors in her lifetime and has continued to do so in the century since she died. She was sensational in so many respects, so I'm sorry my doctor in this book is a bit of a flake.

Another person who had a truly incredible life is the author I paid tribute to in this novel. John Masefield, like the protagonist in his two children's books, lost his parents at an early age. By thirteen, he would leave Britain on a naval training ship and spent much of his teenage life at sea. He also spent most of that time with his head in a book and, tired of the lonely life of a sailor, he eventually jumped ship to explore America.

He lived as a hobo, doing odd jobs and experiencing the wilds, before taking a position in a gigantic carpet factory in New York for a couple of years. This helped fund his addiction to reading and gave him an opportunity to devour hundreds of books and explore a newfound love of poetry, which was the medium that would bring him the greatest success in his lifetime.

When the first world war began, he volunteered in a French hospital and was then sent on a lecture tour of America to promote British interests in the war. During the 1920s, his poetry found a large audience and, in 1930, he was chosen to be the British Poet Laureate by George V. This was the most impressive of many honours that were bestowed on him. He was also a fellow of several important universities and became the president of The Society of Authors, who represent his estate to this day. He produced a vast number of novels, poetry collections and long-form poems, and one of the things I love about his kids' books, and his career as a whole, is that they are so firmly of their time. The books I have read by him are a perfect window into the decades in which they were written, but, for all his contemporary success, he is no longer so well known.

One of the most famous pieces he wrote is the short poem 'Sea Fever', which begins "I must go down to the seas again, to the lonely sea and the sky." I didn't know the poem until recently, but even if you don't take the time to read his beautiful combination of folk tales and ancient magic in "The Box of Delights" or seek out one of his boys' own adventure novels like 'Sard Harker', I urge you to look up 'Sea Fever' as it's a simple, beautiful piece of writing. Masefield died in 1967 and, like other important figures I've mentioned in previous books, his ashes are interred in Poet's Corner in Westminster Abbey.

Moving from poetry to songs, I restricted myself to two and a bit in this book. The tune of the first hymn is called Cwm Rhondda (or the Rhondda Valley in Welsh, i.e. where my mum was born and raised) though it is often referred to as "Bread of Heaven" as that is the line that Welsh rugby fans often sing with the greatest relish during international matches. I am half Welsh and spent most of my holidays as a kid in Mum's tiny mining town in the Rhondda, and so it was nice to put a little tribute to that side of my family in the book. Of course, "Guide Me, O Thou Great Redeemer", as the English hymn is called, is not only sung in Wales but is a popular hymn that was included in both Princess Diana's and the Queen's funerals.

293

Moving from an unofficial Welsh national anthem to an unofficial English one, "And did those feet in ancient time", or as it's more commonly known, "Jerusalem", is a truly stirring song and was preferred by George V himself to the real British anthem, "God Save the King". The lyrics are taken from a poem by William Blake, which is a touch ironic given that he was once up on trial for high treason for muttering such offences as "Damn the King!"

It is also associated with the Women's Institute, after suffragette Millicent Fawcett suggested singing the song in 1918 at their meeting at the Royal Albert Hall. It was adopted six years later as the WI's anthem, but who was Millicent Fawcett, I hear you ask? None other than Dr Elizabeth Garrett Anderson's little sister. Is this some kind of conspiracy that links up completely unrelated elements of my novels without me planning it? Or perhaps it's just the rich tapestry of history that weaves its way through time? I don't know, but I love the way so many seemingly disparate details end up joining together.

Caracals are an extant wild cat found across Africa and eastern and central Asia. They were tamed and venerated in ancient Egypt and were often kept in luxurious conditions by ruling dynasties. That is why the one in my book is named Sekhmet, after an Egyptian cat deity. They were particularly prized throughout history for their hunting skills. The reason I chose to give Baroness Fane a pet one is that… ummm… I can't really remember, but it was probably to make her look like a cross between a femme fatale and a Bond villain.

Fireworks only get a one-line mention, but it did mean I had to read up on their use back in the time of Lord Edgington. First used in China 2000 years ago, they became popular in Britain after featuring in the wedding of King Henry VII in 1486. Later, Queen Elizabeth was such a fan that she created the official role of Fire Master of England to oversee all royal fireworks displays. Fireworks night (or more correctly Guy Fawkes Night – which, incidentally, is when the burning car murder took place) is still celebrated in Britain today and commemorates the attempted explosive assassination of James I in 1605. Until 1859, it was illegal not to celebrate this night and so, during wars, though fireworks were temporarily banned, people had to celebrate inside. Weird.

Right at the end of the final draft, just a day before publication, I realised that I'd potentially made a mistake by referring to the "ladies and gentlemen of the jury". Although the law was changed in 1919 to allow women to serve in court, by the end of the twenties, the men in charge had found all sorts of ways of keeping juries male. Barristers could simply say that they didn't like the look of a juror in order to dismiss them, and judges could order that a jury be all male if they felt that the content of the trial would be unsuitable for members of the fairer sex. By the mid-twenties, women were essentially banned from murder trials, and so it is unlikely Caswell would have faced any on his jury.

And now, to finish this three-million-word chapter, let me tell you something about idiots. I spend a lot of time on the Oxford English Dictionary website these days looking up the etymology of words or searching for some superior synonym to the placeholder I've used. There are some words which definitely need more synonyms. I wish there were more ways to say smile, for example – grin, smile, smirk; there really aren't very many. But just like Innuits with snow, there is one word that we have plenty of synonyms for and that is 'idiot'.

In the thesaurus for the category "stupid person, dolt, blockhead" there are, count them, three hundred and thirty-two entries. Here are some of my favourites, in case I don't get a chance to use them somewhere… stupiditarian, morepork, boodle, turnip-head, cabbage-head, dunderhead, dunderpate, dunderwhelp, mopus, look-like-a-goose, oatmeal groat and skit-brains.

Right, that's your lot. I was going to ramble on a bit more about the history of life insurance and the fabric of Lord Edgington's top hat, but I think we can all agree that I've said enough.

ACKNOWLEDGEMENTS

I'm lucky to have some very knowledgeable people in my family and among my readership to call upon when I need experts. I have to say special thanks this time around to the Reverend Jane Dicker from All Saints' Church West Bromwich, who checked for any mistakes with religious themes and pointed me in the right direction.

I was also fortunate to have the help of my second cousin, Rhodri Price Lewis KC, who made sure that legal practice wasn't beyond the realm of possibility – and suggested that I rewrite the trial scene. Another cousin, my dear Dr Heather Bluebell, is normally called upon to check any medical issues, and my friend Kerry Donovan was essential to the editing process this time around.

Thank you, too, to my crack team of experts – the Hoggs, the Martins, (**fiction**), Paul Bickley (**policing**), Karen Baugh Menuhin (**marketing**) and Mar Pérez (**forensic pathology**) for knowing lots of stuff when I don't. And to my fellow writers who are always there for me, especially Catherine, Suzanne and Lucy.

Thank you, many times over, to all the readers in my ARC team who have combed the book for errors. I wouldn't be able to produce this series so quickly or successfully without you…

Rebecca Brooks, Ferne Miller, Melinda Kimlinger, Deborah McNeill, Emma James, Mindy Denkin, Namoi Lamont, Katharine Reibig, Linsey Neale, Karen Davis, Taylor Rain, Terri Roller, Margaret Liddle, Esther Lamin, Lori Willis, Anja Peerdeman, Kate Newnham, Marion Davis, Sarah Turner, Sandra Hoff, Karen M, Mary Nickell, Vanessa Rivington, Helena George, Anne Kavcic, Nancy Roberts, Pat Hathaway, Peggy Craddock, Cathleen Brickhouse, Susan Reddington, Sonya Elizabeth Richards, John Presler, Mary Harmon, Beth Weldon, John Presler, Karen Quinn, Karen Alexander, Mindy Wygonik, Jacquie Erwin, Janet Rutherford, Anny Pritchard, M.P. Smith, Robin Coots, Molly Bailey, Nancy Vieth, Ila Patlogan, Lisa Bjornstad, Randy Hartselle and Keryn De Maria.

READ MORE LORD EDGINGTON MYSTERIES TODAY.

- **Murder at the Spring Ball**
- **Death From High Places** (free e-novella available exclusively at benedictbrown.net. Paperback and audiobook are available at Amazon)
- **A Body at a Boarding School**
- **Death on a Summer's Day**
- **The Mystery of Mistletoe Hall**
- **The Tangled Treasure Trail**
- **The Curious Case of the Templeton-Swifts**
- **The Crimes of Clearwell Castle**
- **A Novel Way to Kill** (Free e-book only available at www.benedictbrown.net/twisty)
- **The Snows of Weston Moor**
- **What the Vicar Saw**
- **Blood on the Bannisters** (Coming June 2023)

Check out the complete Lord Edgington Collection at Amazon

The first five Lord Edgington audiobooks, narrated by the actor George Blagden, are available now. The subsequent titles will follow soon.

THE "WHAT THE VICAR SAW" COCKTAIL

Hold on to your hats and get ready for the world's most dangerous cocktail. I came across it by chance when reading up on combustible spirits that could have caused the fire in the Baron's car. The Blue blazer is considered the first flaming cocktail and was described in the first bartender's manual ever printed. The fabled Jerry Thomas, or the "most celebrated barman in American history", took a hot toddy and turned it into an "arc of fire" when he worked at the El Dorado Saloon in San Francisco. He was known for his showmanship as a barman, and it soon became his signature drink.

Let me just say before we go any further that I do not recommend making this drink if you like your house unblackened and your eyebrows where they are. There's a brilliant video on the 'How to Drink' YouTube channel that lets you enjoy the spectacle without the risk, and even that experienced drink slinger burns the hairs of his knuckles.

Here is Thomas's original recipe, nonetheless…

> **"(Use two large, silver-plated mugs, with handles.)**
> **1 wine-glass of Scotch whisky.**
> **The same of boiling water.**
> **A spoonful of sugar.**

Put the whisky and the boiling water in one mug, ignite the liquid with fire, and while blazing, mix both ingredients by pouring them four or five times from one mug to the other…. If well done, this will have the appearance of a continued stream of liquid fire.

Sweeten with one teaspoonful of pulverized white sugar, and serve in a small bar tumbler, with a piece of lemon peel."

Dangerous, but warming stuff, perfect for winter/a good insurance claim on your property. Even Thomas warns, "The novice in mixing this beverage should be careful not to scald himself. To become proficient in throwing the liquid from one mug to the other, it will be necessary to practise for some time with cold water." So, I repeat, please don't make this drink at home!

WORDS AND REFERENCES YOU MIGHT NOT KNOW

Mrs. Nimble-Chops – a rather nice phrase for a chatterbox.

Surplice and tippet – the tunic and long, wide scarf worn by a priest.

Luctiferous – a very rare word meaning sorrowful or gloomy. It wasn't really in use much in the twenties, but I thought it so descriptive that I decided to revive it. It has no connection to Lucifer – the mistranslated morning star of the Bible – but comes from the Latin for sorrow.

Plangent - mournful, plaintive-sounding, but it can also mean loud and booming. So that's… confusing.

Mirific – working wonders and provoking astonishment.

Assizes – an assize is a judicial inquest, and courts of assizes were regular sessions in English counties held to determine civil and criminal matters by a judge and, often, jury. They'd been in existence since the twelfth century but were abolished in the 1970s.

Gownsman – someone in the legal (or sometimes clerical) profession. Fairly common in the 1920s but now rare.

Cat's-paw – somebody used to achieve the goals of another person – a stooge or patsy.

Beshrew – what a brilliant word. It means to curse or invoke evil upon. It's common in Shakespeare plays, and so I imagine most people are familiar with it, but I just wanted another excuse to print it here. Beshrew…. Beshrew… Beshrew… brilliant!

Factotum – is a servant who does a little of everything – just like Todd.

Flurry-scurry / twitteration – both mean excitement of the mind. Flurry-scurry is from the late nineteenth century (and does not appear to have caught on!) and twitteration dates back to 1775 and is still in use today.

He hadn't a tosser to his kick – this is taken from John Masefield's The Box of Delights, which is full of 1930s schoolboy slang. It literally means that he didn't have a coin in his pocket and can be used to suggest that someone is broke.

Reeling ripe, tap-shackled, bumpsy, tosticated – all mean drunk!

Expectoration – that which is spat from the mouth.

Throbber – slang for the heart. I would have used "ticker", but it turns out that was originally American and from 1930 onwards.

Take up the cudgels – to fight someone's corner.

To a tittle – possibly the origin of the expression "to a t", which it predates by a century. A tittle is a small mark that makes up part of a letter or symbol.

A confidence man – though conman is now a common phrase internationally, in the 1920s it was an exclusively American expression. There was a (now lost) silent film called "The Confidence Man", so perhaps that introduced the term to Britain in 1924.

Un nombriliste – the French for a person who is so self-obsessed they spend the whole time staring at their own navel. The joke would have been better if I could have used the literal translation of solipsist, but the French for solipsist is solipsiste, so that wouldn't have worked.

Spifflicated / pie-eyed fool – more words for drunkenness, but from the US this time.

Jobbernowl – one of the many elegant words in the English language for an idiot. See end of the research chapter in this book for a whole lot more.

Scrobble – to kidnap. This is another word that comes from John Masefield and was never in common use except by geeky fans of his books and the 1980s adaptation of 'The Box of Delights'.

Scare-lines - sensational announcements, designed to shock, in newspapers and on posters advertising that day's news.

In stir – British slang for being in prison.

Nosh – I have no idea whether most Americans know this British slang word, but just in case, it means food.

Roses all the way – a nice expression to mean that everything is rosy or peaches and cream.

Out of heart – an old expression that seems to have been quite common through much of the twentieth century and meant disheartened / out of sorts.

CHARACTER LIST

Suspects and Victims

Reverend Adolphus Oldfield – the vicar of the title who may or may not die on the very first page of the book (pssst… he does!)

P.C. Derek Brigham – the but useless police constable of Condicote.

Bill Thompkins – the verger of St Bartholomew's church.

Baron Stamford Fane – brutish landowner, known for gambling, womanising and rumoured criminal activity before his death in a car accident a few days before the start of the book.

Baroness Sorel Fane – his American heiress wife. She has a pet wildcat called Sekhmet for… some… reason.

Adam Caswell – slow-witted friend of Baron Fane. Local of Condicote.

Marcus Alsop – twenty-year-old, aristocratic friend of Fane and Caswell.

Emmeline "Scarlet" Warwick – his girlfriend, a wannabe writer, in her early twenties who is very much in love with Marcus.

Mayor Eric Hobson – nervy mayor of Condicote.

Mrs Eileen Grout – a tough, blunt woman and proprietor of Grout's Grocers in Condicote.

Dr Beresford-Gray – the Condicote doctor. A lady, of all things! In one draft her name was Elizabeth, but I think it disappeared in the edit.

Reverend Bodsworth – the new vicar who replaces the (spoiler from the first page alert!) dead one.

Lady Beulah Alsop – Marcus's mother.

Lord Bertrand Alsop, Viscount Tatchester (mentioned) – Marcus's dead father.

Familiar Faces

Lord Edgington – the Marquess of Edgington himself, former Metropolitan police superintendent and the owner of the palatial Cranley Hall estate in Surrey.

Christopher Prentiss – his well-meaning grandson and assistant in training.

Violet Prentiss – Lord Edgington's daughter, Chrissy's mum. A good egg!

Walter Prentiss – Chrissy's father and something of a stick in the mud.

Albert Prentiss– their firstborn son. A soppy fop who was always having his heart broken until he got engaged to…

Cassandra Fairfax – the lovely future wife of dear Albert (unless he makes a real hash of things!)

Loelia Prentiss – Walter's mother, Chrissy and Albert's grandmother, and a real tough cookie.

Halfpenny – Cranley Hall's travelling footman.

Henrietta ('Cook') – the Cranley Hall… ummm…. cook.

Todd – chauffeur, barman, stand-in butler, lover of adventure books and an all-round stand-up chap.

Chief Inspector Darrington – former colleague of Lord Edgington from his days in the metropolitan police.

THE IZZY PALMER MYSTERIES

If you're looking for a modern murder mystery series with just as many off-the-wall characters, try **"The Izzy Palmer Mysteries"** for your next whodunit fix.

Check out the complete Izzy Palmer Collection in ebook, paperback and Kindle Unlimited at Amazon.

ABOUT ME

Writing has always been my passion. It was my favourite half-an-hour a week at primary school, and I started on my first, truly abysmal book as a teenager. So it wasn't a difficult decision to study literature at university which led to a master's in Creative Writing.

I'm a Welsh-Irish-Englishman originally from **South London** but now living with my French/Spanish wife and presumably quite confused infant daughter in **Burgos**, a beautiful mediaeval city in the north of Spain. I write overlooking the Castilian countryside, trying not to be distracted by the vultures, hawks and red kites that fly past my window each day.

When Covid-19 hit in 2020, the language school where I worked as an English teacher closed down and I became a full-time writer. I have two murder mystery series. There are already six books written in **"The Izzy Palmer Mysteries"** which is a more modern, zany take on the genre. I will continue to alternate releases between Izzy and Lord Edgington. I hope to release at least ten books in each series.

I previously spent years focussing on kids' books and wrote everything from fairy tales to environmental dystopian fantasies, right through to issue-based teen fiction. My book **"The Princess and The Peach"** was long-listed for the Chicken House prize in The Times and an American producer even talked about adapting it into a film. I'll be slowly publishing those books over the next year whenever we find the time.

"What the Vicar Saw" is the ninth novel in the "Lord Edgington Investigates…" series. The next book will be out in June 2023 and there's a novella available free if you sign up to my readers' club. Should you wish to tell me what you think about Chrissy and his grandfather, my writing or the world at large, I'd love to hear from you, so feel free to get in touch via...

www.benedictbrown.net

Printed in Great Britain
by Amazon